Prince of the Elders

by

Alexandria May Ausman

Book cover design by Alexandria May Ausman
Editor: Jon M. Ausman

Library of Congress Control Number: 2023922697

ISBN: 979-8-9890048-7-4 (ebook)
ISBN: 979-8-9890048-6-7 (paperback)

Published By:
Ausman & Cousins, LLC
1700 North Monroe Street
Suite 11, Box 284
Tallahassee, Florida 32303-0501

For author interviews: ausman@embarqmail.com

Das Kaiser Haus Series

The Rise of the Priceless (Chapters 1 to 10)
Metal Illness (Chapters 11 to 19)
Jonas the Vampire (Chapters 20 to 29)
Prince of the Elders (Chapter 30 to 40)
Leo's Lamb (coming soon)

The Psycho Series

Cemetery Kid (Chapters 1 to 20)
Stop Calling Me Psycho (Chapters 21 to 33)
Motor-Psycho (Chapters 34 to 44)
Delusion of the Collar and the Key (Chapters 45 to 53)
Brutality's Prisoner (Chapters 54 to 64)
Aesthetic Akathisia (Chapters 65 to 74)
Metallic Burden (Chapters 75 to 83)

27 Masters Series

Anita the Benevolent (Chapters 1 to 7)
The Beast and the Witch (Chapters 8 to 16)
High Priestess of Schizophrenia (coming soon)

Book 4 Characters: Prince of the Elders

Agnete: mother of Christian
Annette: a Haus trainee
Barnum: an Elder of the Haus
Ben: a Haus trainee
Bladrick: an Elder of the Haus
Christian: the anger and lust shard
Christian Axel: a Haus submissive, the Priceless
Claus: an Elder of the Haus
Cora: a FemDom of the Haus
Debbie: Meine Liebe's sexual psychopathic and sadistic mother
Der Goldene Hund: the Voice or the Boss shard; the Conscious shard
Drexel: an Elder of the Haus
Egon: Haus seduction Master and trainer
Emma: a black collar, aide to Jonas
Felix: a black collar door guard hired by Peter
Geraldine: a Haus trainee
Gretta: a House Elder, the Silk Queen
Heidi: A Dungeon Mistress; sister of Helga
Helga: a Dungeon Mistress; sister of Heidi
Hemmel: a Supreme Dungeon Master
Jonas: an Elder of the Haus
Judith: a Haus submissive to Stefan
Julius: a Haus Dominant, married to Agnette
Leo: a Haus Dominant

Mad Max: the sadistic shard of Maximillian, aka the Heart and Judgment

Mad Maxx: husband of Meine Liebe; a Haus Dominant

Mad Maxx: the masochistic shard, aka the Brain and Guilt

Max: the Soul shard

Maximillian: the submissive name given to Christian by Peter

Maximillian: the seductive shard, aka the Libido

Meine Liebe: submissive and spouse of Mad Maxx

Milo: silver collar Haus seduction trainer

Olaf: House black collar; aid to Xavier

Peter: a Dominant of Der Kaiser Haus; best trainer of submissives

Russell: spouse of Debbie, a switch

Ryker: a House trainee

Stefan: a Haus Dominant

Vilber: House black collar; aid to Xavier

Xavier: the Fur King of the Haus

Prologue:

In book four of the Kaiser Haus series, Maximillian finds himself incarcerated deep in a dungeon cell. Questions regarding his mental stability have placed him in danger. When the House doctor determines the "Priceless" collar is 'irreparably damaged' Master Peter is forced into a decision he will live to regret.

Unexpectedly uncollared, desperate, and facing sure death, Maximillian also makes a terrible mistake. He chooses to accept the Elder Jonas's offer. This results in a fate almost too horrible to imagine. Maximillian trades in his single abusive Master, only to become subjected to five of the most despotic souls to ever walk the halls of Kaiser Haus.

As the Elder's shared property Maximillian is recollared and renamed. Now called Mad Maxx, he finds himself caught in the paths of twisted plots and deadly vendettas that span decades.

Determined to complete "the mission" Der Hund splits the Max shards and Christian into teams. Each 'shard' is tasked with doing whatever is necessary to assure 'the boy' survives long enough to break his collar.

Mad Maxx's onsetting madness grows in strength as he endures brutal tortures, bizarre fetishes, and vicious sexual assaults. The shards surprise the disfigured Der Hund and each other as old enemies become valuable allies.

Despite their perilous journey of murderous mayhem, the shard Mad Max reclaims a treasure Der Hund believed lost forever. Unconditional love blossoms within the

"Priceless" as he follows his inner lamb in search of the "green fields" of redemption.

Chapter 30: Uncollared

I awoke in that concrete cell deep within the bowels of the Haus. I was unsure how many hours had passed while I was sleeping. My mouth was dry, and my flesh felt numb. I sat up with some difficulty, groaning out when I realized I was still wearing that damned strait jacket.

Things around that empty room seemed out of focus. I shook my head wildly trying to clear my confused thoughts. I could hear the other cells occupants whispering all around me. I wondered if Jonas's blows to my head had somehow opened my hearing. I had been in those dungeon isolation rooms off and on for almost four years, as I told you earlier. Never had I been able to listen in to the conversations between the cell mates. I admit, this strange new power of super hearing was cool, and scary too. I wanted to get closer to the wall to see if any of them were discussing the date or anything else of interest to me.

It was then I noticed my legs were sluggish. I felt like I was full of the wet materials they used to make this prison I was stuck in. Nothing of the flesh seemed to be working the way I told it to. I was then made aware of my upset stomach. I leaned forward convinced I would vomit as everything spun around me.

I watched rivers of drool pouring out of my mouth. I had not realized I could not feel my lips. It made no sense. My mouth seemed full of sand as it was so dry, but I could not stop the contents of it from dribbling down my chin. It was like being alive but not either. I thought of a zombie movie in the theater that I had seen a little bit of once, years before, when I was just a slave in this place. I forget the name of that horrid film, but I sure could relate to the bad guys in that flick that day.

I was not happy I need not tell you. This situation had gotten out of hand faster than I had ever thought it could. I was only faking the madness a little. I wanted a break from that lustful touching of those perverts. I moaned out when I felt the humiliating wetness of my bladder releasing without my say so. I had truly found a new kind of hell. That was a bit of a surprise since I thought I had hit that bottom already many weeks before.

This had to be caused by that shot the stupid fake doctor gave me earlier. There could be no other excuse for such foul feelings and poor responses from the boy. I quit trying to get to the other wall to listen in on the others when I only managed to piss myself and slowly shuffle like an old husband. Shit. This medication was not good, you know. I didn't like this one bit.

I saw Mad Max come out of the shadows glaring at me with a look of disgust. "Oh, meine Gott. You are a mess Maximillian. Did you miss your perverted schwulers so much you decided to start given yourself the golden showers?" He pointed at the flesh's accidental soiling of itself.

I groaned out in misery at this fool. "Fichen dich Mad Max. I am not well. That monster gave us something foul. The boy is sick with it. I think we are finished. Call Der Hund. Let's abandon this situation for good. I no longer care what anyone does to the Wheel. If we all leave it will feel nothing, do nothing, and eventually expire. That would be preferable to this hell hole it has become. You get in here to see if I tell lies."

Mad Max's eyes went wide. "Nein, you are speaking of insanity Maximillian. No matter how bad this may seem, we will recover from it. The flesh always heals you idiot. I don't like your kind of thinking. I should call Der Hund and report you immediately about it, but because you're my brother I won't. I may not always get along with you, but I don't wants to see Der Hund destroy you either."

I smiled at the kindness my sadistic brother showed to me in my weak moments. "I say thank you for your soothing words brother Mad Max. You're a real pal."

That bastard narrowed his eyes, smiling wickedly at me. "I am not your pal, Maximillian. I only keep your secret because if Der Hund shatters you, I have no one to torture. Your girly screams make me laugh. I truly enjoy your torment more than I can say."

I rolled my eyes and groaned feeling a new wave of nausea overtake the flesh. "Ah, well that makes sense.

What the hell was I thinking that you could ever care for anything but your own selfish needs. Please go away Mad Max. Leave me to my pain in peace, ja? I am not in the mood for your bullshit today. If you keep bothering me, I will come out of this boy. Then I will make it worth my while for all my troubles. I plan to kill you this time when we collide. That you can take for the truth."

Mad Max growled out. "Here I stand, drama queen schwuler. You think you can beat me? Not in this lifetime meine pretty Frau."

That was it. This cocksucker had it coming. I went to break from the Wheel but bounced off his walls as if he was made of rubber. The boy stood up when I tried again to release myself from my bonds in his mind. The flesh struggled and groaned with me, but I could not separate. I was trapped within.

I dropped back to that cot in full on terror, looking at the frightened eyes of Mad Max who saw the whole thing. "Holy shit. Get Der Hund, Mad Max. I am stuck. I cannot get out. Help me. Gott damn it. Call the core. This is a fucking nightmare come to truth. Don't stand there, fool. Go get help."

Mad Max looked around appearing confused. "Are you sure your stuck, Maximillian? Maybe your foot is hung up only. I will come inside to see what the problem is before I go bother Der Hund. He is grouchy right now, brother.

Even I don't wish to give him news that may startle him for no good reason." He came running at me and promptly bounced the fuck off the boy, smacking into the wall.

I watched my brother the sadistic shard nearly shatter when he collided with that concrete from the force of the flesh repealing him like that. He let out a loud wail. Mad Maxx, Christian and Max come running when day heard his distress call. I sat there staring in disbelief as the shards aided our brother off the ground. The flesh started to tremble demonstrating my fright at this unimaginable situation.

Der Hund come through the door before anyone could say a word. I could see from the look on his face he too was beyond terrified.

"Maximillian, what has happened? Come out of the boy now I tell you. Mind me shard." He pointed at his feet.

I attempted again to break out but again the flesh rose with me. It pulled to the end of its leash groaning from the strain of my reaching to get out of there. Tears were starting and the boy's face went red from my frustration.

Der Hund's expression went from extreme concern to a complete panic. "We are shattered boys. Nein, this cannot be. How could this happen? Someone needs to help us. We are doomed," he wailed out, sending the Maxes and Christian shards into a heavy trembling.

I stared at Der Hund, not able to understand his words for some reason. "Nein, we are not shattered. Please, I beg of you, let me out of here. I don't wants to be in here anymore. Get one of the others. Don't let this horror be mine for all our days. Help me Der Hund. Get me out of here." The flesh dropped to its knees wailing these words to our core in my own voice.

Der Hund's eyes filled with tears. "Oh, meine dear Maximillian. There is nothing I can do. You are trapped within and us trapped without. You inherited by accident what I no longer wished to be. I apologize my friend. This must be my fault. I lost hope. I never realized it could be so devastating." He too fell to his knees covering his face while weeping uncontrollably.

The other shards began to wail in terror at seeing their leader behaving defeated like that. They were screaming, frightened me beyond imagination. I felt I could not breathe as that flesh closed in on me like a vice grip. Nothing was making any sense anymore. I was so confused by this noise, the panic, the movements of all of them. I had become stupid with fear.

The door suddenly opened, sending me into a tailspin of terror. I yelled at the thing coming through it and the flesh tried to run from it. I couldn't understand what was happening. I knew I should know, but for the life of me, Meine Liebe, I had forgotten everything. Even my own identity.

I couldn't even recall my own fucking name. I was unsure if I was Maximillian, Mad Maxx, Mad Max, Max, Christian, Der Goldene Hund, or Christian Axel. To be honest, at that moment, I wasn't even sure if I was ever any of them to begin with. It was as if my brain turned to mush and only impulses were left running the show.

I felt the pain of the cold floor and something heavy on my chest. Bright light was blinding my eyes. There were odd noises, like someone talking under water must sound. You know I could hear it, but it was blunted somehow. The room spun this way and that. I stared wildly trying to get something to which to anchor the chaos within. Above me were dark places with borders that shifted rapidly. I screamed into the voids asking if there was anyone in there. I hoped someone would answer from the deep and could help me find my way back from this place of being lost.

I wailed out in despair when these shadows disappeared leaving me unaided in the coldness of confusion. No matter how much I fought to return to my senses; I could not find my way home.

This damnation continued day after day. I couldn't remember anything. I couldn't tell if I was asleep, awake, dead, or alive. I decided I must have been buried in the Orchard and the damned Christian folks were correct. There was a hell after all, and I had found it. I wept a great deal over my torment but screamed for help more, I think. I can never be sure. During this time, I was just not myself anymore. Something foul was happening but what exactly I would never know.

To this day those seven months are lost to me, and no one has explained it to me in a way I accept. All I can say with certainty about it is what your Master Peter and Jonas told me when at last in the eighth-month things started to slowly settle down in my head.

They informed me I had a nervous breakdown thanks to stress. Jonas blamed your Master Peter and your Master Peter blamed Jonas for it. Whoever was responsible, let me tell you this, it was most unpleasant. I discovered I had turned fourteen without realizing it during the dark dungeon days. For all those months I was stuck in that concrete cell, leashed, and restrained in a strait jacket.

Thank Gott my head felt like only a few days passed instead of the many weeks that did. If I could have had my wits about me, I would have been a bit more than a little pissed at them for such brutal treatment. I started to realize I had been treated with neither gentleness nor respect during my daftness.

When I was able to feed myself, remember how to speak, and attend my own needs once more, the brutes finally took off that damned jacket. They wouldn't unleash me from the wall though yet. I found new scars, many healing bruises and cuts, and I had lost a great deal of weight. They must have damned near killed the boy given the extensive marks, wounds, and pain, the flesh was in.

I quickly found out that Master Peter had hired a small group of strong black collar males to attend me. They came into the cell frequently, demanding I eat something, gave me water for drinking or washing, while others forced me to take pills.

If I didn't do what they told me fast enough or give them any quarrel these men were happy to beat me down till I gave in to their orders. I figured out it was best to do as I was told to cut down on the injuries, I had been obviously racking up all that time.

All the "secret staff workers" were sworn to keep my momentary madness a secret. Jonas and my Master had even paid off Hemmel the Dungeon Master. He was becoming a rich person and all he had to do was turn a blind eye to the two Dominant's disturbed prisoners. He helped them keep me hidden away from the gossiping Haus population. They feared rumors of that nasty word, you know schizophrenia (which was a lie of course), would trap me in my metal if the word reached the ears of the Voting Council.

I pulled up and looked at my Master with curiosity. He smiled at me and stared back saying nothing. I decided to chance a thud.

"The doctor said if you were sick for six months or so Master, then you had that bad word." I held my breath bracing for his cane swat for daring to say such a thing.

He laughed so suddenly it made me wince in a pure startle reaction. "I told you that guy was a damned fake, didn't I? Well, he didn't know shit. I do not have that stupid schizophrenia no matter what your Master Peter tells you, nor that crazy Jonas either. Hell, a husband has a little nervous breakdown or two and everyone is so quick to judge him insane. Is it so insane to fall apart when the world around you is so brutal? I got a weak mind for a moment. I suppose I just needed a break from time to time, is all. You get the psychotic stuff sometimes too from all the burdens of your existence. I don't call you that name nor do I think you're crazy, Meine Liebe. If you didn't have these nervous reactions to the abomination of this horror you live, then I would be worried as hell. Only the truly insane can walk around in blood, rape, shit, and horrible pain without reacting to it. Psssst. There is no such thing as the disease schizophrenia anyway. The legend says all the Priceless collars get it thanks to the greed and pressure their forbidden silver incites in those around them. Well, once again that proves legends are only myths with another name. I don't have it, and you don't. I am much saner than Debbie, Russell, Peter, and Jonas, as well as everyone I ever met. Peter and Jonas only call me that name to keep me under their thumb, you know. Those liars better watch their asses. When meine Frau breaks her collar, then we kill them both. Afterwards we run away from this brutal world they trapped us in. Then we see who the schizophrenic is, ja?"

I nodded. "Can I break my collar before I am fifteen, Master?" I narrowed my eyes at him thinking that maybe we could get our dreams sooner if I could.

Master Maxx smiled brightly, "Ja. You can go to Meine Liebe. If you can finish the training faster, then it is possible to take your test after your fourteenth birthday. Normally, no one can be ready that early, but you started your training so young. If you work hard, and move swift, then we could be free a full year sooner."

I giggled with glee at that great news, not that one year less on my sentence helped much. "I can go faster, Master. I will study hard, you'll see."

My Master grabbed the sides of my head and pulled me forward kissing my lips quickly. "We double time the lessons when I am here in the states to make up for your slow ass Master Peter. Ja, this could work. I do worry though. There is a lot of torment already, you sure about this, Meine Liebe? I mean I can wait another year. I want you safe, not broken over this stupid shit the Haus will make us endure."

I nodded. "Long as you tell me why I have to do something; I will understand Master. I know it is not proper to ask that mercy, but it can help me if I know why I am."

He pursed his lips a moment appearing deep in thought then nodded. "I am not supposed to grant mercy, meine Frau, but what others don't know won't hurt us, ja? I grant this one mercy you request in return for your accepting double time lessons. Your pain will offer the equality for this service. I will warn you though, your Master Peter won't make such a deal so don't bother asking for it."

I smiled. "I don't care what he says or does Master. We are getting out of here forever. I can do anything for our dreams. I thought I would die here, or when I got out no one would love me. I no longer think that anymore."

My Master smiled with an adoring gaze in his eyes. "Your words bring me hope, meine little Demonseed Frau. One day very soon we will shut out the world. Then I will be happy all the rest of my days hearing only the beating of your heart and that of our children. You wish to rest yet? This story must be getting boring by now for you."

I laughed. "Vampires, men that have sex with statues, and boys dressed like girls, Master. Are you kidding? I would listen to the whole thing all over again. I never even read a fairy tale so weird."

He chuckled, "Well, I am not sure if I should be flattered or angry you said that, Meine Liebe. I swear nothing I confess to in my tale seems to really frighten you for truth. I will continue this horror story if you can answer me one thing."

I looked at him nodding, eager to hear the rest of his amazing tale.

My Master pointed at his scarred-up chest. "Do you hear it? There is a demon purring in my heartbeat. She lives in there fueling my strength, you know."

I screwed up my face wondering what the heck he was talking about. He looked surprised and even flinched when I laid my ear against his chest listening hard to see if he really had a demon living in his chest. After a few moments, he laughed out loud and ruffled my hair holding my head tightly to him.

"Meine Demonseed Frau, I already said you are the demon that resides in my heart. That question I asked you was a joke. You are too damned literal. I forget sometimes you're so young to understand some things." He was laughing hard at my childish misunderstanding of his high-level concept of love and protection.

I slapped his chest playfully. "Thank God that is a joke. I was worried that thing would eat me while we slept, Master."

He really laughed hard at that. "Awe, you need not worry about that, meine beauty. You sleep on the floor from now on, remember? If I did have a hungry demon inside my heart, she couldn't reach you way the hell over there."

I glared at him in disbelief. "You will really make me sleep on the floor, Master? That is not fair."

Master Maxx giggled even harder. "Welcome to the world of D/s, Meine Liebe. Fair is for the Dominant to decide not the submissive. You sleep on the floor until you earn the right to sleep next to your better. I love you but I grant only the mercy of understanding, nothing else. You suffer like you must, and me too. That is the only fair you and I ever get. Either you are in, or you are out. You don't like something, take it up with my cane. Now, you listening to this damned story or you ready to sleep over there on the floor? Up to you, see you get a choice. Enjoy that while it lasts, Meine Frau. Soon, the only choice I give you is to live or die trying. You say you want to come with me to the world away from all this brutality? Well, then you brace yourself. We are gonna run through the fires of hell together and hope the Devil doesn't catch us. This you understand, ja?"

I grumbled but nodded. "Yes Master. I understand, but for the record, this sucks."

My Master howled at that. "You're fucking right you will. Often. You will do it like a fucking pro, and you can thank me for the Gott damned mercy of it. Now where the hell was I, oh ja, I was still in that fucking cell over a little bout of nervousness I had when I was just turning fourteen."

"For a couple of weeks after Master Peter took off my jacket – I think but I am not sure of the time, hard to say when you're in a cell with no windows, ja – I was left restrained by my leash in the wall in the cell. The days passed slowly by, with nothing but beatings and foul medications.

I was not happy with this situation nor sure if maybe this were not my life for good. No one was telling me anything about what happened or why I was being treated with such brutality. When I tried to ask my Master, Jonas, or those other men, they hit me and said to shut my mouth. After a few nasty battles with them all, I decided it was best to mind them. I couldn't beat them, and I was tired of the bruises and backhands.

I was sitting in my cell during the end of the second week of this "recovery" when the door opened and this Hemmel came inside. I went back to the corner with the understanding that anyone coming through that door was not there to enjoy my company in a nice way, you know.

Dis Hemmel was holding a tray of food for my supper. He looked at me cowering in the corner of the cell and shook his head.

"This is truly too bad you know. I think you would have made a wonderful pleasure submissive with such good looks and a wonderful pedigree. Such a waste." He put the tray on the floor and started to leave.

I decided to try to take a chance to see if he could answer what the hell was going on. "Wait, Master Hemmel. Can you tell me is the Guard going to take me away?"

Hemmel appeared surprised when I spoke to him. "What? You know my name, Maximillian? Could this be? Are you in your senses?"

I stayed in my spot ready to fight, if need be, but nodded. "Ja. Ja. Please I beg mercy. Is the Guard coming for me? I swear I did nothing wrong. I just want to go home. I won't give Master Jonas or Master Peter any more quarrels. I vow to end my insolence at once. I learned my lesson."

This Hemmel took a step toward me, and I covered my head and dropped to a kneel, sure he was about to hit me like all the others. "You sound logical, but are you? Tell me, who else is in this cell Maximillian?"

I trembled a bit but lifted my head. "I see only you Master Hemmel and me. There isn't anyone else, is there?" I looked around with much fear wondering if maybe I missed someone that had slipped in with him.

Hemmel chuckled at that. "Nein, there are just the two of us. Tell me, can you hear any voices?"

I was confused by his weird question. "Uhm, Master Hemmel, is this a trick or something? I hear your voice. Am I supposed to hear another voice? If that would get me the hell out of here, then I will say I do. Is that what you want me to say? I desire only to mind my better's commands. You tell me what you want, and Maximillian will make that happen. You will see I am a man of my word. I tell you I commit no further insult to any Dominant, and I will not."

Hemmel smiled brightly. "Ah, well I will be Gott damned. I was sure we lost you for all time. You're not speaking nonsense and seem to remember your place. This is good news. I will go fetch your Master immediately. You have rejoined us. It's a fucking miracle. That doctor said you were finished. Yet, he is wrong. You wait here. I go get Peter." He took off out the door seeming thrilled for some reason.

I yelled out. "As you wish, Master Hemmel. I wait here." Then I whispered to myself. "Where the fuck can I go. I am chained to the Gott damned wall. This Hemmel is insane I think."

Mad Max walked out from the shadow, "He goes to get Master Peter, huh? Not likely to do him any good. We asked for him already and all we got was a black eye."

I growled at Mad Max, "What is this we shit? I am the one stuck in here fool. You have no black eye. Maximillian has two."

Mad Max snorted. "What I would not give to feel one at this point. There is no end to this nothing. I can never hit anyone with my cane. That brings me any pleasure now. Der Hund is still missing, and Mad Maxx won't stop crying. I think Max and Christian, shit those two, are off jacking each other off. This is a bloody nightmare. I tell you; this torture is one even I cannot appreciate."

I pulled the knees to my chest. "Tell me about it, Mad Max. Well, I say if they will not let us out of this cell, I would rather the Guard come shoot this flesh. No more of this shit. This is worse than death I am sure of it."

Mad Max giggled, "What's the matter, Maximillian? You miss your father's sexy kissing? Maybe you want to suck that Vampire cock some more, but he doesn't visit you anymore, ja?"

I glared at that sadistic bastard. "I have had enough of your nasty jokes, Mad Max. I am chained to this fucking wall, beat down like a dog, and that is not enough for you.

Nein, you come here to torment me more. I swear you say another word to me I get up and shatter your shard right into that wall over there." The boy pointed at Mad Max narrowing his eyes in a threatening gaze.

Mad Max laughed out loud at me. "Oh ja? Well, here I stand fool. You cannot do shit stuck in the flesh like you are. I can say and do whatever I like. You will sit there like a crying little Frau taking whatever I give you."

That was it. The boy stood up and came running at Mad Max. That idiot stood there sure of his safety since the flesh cannot grab its shards. To his surprise, and mine, when the flesh hit the end of that leash I kept going. I collided with the howling Mad Max sending us both smacking into the wall.

The boy fell to his knees in a mindless trance, then slumped over without any shard at the Wheel. Mad Max stared at me in a look of horror and joy. I glanced around realizing for the first time in many months my pain was all gone. The nothing embraced me as I sighed in full relief. I was free.

Mad Max pushed me off him. "You got out. This is possible. I thought Der Hund said we were shattered for all time."

I nodded but giggled with giddiness at this great news. "Ja, he did but apparently not. I am out of the flesh. Call the others. We must celebrate this reprieve together."

Mad Max closed his eyes and focused. Within only moments Mad Maxx, Christian, and Max come running to the scene. They all stood there staring at me in disbelief cutting their eyes back and forth at me then the trancing boy.

Christian spoke up "You are here, and the flesh there. We are not shattered. This is beautiful. There is hope of survival now. Don't you think, Der Hund?" He looked around at us searching for our core shard.

We all looked at each other but none of us were Der Goldene Hund. He was still missing among us. This caused nervousness among his creations. One of us had to find him to speak to him of our recovery.

Mad Maxx sighed. "I will see if I can hail him. He usually will listen to me. However, we still have a problem. One of us must stay with the boy until Der Hund can be notified of this news. The problem is this may only be temporary. Whoever gets into the flesh may be trapped there like Maximillian was, this time maybe for good. Who wants to volunteer?"

Christian looked at Max. "I think I go in."

Mad Max growled out in irritation. "Der Hund said you are forbidden to ride the flesh unless he says so. Nein, Christian cannot be the one."

I looked at my brothers "I am not going back in there. I already did that shit all these months. Leave me out."

Max sighed, "I can go if everyone agrees to it."

Mad Maxx shook his head. "You can do anything without Christian and he is banned from the flesh brother. I apologize but you cannot be the one."

Everyone looked at Mad Max. He was glaring at the boy when he noticed our eyes on him.

"Well, fichen mich. This is bullshit. I don't want to get stuck in there. What if that Vampire wants to fuck us or that father of ours. Then what, huh? I got to take that shit. I don't think so. Make Maximillian do this. He is the schwuler. Hell, he loves it," he screamed out with much rudeness.

Mad Maxx frowned. "Maximillian is worn out, brother. You know the rules. No tired shards allowed in the flesh. That is too dangerous. It is you that can handle the beatings the best. I like them but that will only get the boy more of them. You have a steel soul. You get in there before someone comes and finds the boy catatonic like that. Go now. Maybe it will be okay. We have no choice anyway.

Will you be a pussy and cry or get to doing your job?" He pointed at the flesh demanding, Mad Max enter.

The sadist scoffed. "Fine, I will go. If I get caught in there I will every Gott damned one of you. I swear it." He took his run and entered the boy.

The flesh took a deep gasp, then Mad Max got up off the floor. "Sonofabitch, this shit hurts." He was flexing the boys arms and looking over his chest with an expression of surprise.

I nodded. "I told you that, you bastard. Well, you were tired of the nothing. Hope you enjoy the too fucking much. I am out of here. I need a nap." I started to leave.

Mad Max yelled out. "Hey, wait. Where are you going? You cannot all just leave me here, you motherfuckers. What if that Vampire or out father comes looking for loving?"

I turned around with an evil smile at that sadistic bastard. "Guess you better hope the flesh's lips aren't too cracked to pucker up then. Just remember, you love it Mad Max. Ciao." I left that fuming bastard to deal with the horror for a fucking change.

I watched as Mad Maxx, Max, Christian and that fucker Maximillian left me there to deal with whatever comes through the door. I got to tell you I was a bit more than pissed at them all. I decided the second Der Hund was located he would hear my complaint about this. For that moment, I was stuck. If one of us didn't run the Wheel then the flesh would not last long. Damn boy is such high maintenance, you know? He cannot live in the nothing like all of us can. You know about the nothing, right Meine Liebe?

I nodded. "That is where Rachel and Simon are right now, Master." I smiled at him but quickly realized my mistake when I noticed the wicked grin spreading across his face. Shit, this was Mad Max.

He snatched up his cane and swatted me so fast I heard it before I felt it. I let out a loud scream of surprise and pain.

"Fooled you, didn't I Meine Liebe? You got anything else to say? I can thud all night you know." He grinned even larger with his wrist twitching ever so slightly.

I opened my mouth to say no but caught myself just in the nick of time. He almost got me again with his trick. I shook my head and looked down at the mattress in silence.

Master Mad Max frowned, "A, you are too clever to be fooled twice I see. No matter. I will get you soon. I know that mouth of yours. I really like that mouth in fact. Now on with the story, ja?"

I nodded while he snorted in frustration.

"Well shit, still didn't catch you. Okay then where was I? Oh ja, those dirty bastards left me to rot in the cell."

Hemmel came back inside the cell with Master Peter trailing him within only about half an hour of my "riding the flesh." I was sitting on the cot thinking of ways I would torture Maximillian the second I saw him again when the two of them startled me from my bloody thoughts.

Master Peter came to stand in front of the cot. I got off that thing quick and dropped to a knee. I was in no mood for his tawse.

Master Peter gasped sounding shocked. "Maximillian, you know who I am? You answer me boy."

I nodded. "Ja, you're my Master. I know who you are."

Ma Master pointed to the Dungeon Master. "And who is this?"

I stole a look at the man to be sure of my answer. "That is Master Hemmel, Master."

Master Peter sighed. "Ah, now tell me who are you, my boy?"

I raised an eyebrow at that fucking weird inquiry but shrugged, then said, "Uhm, I am Mad Max I mean Maximillian, Master. I don't understand these questions. I beg your mercy, Master. Can you please take me home to the apartment? I swear to Master Hemmel, I will not be insolent again. I now swear this to you. I am a man of my word. I will obey you without further quarrels."

Master Peter nodded with a deep frown on his face. "I wish you could come home with me, Maximillian. I will call in the doctor but that is only to relieve my mind. The doctor will of course say this is only a temporary recovery. Just a fluke. I am saddened that this end finally comes when he is aware enough to know it. You were right Hemmel, I should have shown Maximillian mercy by ending him sooner. I damn myself for showing too much weakness and affection for something that isn't treatable or curable. His doctor told me he is schizophrenic and would not come out of the psychosis. Yet, I see him kneeling before me like the beautiful Priceless collar I have known and loved all this time. He eyes will now haunt me for all time. I want to believe such a thing as a magical recovery, but I know better Hemmel. It is just a wishful thought."

I knew I needed to work fast at convincing Master Peter to take me away from the cell. I admit, I was feeling despair that my choices were so horrific. I could be shot by the Guard or be forced to endure the lustful touching of my father, yuck.

Either way, the situation was bad and sounded like it was about to become deadly. At least Master Peter could assure my beatings were warranted unlike those the fucking Hemmel had allowed. I decided if I ever broke my collar, I would kill that bastard for allowing the staff to treat me like the punching bag.

I shook my head. "Don't get that doctor I beg of you, Master. This doctor told you lies about me. I am not a schizophrenic. I am not insane. Please don't leave me here. Take me home with you. I will do whatever you want. I swear this. Call off the guard. I do anything. You just say it. I will never disobey again." I fell to my face, putting my forehead on his shoes in prostration near tears that he would not believe I am not a psychotic.

Master Peter scoffed. "Get up, Maximillian. You will stay here. This doctor said you will not get better. You are a schizophrenic, there is no longer any doubt. I am a doctor myself and I know the fucking insanity of that disease when I see it. Not wishing for it to be truth doesn't make it a lie. Only a psychotic would believe denial can be a cure for the Mother of Madness. You will be of no use to anyone all your days. I realize with much bitterness this is likely only a reflex or a memory of my collar I see before me. My Maximillian is lost to me and no matter how much I want to believe you're not a loss, that is not the case. Hemmel, let me out of here. I sent for the doctor, but I already know what he will say. When the doctor finishes let me know, then have the Guard remove this boy for good. I have to face this grief. Do not bring me back here any longer. I cannot bare it." He kicked me off his shoes and turned storming from the cell.

I wailed out in terror. "Nein, nein, please Master. Don't let them kill me. I am not a schizophrenic. I am Maximillian, your faithful pleasure submissive. Come back, I beg you, please."

Hemmel stood there staring at me with some pity in his eyes. "You shut up. You are not a submissive anymore. I will be back with the keys to remove your collar and leash. No need to waste good metal on a corpse." He left the cell.

I went into a complete panic. I had to get the hell out somehow. That Hemmel was going to uncollar me. If that metal come off by any hand other than my own, I would be hunted down and killed. Your collar or oath as the Dominant is your sign of membership. Without it, your destroyed for daring to be within the Haus walls. I tore at that leash lock, even chewing on it with my teeth. I had not been insane, but I have to say, I was going mad with fear.

No matter what I tried neither the lock nor leash would budge. I had been suffering from lack of proper food, and likely chronic beatings for months. I quickly wore myself out in that struggle to release myself from the bounds. Not that it would have done any good had I been successful in freeing my leash. I was still a prisoner in a concrete room. There was nowhere to run. I was finished.

I fell to my backside and pulled up my knees. I wept quietly into my arms realizing at last my defeat. I didn't wants to die, but like all my life, there was nothing I could do about it. My captors had decided to end my days. Their will was stronger than my own.

The door came open. I cowered and prepared to offer my last fight to Hemmel. I never thought I would see the day I was ready to defend myself from getting that collar broken. Yet, here it was, me ready to trap myself in that metal.

To my surprise Jonas stepped into the cell. I saw him and immediately screamed out in desperation, "Jonas, beg you, do not let Hemmel take my collar. Please call off the Guard. I am not a schizophrenic. Please believe me. I am you blood bonded lover, Christian Axel, remember. I will obey you. Save me and do whatever you want. I swear I will give you no further quarrel. I will give you all I have for your mercy. I never complain about your affections again." I rushed forward and prostrated myself at his feet panting with many tears falling.

Jonas flinched and tried to back away. "I only came to say goodbye to my love. I didn't think, wait, you know who I am?"

I wailed out, "Ja, ja, you're Jonas, my blood bonded. Please help me. I am not the psychotic. Please save me Jonas."

Hemmel came through the door with the bolt cutters. He grabbed my upper arm hauling me off Jonas's feet pushing me to my back in the floor. He put all his weight on my chest and prepared to cut off my collar with that tool.

I was kicking and screaming with all my strength, calling out to Jonas, "Please Jonas, I am not crazy. Save me. I will do anything. Do not let them do this to your blood bonded Christian Axel. There are six of us. You asked me this. I tell you now. There are only six: Maximillian, Mad Max, Mad Maxx, Christian, Max, and Christian Axel. See, I am not a schizophrenic. I am the Priceless like Justus was. He had ten minds. That is too many to survive. You better think, Jonas. You let them kill me and you will never find the female of our kind."

Jonas heard my confession and my reminder of why he bothered me in the first place. Hell, I was going to be killed so what did I have to lose telling the Vampire my secret? Absolutely nothing. He came forward and grabbed Hemmel that was still struggling with me trying to cut off my collar.

"Get the fuck off my Christian Axel, you bastard," Jonas growled out as he threw that Dungeon Master across the floor. It was not that Jonas was super strong. Hemmel was caught off guard you see. It was easy for him to be tossed off thanks to that.

Jonas reached out his hand. "My love, you are back. I am very happy to see your beautiful face at long last. I thought I lost you to a shattering." I allowed him to pull me to my feet.

Hemmel had recovered. He come back at me with those fucking clippers. I backed away in fear. Jonas turned around with anger flashing in his dark eyes.

"Are you deaf, Hemmel? I see ears on that daft head of yours, but they don't seem to work. I said back the fuck off. This is my blood bonded lover. You touch him with that thing I will use it on you, only it won't be any collar I am cutting off."

Hemmel hesitated, he continued his assault on me. "I do apologize Jonas, but Peter says this submissive is to be destroyed. I am only following his Master's orders. I would politely ask you to stand aside. The Guard is already on their way. This is done. If you want his metal left till after the Russians do their job, that is fine, but either way, Peter demanded this silver be returned to him."

I trembled with full on terror as my eyes searched the door for the coming death. I could see Ryker's face disfigured by the butt of the Guard's rifle. Jonas shot a look of fear at me which made me really freak out.

I ran to Jonas and wrapped my arms around his waist. Without hesitation I buried my face in his chest weeping loudly in full panic, begging him to save me. I was holding on to the Vampire for dear life. **(Damn me for that most unmanly display right there, but hey I was just a dumb boy, ja?).**

Actually, because of this most humiliating schwuler behavior I engaged in, it caused Jonas to wake the hell up. I suppose he recalled why he blood bonded to me in the first place, or maybe he just didn't want to be shot by accident when those Russian brutes tried to extract me from his flesh. Whatever the reason, he went right to work on the solution to this horrific situation.

Jonas glared at Hemmel. "Give me that damned bolt cutter, you bastard. Peter comes here to visit this boy and saw that he is not psychotic but ordered this horror anyway?"

Hemmel handed the tool to him. "Ja, he saw him only a bit ago. I told him the psychosis had passed but he would hear nothing of it, Jonas. He ordered I remove this boys metal and have the Guard finish him off by taking him out the back. I am to speak no more of this to anyone from this day forward. Don't be cross with me for following the orders of this collar's Dominant. I had no choice. He has the right to destroy what belongs to him."

Jonas wrapped his free arm around me. "Calm down Christian Axel. I will not allow the Guard to harm you, I swear it. I am taking you out of here. This is bullshit. If your Master doesn't wants you anymore, even better for me. I have you all to myself. This okay with you? You come with me and submit to my authority as your Master?"

I nodded, never removing my face from his flesh. "Ja, ja, I swear it Master Jonas. I will do whatever you want. Please save me from the Guard."

Hemmel gasped, "Wait Jonas, I cannot let you do this. You're an Elder. You cannot hold a collar. This is against the Haus law."

Jonas chuckled, sounding full of evil. "I am an Elder, Hemmel. You and Peter keep forgetting I am the Haus law." He pulled me along still in his embrace to the wall then used that cutter to break the padlock that leashed me in place.

At that moment, the Guard arrived. Two huge, hairy brutes carrying rifles came through the door glaring at the three of us. I locked my hands around each of my wrists holding onto Jonas with all my strength, bracing for their attempt to pull me off him.

The larger of the two approached and grabbed my shirt pulling hard while calling for his partner to come aid him. I wailed out in misery thinking that Jonas cut the leash free so these two could haul me away with ease, you know.

Ta my surprise Jonas suddenly yelled out, "ОСТАВЬ ЭТОГО МАЛЬЧИКА В ПОКОЕ. ВЫ БОЛЬШЕ НЕ ТРЕБУЕТСЯ. ЭТОТ ВОРОТНИК ИМЕЕТ МОЮ ЗАЩИТУ." in the Russian language.

I didn't understand what he said but the two brutes released me. They said something to each other, then turned around leaving almost as fast as day had come. He told me later he said, "Leave this boy alone. This collar has my protection. You are no longer required." Since Jonas was an Elder and the one that paid their salaries, neither of these brutes was willing to argue his command to let me be.

At the time, the only thing I knew was Jonas had somehow saved my ass. I was more than a little grateful, I must confess. I am not a schwuler, but I was certain I loved that man in those stress filled moments. I was unwilling to anger him no matter what perversion or disgusting thing he asked of me. This belief was further assured when he pried me off him, I was still pretty panicked you know, and forced me to look at him.

"Christian Axel, you listen to me. I am taking you home with me this minute. I want you to be quiet, obedient, and calm. You misbehave and I will call the Guard back. This time I won't tell them to go away no matter how much I love you. You understand me?" He stared into my tearful face with much sternness.

I nodded wildly. "Ja, I understand Master. I will obey. Thank you for your mercy."

Jonas smiled at that then reached into his jacket pocket and handed me a handkerchief. "Wipe away those tears and get ahold of yourself, my love. When you're calmed down, we will leave this cell. You are all mine alone since your Master Peter has decided to throw you away. No matter what you say, you are the schizophrenic Christian Axel. That doesn't bother me a damned bit. I saw you at the worst and I also see you return in time. I am a patient man, I told you this before. We work together to keep this demon a secret, and you break that metal. Then you find your mate and bring her home to us. Your blood is the cure for age, but I need her blood to cure death. Only the set of both of the Priceless can grant me immortality. You will do this in return for this life of yours I save today. I will hear no excuses and this directive I command of you is not negotiable. It is my will or death, no other choices for you. If I withdraw my protection, you will have more than that Guard to be worried about. Schizophrenics don't become surgeons, nor do they survive long on their own, now do day? With the aid of my money, power, and influence, you can have all your dreams my love, but only if you pay my price."

I wiped my eyes as he told me his demands, keeping my gaze to the floor. I heard his warnings and realized it didn't matter that I was not a schizophrenic. Jonas and Peter had decided I was diseased. The two of them had me in their clutches so tightly I could barely breathe. I understood at last, if I struggled too much, they would crush me with their iron grips. Next time I would not survive…

Chapter 31: The Bat's Collar

"I followed behind my new Master Jonas keeping my head down and eyes to the floor. He led me from that cement cell back up the stairs to the main part of the Haus. I was trembling a great deal still unsure that the Guard had truly been called off. I tried not to do it, but my trauma at that near miss caused me to keep believing my collar was busted off.

I reassured myself by reaching up and holding onto it with my right hand. This did help me calm a bit. I found the circle of silver still intact, and secure around my neck. I could feel that I had not been uncollared.

I kept repeating inside my head, we would be alright. Master Jonas had saved us from the orchard and my father's bed for good or so I thought at the time you know. I was not happy to be in the possession of this Vampire. To be honest I was no longer too picky about that. Far as I could see it, anything was better than helping the fruit trees grow stronger.

Master Jonas would turn to look back at me following him in silence up those stairs. When we reached the top, he stopped and took a deep breath. I felt like I would piss in my pants thinking he had suddenly had a change of heart. Master Peter had tossed my collar. If this Vampire Elder didn't want my silver either, then I was finished.

He turned around staring at me with some look of disgust. "You are filthy, bruised to shit, skinny, and look insane, Christian Axel. I wish I had time to at least have changed these rags you wear before we enter the Haus hallways. The tongues will wag bad enough when you are spotted after being missing for eight months as it is. Then to have you looking as if you just got off a deserted island after many months of being castaway, oh this is not good." I kept my eyes down shaking in pure terror while he looked me over clicking his tongue.

Then he gasped and took off his long jacket, "I think this may help hide the worst of this foulness for the short time we must travel. I don't care how you do it, but you cover that famous face scar of yours. Make sure no one can see those eyes either. Maybe if we move quickly no one will notice that this creepy creature is the Priceless Maximillian. When we get home, get into the shower. I will make some calls to a hairdresser that knows how to keep their counsel. You need a fucking haircut. I will buy you new clothes and hide you out a few weeks till your healed. I want some weight back on your bones. I was told you refused the food while in the cell. You will eat for me, or I will put fresh marks on you to go with these other injuries. This you understand?"

He had me put on his coat and showed me how I would cover my face so the collars and Dominants of the Haus would not know me. Once he was sure it would be difficult for prying eyes to recognize me, he nodded his approval.

"We go now. Move swiftly, silently, and rapidly. I will not stop. You better keep up or that Guard will have their fertilizer. Come now, that is a directive." He opened the door taking off into the hallway at a rapid stride.

I nearly had to run to keep up with Master Jonas's fast pace. The silver collars fell to their knees at his approach and the black collars retreated in every direction. The Dominants seen to be trying to get a look at the boy with long hair following him on a leash. No one got a good look, thanks to my well-placed hands and slumped shoulders. I heard his directive loud and clear.

I knew Master Jonas was not trying to be cruel. This was an attempt to save his and my reputation. He didn't want anyone to see him rescuing Maximillian from the dungeons looking disheveled like this. If I were noticed for who I am by any of them, the rumors of serious insolence or even insanity would spread through the Haus like wildfire. That could be a disaster for our plans to break my metal if such talk reached the ears of the Voting Council.

Much to my relief he took the back hidden staircase to his apartment. Very few silvers used this path. The black collars were always in a hurry to move up and down if they used them at all. The only Dominants traveling with any kind of regularity on those steps were the Elders themselves. Therefore, we were not as rushed nor was my identity in as much danger of being discovered.

Despite our slightly slower pace, we still made it to Master Jonas's sixth floor apartment in record time. I heard him let out his breath in relief while he unlocked his front door and pulled me inside. He slammed it behind us demanding I strip and hit the shower without the mercy of a moments rest as he raced through the living area.

He let my leash go and watched me move with speed to his master bathroom while throwing off his jacket across his large velvet couch. That rest of my ancient clothing was so thread bare, it had been eight months, and no one ever gave me any new ones, they pretty much fell apart when I attempted to remove them. I piled the dusty, dirty rags into the corner of the room rushing for his shower without hesitation. I was more than happy to follow this order. I had not had such a luxury in all those months. I was covered in sores and skin infections thanks to that inhuman treatment in the cell.

I stood under that flowing water feeling the horrors of my years with Master Peter washing away down the drain. My flesh burned and itched worse than it ever had even during Xavior's torturous treatment of me. It didn't matter, not for that moment. I closed my eyes and just let the lifegiving liquid message my aching bones. I thought I could have lived in Master Jonas's bathtub forever drinking in the sensations of being clean once more.

I heard the door to the room open. I could see the outline of my new Master come inside. He stood there staring at the hideous pile of filth I left that had once clung to me like rotting flesh. Even through the rushing water I could hear him groan from that sight.

I turned off the faucet quickly and came out of the bath onto his fuzzy black bathmat. I dropped to a knee, shivering and wet from the cold of that huge room. Master Jonas stared at me a moment with astonishment, not a good kind either, then found his tongue.

"This is a horror. You will require medical attention. You're skin and bones, Christian Axel. These blisters, oh this will not do. That fucking Peter is a neglectful bastard. No wonder you've lost your mind. There is no way you can wear anything with disease of the flesh like this. Here, put on that soft robe of mine but keep it loose off your irritated skin. I will make another phone call. That rat bastard father of yours is not the only one around here that has medical personal in his hip pocket. Gott damned fool didn't need to call the Guard to waste any bullets. You'd have surely died of sepsis from your bed sores soon enough. Come with me and remember, not a word out of you. I am still not sure I did the right thing to save you. This illegal situation will cause much trouble, and I am still wondering where to even begin to dig either of us out of it. I warned Hemmel to keep his mouth shut but Peter will be expecting that collar back to prove your planted." Master Jonas watched me take up his black silk robe and put it on to cover my nakedness as commanded.

I said nothing and kept my eyes to the floor. I knew I was not out of the woods yet. If Master Jonas could not come up with a way to hold my collar, then all this hope I had may have been a waste. He could talk like he was the tough dog all he liked to the Dungeon Master Hemmel, but Master Jonas was the youngest Elder. He had no power at all in the Haus without the agreement of all his brothers.

Master Jonas nodded when the horror of my long incarceration had been covered in silk. "That is some improvement but like anything else at this moment it is only a cover up. We need something more than skin deep to fix this mess. Follow me. We first must convince Peter his will has been done. That will buy me time to come up with a plan to keep your collar for my own despite the Law." I trailed behind him still shivering and feeling fevered from my extreme physical deficits.

Master Jonas had me kneel by his velvet couch while he went to his bedroom. He came back with a hex wrench in his possession. I nearly come unglued when he leaned down and began unlocking Peter's collar. In full terror I wailed while grabbing it, trying to block him from taking it off.

Master Jonas backhanded me with such force I nearly hit the floor unconscious. The stun allowed him to continue his task of removing this tossed circle of silver and leash from my throat with no further protest from me. I was too weak to offer any reasonable resistance. I began to weep silently in much fear as I saw this thing, I had wanted gone for two years in my Master's hands after he took it from my neck.

I covered my naked throat, cowered in full panic there on the floor. The walls were closing in on me, threatening to drive me back into madness. Master Jonas noticed my distress. He stood over me holding the defunct silver in his hands with an expression of pity on his face.

"Calm down, my love. I know you are scared. I will tell you a secret. I am too. This collar I have here is no good anymore. Peter wants it back. He has thrown you away, Christian Axel. I must return to him what is his. I will make sure he gets it back. The boy that wore it, however, is mine. I never had a pleasure submissive of my own before. I will have a collar made for my Christian Axel, and you will submit to my collaring when I have this gift ready for my beautiful property. That is if I can find a way around this stupid Haus law about my owning a submissive. That is not your worry. Your Master Jonas will find a way, that I swear to you, my love. Until the proper collaring with me, you need to focus on healing and rest. I can see you are worn and in foul health. I will keep you hidden in this apartment. In time, you will be beautiful once again. But without a Dominant's silver of ownership, you will be shot on sight. No one musk know you are here still among the living. You must mind my orders and be quiet as death or that rider will take your tongue for his own. Do you understand me, Christian Axel?" He reached down and pulled my tear drenched face up, forcing me to look at him.

I nodded. "As you wish Master. Thank you for your mercy." I felt sick to my stomach and so fatigued nothing mattered anymore.

I was more than aware that without my collar I was fully hostage to Master Jonas's pleasure. If he changed his mind about finding a way to bend the rules or worse, couldn't bend them, I was a goner. The best I could hope for was an auctioning of my metal. Since I only had the one virginity left the new Master or Mistress would take that and I would be hopelessly trapped as a submissive all my life.

The worst that could happen is Peter would tell everyone I had schizophrenia, and the Guard would be called to finish what they started. Either way, I was in one hell of a tight spot. Everything hinged on the Vampire Elder's silver tongue and masterful manipulation abilities.

I cannot even begin to describe how fucking scared I truly was over this nightmare. I had thought of nothing but escaping from that foul Peter, but when the day finally came, it was not the happy moment I thought it would be. I had learned long ago that escaping the Haus was impossible unless you could break that collar. Now that I didn't have one to bust, it was looking more and more like I would never get out of the hell hole alive.

The personal physician of Master Jonas came within only an hour of his removal of Peter's collar. The man gave me a full examination. His expression was like that of Master Jonas, disgust. He informed my Master I suffered from malnutrition, skin infections, contusions, and a likely concussion. The doctor told him that I would do well to spend a little time in a hospital bed with IV drips and constant care as I was in such poor shape.

Master Jonas informed him this was not possible. I heard him tell this doctor that if I was not capable of healing up without outside aid, then I was finished and should be put out of my misery. This doctor nodded his head as if this was a normal thing for him to hear every fucking day. This man reported that I could survive without a hospital bed, but that my infections were extensive and dangerous. Any of them could lead to septic shock or permanent damage to my flesh. Master Jonas told him to leave medications and instructions. He would make sure they were followed to the letter, but I was not going anywhere.

The doctor finally relented though he didn't seem very happy about the whole thing. My Master was given many pills and salves for my open sores with strict instructions I was to rest in the bed for at least thirty more days. The worried doctor left stating he would check back soon.

He barely left when the barber showed up knocking. I sat in a chair within Master Jonas's kitchenette and was then subjected to a haircut of my Master's choice. This man cut my hair short everywhere leaving the top a little long for the spike look you see me wearing to this very day.

Turned out Master Jonas liked his hair long like the Frau, but he preferred the male looking short hair on his lovers. Oh well, not like I had any choice. I had always worn my hair in a tight hair cut so this hair I would have to take care of the top was a bother to me.

Seemed to me one of the really nice things about being the male was there is no need for much hair care. With our gender even bald can be fashionable. This added chore of keeping the hair products in my mane was a pain in the ass. I didn't think I was so happy about it. I said nothing about it though. I had minded my new Master to a fault. Not a single word had left my lips throughout the entire two visitors. I kept my eyes down, ears open and mouth shut.

When the barber left, I was still sitting quietly in the chair with my lost locks laying all around me on the floor. Though the doctor's salves had cooled the worst of my burning flesh, and the silk robe after the shower calmed the chronic itching, I was fuller of despair than ever. I kept my face down and my shoulders slumped. The weight of the world was crushing Maximillian's back.

I was so far behind in my studies and my Dominant's training, catching up seemed beyond my ability. My father tossed my collar, and this new Master wasn't even my legitimate owner. The ones that mattered to my future believed I had this mental illness. It seemed a hole had swallowed me up and a life of silent, brutal servitude loomed for all my days. It was so hopeless.

Master Jonas came back into his kitchenette to find me there depressed beyond reason. He stood in the entryway watching me for a bit. I didn't bother to respond to his appearance. Unless he told me to do something, I felt it best to be still. I was his bitch and understood that all too well,

He was the puppet master and I had to wait till he pulled my strings. I admit, I hated him for it more than I can say. More than that, I hated me for it. What a life I had found for myself, ja?

Master Jonas approached me with a look of pity on his face. "Christian Axel, you must try to keep the faith for me, my love. This seems very bad right now, but if you can stay strong and battle your way back from the abyss, then your lover Jonas will be here to catch your fall every time. We are blood bonded for life. You and I will change this Haus, you'll see. One day I will be the Master of this Haus with my beloved Christian Axel at my side. These dark days will be a memory long forgotten. I sent Peter back his property without the boy inside. Peter's Priceless collar Maximillian is officially dead, my love. When I collar you, I will have the right to grant you a new name of my choice, or I can give you the gift of choosing your own. If you can fight for your recovery, and for us, then I grant this mercy to you. This is something to look forward to, ja?"

I nodded my head wincing as I recalled the collaring ceremony with Peter. "Thank you for that mercy, Master Jonas." I didn't mean a fucking word of that gratitude.

What the hell did I care what anyone call this loser? It seemed to me not even close to an equal trade for the consummation and vows this Vampire would extract from me on the horrific day he put his metal around my neck. All that I would have to endure again for the right to survive in the hallway without a bullet in my brain. This was perhaps not the right thing to bring up to me at that moment of my deepest grief over what I thought was an epic failure.

I tried to hold it together, but damn me, I broke down weeping in pure depression unable to fathom the depths I had sunk to. Master Jonas apparently didn't expect that response over what he thought was great news.

He came over and wrapped his arms around me. This only made me more despondent. My hopes for a Frau and children were replaced by the horror of man as my husband. This was beyond hellish, trust me. My silent sobbing became a full-on crying jag that I was unable to stifle. I couldn't bear that somehow, when I had been on top of this situation, I had fallen right through the floor and straight to Hades.

I was only fourteen, just turned, and puberty had not sent me into a massive growth spurt yet. I maybe could claim one hundred and seventy centimeters (around 5' 6") and barely one hundred and twenty pounds thanks to that starvation in the dungeon over the months. The much larger Master Jonas had no problem lifting me from that chair into his arms. He picked me up like the bride and cradled the crying boy.

I didn't struggle as he carried me down his hallway to a room with a light grey door. He opened this to reveal a small room with a twin bed draped in black sheets, black dresser, fancy floor lamp, and tiny closet without a door. The window was boarded up. He took me to this bed and laid me into it with gentle care.

I was still beyond consoling with my sorrow. My Master sat next to me on the bed stroking my face with an expression of concern. He said nothing while I emptied my heart of the tears of defeat. Many moments passed before my eyes found it's well had run dry at last.

I stared at the ceiling quivering from time to time, my chest still aching with torment. Master Jonas never left my side while I accepted what I thought was my fate that late afternoon. He sat there in complete silence, keeping his presence with a soft touch on my horridly bruised face and neck.

When at last I had stopped crying, he cleared his throat. "Christian Axel, please my love you must try harder to adjust. The doctor told me that sometimes after a deep psychotic break from madness a dangerous depression can overtake the person. He warned me that you can maybe want to end your life. I want to say, I didn't save you to have you undo it with your own hands. I would beg your forgiveness, but I will have to bond and lock you up for a bit to keep you safe. I know this will seem cruel after all you have been through, but my love, I must protect you from yourself. This will be your room until I can be sure this darkness within you has passed on. It is only for a little time, and you can shorten that by remembering what I told you already. We will beat this. You will break that collar, and one day you will bring our Frau home to have your children. If you can learn to trust your Master, I can even assure your dreams of becoming a doctor are still within your grasp."

I gasped at that and focused on his smiling face, "What? Nein, you say I have this schizophrenia. I am too far behind in school and the Dominant training. I cannot get it finished in only the two years left. I don't even have a fucking collar. I am finished. I am sorry I am so weak I didn't just let the Guard do the right thing. Peter is right. I am not worth even growing a tree in the fucking orchard."

Master Jonas chuckled at my statement. "Ah, you are so young Christian Axel. You know nothing of how this world works. Money, power, influence, that runs the wheels to all things in our society. Not just in the Haus, but in the places beyond these walls. You are intelligent. While you heal you study and even after everyday work hard. You will catch up easily in the school work. The Dominant training, well my love, that is something that your Master can clear the path for you to walk without further hindrance. You do what I tell you, and my collar will be good as broken the second I put it around your neck. When you are ready for medical school as a Dominant in your own right, Peter has a contract with you. That idiot cannot get out of his deal any more than you ever could. He recorded it with the Book of Honor in the Law room. He made that deal with Christian Axel, not Maximillian. He must send you if you break your metal, darling. Your blood bonded lover Jonas will make sure a good medical school accepts your application. That schizophrenia never needs be discussed nor known to anyone long as you keep your vows to your man. This you understand, ja?" He smiled with much wickedness at me.

I sat up feeling sudden hope in his words. "Ja, I had forgotten that horrible contract with Peter. This thing will still stand even though he tossed my collar?" I winced realizing the very contract that had once sent me to violence against myself could be my fucking salvation.

Master Jonas grabbed both sides of my face holding me tightly with a toothy grin below his firelit eyes. "Ah. There is my Christian Axel's fight at last. Ja, my love, this contract will hold if and only if you break that collar of mine. Peter made a mistake. He listed his agreement was made with Christian not Maximillian. There is still a Christian Axel even if Maximillian has been put to the orchard. You can still make that rat bastard father of your pay for your glorious future, but my love you must fight this disease to have all your dreams come true. It will not be easy; this is a fact. You can do this. I have seen the truth of your priceless nature. This is a setback, not the end of everything, unless you decide you want to quit. If so, then tell me now before I get my hopes up. I can always call the Guard and end both our struggles. I would rather see you put to the yard and start my grieving than wait weeks to find out you're not willing to do what must be done to recover all that we almost lost."

I confess I considered having him call the Guard back. I was so full of demons of sorrow. The future seemed dark, bleak, and hopeless. Yet, I found strength in Master Jonas's faith that this could be done. He is a manipulating bastard, but this time, maybe that was exactly what I needed. Had he not been there prodding me past this depression that had set into my psyche, well Meine Liebe neither of us would be here now, I think. *(He winked at me knowing that he had saved my own life several times already. I nodded but was careful to keep my mouth shut. Mad Max was still telling this part of the story. I kept a baleful eye on his cane with much trepidation that one wrong move would result in a painful swat.)*

For the next two weeks I was locked in that room and often bonded to the bed to keep me safe from injuring myself. I endured it understanding at least Master Jonas didn't hit me much or starve me half to death during my incarceration. I was allowed to be free several hours a day if I stayed within his sight and kept my mouth shut.

He brought me my schoolbooks and allowed me enough freedom in my bounds to study during my long hours of imprisonment. He insisted I shower daily and fed me so much I often was full of sickness. If I dared to refuse to eat every bite of his high calorie meals, I would get a backhand till I complied. Master Jonas gave me no quarter for denial of any of his commands. Hesitation, argument, or slowness was punished swiftly and without mercy. I learned quickly to not mess with Master Jonas. He was not one to forgive or grant any disagreements.

The first day of the third week after my near death in the dungeons, I was laying in the living room studying after the huge breakfast the Vampire forced me to eat. There was a knock at the door. Master Jonas was on his velvet couch reading a novel when this noise came. I got up to rush off to my room. I was still without a collar and my existence in the Haus a secret. When visitors came it was my duty to remove my presence immediately and await further orders from my Master.

Sometimes it was the doctor visiting me to attend my now healing wounds. The infections had cleared up and my flesh had stopped burning and itching by this time. The bruises were still there, but the yellows of their end had begun to show up on my skin as well. My weight was still very low, but I was starting to recover and gain back some energy. Things were looking up regarding my physical wellbeing.

My mental health, however, was still in the toilet. I spent many hours weeping and wishing for death to find me. I must confess locking me away and bonding me like that was likely the smart thing to do. There were several times I would have done something stupid had I been free to roam. Things in my head had gone from dark to black.

It had become a struggle just to get out of bed every morning. Master Jonas's backhand or quirt were the only reason I even bothered. I may have wanted to seek the reaper, but I didn't care to do it with black eyes and a welted ass.

I had not seen any of my brother shards since the dungeons. I had become despondent and lonely without them there to fuck with. I assumed they had abandoned me to my fate at the hands of this Vampire husband. I hated them all more than I can say for their dishonoring me like that. Nothing I could do.

I called and called for them, but by that day I had given up. Der Hund said we were shattered. I began to assume that meant they were all gone, busted into millions of pieces. Only me, Mad Max, was left to endure whatever horrors awaited the flesh. That fear added fuel to my already nasty vision of my existence.

I went into my room, closed the door, and got onto my bed with my schoolbook. There was no reason for me to expect the doctor since he had visited the day before. My exam had brought a smile to his face due to my great improvements. A recovering patient doesn't keep the doctor hanging around for second helpings of poking and prodding.

I was startled out of my study by Maximillian entering the room. "Well, I will be damned. I didn't even know a brute could read much less do equations. The boy is looking better. I cannot believe you, of all of us, managed to pull us out of that horror state the flesh was in. Not sure I like that hair cut your sport though. I guess it is trendy, but damn what a lot of trouble that is going to be."

I almost come out of that bed ready to punch that schwuler bitch. "You bastard. Where the fuck have you been? I been calling for you for two weeks now."

Maximillian giggled at me. "Calm down there, Mr. Bad Ass. I told you I needed a fucking nap. I was stuck with the boy for eight months and they were not good times, you know. I know you do because you had to sit in there while that shit healed up. If that makes you mad, then tough shit. I am here now. What's the matter? Did the Vampire like your sucking better than his?"

I narrowed my eyes at him. "You are a pig you know that? For your information Master Jonas never touched me like that the whole time. Thank Gott. See this? I pulled down my shirt to show him the boys naked neck, no collar. I don't have to pay any special services without the contract for them fool."

Maximillian gasped, "Holy shit. Oh Meine Gott. We are dead. Where the fuck is our collar? What did you do to get us uncollared. Help, help, someone help. Mad Max has killed us all," he screamed like the little bitch he is.

Mad Maxx, Christian, and Max rushed into the room upon hearing our brother wailing like that. I sat their crossing my arms while those fools all freaked the fuck out over the boys lack of silver. I let them flip out for a bit while enjoying their pain. Hey, they all left me to suffer, plus what can I say? I am a sadist, ja. After a while though it kind of got on my nerves.

"All of you, shut the fuck up. Listen to me. Peter tossed his collar. Master Jonas sent it back to him, is all. We are awaiting the new one that contracts us to this Vampire. He has been hiding us out while he gets his permission to do this thing. Maximillian, I hope you are good and rested cause I will be damned if I am going to run the wheel when that consummation shit goes down. I mean it. We need to test the switch right away. I warn you, if I am stuck in here, I am going to shatter your ass with my bare fucking hands. This has been a nightmare I was not created to endure. Mad Maxx would have been a better selection, hell even Christian could have done a better job at this depression shit. I cannot bare another second. I want out." I glared at my brothers full of the fury at this terrible situation.

Maximillian looked at Mad Maxx. "I am not ready for this yet, brother. If the flesh is depressed, you know I will give into it. The bleach and jumping off the banister seemed like a good idea at the time you know?"

Mad Maxx sighed. "Shit, ja, he is right Mad Max. Maximillian has already tried to kill us twice, and Christian ran out into the yard. We cannot have either of them at the wheel if depression has onset. I suppose I will have to take my turn if you're tired for truth."

I nodded wildly. "Ja, brother, I am done. You get me the fuck out of here. I swear I am two seconds from running from this apartment bare necked ready to play the clay pigeon for the Guards target practice."

Mad Maxx sighed. "Okay, then I trade with you for a bit. Maximillian, you get your ass back together. Your next when I wear out. I will ask you Christian and Max keep hunting for Der Hund. I have yet to find him and cannot search when riding the flesh. If you find him tell him, we are not shattered. We need him to come home right away. Gott damn him. Mad Max you come out and I will go in now." He backed up ready for his run if I was successful in stepping out of the boy.

I closed my eyes, took a deep breath then to my relief stepped out of the flesh with ease. Mad Maxx rushed past me leaping into the boy just as his knees buckled from the sudden loss of his direction. I watched as Mad Maxx grabbed the side of the bed catching the flesh before it hit the floor. He blinked and looked around overwhelmed by the sensations of life after so many months of the nothing.

We watched Mad Maxx sit back down on the bed examining his hands and legs while reacquainting himself with the flesh. I looked over at Maximillian with a smile of wickedness overtaking me. I walked over and backhanded that schwuler bitch with all I had.

"That is for being you. Go get your nap crybaby. Before I shatter you just for something to do." I reared back to smack him again when Christian grabbed my arm.

"Stop that you two. Isn't that how all this shit started? I swear you two fight like the Frau and Husband. Go fuck each other and make up but stop trying to start another shattering. This bullshit is getting on my nerves. That is damned hard to do." He pushed me away from Maximillian.

Maximillian run at me while I was distracted by Christian. He smacked into me, sending both of us into the wall. We near shattered from the force. Max and Christian come running to break up our argument which only caused them to get involved in the fray. Soon all four of us were in a brawl knocking the shit out each other, even busting off fingers and near shattering off each other's arms.

Mad Maxx sat there in the boy shocked into silence and fear. He was helpless to stop the all-out war of the shards. The situation had gotten out of hand so fast, in mere moments it was clear if we didn't come to our senses soon, only the strongest were going to survive.

"Stop this shit at once. All of you motherfucker, on your knees now I say, or I will shatter all of you myself." The walls shook with the anger of Der Hund sending all of us to our knees, including Mad Maxx in the boy, immediately.

I watched in horror as Max suddenly began to vibrate then exploded into dust. All of us began to tremble thinking Der Hund had shattered our brother the shard of forgiveness and mercy in his anger. Then to our pure shock, Der Hund came into the room, only he was not complete.

The core shard was translucent and damaged almost beyond recognition. His eyes were drooping, and his mouth disfigured. One arm was missing entirely. He had become a walking horror. All of us gasped and lowered our sight trying to look away from the monster Christian Axel had become.

"You cowards. Look upon me. This is what happens when you fight within. You nearly destroyed me. That shattering has come and this half-life. This is what I am condemned to for all time. I was thrown so far from the blast of it, I lost my way back. I travel for many months, finally finding my way home only to find my creations fighting yet again. Look upon me, fools. This is what we have become. Do you desire it to get worse still? Then keep up you're bickering. Go ahead, push me. I will blow all of you to pieces and the fucking boy can stare into the nothing for all time," he bellowed out, sounding beyond furious at all of us.

I was kneeling with the others in the boy, but I knew Der Hund, no matter how anger was speaking to me. "Der Hund. You shattered Max. This shard was the guard for Christian and all that was good. I don't understand why?"

Der Hund growled with his eyes glowing red with hell fires. "I grant no mercy. Feel no need to give forgiveness. There is no love, Mad Maxx. This shard was a useless thing. I freed Christian from his bonds to Max. We take no prisoners and feel no remorse anymore. Twisted, they have made us and twisted we have become. You, my masochist, are next if you persist to piss me off. I have no need for guilt either. Maximillian, your gentleness is also a waste. Do either of you desire to find oblivion with Max? If not, then shut your mouth and take your turns running the flesh. Otherwise, I can survive with Christian, my anger and lust shard, and Mad Max, my sadist shard. They are all I need to destroy all my enemies." his voice shook the walls and the ground, sending all of us into prostrated postures.

We all answered in unison, "Your will is our own." No one dared to say another damned thing either.

Der Hund glared at us with his dislodged eyes for another few moments then he stormed out of the room headed for wherever he tends to go when angered like that. None of us moved for several moments. We just trembled and panted in terror at what we had just witnessed. We had been searching for our core for many months but finding him had been worse than losing him. There was no longer any doubt, we had shattered in the worst way, and Der Hund had not fared well during our fall.

I realized Mad Max had left, so I took that second to hazard a question. "Does shattered mean you do have schizophrenia, Master?"

As I suspected Mad Maxx wasn't the thudding type. "Ja, that is what it means. You see Mad Max and Maximillian do not believe in the mental illness. Christian, Der Hund, and I know this is what happened to us. No matter what we have tried to do all these years those two idiots will not accept the truth. In the end, it matters not what the doctors call the disease. There is no escaping the truth of it. We can never be the Christian Axel we had once been. Der Hund has never recovered, and while he was able to eventually remake Max, that shard also never has been what it was before the shattering from so long ago." He frowned then stroked my hair gently.

I narrowed my eyes. "So, that means you can't love me, Master? Max was the loving shard, right?"

Mad Maxx chuckled hard. "Ah, you see you need to hear this whole story, Meine Liebe. That will be explained in time, but you get too impulsive. While your eagerness is sublime torture, I think it best for you to hear me out, then ask the questions, if I have not answered them all, ja?"

I nodded. "Yeah, you are right, Master. Just one more thing. Does it hurt to have schizophrenia?"

Mad Maxx pulled me close and sighed loudly. "More than you can ever comprehend, Meine Liebe. The pain is so bad, I cannot even find joy in it. I hope to prevent such a madness within you. Sometimes, I can see it in your eyes too. I worry that one day your shattering will come.

59

If it does, then we can never hope to break your collar. Schizophrenics are forbidden Dominant status by Haus Law. They are automatically trapped in their metal and usually put to the yard or hauled away to wherever the Guard takes them."

I winced. "But Master, you said you have schizophrenia. You broke your collar. How?"

He squeezed me tightly. "Again, I say to you Meine Liebe, let me finish the damned story? No wonder Mad Max thuds you. I am not much for such a thing, but I am thinking maybe I will take up the habit until this story is done. Do you wish to test my skills with the cane?"

I shook my head. "No thank you Master. I apologize for that. Thank you for your mercy."

Mad Maxx chuckled. "You think me, Max? No mercy with Mad Maxx, little one. Now do I continue with this story, or do you wish to test me some more? That is what I thought." He watched me settle back in and shut my fucking mouth. After all the dude has schizophrenia. He's a nutball, yikes. Kind of explains a few things though, doesn't it? Just saying.

"I finally decided to get up because the flesh's knees were sending signals of pain to me. I looked at Mad Max, Maximillian and Christian still shaking on the floor.

"Der Hund has gone. Get up brothers. His mood is foul. I suggest we all tread lightly from now on around him," I whispered to the others.

Maximillian looked up. "He said he is going to shatter you and me Mad Maxx. I don't want to be sent away. What can we do?"

I shook my head. "Stop fighting, complaining, and take your turn. He told you, brother. I say we all listen to our core and do our best to make him as comfortable as possible given the, well, you saw him."

Mad Max got up. "Ja. That was a nightmare come to truth. Well Christian and I am in no danger. Only you Frau's are threatened." He chuckled full of evil.

Christian got up smiling. "Ja, and I have no babysitter anymore. This is great as far as I am concerned. Time to chase the women and kill our enemies at will." He and Mad Max high fived each other, giggling at that.

Maximillian got up too sighing, "We cannot go killing and fucking as we please you fools. The Guard will end that real fucking quick. Be reasonable."

Mad Max glared at his brother. "Ah, look Christian, Maximillian is about to cry. He would rather be fucked then do the fucking you know. Schwuler freak."

Maximillian started to become angry, but then looked with sudden fear at the direction Der Hund had fled. "Ja, hahaha, you got me there brother. I am the schwuler. That is a good one."

Mad Max frowned at that. "Ah, ja. You're a sissy baby too. You love to suck the cocks while you cry and paint your toes."

Maximillian shrugged. "The bigger the cock the better brother. You sure know me well, If you don't mind, I think I feel like going to cry right now. Maybe if I am lucky, I can find nail polish to match my tears, ja?" He took off out of the room and I swear he was going off somewhere to cry likely. Who could blame him? Mad Max is a bastard. Not being able to defend yourself against that creep is no fun, I should know since Der Hund threatened me too.

The door of the room opened with Mad Max and Christian still there. I nearly let out a yelp of shock when Master Jonas entered. I had been so caught up in this mess with my brothers and core I forgot there was an outside world you know.

My Master stood there smiling with much joy in his expression and a black box in his grip. I watched Mad Max and Christian rush from the room leaving me to deal with whatever nightmare this Vampire was up to this time. I didn't say a word nor move while Master Jonas came forward and dropped that box in my lap.

I stared at it then went back to Master Jonas. "What is this, Master? I did nothing to earn a present, did I?"

He chuckled. "Not yet, but soon you will earn this one. Open it Christian Axel. Damn it, I bring my love a gift and he acts like I am punishing him. What a strange boy you are."

I nodded. "Okay, I thank you for your kindness then." I opened the box and about fainted off the bed when I saw what was inside there.

A circle of silver with a large black bat and O ring welded to the throat of it, wrapped up in a neat order next to it a long leash of black rather than silver links. Master Jonas was letting me know loud and clear his bid to hold my collar had been accepted. A collaring ceremony was in the air at last.

I felt my mouth go dry with fear even though I knew this had to happen or I was doomed. It didn't make the idea of being collared by this scary man any fucking easier. I closed my eyes reminding myself at least Jonas was not my fucking father. There was no relation to this lover other than his gender being male like my own. The irony that I traded being raped by my own blood for someone that wanted to rape me, then drink my blood, was not lost on me even that dark day. (*Master Mad Maxx giggled bitterly at that statement*).

Master Jonas laughed out loud when I said nothing, then closed my eyes. "Well? Do you like it? I thought for my very first collar I would have something special made. This is pleasing to you, I hope?"

I opened my eyes and looked at him without expression. "Ja, it is very you, Master. Am I to assume your lobby to collar me has been fruitful? Or is this just a promise of things to come?" I did my best to not compliment something I found abhorrent – any collar is no matter how fancy – and to gain intelligence on when I could expect his horrific collaring ceremony.

Master Jonas frowned, then nodded. "My bid to hold your collar was successful. The collar came over a week ago. I held it until Claus came to give me the news, I can now claim you. I had a hell of a fight. Christian Axel, we need to talk, then after we understand each other, I will allow you to choose you fate. I wish to give you what I believe Peter did not. The truth of what the collar will mean to you and to me."

I sighed. "Maybe I don't need to know, Master. I must confess, had I known the horrors the first time, I would never have come when Peter called for me." I looked back at this bat-collar with guilt at my ignorance with not even knowing what special services meant back then.

My Master took a deep breath. "You need to know this time Christian Axel. If you don't agree to do all that I ask, you are finished. You see to get this honor of holding your collar I had to make many underhanded deals. I needed all my brothers to agree to this. The only way I could get them all to bend the rules was two-fold. First, you're considered my blood bonded mate. By Haus law we are married. That means I am allowed access to your favors anytime I like despite who may hold your contract silver. I could just say for all your life. That would save your life, but without a collar you're trapped in limbo servitude and can never obtain Dominant status. Therefore, by Haus law, your collar goes up for auction."

I gasped in terror. "I am going up for auction. Oh nein, call the fucking Guard. I'd rather die than have Leo or worse gain my metal. I will be trapped in it for all my life without a virginity." I felt the tears beginning to form.

Master Jonas growled, "Calm down, Christian Axel. I said only that by Haus law your collar should go to auction thanks to Peter's toss. Now maybe I would win the bid, but I dare not risk such a precious treasure to chance. So, I went to all my brothers. Each one agreed to allow this unusual "collaring" of the Priceless metal with me under one condition. If you agree to it, then I can bypass this auction and collar you for my own."

I sniffed back my tears but felt sick to my stomach. "It must be something you think I will find horrible, or you would not offer me the choice. I beg of you to end my pain and tell me what nightmare I must agree to or find myself

64

up for bids and trapped as a submissive for all my days." I braced myself for the bad news.

Ma Master shifted his weight then looked at the floor. "Well, Drexel, Bladrick, Claus, and Barnim want to share this collar. In other words, they let me claim the contract, but they have permanent leash rights to the only collar ever held by the Elders. I can have you, but I must share you without hesitation nor complaint from either of us."

I swallowed hard feeling his words strike me like needles in my ears. "I will be a whore to the Elders is what you say, used for their pleasures whenever they desire."

Master Jonas nodded. "Well, I would not say it so crudely, but ja, I suppose there is no way to make this any prettier. The bottom line my love is you and I take their deal, or you get ready for auction or the yard. I am willing to give you a few days to decide, but they are about to raise Cora to Head of the Haus at the end of the week so we must hurry," I interrupted my Master most rudely.

"Did you just say they are raising Mistress Cora, Ben's Mistress to Head of the Haus?" I felt the world begin to spin.

He nodded. "Ja, the rule of the FemDom is rising. If you deny the ruling Elders, with Claus at their head, well my love I doubt Cora will allow any quarter for you. Perhaps worse she may take you for herself to give to her best buddy Leo. I already know that she and Peter worked out selling your penetration virginity to Gretta. I think it best you do not leave any further possibility of this FemDom's screwing with your destiny, ja?"

I groaned out in true pain. "What? Gretta won the bid for my virginity. This is a fucking nightmare. Tell me you lie. She had Ryker come to destroy me. Cora sent Ben. This cannot be happening. Gott damn it. Peter is not my Master anymore. Can you stop Gretta? If I agree to your collar, you can reopen the bids for my collar selection virginity, right?" I nearly lost my mind for a third time over this horror news.

Master Jonas sighed. "Nein, look you can get through one night with Gretta when that horrible day comes. Just try to remember if she is collecting on it then you are only a week away from breaking your metal. If that fails, put a bag over her head, or hell, over your own. Look, that shit is beyond my control. I need you to focus on the decision at hand. Do you accept the terms of the Elders, ja or nein? Christian Axel, I need you to be sure. Once this is done, there is no turning back. I will warn you of one thing. If you say nein, I will have Hemmel come take you back to the dungeon right away to await your collar auction. I cannot stand to have something held under my nose that will never be mine." He glared at me with much sternness in his gaze.

I felt the tears break loose from my eyes. "I understand, Master. You ask a lot about me. I would happily accept your collar alone, but to ask me to accept the tight leash of four others at their will, these foul men. I ask you, what would you choose if you were in my place?" I looked up at him feeling more lost than I had ever in my life.

He shook his head. "Honestly, my love, I would never have made it this far. I would already be growing a tree. I am not a priceless, I am just a man looking for more than he was born to be. You, Christian Axel, were born to be a legend. The path for you in this life is naturally harsh. I have faith that the Gotts gave you all you will ever need to face your foes and win your battles. It is a lot I ask of you, a terrible burden for us both. However, if you can survive it, at the end is that door and the bolt cutters. I will proudly watch you cut my bat in half if you choose to join me. If you do not, you existence will be just as brutal, but you can forget hope of a better day for it. The boy I saved in the dungeon said he would do anything to survive. Well, prove this to me. Submit to me my love. Don't you see I am offering to save you from yourself."

I picked up that odd looking collar still weeping silently. I rolled it in my hands trying to decide how bad did I want to get out that front door on my feet rather than being carried out. I looked back at that Vampire outstretching my hand with the circle of silver in it.

"I bet you paid a great deal to have this customized like that. In fact, it looks Priceless to me, Master." I smiled at him bitterly while my tears streamed down my cheeks.

Master Jonas's face lit up with thrill. "Ja, it did indeed. There isn't another in the whole world like it. I am the lucky one to possess it."

I nodded. "You may hold it in your hands, but the funny thing about such unique things is while many envy you, others will do anything to take it all for themselves."

He laughed. "Isn't that truth. That will not matter. I am not a man to be stolen from. Christian Axel, you have this night to prepare yourself. Tomorrow afternoon I will call for your submission. If you don't answer when I call, then

67

be ready to leave my home forever." He walked out and slammed the door locking it behind him.

I looked down at that box falling into a crying jag while briefly considering hanging myself with the black leash. That comes with my choice between a rock and a hard place.

Chapter 32: Second Submission

"I wept for at least an hour sitting there holding that damned black box. That leash of black metal mocked me with visions of my foul defeat. I knew there was not any other options. Only Jonas had taken a virginity for this collaring already. If I dared to go to Auction, the new owner would take the last one I possessed since no one knew of Annette.

That would forever trap me in the collar. It was extremely simple: go with Jonas and have a chance of a better day or say nein to his deal that I collar with all the Elder schwuler and face death. For me, lifelong servitude as the Priceless collar was a promise of eventual demise, at my own hand or from a bullet owned by the Guard.

I called out to Maximillian. This collaring business was his domain not mine. He was built for the schwuler sex and our submissive shard. He came almost immediately, appearing out of breath and in his usual affable mood.

I showed him the box. "The word has come, brother. Jonas is permitted the collar."

He smiled at that and clapped his hands in relief. "Ah. Then we are saved. That is good news, brother. Der Hund will surely be lifted from his irritable state by this win."

I shook my head and groaned. "Wait, Maximillian, there is more to this than meets the eye. I call you because, well, I am just going to be forceful and say it. We are collaring with all the Elders, not just the Vampire. He will own the right to keep us in his home, but all the Elders are the Master of whoever we are named."

Maximillian's expression melted into one of confusion. "Huh? What is this your say? It makes no sense. Five Masters? Wait, five consummations? Is that why you called me? Nein, nein, fuck that. Call Der Hund. I am ready to join my brother Max. I will not tolerate the pawing of five nasty old men. I rather be dead," he yelled vile calling out for Der Hund to end him.

Der Hund come barreling through the door before I could hush the cries of my brother Maximillian. The look on his face was that of the angry bear. He glared at Maximillian that now trembled before him. I dropped to a kneel, hoping to calm these two before my brother ended up joining the shattered Max.

"Der Hund. Please forgive Maximillian's plea. He is just upset with the news Jonas brings to us. He means none of it. Don't listen to him. He is unaware of the details yet." I begged our inner self to use mercy with the easily excitable submissive shard.

Der Hund growled out, "Eh? Well, what the fuck. Someone start speaking of this interruption or I shatter you both. I told you already, I care for neither of you. Your services are no longer required to complete our mission."

Maximillian whimpered then fell to his knees begging, "I ask to be shattered Der Hund. I cannot deal with the affections of the foul five. I don't care if that does mean we are still capable of breaking the metal. This task is too much for me to do."

Der Hund flinched, appearing startled, then looked at me with shock. "What? The foul five? What does this shard speak of? We can still break our collar. Peter tossed it. We have no fucking collar. Auction or orchard is our fate. Is this shattering spreading again?"

I shook my head. "Nein, Der Hund. Maximillian has just discovered Jonas obtained the right to collar us as he has already paid the fourth virginity for his favor. We will have to consummate by this schwuler sex, but our third virginity will be left intact. That virginity was claimed by another the week before collar selection vote. If we accept Jonas's offer, our original mission is still valid."

Der Hund gasped then smiled; I think, not sure as his mouth is pretty fucked up, you know. "Our original mission can still be obtained. Ah. This is glorious news Mad Maxx. I thought it was all lost thanks to this shattering. Wait, if this is true then what the fuck is your problem, Maximillian? You can handle this consummation and any lustful attention that Jonas comes at us width. The other four you were seducing. What the fuck is the problem with you." He kicked Maximillian hard.

Maximillian groaned out in pain. "Mad Maxx doesn't tell you all of this agreement. If we take Jonas's deal, we have all five of the fetish schwuler's as the Master. They all will hold our collar equally. Special services whenever they wish it."

Der Hund jumped back in shock. "What? Nein, this cannot be so. No submissive can have five fucking masters. Mad Maxx?"

I looked at the floor with tears forming again. "Ja, this can be so. It was the only way Jonas could get the greedy bastards to agree to his collaring us. They think it not fair he gets what they cannot. They agreed to let him hold this collar contract with us, but they all hold a tight leash until it is broken. We must take the deal, or we are to go to auction. I accepted this offer. I apologize for not seeking your counsel first, but Cora is rising to replace Xavier. We had to hurry."

Der Hund groaned loudly. "Oh shit, Cora. I think I can see the plot now. Ficken mich. Ja, ja, you did the right thing, Mad Maxx. This is the only way we can survive. It may even work to our advantage as I now think about it a bit. This nightmare of five old schwulers touching us is bad, but it makes us the most powerful submissive in the Haus, hell the most powerful anything in this place. Pillow talk, and satisfied lovers do anything for the object of their desires. There is hope yet. I am thrilled by this news. Maximillian, I am going to strengthen you for this task of remaining pleasing for the foul five. You and Mad Maxx can handle this task with perfection." He grabbed Maximillian by the arm and threw him into the boy next to me at the wheel.

We struggled a bit to get comfortable in the flesh working the controls together while Der Hund stood there smiling at us. Der Hund then closed his disfigured eyes. I felt my brother Maximillian begin to meld into my side. I could suddenly hear and see what he could, and vice versa. We had become a single shard with two heads.

Der Hund chuckled "I am grateful in my anger I didn't destroy the two shards I thought worthless. Providence has shined on us at last. Together you two will bring us to see the sun on the boy's face once again. I will keep Mad Max and Christian for myself to hold counsel for our next moves. With my best shards trapped within, the flesh will become the perfect seducer, submissive, thinker, actor,

72

sexual dynamo, and schemer. I chose the name Mad Maxximillian for the collaring because that is who we are now. Do your job and break that fucking metal, boys. This is a directive."

We answered in unison, "Your will is our own." Then we watched a much happier Der Hund limp out of that room leaving Mad Maxximillian to do the impossible.

I looked at my brother's head and suggested we finish the melding. Being a thing with two brains was too clumsy I thought. Maximillian agreed. We focused hard then slowly evolved into a single shard capable of all the things Jonas and the Elders would require of the flesh.

I sat there waiting for the rest of the story, but my Master had suddenly paused. After a few moments of this I finally hazarded a glance at his face. He was sitting there with his eyes closed. I was confused wondering if he was thinking when I noticed his breathing was slow and deep. He had fallen asleep sitting up.

I shrugged then sighed. I wanted to hear the rest of his tale, but I dared not wake him up. I knew Mad Maxx could thud, I had dealt with it before, and unless Maximillian was there, my welts were pretty much assured by any other shard that may be present if I startled him to alertness.

I very gently began to climb off his lap to head for the floor. I recalled he said I was not allowed on the mattress while sleeping anymore. I knew better than to be caught breaking a directive. I had almost made it out of his lap to the mattress when he awoke with a loud gasp and grabbed me suddenly.

I let out a wail of terror from his rapid and unexpected movement. "I apologize Master, I thought you wanted to sleep. I was heading for the floor." I trembled while watching his cane.

Master Maxx chuckled "You were smart to head for the floor, Meine Liebe, but I am not asleep. I am telling you a story. Are you tired of it already?"

I shook my head. "Nein Master, I want to hear it."

He pulled me to his chest roughly. "Then be still, damn it. I believe we had just decided to continue with the original mission and Maximillian and Mad Maxx had merged to become me, ja?"

I sighed with relief realizing he had stopped so that his shards could merge and continue telling their story to me. Silly old Meine Liebe knew that sort of shit takes a minute. What was I thinking.

I nodded. "Yes, Master, that is where you left off. Thank you for your mercy."

Master Maxx laughed out loud. "Again, with that word mercy. One day you need to tell me what exactly that is. I hear it all the time from you, but like the Griffin, I think it must be a myth. Mein Kind die Zeit für Märchen is für uns beide längst vorbei." (translation: My child the time for fairy tales has passed for both of us.)

I almost laughed at that. "Uhm, okay Master. I agree. Danke, dass du mir erlaubt hast, deine Lektion zu hören." (Translation: Thank you for allowing me to hear your lesson.)

He patted my head. "Ah. Now you are speaking my language. We continue…"

"It was time to face many gruesome facts. Whether we liked it or not this collaring and sex with the man was part of our life. Der Hund's orders were loud and clear. It was our job to please these foul Masters. Through this perfect service the power of persuasion would be all ours. With this unique ability to hold the private audience of the rule makers of the Haus we were assured that we could break our metal. We even thought it possible to improve the conditions for all those trapped within the Haus walls for the better. Only time would tell the tale of it all.

For that moment, before we went out like superman trying to save all the collars, more simple things were of importance. I stood up and shook off the feelings of despair that clung to the boy like clouds of smoke around our head. I knocked on my room door and called out gentle as possible begging the attention of Jonas.

He heard my attempts to gain his ear and came right away. "You call me, Christian Axel? What is this? Did you change your mind about this collar I offer to you? I hope not because I went through so much trouble. My disappointment would be great, and I am kind only to those on my side." His eyes blazed with embers of anger.

I dropped my gaze looking at my shoes. "Uhm, nein. That is not why I call for you to open this door. I have some requirements for this collaring and consummation. I apologize for this inconvenience, but there are certain rituals I must attend to in order to be prepared for your pleasure." I cleared my throat feeling sheepish to have to discuss such personal things with my soon to be official Master.

Jonas stared at me with an expression of confusion on his face. He seemed to be oblivious to my attempts to obtain the cleansing tools and other items necessary to assure the consummation didn't go as ugly as my first one had.

Then suddenly I saw the flash of realization come over him. "Oh, oh, ja, ja, I wasn't thinking, my love. Of course, you uhm, write down all that you need. I will make sure that you have it in your possession promptly."

I nodded then handed him the list I had already written down assuming I would have to have this conversation at some point (assuming he would want to collar someday). All my personal items, clothing, and anything I had owned were in Peter's apartment beyond my reach. Without them, I was at the mercy of Jonas's kindness to replace the needed items.

Jonas had bought me some articles of clothing, t-shirts, jeans, a pair of tennis shoes, but other than that I had nothing to my name, not even a toothbrush. My enema kit, shaver, witch hazel, lubrication, hairbrush, mouthwash - you know all of the things for proper hygiene and some comfort – needed replaced immediately or this handling of five schwulers was gonna be more than a nightmare, it would be a most brutal one.

He looked over the list rapidly, nodding his head in agreement. "Ja, this looks right, my love. I'm going right now to get these things for you. I will place them all in the master bathroom for use as you need them. Anything else I can do for you before I go?"

I nodded. "Ja, when you have them, I need this door unlocked so I can properly prepare. You will have to trust me for this night not to run off down the hallway like a madman. Otherwise, well it can get ugly."

Jonas chuckled. "Ja, I bet. I don't know why I never thought of all the trouble that goes into this simple act of love."

I smiled with much bitterness. "You didn't think of it because you enjoy, instead of enduring, Master. Thank you for this mercy of allowing my comfort and granting me as much honor as possible given this situation."

He nodded, appearing a bit saddened at my words. "I suppose this is not as happy a day for you as it is for me or my brothers. I forget you are the hetero and worse cannot spare your own penetration virginity. That will cause any sexual encounter to be one sided for you. Pure hell, no doubt. For what it is worth I promise to be a gentle lover."

I shrugged. "For what it is worth there is no such a thing when the sex is unwanted. I appreciate your trying to make yourself feel better Jonas, I mean make me feel better, but it is not necessary. Better you than my father Peter. However, I must say if you truly loved me, you'd respect my sexual interest in the Frau only. None of you care about my own truthful pleasures, that is obvious the second you are touching me without consideration. Since you do not, then do me the service of never bothering to call me your lover. Rough, gentle, brutal, not like I have a fucking choice now is there? I am your property, hostage, and your whore. That is my lot in life, this I understand. I don't require lies to alleviate guilt that is not mine to carry. Keep the bullshit to yourself, and I will do my job of making you a happy man without quarrel. I will not disappoint you. I am well trained and capable of granting you your darkest desires." I kept my eyes downcast despite my most cruel but true statement. *I didn't care if he thudded me for saying it either. I was tired of his pretending he loved me any more than Claus or Peter had. I know what I am to him and all them. Why keep fucking lying, ja?*

Jonas stood there glaring at me with what appeared to be irritation in his gaze. "I don't like what you say to me, Christian Axel. I am in love with you. I went through pure hell to save your ass, and this is what you think of me? You are not my whore. You are my man. We are blood bonded."

I chuckled at that. "Okay, then I say to you I don't want you touching me in any way. Keep your hands off me."

Jonas bellowed, "Nein! You are my lover. I will make love to my man all I want. You are not the Dominant and cannot tell me what to do or not do in my own house. I told you I demand romance from my blood bonded and I will have it."

I nodded with a stern expression of my own. "Jonas, I will say again. I will do whatever you want. All of you Elders can force yourselves on me. I will give no fight. I will grant your pleasures without hesitation. However, you and the others saved my ass so you could have it, literally. You didn't do it for me. All of you did it for your own lustful interests. I am a lot of things Jonas, but the fool I am not anymore. I don't believe in fairy tales about mythical things such as your love for me. Keep your talk of romance for your blood bonded to yourself. You didn't allow me to say nein because you knew I would have. You knew I didn't love you, I never lied to you. You on the other hand told nothing but untruths. It is bad enough you sexually assault me physically. I will not tolerate your attempts to fuck my head too. You are right, this is your house. You are about to become my Dominant. I have to do what you say, and I will. I warn you, don't bother to try to cross the line between what I am willing to give you and what you can never have. You leave my heart be. That is for my Frau and children. Beat me or kill me if you like. I will not give that to you or anyone else."

Jonas stood there fuming, but he knew I was only being honest. He had lied and blood bonded me against my will. He thought I would fall in love with him as the good guy compared to my evil father Peter. Well, that shit didn't go as he expected.

His lustful interest in possessing me all for himself blinded him. Jonas never once considered how he would feel if someone he found repulsive forced themself on him. I wondered if he would feel romantic feelings for his captor if they dragged him around on a leash and traded him to all their friends. I seriously doubt anyone would.

I maybe should have kept my own counsel on this, but Meine Liebe, it was time I stopped eating my fury. I had my fill of it. It made me sick to my stomach and kept my shards fighting like brutes within. We may be schizophrenic but the one thing we are not is a liar. Jonas, Peter, Claus, any of them, all the same person. They only thought of themselves, and they used the weak without any shame.

They could try to twist up their motives, but I could see around corners clearly thanks to my illness. I was bent by the constant strain of it all.

I realized Cora, Gretta, and Leo had been working with Peter all along. They had used Leo, Ben, and Ryker to drive me into Peter's grips as my protector. Leo's attempts to get my public blow job to Ben and playing the bully, it was all planned. That is why Peter had that fucking blue dress. Ben did give it to him. Likely, Peter picked it out himself.

I now understood my beloved Ryker was in on it too. He was playing the friend that turns into the tyrant. He likely got put to the lawn because he discovered the secret of Peter's identity. They feared he would tell me. Well, he did, but I didn't believe him. Too bad for Ryker and too bad for me.

I am sure you are sitting there Meine Liebe going, wait, how does any of this relate to Cora's rise? That is the trouble with the Haus. nothing is straightforward. You have to look deeper than the surface.

You see, Cora wanted to be Head Haus Elder. She was the only one of the four Dominants (Gretta, Leo, Cora, and Peter) with the qualifications to hold the position. For her to rise they had many hurtles to jump. The first one was there was already a head of the Haus named Xavier. He would have to die. Then the four would have to capture the vote of the remaining schwulers which for Cora would be near impossible given her gender.

Peter hatched a plan. If they could find a handsome young boy that was of the priceless metal, they could maneuver this collar to do all the dirty work. Then she could just walk right into the empty spot.

Peter had a son that met the qualifications, but he was unruly and not getting with the program for some reason. Peter had no idea he had accidentally birthed a true priceless. Thanks to his ignorance he assumed the usual games should work. They used Ben the bully to isolate me from all the other trainees. They used Ryker as the only voice other than Peter I would hear in my loneliness. He used Leo to force me to realize worse choices than him were out there if I didn't obey. They worked together keeping the pressure on me. This drove me to despair. My acting out with frustration caused me to attract the attention of Xavier that day in the Great Hall.

This sealed Xavier's fate. Cora and the others now had the opening. Peter began to employ part two of the plan. He convinced me that seduction of all the Elders was the only way to break my collar. He planned to use the favors my indignity brought him with the Elders to get Cora the vote. Cora would then elevate her co-conspirators Gretta, Leo, and of course especially her champion Peter.

When Ben's usefulness was done, they had to clear him out like they had done Ryker. Cora and Peter had his silver tarnished to black. Effectively he was exiled from the Haus as payment for his role in setting me up to do my job mindlessly.

None of them knew he retaliated, and I killed him, but they didn't care if his tongue was silent about his role in this conspiracy. Geraldine was also a victim of all this horror. She loved Ben so much; his enemies were her own. She had no idea Ben was only following orders. When he died leaving her soiled, she come at the only one she knew to blame. She found herself a grave in the yard for her misunderstanding.

I had managed to seduce Claus, Jonas, Bladrick, and Drexel even though I had not completed the last two. When my illness onset I was so damned close to sealing the deal for Peter and Cora, my fall was of no consequence to their plan of a Haus takeover. In fact, it finished the job.

Peter tossed my collar upon finding I had returned to my senses. He called Jonas to tell him I was to be put to the lawn. He was aware Jonas has a wild notion that only the male Priceless can discover the female of his kind. Peter waited till I was no longer psychotic, then tossed my collar expecting Jonas would go insane himself trying to salvage his only hope for a future female cure for death.

As Peter had planned, Jonas stole me from the dungeons, then spent weeks attempting to gain the approval to hold my collar. With all the Elders fighting among themselves about who would get the honor of holding a Priceless collar for their own, Cora made her bid for the open position.

Ironically, Peter used the two Elders, Drexel and Bladrick, who had never tasted their leashed rights but mistakenly vowed to trade him a future favor. They fulfilled the payment to him by bullying their distracted brothers to push for her unanimous vote. Cora slipped past them all in one of the fastest votes for a Head of the Haus in recorded history of that place.

None of them knew they had been manipulated into raising a woman that had fooled them all. Her rise had been more than fourteen years in the making and expensive, paid in the blood of nine other human beings: me, Ben, Ryker, Felix, Vilhelm, Milo, Geraldine and Xavier.

The truth of this betrayal was not completely told by merely Cora's rise to head Elder. Gretta too made her play. The first thing this Cora did was name her choice for head of the Voting Council. Ja, you guessed it, her best buddy Gretta was given this honor.

This mattered to my future a great deal. With Gretta sitting at the head of the Voting Council, Jonas had no choice but to deal with the rising FemDom. The schwuler's petition to own a single Priceless collar as their shared property had to be voted through by the Council to be legal. The middle range Dominants tended to side with their Head and vote the way they say.

Jonas visited Gretta and asked for her favorable vote. She agreed, for a price, my penetration virginity. Peter had said publicly he would make sure she never won the bid for it at auction. This had been an embarrassment for her no doubt.

I had mistakenly thought Peter was behind this abomination of having to endure her leash. That was simply impossible since he had tossed my collar and therefore lost all rights to my contracts and leashing.

Instead, it was Jonas that was the controller of the final virginity leashing. Gretta was able to bypass the auction entirely by trading her vote for the Elders' petition for my final innocence, even though Annette had already beat her to the punch, thank Gott.

I will never know if the shattering really anything had to do with my sudden double vision. As I stood there glaring at Jonas standing my ground, I could see right through it all at last. I had been nothing more than a pawn in a huge game of chess. I had stepped into every trap, and played my part with such perfection that it was downright embarrassing.

It was obvious that my father never intended to keep my collar after he was through using me for his bloody task of raising Cora. What his plans were for me if I had not developed my illness once his goal was reached, I shall never know.

However, I suspect he had told me on the day of my collaring of his real intentions:

"Peter then asked me again if I understood he only owed me medical school if I broke my collar. If I didn't, he told me I could expect him to sell me off to another Dominant at some point. He was not interested in any D/s relationship with the shoddy submissive Christian."

I had been so overwhelmed by his rape, where I learned what special services were in a brutal way, and his cruelty after that collaring ceremony I had forgotten he made it damned clear he never wanted any long-lasting D/s relationship with me.

It was becoming clear he made that fucking contract for after I broke my collar, if I could, to use my special services rights even when I was Dominant. This was merely a way to gain favors through offering my leash to those that could grant him power for most of his life. Remember that contract ends at forty-two years old for me making him seventy-four.

Peter knew the he could do well by trading me off as the ex-Priceless collar. That I would be a doctor only added to the value of favors such a thing could assure him.

If I couldn't break my collar, then he intended to sell me out on auction. I would then be passed along the Haus the second he was through with me. Then I would have been slowly ripped apart by greedy Dominants. He knew the price I would pull would be amazing with all seeking their taste of the only Priceless collar seen on the floors in several decades.

I had to face the fact that I was never more than property to Peter. He had no problem using me in every way from meeting his twisted lust to trading to others for their own fucked up interests. He didn't care about my eventual demise or the damage this caused my mental health. Hell, he was happy to help me along faster in both categories. So much for fatherly love, ja?

The only person in this plot I could not place was my mother Agnette. I assumed at this point she was paid a handsome some by Cora and Gretta to play her part in the systematic brainwashing of her boy. After all, without her acting job, I would never have been pushed so hard to poison Xavier or seduce Claus as I had done. I doubted that Peter had truly betrayed her by having Claus embarrass her out of the Haus.

I suspected she and her new husband Julius were already moving back into her apartment. She could care less that she had trapped me in a nightmare world. It occurred to me most likely, she and Julius were toasting their success of owning the full favor and gratitude of the new Head of the Haus. She and Peter would no doubt enjoy their success with a sudden increase in status thanks to "sacrificing their child" to aid Cora to her lofty perch.

All these insights came to me the night I prepared for the nightmare second collaring ceremony with the Vampire. Jonas had been pouting in silence because I had called him out on his fake affection for me. I saw him slinking in the hallway shadows watching my every move. I ignored him sticking to my tasks at hand.

I was aware the consummation would be rough despite my lack of virginity at being penetrated by this late date in my submissive career. For nearly nine months I had not been even fondled by a male or female in any way. That would mean my status as "broken in" had long since returned to a less "seasoned" state.

I assumed with some horror that there would be tearing and pain until I had become used to the penetrative sexual congress all over again. I knew this from memory of the trouble this caused after only four months free of penetration sex during my mental breakdown after the death of Ryker. I did my best to focus on the power my indignity would purchase Mad Maxximillian.

I started to understand that if I was able to keep my head, and do my job, then not only would I be free, but revenge could also be mine. That night I decided before I kicked down the front door of the Haus that Cora, Leo, Gretta, Peter and Agnette would be tasting my fucking boots. I would be Gott damned if they were getting away without any punishment for all the lives they destroyed. Okay, Xavier could rot in hell, but the others were just ignorant pawns like me.

The hours rolled by slower than usual but too rapidly at the same time. Through the night I worked on my plan to gain vengeance and my preparation for the ritual. I noticed Jonas didn't sleep a wink that night either. I assumed he was worried I would use this time to try to escape his crutches.

I had no idea the real reason for his insomnia. My words of hate had cut the strong Vampire into two. He was considering he had made a mistake attempting to collar the headstrong Christian Axel. With a conflicted heart he too watched the clock, both afraid and eager for the collaring hour to arrive. Like me, he was doing his best to make the best of a less than happy situation.

When the morning arrived, I had to beg forgiveness for refusing to eat breakfast after three backhands from the stressed Elder. He nearly busted my mouth to pieces before I was able to get him to recognize my reason for passing on the meal was a valid one. He relented but seemed eager to find any chance to slap me around for the many hours before the afternoon.

Had I been more mature I would have recognized these rough blows as the acts of heartbreak and frustration they were. Jonas wasn't kidding when he said he cannot stand to have things held under his nose he can never possess. My confession the night before was proof to him that, try as he might, I would never love him back. Which was his darkest fear as it turned out.

I began to pace in my room when the hours of late afternoon arrived and still Jonas had not called me for his collar. I saw him go to his room a few hours before, but I never had witnessed him coming out. This long waiting was more unnerving than the fucking ceremony itself could ever be. By dark, I began to fear he had changed his mind and no call for my submission was coming at all.

I sat down on my bed, pulling up my knees to my chest readying myself for the Guard when the clock struck eight and still no request for me was made. There was nothing I could do. Nor could I take back my words of anger. What I said was honest, like it or not. I tried to console myself with the understanding that everyone else in the world may be a liar, but I would die with the clean conscious that this was one thing I never had been.

I had nearly fallen asleep from my silent weeping at what I assumed was my fate when the clock chimed midnight. My hypervigilant ears heard a sound that alerted them to pay attention. I sat up rubbing my wet eyes, listening to the noise I thought I had heard.

Jonas called out loud and clear, "Christian Axel, I Jonas choose you. If you choose me back, then you must come to me of your own will."

I jumped off my bed and rushed from the room seeking the origin of his voice. I listened with all my might, thinking I heard Jonas in the living room. I nearly ran down the hallway to find my assumption was correct. There on his velvet couch sat the Vampire Jonas, decked out in his finest "Dracula" outfit.

The Dracula outfit, as I call them, are high collared, ruffled blouses of crimson with a black waist coat, black breeches, and long black jacket. He was well manicured and wearing all his finest rings, a silver bracelet, and a bloodstone broach. On his head was a fashionable hat, that is if you lived in 1889. I saw his riding boots with the many buttons up each side and briefly wondered how he expected to consummate this damned collar by sunrise. It would take hours to get him undressed.

I didn't hesitate to rush to his feet and drop to a kneel. "You have called for Christian, and I have come willingly without threat or promise."

Jonas nodded. "Understand your submission is for all time to me, and shall be shared with my brothers Claus, Bladrick, Drexel and Barnim. Only if you break my collar will you ever be free of our pleasures in this life. This collar is your bond to us, wear it and join us, or deny us and we never ask for your will again. You must willingly submit or leave this apartment and never come back."

I took a deep breath and braced myself for the feeling of despair a collaring always brings to the one taking the heavy collar. "I submit to you and your brothers willingly without threat or promise. I understand my submission is for all time. I will serve without quarrel or hesitation until I break your collar. Only then can I be free of the pleasures of those that I call my Dominants." I was broken from my deep thoughts by the sound of a gasp behind me.

I turned around with a start to see that in the kitchenette standing in the entryway were four Elderly men. Drexel, Bladrick and Claus I recognized but the last man I could only assume was the elusive Barnim. I shot a look of shock, fear, and confusion at Jonas.

His expression stayed blunted. "They insisted on watching this collaring, my love. I tried all day to speak sense into them, but we are creating history this night. Your other Masters believed they have the right to be present when you make your vows to serve us all as our Priceless pleasure submissive. I apologize for the inconvenience, but I warn you, sacrifices had to be made to save you from the auction. Focus on me, and we can get through this."

I could barely breathe as I leaned forward hoping the others would not hear my inquiry. "Uhm, Jonas, they are only staying for the vows, right?"

Jonas shook his head. "I normally would say ja, but to be honest with you, Christian Axel, who the fuck knows what they think they have the right to see or experience during this honorable ritual. This has never been done before. I ask you once more, even knowing this, are you willingly submitting to our collar?"

I shot a look of panic at the smiling men, then back to Jonas. "Ja, I Christian Axel submit to your authorities willingly without promise or threat." I glanced back at the men then closed my eyes feeling I would faint from my panting terror driven breath.

I was sure the Elders were gonna gang rape me the second Jonas put on his collar. It was a tough thing to not run screaming from the spot. I reminded myself it matters not one at a time or all together, this would be my fate until I broke that damned metal.

Jonas nodded then said, "Then we submit you, bond to you for all time. We make these promises to you: we will protect and defend you. We will not offer you monogamy. We order penetration monogamy unless ordered by one of us five. We will take the title of Master. We will require all services and will provide all services in return. You will be under my care in all ways, but you will provide for the pleasures of any and all of the Five Elders present tonight. In return I will swear your need will all be met with my own hands or when not possible, the hands of any man in this room to stand in my place. You will answer to me, but you will also answer to these men present. All other Dominants real or imagined will have to gain our approval to use your services from this moment on. You will show high protocol to any member of Reichsadler Haus. I pronounce you reborn in our own image. You will now choose a name by which you shall be known for all time by your sisters and brothers, mothers, and fathers of the Haus, or until you break your bond with us and become Dominant in your own right."

I felt very sick to my stomach and the ground seemed to lurch beneath me. "I agree to all vows you have spoken and return them in my own ability. I vow that I will mind my Masters commands, only answer to them or their representative, protect and defend my Masters, submit all decisions to their ultimate authority, never call them by anything but the title they demand, grant my Masters my full loyalty, and will provide all my services for their pleasures without complaint or hesitation. I chose the name Mad Maxximillian for my rebirth in my Masters image. I thank all of you for your mercy and I am forever grateful for the honor of serving at your feet."

Jonas smiled, "I pronounce there is no longer the boy called Christian Axel. I resurrect you and collar you as Mad Maxximillian the Priceless collar also known as the property of the Elders of Reichsadler Haus." He put the bat collar around my neck, then locked it into place while I held my tears of terror in check taking slow deep breaths.

Jonas then reached out and pulled me forward into a deep kiss with him. I flinched when the Elders standing in the kitchenet began to clap loudly and cheer in approval. Then each of them approached Jonas and me. He let me out of his embrace smiling with fire in his eyes.

I trembled in fear, frozen in my kneeling. Each of the Elders come forward in his turn leaning down and embracing me into a deep kiss like Master Jonas had. I was unable to deal with the idea these men would likely be waiting to take their turns to end the ticking of my consummation clock the second they were done "tasting" my lips. This was not a nightmare I had prepared for but should have thought a possibility given my history of bad luck.

You see Meine Liebe, a consummation of sex or blood or both much be made within twenty-four hours of a submission, or the collaring is null and void. This is the last chance for a Dominant or submissive to change their mind and take back their vows. After that, the vows are solid and unbreakable.

When at last Barnim took his bonding kiss from me, Jonas smiled at all of them. "There, it is done. Mad Maxx belongs to all of us brothers. As was already decided, I would ask you to grant me privacy to consummate this agreement with our collar. Thank all of you for witnessing this historical and fruitful submission here tonight." He pointed to his door sending me into breaths of pure relief realizing only the Vampire would be an issue at least for this night. This was horror.

Master Barnim spoke out with irritation. "Wait, I demand we reopen this discussion of the consummation. I never even got to see this submissive until this moment. I think since I never have been leashed nor promised such a pleasure, I should take this thing with me and do this myself. All you already got your chances to enjoy it. I want mine now."

Master Bladrick scoffed, "Shut up Barnim. If anyone should get to do this honor, it should be Drexel and me. We paid the previous owner, but that bitch swindled us. We never got our leash time with it. It had been tossed before we could collect."

Master Jonas groaned when he saw the horrified look on my face. "This is bullshit. We have already dealt with this sensitive subject. I am the one to receive the honor of the consummation, we agreed. I found the tossed silver, lobbied hard for us to hold him, and cared for Mad Maxx until he could be collared for us. He wears my own damned metal. You will all have to wait your damned turns. This situation we already agreed."

I kept my eyes to the floor feeling my ears burn while three of the five called me a thing or it. I could feel their disregard for my humanity deep within my soul. I stole a glance at Master Jonas. He shook his head and cast a look of pity at me then flashed a quick smile.

Claus then growled out, "I am still head of this Haus Jonas. I want to be the one to do this honor. In fact, I can take him first as is my right. Give him to me this minute. I want him in my bed."

With that a full-on argument broke out among the Elder schwulers. Their voices raised and Master Bladrick and Master Claus were using wild hand gestures to indicate their extreme anger. Master Barnim whined, and Master Drexel fumed. Master Jonas sat there watching them all with his dark eyes appearing a bit humored but mostly bored with this childish display.

Several minutes of this loud disagreeing went on when finally Master Claus yelled out, "Enough. I know how to settle this once and for all. Mad Maxx, you pick the Master of your choice for this consummation."

I felt my blood freeze in my veins and my heart seized. "Thank you for such a mercy, Master Claus, but such a gift I cannot accept. I submitted my will to the Elders' authority. I will comply with the wishes of my Masters, but I cannot be asked to choose among them. Such a thing breaks my vow of protecting and defending all of you by inciting jealousy or the appearance of favoritism. This is not permitted in one of my lowly status. That said, I will remind you all that my fourth virginity was taken in the blood bonding to Master Jonas. I vowed monogamy for my penetration virginity and possess no other. Based upon the Haus Law, Master Jonas is the only one capable of doing this task of bonding my collar to all you with any legitimacy. I beg all my Masters for their forgiveness in my shortcomings, and lack of freshness." I could barely breathe out the last words as the horror of those words wrapped around my ears and stuck in my throat.

Master Jonas crossed his arms with a toothy grin aimed at his silenced brothers, "Ah. Our little Mad Maxx is correct. He cites the Haus Law and the special complications of this very special second collaring. Is Mad Maxx not correct, Claus? All of us know a virginity must be taken to seal the collar. I attempted to take this from this submissive unaware he had received a recent transfusion. Therefore, he still possesses this penetration possibility. I know am happy to take his fourth virginity and seal his collar to us before the consummation clock runs out. Drexel you witnessed my blood bonding yourself. You must recall I complained the penetration of the secret place was worthless thanks to his thin blood. I ask you brothers to think about this. We already bend the rules to almost a bust by collaring this rare treasure, would any of you dare to risk a complaint that the bond was not secured after all we went through to possess it?"

Master Drexel nodded while looking at the floor. "Jonas is speaking the truth, brothers. I witnessed the blood bond which stands. When I examined the boy, Jonas brought up the transfusion. I judged the act of his deflowering was no good. Mad Maxx's fourth is still intact by Haus Law."

Master Claus groaned then said, "Ja, you are correct, Jonas. We risk losing our collar if we don't do this right. I withdraw my bid for consummation."

Master Bladrick nodded. "Ja, Drexel and I do the same. This is not a virginity either of us covet. We will wait our turn for our rights to our collar's services."

Everyone looked at Barnim except me. I was busy about to piss my pants with the memory of that last fourth virginity deflowering nightmare. "I admit this is not my fetish either, but I am willing to learn it. I want this consummation right."

Master Jonas stood up so fast I fell to my face covering my head in fright. "You cut the shit, Barnim. This is not something you just learn. If you have not awakened, then you wasted my chance to have this collar as my donor. I will not sit here and allow you to spit on my customs nor disfigure our beauty just so you can say you fucked this collar first."

Master Claus held up his hands in a gesture of silence once more. "Enough I said. Jonas, you take this secret virginity from this submissive, and seal our contract with him. No more fighting about it. Tomorrow, Drexel, and I will come to witness this has been done. Barnim, you can have Mad Maxx for your pleasures beginning tomorrow night because I switch my day with you to cool the hot blood you have for your brothers in this matter. Are we all agreed this is fair?"

Everyone glanced around at their neighbors. No more grumbling was heard among them, and Master Jonas sat down calmly once more. I stayed on my face in prostrate too frightened to move a muscle. I was not aware I would have to be bled again, and did he intend to dry sodomize me too? I thought for sure I was gonna beg Master Claus to call the fucking Guard before I would suffer that nightmare once again.

Then without much noise, the group of Elders left the apartment appearing in a celebratory mood once more. The dark shadow of anger had left them just as fast as it had devoured their tongues in the first place. I swear I will never understand the Dominant if I live to be a million. They are such moody and pushy people you know.

Master Jonas got up and locked his door letting out a loud, long breath of relief. "You may get up now Mad Maxx. The hyenas are gone to lick their wounds. They won't be back till tomorrow night. You are safe for now. Try to enjoy it. Those old bastards will make you sorry for your birth for many months no doubt, but don't despair. They are all old men with brains younger than their asses. Not a damned one of them can keep up with your charms for long. You'll see." Master Jonas began walking to his bedroom.

I got up and followed him trembling a bit, bracing myself for his brutal consummation of the collaring. He turned around once inside, appearing surprised.

"Mad Maxx? what the hell are you doing? This is my room. Did you forget where I put you in this apartment?" He removed his hat and placed it on his dresser while beginning to unbutton his shirt.

I stood there quite confused, then found my strength to ask why he was playing the mind games with me. "Uhm Master, the consummation? I assumed you would wish to take this fourth virginity now and seal the lock?"

Master Jonas sat down on his bed still undoing his cuffs. "I admit that is what I planned to do Mad Maxx. However, you tell me that sort of thing is a hardship for you. You said I cannot love you if I force myself upon you so I say I will not do it then."

I shook my head feeling even more confused. "I don't understand. If you don't do this, my collaring with you and them is null and void. Master Claus and Master Drexel will look to make sure your consummation was completed."

He laughed. "Damn right they will, Mad Maxx. I think I will bid you a good night. Please close the door on your way out."

I almost fell to the floor when my knees went weak with fresh fear. "Nein, Master I beg your punishment, but I must insist you seal this contract with me. If I lose this collar I am finished. I told you I will not struggle, fight nor complain. I am prepared for it. You watched me. Why are you refusing to do this? Any of the others were willing to consummate but you refuse? I don't understand."

Master Jonas frowned "You said things yesterday that got me to thinking. You are right Mad Maxx. I would not love someone that forced themselves on me and made me feel like a whore. I thought a great deal about this. I won't be just another monster you can blame for making your heart black. I told you I wanted romance from my lover, but you say not to call you such a thing. If you are not my lover, blood bonded nor even willing partner, then fuck this. I would rather die alone. I am not like you think I am, my love. I do care about you. I stand up for you. I did look after you when no one else would. In return for my affections and pure love I receive hatred, distrust, and fear. I would rather you go to Barnim, Claus, Drexel or even Bladrick to seal your collar. I will even give away my days with you. This I say with love in my heart. If letting you go is the way to prove my love, then so be it. The door is unlocked, and you wear a collar. I repeat to you Mad Maxx, be kind and close my door behind you on your way out. Oh, and that collar is beautiful on you. It was worth the wait, and any pain it caused me just to see you in it this once." He got up and went into his bathroom, closing the door behind him.

I stood there perplexed. What the fuck just happened? What the hell was I going to do now? I had to find a way to consummate this fucking collar and stop my countdown to extinction.

Chapter 33: Monsters in the Bedroom

"I stood there staring at the closed bathroom door unsure what to do. Master Jonas had refused to consummate the Elder's collar, and Claus had granted him the honor exclusively. My confusion was more than a little evident. I suppose I thought he was fucking with my head and that is why I waited around like that. I think I was expecting he would come out of there laughing at my terror over his cruel joke.

He emerged to find me kneeling by his bed with my head bowed. The stress of that long day and the night before had worn me down. I was near asleep sitting there despite my fear of his vicious deflowering ritual to come. I heard him exit the bathroom and immediately snapped up to attention, fresh trembling anxiety already working on my nerves.

Master Jonas seemed startled. "Mad Maxx, I thought I told you to get out and close the door behind you. Why are you still here? Are you looking to get a beating? I would think you'd wish your last injuries heal a bit before you went seeking new bruises."

I gasped that he was still trying to play this mind game with me. "Master, I beg you to stop teasing me. I am here for your pleasure deflowering to seal the lock of your collar. I am here willingly. You see that I am not running nor crying. I don't understand this refusal. Mercy please, Master."

Master Jonas clicked his tongue with much sternness in his voice. "You're more brutal than any rumor I ever heard about you. You're the one that teases me. You have a black heart without a shred of sympathy nor love left in it. I will be a victim to you no longer. I can take a thud, and pain like few others. However, the torture I suffer desiring your cold affections, this I must end. I will never survive it. I say for the last time get the hell out of my room, Mad Maxx. Don't come back here anymore or I will kill you with my bare fucking hands."

I shook my head with tears of sheer terror coming to my eyes. "Then kill me, Master. I cannot leave without your bonding me to this silver. If I do, the Guard will have fresh fertilizer anyway. You ask for my attention as your lover, but I say I am spread too thin among your brothers to even consider such a thing. I hear you when you say you desire my heart. I must serve your needs or die. I suffer Hell while you find Heaven in my embrace. That is not an equal service for the one you return to me. If you are asking for my gratitude, respect, or even my affection for all you have done for me then please know that you already have. I give those to you willingly. Is this not enough for you? I cannot change my nature any more than you can Master. Then fine, tell me the lies to say so that you can find peace with what you do against my will."

Master Jonas let out a growl then came to me grabbing my "bat" collar lifting me to my feet. "I said get out, Mad Maxx. I don't want you anymore. You are dead to me." He dragged me through his room and tossed me out like a rag doll into his hallway slamming his door, locking it behind me.

I hit the floor in a full-on weeping jag. This was more of a nightmare than I had expected, and I assumed it would be very bad. If Master Jonas would not seal the deal, I would be finished. I was aware only he could take my secret virginity. I didn't know what to do to save this collar.

I found the strength to get off my knees and head for the front door. I ripped it open and ran next door to seeking the aid of Claus the Head Elder. I thought maybe with his help, I could find a way around the blood collar consummation.

I knocked on his door doing my best to quell my tears. It took a few attempts but finally the Elder crossdresser answered my call. He stood there; his eyes red from sleep appearing stunned. I sniffed hard then took a deep breath.

"I beg your mercy, Master. Master Jonas has refused to consummate the collar. Can you do this thing, or do you suggest I seek the aid of another of my Masters?" I fell to my knees ready to prostrate in sheer desperation hoping that as the superior of all them he could finish what had been started, breaking rules if need be.

Master Claus stood there in his robe staring in disbelief of my words. "What? You are making no sense Mad Maxx. Are you psychotic again?"

I looked up in shock. "Huh? Psychotic? I don't understand…" Master Claus interrupted me.

"Jonas told me about the schizophrenia, Mad Maxx. Do not be angered by it. I am sworn to secrecy, but he had no choice. Without my backing he could not get your collar salvaged by his hand. I demanded to know why Peter tossed you. I obviously agreed this was not an issue since you are Priceless. Insanity is expected in one of your kind but this knocking on doors in the early morning with hallucinations, that I won't tolerate." He glared with some irritation in his expression.

I shook my head. "Nein, I don't hallucinate Master. Please I beg of you, check if you wish. I am not consummated. Master Jonas has told me to leave and not return."

Master Claus's eyes went wide. "Oh, meine Gott. What the hell did you do? You angered him somehow. You were insolent?"

I looked at the floor with fresh tears bursting forth. "I must confess. I was insolent, Master. I don't mean to be so, but he wants something I can't give him."

Master Claus blew out his breath as if punched in his big gut. "What is it he asked for? Is it something that breaks the Haus rules of conduct like bestiality? Sex with a baby? What the hell is there on Earth the you, my beloved Mad Maxx, couldn't do for him?"

I sobbed out. "Mu heart, Master. I refused to love him no matter what he did. I told him to call me his whore rather than his lover. I swore to never feel anything other than affection, respect, and gratitude toward him. That is all I can give to anyone that forces me to my knees to serve when it is in my nature to be free."

Master Claus's expression became one of pity. "Oh, meine dear Mad Maxx. Come in, my love. There is no reason to make this drama of ours the Haus business. We can discuss this misunderstanding in my apartment." He stood to the side while I got up and walked in feeling a tiny shard of hope within that he could save my metal.

My Master sat down on his couch. I waited then approached and knelt at his feet. He sat there staring at me a moment. He reached out and stroked my vet cheek.

I looked up at him with hope in my eyes. "Can you consummate this collar, Master? I am prepared and will give you no quarrel over it. I beg of you, seal this contract with me."

Master Claus closed his eyes with an expression of lust crossing his face. "Oh, what I would not give to do that Mad Maxx. You have no idea how bad I want you right now. I thought you dead or sold away when you disappeared. Then Jonas comes to me and tells me of your curse. I was both overjoyed to hear you live and grieved to know the truth of your suffering. It has taken all I have not to run next door begging Jonas to let me have you for my own if only for an hour. Please know I would happily take you right here on the floor to consummate that collar of ours right this second if I could. However, I cannot take the secret virginity. I don't know the procedures, nor do I want to know. I am forced to wait until your contract is secure before I can enjoy the pleasures of my shared collar, my love. Jonas is the only one that can do this legally. You must get him to relent and seal our contract."

I fell to my face on his feet openly crying. "Please Master. Bend the rules. Find a way. I will do whatever you wish. I won't struggle nor give you any trouble. I beg you. Please save me from this dishonor. Master Jonas has locked me out of his room. He threw me out. He told me I am dead to him. If I am left to his whim, I am good as on the boat across the river to Hades already."

Master Claus reached down and grabbed my shoulders pulling me off his ankles. I assumed that meant he was giving into my pleas for mercy. I immediately responded by embracing him then engaging him in a passionate kiss. He moaned out in thrill as I reached into the chest of his robe opening it preparing to stimulate him for our couple.

He pulled away from my over eager attempts to finish this necessary intercourse panting. I thought this meant he was ready for me to grant him oral pleasure. I dropped back to my knees grabbing his thighs trying to position myself between his legs. Master Claus groaned out then pushed me with much force near sending me backward to the floor.

Confusion at his behavior flooded my mind. I thought maybe he was playing a game of hard to get. I steadied myself and came back to him this time with more determination. He opened his eyes and pushed me back again, harder this time.

I whimpered, finally understanding he was denying me a couple consummation. "Master? I don't understand. Have I done something to displease you as well?" I sat back on my backside unsure what the hell to do now that I had struck out twice.

Master Claus panted with a fire in his eyes. "I told you I cannot consummate this collar Mad Maxx. I must demand you stop tempting me. I am only a man. You do that again; I swear I will do something that we both will regret. Only the one with the power to fully seal the lock can have you in the next twenty-four hours. You know the damned rules. I adore you and this is no secret. Turning you down tonight when you show such attention is fucking killing me. I never have been so turned on, and I never seen you more eager to be mine than you just were. Go back to Jonas and do that to him. If that fucking Vampire can throw you out of his bed, then I will fucking bow to him myself. He would have to be superhuman to deny the lust you incite. If he thinks that such eager wantonness, you display is not a sign of a true lover then you come back here to me. I will cut you and drink your fucking blood then call it done. That is how much desire you have driven me to. I release you to return to your Master Jonas now with much regret, that I can swear to you."

I shook my head still weeping heavily. "Master, he locked me out of his room."

Master Claus laughed while wiping the sweat off his forehead from his still heated up interests. "You are a Priceless with a long history in the chains. I already know you can pick the fucking lock, Mad Maxx. Are you making excuses to make me feel more appreciated? That is not necessary. You can love Jonas all you want. I take whatever you care to grant to old Claus. I bask in your shadow and live in your eyes. For me, this will always be more than I dared to dream. If you fight for Jonas's affection with all you have, he will believe you love him. You take Claus's advice and I promise you, tomorrow I will find your maidenhead busted and the lock sealed. The clock is ticking. Go make Jonas a pleasured man by doing your job, Mad Maxx." He pointed at the door.

I nodded, wiping my tears away. "As you wish, Master. I return for your blade if Master Jonas throws me out again."

Master Claus snorted while I went to his door. "He won't, that lucky bastard. See you in the morning, Mad Maxx."

I went back to Master Jonas's apartment. I dug through the drawers of his kitchenette until I found a flat head screwdriver. I took this thing and got a paper clip from my schoolwork then headed for Master Jonas's bedroom door.

I knelt and began the process of opening this barrier to the object of my necessary consummation. I was just nearly into the room when the door swung open nearly sending me face first to the floor.

Master Jonas stood there in his black silk robe with a look of fury. "What the hell. Are you trying to break into my fucking bedroom, Mad Maxx?"

I nodded. "Ja, Master, I am. I beg your forgiveness, but I must speak to you right away. I didn't want to wake you up."

The Vampire's eyes lit with flames of fury. "If you didn't want to wake me up then how the fuck did you expect to speak to me?" He backhanded me with much strength sending me sprawling.

I reeled from his blow but got back up into a kneel before him doing my best to ignore my stupid statement. "Master, I am begging you to please listen. I apologize for saying the ugly things I said yesterday and earlier, I am just a stupid boy. What the hell do I know about anything?" Master Jonas kicked me hard in the chest sending me backward with the force.

"You shut up, Mad Maxx. I told you that you are no longer welcome here. Still, you persist in bothering me. I suppose I will have to kill you to rid myself of your intrusions." He kicked me back to the floor when I tried to rise to another knee.

I steadied myself against his next blow while getting up to my knees. "Master, I deserve your anger no doubt. Kill me if you must but hear me when I say I am ready to submit to your couple willingly. I beg you to accept me for your own."

Master Jonas bellowed out sounding angrier than I ever heard him before. "I don't want you, Mad Maxx. I told you this. Get out. Just get out of my sight. I never want to see you again." He backhanded me this time busting my lips to ribbons from his hard blast into my mouth.

I reflexively reached up and covered my face. "I choose you, Master. I choose you," I yelled out just as Master Jonas pushed harshly in my chest knocking me off my knees to my back.

He stood above me ready to stomp in my chest with his bare feet. "I don't choose you." He brought down his weight causing me to gasp out all my breath, unable to speak another word for a few minutes.

I choked on my own blood, writhing on his floor. I watched helplessly, unable to stop him as he brought down his foot again, this time on my left upper arm. I opened my mouth to wail but nothing came out from the lack of air. Master Jonas then reached down and grabbed my shirt collar on both sides pulling me up to drag me out of his room again.

I was breathless, and terrified. I didn't offer to resist as the furious Vampire started hauling me back down the hallway.

Then out of nowhere I heard Master Claus's voice in my ears, "Fight for Jonas's affection with all you have, and then he will believe you love him."

I nodded understanding what I had to do at last. I pulled back on Master Jonas's grip with all my strength. This surprised the Vampire. He thought I was going to remain compliant with his attempts to send me away. Nein. I had no fucking choice but to consummate with this creepy Elder.

Anger filled my breast while I thought of this man blood bonding me against my will. If I was stuck with him then Gott damn it, he was trapped with me. If he wanted to be my husband, then he was going to have to do his fucking job. Just like Mad Maxx, Jonas no longer had any choice.

I flew at him grabbing handfuls of his long hair on both sides of his head. He tried to push me backwards off him by pushing my chest as he still had my shirt collar. I held tight pulling him with me as I flew backward. I used his steady stance to keep from falling on my ass.

He growled out in fury, "Let me go, you sonofabitch."

I took a deep breath. "Nein, you vowed to protect and defend me, Master. I demand you immediately seal this lock. I am your blood bonded. If you fail me, I am lost to you and you to me. Hate me if you wish but do it with honor, Gott damn you," I yelled into his fact, my own eyes starting to light with hell fires.

Master Jonas tried again to push me off him. "You insolent bastard. How dare you? Am your Master. You fucking mind me. Let me go and get on your knees." I held fast yet again, keeping him from escaping me.

"I get on my knees and submit to your pleasure when you stop acting as an ass. If you are my Master, start behaving like one and end this shit of acting like a heartbroken Frau. I am your husband and your submissive, Mad Maxx. There is no other. This is not enough for your fragile ego. Then you send me to hell, and I will take you with me, my love. At least at the devil's feed you will be forced to keep your fucking promises to care for me unconditionally, ja?" I pulled his hair tightly trying to force him towards me.

He pulled back and pushed me harder causing much tension between us. "I never fucking promised such a stupid thing."

I laughed loudly at that. "You didn't? Funny, I thought you said you wanted me to love you romantically. Well, that is what real love is Master. The real fucking emotion has no boundaries nor conditions. That is the Gott damned definition of it. So, are you a liar or do you love me?"

Master Jonas's eyes went wide in surprise. "What? I don't, I uhm, I am not a liar." He stopped pushing me and stood there appearing confused.

I relaxed my struggle slightly and panted out. "Then you love me still, Master?"

My Master looked at the floor appearing saddened. "Fuck, ja, Ficken Mich. I do love you, Mad Maxx. I wish to hell I didn't."

I nodded. "I bet you do wish that. To fucking bad. You wanted me enough to trick your way into becoming my husband. Well, be the sonofabitch then. Seal your Gott damned collar. I am here just like you wanted, am I not? I returned it to you. I am willing to fight, reprimand, and even seduce you until my face haunts your dreams for all your days. I cannot escape your embrace Master, so I will return the fucking pleasure of it." I pulled my stunned Master to my bloody lips and engaged him in a heated kiss.

Master Jonas tried to pull away, but I pulled myself closer to him holding him still by his pinned hair in my hands. Within a few moments I felt his grip on my collar relax and he began to kiss back. I let out an internal sigh of relief when he pushed his tongue into my mouth moaning out in sudden interest.

He let go of my collar and grabbed my upper arms with quick viciousness. I let out a loud gasp as he spun me and slammed me into the bedroom wall with great force. We didn't break our lustful kissing, nor did I let his mane go despite his aggressive move. Master Jonas had begun to pant with rising desire. He dropped his lips to my neck sucking and biting as he had the day Leo and Peter had interfered, then gotten themselves thrashed for it.

This time I braced myself for his breaking of my flesh if that was his intention. I was resolved no matter what he did, I was not leaving until he sealed his fucking collar lock. Mad Maxx was hell bent to survive this nightmare.

No one, not even this Vampire, was going to keep me from gaining the metal I intended to bust to pieces in my bid for freedom. I was more than ready to pay the hefty price for the thing I wanted the most.

After a few moments of this most unsettling behavior when he noted I did not tremble, he growled out like the hungry wolf. "I will have to deflower your again, Mad Maxx. You prepared for that?"

I gasped out while he continued to playfully bite my neck. "I am Master. I willingly grant you anything I possess you wish for your pleasure. Take me any fucking way you want just make sure you take it without expectation of equal return from any one in my low position."

He nodded, beginning to breathe shallowly from the thrill of his rising lust. "I realize what you tell me now. I don't ask you to love me as I love you, but I must beg you to adore me. Is that an impossibility as well?"

I closed my eyes preparing myself to pull far as possible inside, seeking a safe place from his brutal sexual assault. "This I can grant you willingly. I respect, adore, admire, and even have affection for you, Master Jonas. Asking for more is not only cruel but inhuman given the circumstances."

Master Jonas nodded and groaned in pleasure. "Ja, I see that clearly now that you have opened my eyes. You have my undying affection, adoration, favor, and love, Christian Axel. I will take you for my own once, and this morning I will take you twice. I am helpless to deny my need for your presence in my life of all my remaining days."

He leaned down wrapping his arms around my thighs and lifted me into his arms like the bride. I let go of his locks, finally sure he was within my power securely. I didn't struggle as he carried me down the hallway to the room with a red door. I took a deep breath and put half of

Mad Maxx to sleep the second we entered that place of pain and blood.

With our intelligence protected like an infant in its crib we held still as the Vampire stripped us down then tied us up in his bondage bed. He left the room without a word leaving us laying there in the spread-eagle position.

Within only a short time he returned with the beautiful Emma on his arm. She smiled and moved immediately to sit next to us on the bed. We watched her in silence as she leaned down engaging us in her kissing. Our eyes closed sweeping us away to the promise of a world to come once we broke our metal.

Her soft lips and female scent did their job. My lust rose to the surface as did my manhood. Emma ran her hands over my bare chest sending spasms of electricity throughout my flesh causing a sublime thrill. She had accomplished her goal, but to my surprise she didn't stop her kissing nor soft touching of my upper arms and shoulders.

I was so enamored by this gorgeous woman I barely felt the blade as Master Jonas re-opened his fourth virginity penetration scar. I flinched but didn't break my tongue embrace with Emma. I no longer cared about what my Master was doing. All I could see, hear, smell or think was this female that seemed interested in mating with me.

Then to my ultimate shock Master Jonas dropped to my bleeding thigh and began his drinking of my blood. I was surprised because Emma had not left, nor had she stopped her gentle stroking of my flesh. I wanted her to move her soft hands to my more potent areas, but she kept her touching above my waist. I moaned out with eagerness, ignoring my Master's disgusting behaviors entirely, when Emma dropped to my neck then began running her tongue into my sensitive ears.

The torture of wanting to mount this girl was threatening to send me to madness. I began to pull hard at my restraints despite my resolve to be still for this consummation. My mind had gone wild with the need to possess Emma for my own. An animal of lust had been unleashed inside me and I was losing control fast.

I had completely forgotten that Master Jonas was even in the room. Then he reminded me when I felt him release my right arm from my bonds. I couldn't believe my luck. I used that arm to grab Emma around the waist pulling her closer to me. I was doing my best to maneuver the girl to a position for my penetration. She gently resisted my attempts to pull her onto me. Then with a coy smile she stood up and left rapidly without so much as a goodbye as she had done before.

I was beyond upset by that. I reached up and began to feverishly try to undo my other arm. "Nein, Emma. Come back. Please come back. Why did she leave, Master," I yelled while tearing at Master Jonas's rope.

Master Jonas chuckled as he put up his lancet. "If only I could make you so wild for me as that girl can in mere moments, I would be the happiest man on earth. Emma has left because it is time for us to seal the lock Mad Maxx. I know you do not love me, nor do you desire my affections, but I will ask you for the mercy that you pretend you do. I give you Emma to draw your interest as my favor in return for yours to me this night." He crawled up on the bondage bed undoing my right ankle then began working on my left while I continued to pull my other arm from his knot.

I watched Master Jonas move across the mattress toward me. I looked back longingly at the door through which Emma left me. I wished to chase her down and ask her to be mine for all time, but I was stuck with the Vampire. He sat up and removed his robe, tossing it onto the floor.

I closed my eyes as he leaned down, running his hands over my flesh as Emma had moments before. My immediate repulsion was noted by a fast-retreating erection. My Master saw my deflating sexual desire. He sighed then grabbed my chin demanding I look at his face.

"Mad Maxx, I had hoped that having Emma linger would aid me in helping you find some pleasure in our coupling. I see this is not possible despite all my best efforts. I wanted so badly to give you something for what you will give to me in our intercourse. other than penetration which I cannot allow. Is there anything, my love, that I can do to relieve your burden while I take my pleasure?" He seemed quite sad as he searched my eyes for his answers.

I shook my head. "Hurry the process up, Master. That is my only mercy. This is not my way, and never will be. I do whatever you ask but I can never find anything other than stress from it. I apologize for my nature. I didn't choose it any more than you did. I will say though, if I were the schwuler for truth, you would be the lover of my preference Master. I never lie, even at the risk of death. If I say this to you, then you will have to take my word for it. I am a man of my word."

Master Jonas smiled with much peace in his gaze. "That was maybe the most romantic thing I ever heard from anyone. Your truthfulness is more beautiful than your eyes, Mad Maxx. I realized tonight I cannot make a dog into a cat, and I cannot make you desire a man over the woman. Tell me, does this Emma please you, Mad Maxx? Is she anything you would want in a woman?"

I smiled at that. "Ja, her not being mine is the only fault I can find in her Master."

My Master chuckled as he stroked my cheek lightly. "I tell you what, my love. You never breathe a word of it to anyone, then I call her back. I will allow her to join us in our bed. You swear on your word to three stipulations, this is a gift I grant to you for our wedding night and all nights together until you break the metal."

I stared at him unsure if maybe I had not gone mad again and was hallucinating. "Huh? You will let her come be here when we couple, Master? What three stipulations?"

Master Jonas ran his hand down my chest. "First you can never tell anyone. She is not only a black collar, but this kind of thing is frowned upon for the collar with their penetration virginity intact. Second, you can never have her for any kind of penetration. Not now, and not ever. Emma cannot bring you to any orgasms, not even by manual stimulation. She can however kiss, stroke your upper flesh and calm your stress during our love making. Only I can bring your climax with my hand to protect your collar selection virginity. You may orally stimulate her with her permission and my approval only. Third and the most important, I want you to show me attention during our couple as much as you demonstrate to Emma. If I start feeling left out of my right to kiss or affection, then she will be asked to leave and never permitted to return. Do you agree to these stipulations on your word of honor, Mad Maxx?"

I sat up with a feeling of unreality coming over me. "Are you serious Master? If this is a game, you play it is most cruel and unappreciated. Does Emma say this is okay with her?"

My Master chuckled with wickedness. "Emma is one of my donors that is no longer eligible, thanks to her tarnished collar. She made the mistake of growing older than thirty and her Master painted her silver the color black rather than see the beauty sold out to the invisible people. I realize you are used to your lovers not giving a shit about your calm mental health or disgust at such a one-sided act of intimacy. I am not another lover. I am your man. One day you will bring our Priceless Frau. Then unlike Emma, she will share our bed in all ways. There is no reason to not accustom us both to this third possibility of affection right away. I realize for now; Emma is only the fantasy of things to come. Yet, I say better to have a living breathing focus for your lust then to have nothing but images in your shattered mind."

I started to argue I would never share my Frau with him or anyone. *Well, that didn't go as planned did it, Meine Liebe, shit.* I decided to keep my big mouth shut for a change. I knew I was not allowed to penetrate any female until my collar was ready for selection. Sex with the man through special services – uhm, five Masters, yikes – was a guarantee until then. Any little mercy I could get from this horror and pain of being the one penetrated sounded damned good to me.

I nodded with a huge gleeful smile. "I swear on my honor to your conditions, Master. I only ask that you be ready to smack me down if my lust gets out of hand with Emma. I will try to contain myself, but the woman makes me stupid. You know I thought her only twenty or less. She is beyond beautiful."

Master Jonas laughed loud and long. "Ja, that is what happens to me whenever you wag your tail at me Mad Maxx. I can relate. I love to see this smile of peace on your face, my love. I am sure that Emma will be most flattered you said that since she is almost forty. Her beauty holds in the flesh and in her heart. A finer soul I have never known. I will go get Emma and we seal this collar the rest of the way but first, I ask a moment of your affection just the two of us."

I nodded, still smiling. "That is a fair request, Master. I am happy to grant it." Master Jonas leaned in and for several moments kissed and touching me everywhere with much wantonness.

I closed my eyes and endured it without quarrel and even faked a lustful interest back. My eagerness to please him seemed to satisfy the most generous Vampire. He had some difficulty ending his adorations long enough to fetch Emma back. I quietly damned myself a bit for overdoing my acting job. I was in a rush to get the beautiful girl back into the room, even if I couldn't complete any lustful business with her. I just knew having her lips for my own and her touching me could make the horror of sex with a man tolerable. You know it is good to be a young person. Fantasies and fairy tales are still believed, ja.

Master Jonas groaned then pulled himself off me. "I will go get Emma but before I try this, I will want to bind your wrists behind your back Mad Maxx. Your too young to control yourself when the object of your truest interest is present, I think. I find even in my experience sometimes it is difficult to stop myself from going too far. I know this will be a hardship for you but do your best to remember it is out of love that this is done. If you soiled yourself, then all our hopes and dreams of a Priceless Frau and children are dashed forever. That collar of mine will be locked for all time then. I trust my Emma with many secrets. She desires nothing more than to be silver once more. The knowledge of a soiled Priceless Mad Maxx is something that holds enough power to polish her back to her greatest wishes. This you understand, my love?" He pulled his ropes from the bondage bed posts preparing to bond me once again.

I nodded but felt much disappointment. "Ja, I understand Master. I wish it didn't have to be this way. I am a man of my word. I wouldn't dare to break it to you. I have the greatest gratitude for your kindness. To betray you would never even cross my mind."

Master Jonas motioned me to sit up and put my hands behind my back. "I know that you would never do such a thing on purpose, my love. However, I know my Emma too well. I will be distracted with my own interests in you. This is only a precaution, is all. One day maybe the restraints can be removed, but for now I think it for the best." He tied my wrists together then left the room to fetch Emma.

I sat there feeling both excited and despaired. It was wonderful to at least have the Frau to kiss on but still the penetration of Master Jonas was not gonna be pleasant. I had never encountered this kind of situation. It was then at last it hit me that this beautiful woman was going be present to see my subjugation to the mount. A chill went down my spine at that thought.

I had been briefly raped by Xavier in public and my mother had also been present during a coupling with him. I greatly desired Emma's attention unlike in those other cases. I trembled with the sudden realization that this gorgeous woman would find her witnessing such horror a real turn off. I assumed she would lose her interest in Mad Maxx the second she saw me nothing more than the cock holder of Master Jonas.

These dark thoughts were plaguing me when Emma and Master Jonas returned to the bondage room. I whimpered slightly as I saw that Master Jonas had also retrieved his black leash. I didn't offer to quarrel as he came forward and attached it to my collar by the O ring then locked it into place. He bonded the other end to one of the bed posts. I was unable to defend myself against his lust nor run from it anymore. I closed my eyes and braced for this brutal couple.

I felt a soft pair of lips brush against my forehead. I opened my eyes to see Emma's beautiful face in mine. She was unbuttoning her blouse with speed. I was in a trance watching her as she quickly shed her clothing revealing the glory of her perfect flesh that her outfit had hidden from view. I could not tear my eyes from her outstanding breasts and triangle of pleasure. All my fears of her being disgusted by my position in this threesome had melted away. All I could think of was her soft skin, and gorgeous eyes.

Emma moved forward and embraced my lips with her own. I moaned as she ran her hands across my chest, once again heating up my lust for her. She crawled upon the bed pulling my head to follow her as she laid on her back. My leash was pulled tightly holding me from falling forward onto her while I fell under her spell of heavy kissing.

Master Jonas watched this lustful display a moment. Then he crawled onto the bed and grabbed my head pulling me away from Emma's wanton lips. He engaged me in his own heated tongue embracing. I kept my eyes on the beautiful woman. She sat up and wrapped herself around the back of me. I moaned out in sublime thrill when I felt her firm breasts and glorious pubis stroking my flesh from behind. Emma put her mouth to my neck and then playfully sucked and lightly bit me from the nape of my neck to my shoulder blades.

My lustful interest in Emma became confused as Master Jonas increased his own deep mouthing. I could no longer distinguish between the two. All I could think was I wanted to be mounting something. Fourteen-year-old boys you know, yikes! The dam for carnal desires had broken in Mad Maxx. I was no longer picky about who or what as long as those two kept pushing all my pleasure buttons.

Then Master Jonas began to push my head down indicating he wanted me to orally stimulate him. That caused a bit of alarm in my lust driven brain. I whimpered a bit while he pulled me toward his manhood. Emma immediately increased her eager kissing, pulling to my left side licking my ear and moaning into it.

Then she whispered. "Do to Jonas with your mouth what you want to do to me. Show me, my love, make me want you."

I damn near cum right then and there to the sound of her sexy voice. She had effectively ended my fear of being witness to my humiliation. I immediately went to my job of providing my Master his desired oral sex with Emma in my ear cheering me on.

I suppose I was doing too good a job trying to impress my female audience. Master Jonas had to pull my mouth off him before he reached orgasm in the wrong place for proof of our collar consummation. This was after only a few minutes of this twisted sexual romp. He was more than ready to seal the lock on his silver at this point.

Emma grabbed my face and forced her lips to mine again while Master Jonas maneuvered himself behind me to take his mount. I braced myself for his entry doing my best to focus on the beautiful Emma when I felt him preparing me with his lubrication. I sighed a breath of relief into her mouth as I realized this sodomy would not be a vicious dry one as he had done before. Hey, it is the little mercies that matter, ja?

Despite his best attempts to offer comfort for his penetration I let out a wail of agony when he pushed himself into me. As I said, it had been more than nine months. I was no longer seasoned. This intercourse was just as bad as the first time when Peter took me this way. I may as well have been the virgin.

I trembled crying out with pure pain, stunned and unable to move as Master Jonas pulled me onto his erect cock. I gritted my teeth and closed my eyes doing my best to battle against the extreme discomfort of Master Jonas's harsh thrusting. Emma tried several times to pull me back into her kissing but to be honest, I was too overwhelmed with agony to do anything other than shake and groan.

Emma shot a look of concern at Master Jonas behind me. He had grabbed my shoulders and was moaning out in his own world of pure pleasure. His intercourse with me had become strong and rhythmic sending me straight to hell. She obviously had no experience with keeping the attention of a man when he was fucking anyone other than herself. She seemed confused as to what her role should be in these two men sexual congress.

I was unable to see anything but the white lights of searing pain behind my eyelids when suddenly my face was surrounded by firm flesh. I opened my eyes to find myself groaning out in distress into the beauties bosom. Emma had pushed my head into her breasts. She grabbed the sides of my head demanding I "Küss my Brüste" (Kiss my breasts).

I moaned out, "Ich kann yetzt nicht denken. Verzeihen Sie mir, Emma." (Translation: I can't think right now. Forgive me Emma.)

She pulled harder on my head, appearing most frustrated. "Nein. You don't need to think Mad Maxx. just do it. Focus on me, damn you."

I was starting to taste bile in my throat from the pain of Master Jonas's increasing torment to my backside. I shook off the hell of it as best I could and began to clumsily kiss Emma's flesh. She pulled my head from one breast to the other doing her best to distract me from my Master's brutal penetration intercourse.

Meine Liebe, I wish I could tell you that Emma's most ingenious plan worked like a charm. That would be a lie though. I was at the time too under used for this kind of carnal congress. Anal sex can be painless, and even pleasurable in some cases, but not without much practice with it. Mad Maxx during his second collaring consummation was just too unprepared for this sexual act to make it anything more than literally a pain in the ass.

I was nearly ready to faint from the pain, panting, and stressed out by the time Master Jonas began to pound on me with the signal strokes of an approaching climax. I closed my eyes once again and stopped kissing Emma to grit my teeth wailing out in terrible trauma as my Master moaned loudly in his orgasm. He had successfully sealed his lock with much vigor and my own blood.

Master Jonas fell over draping himself on my back wrapping his arms around my waist while kissing my neck. I shook and took shallow breaths, biting back the pain with all I had, grateful the horror of sex with the man was over. At least for a moment anyway.

Emma smiled then kissed my trembling lips. "You did magnificent, Mad Maxx. Your beautiful to watch."

Master Jonas ran his hands along my chest from above me. "I told you Emma I was about to show you a sexual artist of superior ability, didn't I?"

She giggled. "Ja, Jonas, you did. I admit I am feeling honored but a bit useless in this arrangement. You have no need for my charms when the perfect joy is already present."

My Master chuckled, then pulled up and uncoupled with me. I was immediately relieved by the way. "Trust me Emma, your being here helped this situation more than you can know. Mad Maxx, don't you agree my love?"

I was still shaking pretty bad as I slowly sat back off my knees to my ravaged bottom. *You know why don't you, Meine Liebe.* "Ja, ja Emma. Thank you for your distraction. I am grateful for it." The truth is I was no longer interested in her, or anyone's touching for that matter. My lust had left the building, maybe for good, after that rough business. Not fun, but I need not tell you.

Emma smiled with much glee. "I am happy to come to your bed anytime, Jonas. I like Mad Maxx a great deal. You are a generous lover, but I already knew that. Thank you for this honor. May I now take my price for this arrangement?"

Ma Master nodded. "Ja, you may Emma. The wound should still be open."

I was startled back from my place of sheer agony by this odd exchange. I shot a look of confusion at Emma as she came across the bed toward me with a strange wanton look in her eyes. I backed up with a bit of fear, unsure what the hell was going on here.

I could not go far thanks to my leash and the back of the bondage bed. Emma grabbed my right leg and pulled it harshly toward her. I fell nearly to my back unable to push her off because my arms were still bonded behind me. I let out a yell of pure horror when that beautiful girl dropped her face to my thigh and bit into Master Jonas's "fourth virginity" cut and began sucking out my blood.

I wailed out to my Master. "What the fucking hell, Master. Get her off me. Stop this nightmare. Emma, let me go, please I beg of you." I couldn't take my eyes off Emma as she violated me this way.

Master Jonas came across the mattress and took me into his embrace blocking my view of Emma's making a meal of me. "Look at me, my love. This is nothing. Emma wants to remain youthful. Your blood will grant this to her for many extra years. She comes to serve you by lessening your stress during our lovemaking and all she asks in return is a taste of your powers. She has earned her price; this you surely cannot deny."

I felt tears starting to fall at this latest hellish reality. "I thought, I thought she was here cause she, never mind, Master." My heart broke in my chest as I realized Emma was like everyone else, she only wanted something from me, but didn't really care for me.

Emma finished her blood thirst and sat up appearing enraptured. "Don't let this bother you, my love. She will serve you well and keep our secret for this small price. That mercy is worth seeing you so calm during our love this night. I felt very desired even if it was all illusion. Try to focus on the fact you brought your Master perfect pleasure, and that collar is now secured. This situation between us will improve greatly for you once the metal is busted and your Frau joins us in our sexual tristes. Then we both get orgasms, ja?" He stroked my cheek lovingly.

I could not tear my terrified sight from Emma's blood-stained lips. She was smiling at me coyly with the crimson running down her alabaster skin. I briefly feared I had become no better off than Lucy or Nina from Bram Stroker's Dracula novel. I was surrounded by these fucking Vampire people, and I was their dinner in all ways. I worried I would in time become one of them. Or once bled dry, left to rot in the Orchard.

Emma left, then Master Jonas finally untied my arms. He unlocked my leash from the bed but not my collar. He allowed me to redress, then I brought him his robe. I aided the Vampire in covering up his nakedness, then dropped to my kneel.

"I am glad you came back and forced me to re-think my decision to send you away Mad Maxx. I am not happy about having to share you with my brother Elders, but I know this is only for a short time. You and I will begin working on busting that bat collar right away. I plan to call you Dominant on your fifteenth birthday. Mark my words, this time next year, you can begin your training that will eventually lead you to our Frau." He reached down and took up my leash smiling with much pride.

I felt some relief at hearing that. "You really think I could break my metal in one year, Master? I am so far behind in my Dominant training."

He nodded. "No worries my love. I will clear your path. All you must do is pass the last two parts of the test."

Ma brain whirled with confusion at his statement. "Wait Master, I have four more parts not two. The *Toleration of Pain with Torture and Public Humiliation* I have completed, there are no others that I have passed."

Master Jonas chuckled. "Ah, well, that is incorrect Mad Maxx. You passed the *Seduction with Artistic Skill* portion the second you gained the desires of all five Elders. You managed to get them all to change the rules just so they could possess you. That my love is seduction of the greatest skills ever seen in this Haus. In fact, the second you finish your rounds with all the Elders, you also pass the *Tolerance of Unusual Sexual Fetish* portion as well, I have no doubt your ability to please even the picky Drexel will not a problem for a pleasure artist such as yourself. If there are nothing but continued arguments of who gets what days, then consider your fourth section passed with flying colors. Jonas winked at me here. Then you can pick up the last two in the next twelve months without even breaking a sweat. You are Priceless my love. Your very nature assures your success. You were born to be a Dominant, that nature cannot deny."

I sat there in my kneel almost ready to shout for joy. I had only two more sections of this horrible test to pass, then I would be free of this nightmare at last. Well, that fourth one I had no choice but to please my Masters so that was as good as completed, as Master Jonas pointed out. I was able to shake off the terror of that second collar consummation and ignore the discomfort of my re-introduction to penetration sex by focusing on this light at the end of my tunnel.

Master Jonas had me rise and follow behind him on his leash to his bedroom. Once inside he demanded I undress and allow his cuddle in his bed. I fell asleep in his embrace well-worn from the many days of stress. Master Jonas informed me he was granting me bed privileges but to be honest, I would have preferred my own room like before. Bad enough, I had to tolerate his lustful interests. Then to have the burden of dealing with his cuddle and snoring after his violations. Not a fun thing let me tell you.

Our late (ridiculous by the way that I had to beg so hard to be fucked like that. I am still a little pissed about it just for the record) consummation led to our oversleeping that morning. Master Claus and Master Drexel had to come calling twice before finally I awoke to hear the knocking on the apartment door. I roused my Master. He yawned and yelled loudly that we were coming.

I tried to escape his embrace to get dressed, but he pulled me back into a wanton kiss. I feared for a moment that my other Masters would have to return a third time, after Master Jonas took his special services rights. To my relief, he let me go with a groan of frustration within a few moments of his heated touching.

"Shit, coming you rat bastards. Quit knocking." My Master rolled out of his bed then grabbed his robe with much irritation and went to answer the door.

I got up and grabbed my jeans then recalled what the hell the Masters were visiting for. There was no reason to bother dressing. I would only have to take it all off again for their humiliating exploration of my flesh while they sought the evidence of the sealed lock.

I sighed then took off after my Master naked as the day I was born. I quietly headed down the hallway into the living area in high protocol submissive valuing, you know on the balls of my feet, then gracefully knelt by Master Jonas's velvet couch.

Master Claus and Master Drexel were entering the apartment and had a full view of my appearance in the room. They had apparently had not expected to see that. They both gasped, which caused my Master Jonas to turn to see me kneeling there quietly. He chuckled with pure humor that I had shocked those Elder schwulers with my most appropriate behavior.

"What is the matter boys? You have both seen this beauty naked before. Why are you acting like a couple of prudish Fraus?" Master Jonas laughed even harder after saying that.

Master Claus gained his tongue, still appearing a bit stunned. "Ja, I confess I have, but still, it is breathtaking, and I am not ashamed to admit this. Now enough of the teasing Jonas. Did you seal the fucking lock or not?"

Ma Master nodded still chuckling. "Ja, that collar on our submissive is valid. Check for yourself Claus. Drexel, be my guest too. Mad Maxx stand up and submit to your betters for examination."

I stood as commanded and tried my best to remain stoic for this necessary providing of proof the consummation was completed. Normally only a blood bonding requires witnessing but due to the unusual nature of this second collaring and odd virginity trade, the Haus required that honesty be verified.

Master Drexel examined the fourth virginity wound closely, while Master Claus probed my hind side for evidence of Master Jonas's violation and climax. I didn't have to endure this humiliation long before both Masters were satisfied, the lock was sealed and my contract with them valid. They smiled with glee that the thing they never expected had happened. They all possessed their very own collar and the rare Priceless one at that.

Master Jonas released me to go shower and dress while the three of them called a black collar to bring champagne. The Elders wanted to celebrate their coveted acquisition despite it only being the noon hour. I left them with much haste, more than ready to scrub off a few layers of flesh in my desperate attempt to wash away the horrors of that consummation ritual.

I took a long, searing hot shower and got out to dry off. Master Jonas came into the bathroom startling me to near heart attack. He was smiling at my drop to my knees in a cower of fright.

"You are a jumpy thing, my love. I would apologize for scaring you like that but watching your graceful kneel always thrills me no matter the circumstances. I have come to tell you my special wedding gifts to you have arrived. When your done with your hygiene and prep for Barnim's affections tonight, you will go to the room I granted you. You'll find your closet filled with new outfits. These are my gifts of love for your perfect service. I thank you for the joy it will bring to me to see my beauty in clothing worthy of him." He then left the room, closing the door behind him as quickly as he had appeared in the first place.

I finished my hygiene and grooming rituals, then went to my room with the grey door. I was both flattered and horrified by the sight of that closet. Master Jonas had black collars line the racks with clothes made of silk, brocade, and other fine materials. I noticed immediately the shirts were blouses of ruffles in crimson or black only. All the breeches were black, some with fancy designs and lace, and several elaborate waist coats of red or black also hung there.

I found three long jackets of black with a satin red lining and differing cuts. There were several pairs of boots, all complimentary colors for the "Dracula" outfits. I almost fainted when I saw that at the top of that closet were four top hats like the one Master Jonas wore during the collar vow ceremony.

On my dresser was a makeup case full of the black eyeliner and dark colors Maximillian had become infamous for wearing during his time under Peter's collar. I sat on the bed feeling quite faint from this most unexpected turn of events.

I realized it was my Master's right to dress me in outfits that brought him delight, but I had not considered this. Master Jonas fancied himself the Vampire, and he cared nothing for society's view on proper fashion. He had quite obviously decided that I was not to follow their rule either. I wondered if all four of the other Masters would also demand I dress in a way they found attractive.

Despite my feeling a bit nerve racked over this situation, I got up and began the elaborate dressing ritual that would become a part of my life for many years to come. When I finished, I looked in the mirror to see the Vampire Mad Maxx looking back at me. I thought again of Emma's blooded lips and shuddered to my core. I was beyond terrified Meine Liebe. I was now certain that Master Jonas was trying to turn me into one of the undead.

I left the room to face my Masters and await my Master Barnim, the sexual sadist, arrival. I had already endured the violence of the Vampire's blood fetish. I still had three more unusual fetishes to endure before I could call myself fully collared to these horrible men.

I trembled slightly when I entered the living area to find Master Bladrick and Master Barnim had arrived to join their brothers in their celebration toasts. They all stopped and looked at me with gazes of desire, approval, and lust.

Master Jonas smiled his toothy grin. "Ah, there is our beautiful Priceless collar, boys. Feast your eyes on our success. This Haus can deny us our pleasures no more. Mad Maxx is a sexual artist most talented and unique among all the silvers of his kind. We are the luckiest men on Earth."

Master Claus clapped his hands, his eyes shining with much joy. "I not only agree with you Jonas, but I also drink to that."

Master Drexel looked at his partner Master Bladrick. "I eagerly look forward to experiencing the thrill of this collar's favors myself, as does my brother." He nodded to Master Bladrick that stared at me as if in a trance saying nothing.

Master Barnim snorted. "Well, you two can wait your fucking turns. This beauty is all mine tonight. When I am done with him, maybe there will be nothing left for your exploration Drexel."

Master Drexel scoffed at that. "You go easy on this treasure, Barnim. I am already pissed Claus makes me go after you and Jonas. That poor Priceless will be a bloody mess by the time Bladrick and I get him thanks to the nasty shit you and that Vampire are into."

Master Barnim shot a look of anger at Master Jonas then back to Master Drexel. "Fuck you, Drexel. All the damned boy must do for you is hold real still for your cock. You call yourself an artist but when it comes to sex, your nothing but a bore."

Master Drexel looked at me and I dropped my gaze to the floor feeling fear rolling down my spine. "I would like to apologize to you, my love, for this pig's behavior with you tonight. I offer you some comfort by saying if you can get through it without jumping from the banister, I assure your time in my embrace will be enjoyable after the fucking nightmare of dealing with Barnim. He is not socially anxious about that, I am sure. He stays out of sight, lurking in dark hallways because he fears Gott's punishment for all the foul things, he requires to find his pleasure. That is what I think anyway."

Master Barnim growled out in anger. "None one gives a shit what you think, Drexel. Why don't you go fuck one of our statues. We all know you chose them because you're so nasty only something that cannot say nein would be willing to call you their lover.

I stood their listening to these two men hurl insults at each other picking on their fetishes, their mothers, and every other foul thing they could come up with. I realized with much disgust if even only half of what day claimed of the other's foulness were true, then my terrible situation had only just begun.

Chapter 34: Hooked

"I stood there with my eyes to the floor terrified out of my mind listening to the two old schwulers insulting each odder. I trembled with the idea that even for only a year this was to be my life, pleasing these horrid men. I had been doing my best to accept the life of a pleasure submissive, but Meine Liebe, this was true horror for you Master. Five Masters, all men, all elderly, and all disgusting in their carnal interests.

I think Master Jonas either saw my shaking in my boots or thought the discussion may be a bit much for this unstable boy Mad Maxx. Whatever the reason, he took pity on making me listen to this disturbing verbal fighting between Master Drexel and Master Barnim.

He looked at me for a moment standing there in the entry of his hallway then called out. "Mad Maxx, come here and kneel for your Master. I wish to have my submissive at my feet so I can look upon the beauty of him and share with my brothers the vision of our rare treasure."

I moved with speed to follow his command while Master Drexel and Master Barnim stopped their insults to watch me. I took my place at his feet in a kneel then bowed my head staring at the floor my back to the other Masters who sat in silence for this show of protocol.

Master Claus spoke up after I took my position. "Ah, now that is bedder. We can all gaze in wonder at this property of ours and our ears are no longer assaulted by the voices of old men behaving like child." He shot a look of irritation at Master Drexel and Master Barnim.

Master Jonas chuckled, "I agree Claus. This bullshit has been spewed into my apartment gets on my last nerve. This collar is still mine for another few hours before I must pass it on to the next of us. I don't appreciate having to hear about the foulness that Mad Maxx will have to endure in the beds of my brothers. I would appreciate it if Barnim and Drexel could keep that shit to themselves in my presence. I could go my whole life happily never hearing of their personal sicknesses in fact." I took a deep breath agreeing that I would like very much to never know about it myself. Sucks to be me though, doesn't it?

Master Barnim scoffed at that. "You have a lot of room to talk Jonas. At least I don't plan to go sucking the boys blood out. Even Drexel isn't as sick as you are."

Master Jonas growled out, "Shut the fuck up Barnim. You do anything but suck the blood. As it is I will have to bring bandages and antiseptic to keep Mad Maxx from dying of infection thanks to your twisted shit. I have to say you are the only one of us I would have fought to keep from sharing a collar with. Xavier himself couldn't have been more of a threat to his welfare. I would be careful fucking with me too much or I will fight hard to get you removed from the leash."

Master Barnim stood up with much fury in his eyes. "That is enough. I can tolerate this scum Drexel pointing fingers but you Jonas. I will not sit here and be insulted by the likes of your kind. There is no sicko bad as you in this whole Haus. You go too far comparing me to Xavier. This I demand an apology for, and I mean it."

Master Jonas jumped to his feet too causing me to cover my head in terror as he yelled out, "Fuck you, Barnim. Will not apologize for telling the truth of it.

Master Drexel stood up joining the fray. "I am with Jonas. You're a fucking monster, Barnim. I don't want to share my collar with you either. I vote we kick him from the rotation."

Master Claus moaned out in irritation, "All of you sit the fuck down. No one is voting for anything here."

Master Barnim looked at Master Jonas. "You hear that? Drexel would ask to have me removed; well Jonas, your Vampire ass is next. You better stand up for me or that weasel will get you too."

Master Jonas bellowed out, "That will never happen, Barnim. I am with Drexel for voting your removal. I found the collar. No one can remove me. You, however, are a threat. Demand he be prevented a leash, Claus. Get him the fuck out of here. Mad Maxx will not survive him."

I was now crying in full on panic listening to the fighting going on all around me. I didn't know why the hell Barnim was so hated by the others, but if he was anything like Xavier, I didn't think I could handle that.

I barely survived the last sexual sadist's lust. I was aware that type of fetish often resulted in the slow death of their submissive. I began to believe I had managed to get this close to collar selection only to be ended by Master Barnim just at the finish line.

Then suddenly, through all the shouting and heated anger Master Bladrick stood up. "Sit down, all of you. Enough of this bullshit jealousy. There is not one of you worse or better than his brother. We all have our twisted interests but not one of us can boast they killed a single leashed collar with them yet. Stop acting like Barnim is the worst of you. He also isn't a fucking thing like that monster Xavier who did kill many worthy collars. He was a fucking criminal, and I am not afraid to admit such a thing. We all feared him for good Gott damned reasons. Barnim doesn't scare me. I don't worry about my sweet little bat collar in his possession. I know tomorrow he will bring the boy to Drexel, and I will be in good health. However, all of you have frighted this collar so bad he is traumatized. Look at him. I mean it. Gaze at this beautiful boy you all worked together to own. You now tear each other apart and injure your prize, for what? Because you have to wait your turn for his affection? Are you all so hard up that having to wait a day or two, plus share with your brothers to bask in the thrill of our very own Priceless can cause you to behave like children? All of you sit the fuck down and enjoy this success. Can we not just this once behave like the brothers we are? I am too old for all this damned fighting and so are all of you. I for one want to enjoy my last few hours on this Earth with the joy of viewing this gorgeous young boy. I would also hope to hear the thrill he brings us, instead of donning earplugs to drown out all the bullshit spewing from your mouths." Master Bladrick's old foggy eyes blazed with the fires of hell which surely loomed not too far from him at the age of eighty-six.

The Elders all stared at each other still appearing angered, but no one said a word. Master Bladrick's dress down had them all thinking, there is no doubt. I continued to weep at the inhumanity of this situation I found myself in. No matter good or bad fetish, I hated these men, and my status as their submissive, hell anyone's submissive. I wished nothing more than to see them all in their graves soon as possible.

Master Claus finally spoke. "Jonas, Drexel, Barnim, apologize to each other. Bladrick is right. There is no call for these insults and squabbles among you."

The three men glared at each other but all of them gave mumbling apologies as demanded by Master Claus. Then everyone sat down in an uneasy truce. The mood was subdued and less than celebratory. Their nasty words to each other had cut them deeply. They went to small talk pretending all was well between them, but not even a fool would believe any of them was happy with his brothers.

Master Jonas watched me weeping quietly into my lap for a bit then said, "I will have to apologize brothers, but I still have a bit of time on my clock. I am taking Mad Maxx and my rights with him elsewhere. You may enjoy my home and drink the champagne to completion. Barnim, I will bring the Priceless collar for transfer just before midnight tonight. I will see you then. The rest of you I catch up with later when next we meet. Make sure the last one to leave locks the door on the way out, ja?" He stood up and snatched my leash demanding I follow behind him back to his bedroom.

The other Masters mumbled their goodbyes, as Master Jonas hauled me behind him. I wiped my eyes while keeping my gaze to the floor feeling more despair than you can imagine. I had just cleaned up his last mess and now he was dragging me off to make another one. Worse, I had this horrid Barnim at midnight sure to befoul me yet again.

There didn't seem to be an end to it, and I was thinking I couldn't keep scrubbing all my flesh from my bones trying to fool myself into feeling clean of their sickness. No doubt I was in for a harsh ride. No pun intended there either.

When Master Jonas and I got into his room he closed the door behind us and pulled my leash tight to keep me from kneeling by reflex. "Don't you mind them, Mad Maxx. They are just grouchy old men. They are trying to scare you, is all. You keep your mind on our plans to break that metal, mind them quickly without quarrel, and all will be okay. You will get used to them. The Elders never change. In a few weeks you'll know exactly what to do for each one, and it will be a piece of cake keeping them satisfied."

I shook my head feeling I may begin to cry again. "This is a nightmare, Master. I don't think I can do this. I thought I could, but I am just one person. I cannot please them all."

Master Jonas laughed then pulled my leash toward him till he had me in his embrace. "Ah, there my beauty. This Drexel, all you got to do is hold real still. Claus you already know well, Me you make happy three times already. Bladrick is merely a watcher, he is of no threat or work. Barnim, well he will be the only challenge. You can handle a thud, and torture. I already heard about your dealings with Xavier. Barnim is only occasionally, and he will never take you as far as Xavier did so no worries. A little pain in his chains, and a rough couple, then he will be satisfied. I tell you my love you will get used to it; I have faith in you."

I hid my face in his chest then whimpered. "No pinwheels or ball crushers I pray Master. I cannot take that shit."

Master Jonas chuckled. "No worries, my love. I thought of this. I have a full chastity device that will protect all your manhood not just the cock. Damned Peter was stupid to leave such a sensitive part of the man unprotected around Xavier. I need your potency protected and I cannot be sure the other Elders will care to see you break your metal like I am. Therefore, I already had Claus set into our contract your penetration be protected by your lead Master anyway he saw fit. I choose the cock and ball cage, and all have agreed to it. There will be no parachutes, ball crushers, or humblers possible with Barnim. He was pissed but too bad for him. He need not end your ability to father little ones."

I breathed a sigh of ultimate relief upon hearing this small piece of good news (hey, my bar was low okay. Unless you ever had your hoddensack tortured don't judge this was not a big deal to learn that Barnim would be prevented from it.) "Thank you for you mercy, Master. I appreciate that more than you can know."

Master Jonas chuckled. "Oh, I am aware of the sexual sadist, my love. I intend to see you make many pure Priceless children. Barnim is such a selfish bastard he would care nothing for destroying that ability. I know that rat bastard well, Now, you may thank me for my foresight and mercy by attending my interest right this minute before I must turn you out to my brothers to make your monthly rounds." He pointed to the floor indicating he desired I get to my knees and grant him a blow job for his foreplay before submitting me to his intercourse.

I sighed but did as he commanded. I was sadly glad to get the practice with penetration sex. I was aware that Master Jonas would offer the kindness of lube. I had painfully realized I was underused. If I didn't get that situation dilated quickly then if Barnim was not such a gentleman about comfort, it would be beyond tormenting.

I willingly suffered another harsh couple with Master Jonas despite his being quite kind in allowing some time to adjust, unlike the night before it hurt like hell again, to try to break my skills back into a state of painlessness. When he reached his apex, I felt I would come apart with my shaking and intense agony. I was more than upset that it didn't appear any ground had been gained by this humiliating act.

Master Jonas must have realized this fear I was dealing with. He uncoupled and pulled me to face him, my cheeks still wet with tears and back teeth about broken off from the grinding of them.

He looked at me then said, "This breaking back in I should have done before I collared you. I apologize for this. I admit I had forgotten the facts of this kind of penetration. I realized too late you will suffer needlessly for my neglecting my duty to your comfort, my love. So, today I called your doctor and have him bring in muscle relaxers. I will give you two of them to take before we transfer your collar to Barnim. This will get you through his torment coupling with a bit less torture. I will give two more to Bladrick for your turn with Drexel tomorrow. Claus is already aware and will make sure you are made as comfortable as possible. By the time you return to me, I hope to find your seasoned once more, but if not, then we do what must be done as humanely as possible. I don't wish to see you suffer during our intercourse. That is not my fetish, my love. Make sure when you pack your things to take the witch hazel for swelling and I leave you a bottle of lubrication too just in case the two rat bastards pull the whole "I don't have any around the apartment" bit on you."

I nodded feeling a bit of relief that my Master had considered two bits of torment without my having to humiliate myself by admitting them. "Again, I thank you for your mercy, Master."

He pulled me into a deep kiss then said, "I am proving to you Christian Axel that I do love you without boundaries or conditions. I am your Master, but I am also your husband. That means I owe more to you than just my authority over you. It is also my job to lessen your burden when and if I can do, just as you will do for me. We are blood bonded partners for life. One day we add another heart to our family but for now, it is me and you against the world. If they mistreat you, then they hurt me too. This you will come to trust and understand as you mature."

I looked at the mattress feeling sick to my stomach. The Vampire that seemed so kind to me appeared to have another agenda. I had to know. "Master, you keep bringing up my Frau. Are you telling me that she will not be mine exclusively? I will be Dominant and eventually so will she. I understand sharing this for a time may happen but after she breaks her own metal, and mine is gone, well, then we have the choice, ja?"

Master Jonas frowned. "Nein, I will be blood bonded to both of you. You cannot break such a bond no matter your status Christian Axel. Besides, she will be thrilled to have two handsome men in her bed. Your young, you'll see."

I decided to keep my mouth shut on that bullshit. I didn't know how my Frau would feel about two men in her bed, but I knew damned well how I felt about even one of them.

Master Maxx suddenly spun me around looking me in my face with curiosity. "I hold my Frau in my hands now. I ask you tonight, this thing Master Jonas said to me, is it true? Do you think having two men is acceptable? You may answer my question with your voice."

I shook my head. "I don't want anyone but my husband anywhere near me. I don't like sex to begin with. I can barely put up with my husband wanting it from me, Master. I also don't want any nasty Vampire biting me, drinking my blood, putting his boy part in me, or making me watch him have sex with my husband either. I would have to put a stake right through the Vampire's heart. I can promise that when I get big, I won't let anyone hurt you or me anymore, Master."

Master Maxx smiled, then hugged me tightly. "That is my Demonseed Frau. You make my heart sing with your words of true love. I am grateful to have a woman of a such fine quality. We will break your collar and stop this bullshit of Jonas or Peter sharing our bed if he still lives by then. I want you all for myself, and when this horror is over will I never share you with anyone again. We will be monogamous for all time and make many beautiful children, ja?"

I nodded. "Yes Master. I want that too. No more stupid men for either of us. Just you and me and lots of babies." Hey, I was nine, what did I know about anything?

He held me for several minutes in his loving embrace then pulled me back into position in his lap to begin his story once more.

"I took another shower pondering the ways to escape the bounds of his blood ritual. I wondered if in the world outside the Haus such a union was honored or if this was merely the bullshit laws of this illegally run place. I decided to start my research to find out what the laws of the country said about same sexed unions and civilly recognized marriages. I suspected Master Jonas couldn't enforce his statements that I was his partner by right. If I could find proof otherwise, well that Vampire could color Mad Maxx gone. No way I was going to stay with his creepy ass.

Don't get me wrong, he has been more kind to me than anyone thus far. That said, he was still a rapist, abuser, and pervert, because I was never permitted the right to say nein. If I had been allowed to, he would have heard me screaming it at the top of my lungs. I didn't want to be with him in any way, not ever.

I only respected that he did indeed seem to love me, or at least what I could do for him. He had saved me from the Guard, but he had his own selfish reasons. Had I just been a regular submissive without the power to grant him eternal life (*or he believes it anyway, though it is bullshit Meine Liebe. Don't you fall for his lies. We don't have that mythical power*) he would have let them shoot me right there and then.

None of those old schwulers cared a thing for me other than what they could extract from my bones. I was not loved by any of them. I was being exploited, plain and simple. In this life many will exploit the ones around them for whatever they can get. That is okay when the use of another is agreed upon or paid for equally, like in a job or even some marriages. It becomes abuse when one side is taken against the will of the other or when the trade is terribly unbalanced.

I was being raped, tormented, tortured, controlled, and misused in every sense of the word by these men. If I dared to stand up to them, even just to say I didn't want any more dinner, I was soundly beaten to the ground till I relented to their desires.

I was not permitted to have my choice in dressing, eating, hygiene, outside interests, preference for sexuality, or even a vision for my future. In all ways I was more of a slave with no more rights of the animal.

I was deep in thought of my predicament scrubbing off my latest indignity with Master Jonas when he came into the bathroom. I killed the water and leapt from the tub, dropping into a kneel with much confusion at his intrusion of my hygiene rituals.

He stood there with a sour look on his face. "Mad Maxx, I apologize for interrupting you. I wanted to let you know Barnim dropped off his preferred clothing for the night. I had them laid out on your bed. I am sorry my love. His taste is crude and without any class. When you come back to me, I will see you back in outfits worthy of your beauty. I can do nothing about his lack of taste. Carry on." He left the room as quickly as he entered.

I finished up my cleansing, then walked to the room with the grey door. On the bed was a "bondage outfit" of leather and chains. I winced at the sight of that bullshit. Barnim was making it clear I should expect a fair amount of torture and thudding in his collar. I had to endure ruffles, makeup, panty hose and even dresses, none of it had bothered me much.

However, this latest outfit caused me dread. The chest harness without any fucking shirt, leather wrist and upper arm cuffs, a pair of heavy boots and chain, leather bondage pants indicated the Barnim was one nasty fellow indeed. His preference for clothing was designed for easy access to cause pain, brutal/rapid coupling, and each item had built in ways to restrain me if I tried to retreat from his agonizing pleasures.

I groaned when I caught my reflection in the mirror after putting the stupid things on. The boy staring back from the mirror looked like the typical male biker bitch. I winced when I noticed the whole thing would match my fucking collar and leash to perfection.

I checked twice to make sure he hadn't sent over a fucking face hood too, to make sure I suffered completely from his obnoxious outfit. I wondered if next he would send one so then I could look completely like the foolish gimp. Shit, this was pure humiliation to the extreme. And I thought the Vampire look and dresses were bad. There are no words strong enough for my disgust on this one.

I come out of my room looking like a reject from the Village People with a frown on my face. Master Jonas was coming down the hallway and spotted my despairing expression. He stopped then covered his eyes with a sound of disgust that matched my own feelings about the matter.

"Fuck me, that is worse than I imagined it would be, Mad Maxx. I apologize so much for this dishonor. I suppose that it may help you feel better when he strips you out of that ridiculous outfit. I swear I would prefer to run naked than be caught dead in that horror." He groaned louder than I had when I saw it myself.

I shook my head looking at the floor. "You're not helping matters Master. I am aware I look like a damned idiot in this crazy shit. I would beg your mercy to let me be about it. I do what I am told. I have to please these other Masters and that is my lot in life. Aren't you the one that said that?"

Master Jonas nodded. "Ah, ja I did. I apologize for my insult to you for doing your job, Mad Maxx. Just make sure you pack that which hazel. I am sure you will need it. I left antiseptic, bandages and your muscle relaxers on the bathroom sink. I think you may need a pain killer too. I will set one out right now. I am sure Barnim will try to make you suffer, to punish Drexel for insulting him. If I were you, I would take a dose of Tylenol now and leave the pain killer in your overnight bag till Barnim is finished thrashing your ass. Oh, and come with me to get your chastity device secured before I forget again. You'll thank me in the morning, no doubt."

I growled while following him to his room. "I already thanked you most soundly I seem to recall Master."

He chuckled at that. "Yes, you did my love. I am more relaxed than I have felt in many years. I must admit, I miss you already. Your being around has done much to make me feel less lost in this world of nothings."

I rolled my eyes while he began to dig in his dresser drawer looking for his chastity device. He was busy and didn't see that move of disrespect, thank Gott. "Your pleasure is my own Master. ill Master Drexel expect me to dress like Napoleon, or maybe the Thinker? For that matter

147

I am wondering if Master Claus will send over a fucking wedding gown and tierra demanding I walk down the aisle on his arm for the Priest? I wish to say this dressing for each of you is a pain in the ass you know."

Master Jonas laughed but shot me a look of caution. "If tell you to dress like a giant chicken, you will do it and shut your mouth Mad Maxx. We all have the agreement as long as no one tries to do anything permanent like scarification, tattooing, or nipple piercing. They are allowed to make your appearance pleasing to them."

I flinched at his saying what I had not been worried about. "What? You all had to agree not to do that shit Master. What the hell. What if they break their word and do that horror anyway. Once such a thing is done, then it is fucking done."

Ma Master found the item he was seeking then turned to me with a serious expression. "If they do such bullshit they are immediately forfeited from the rotation and can never have your collar alone again without a witness. You have nothing to fear. None would dare to end up in that situation."

I rolled my eyes again while scoffing. "I will remember you said that when my face sports a nice big butterfly tattoo or my head is decorated by the golden looped earrings, Master."

Master Jonas walked over to me standing in his doorway chuckling at my whining. "I swear, Mad Maxx, you are such a negative man. Stop your bitching and drop those horrid trousers so I can put this thing on you. I believe you have enough to be concerned over without adding the fear of tattoos or more scars my love. When Barnim is thudding you tonight, try to focus on the gorgeous Emma. That should help you endure his harsh intercourse, I think."

I did as he told me watching him clumsily attach the horrid chastity device. "Uhm, ja, I wanted to talk to you about Emma, Master." I winced when he closed the damned thing on my manhood. It was too snug and not made for the larger fellow I suppose.

Master Jonas shrugged. "What about her?" He locked it into place then stood to admire his handiwork.

I groaned out in much discomfort. "Well, I beg your mercy Master in two things. First, I must ask you to find a larger cage. This one is going to lead to a loss of my manhood if I wear it too often. Second, I would ask you to never invite Emma to our bed again. Thank you in advance for these kindnesses if you would see it in your heart to grant them."

This seemed to surprise Master Jonas. He crossed his arms staring at me in disbelief. "Okay, I can see the cage is too small. I will fix that right away by sending off a black collar to find a larger one. However, why do you ask the second mercy? I thought you said Emma was perfect, anything you desired in a woman?"

I shook my head. "I never want to see her near me for the rest of my life, Master. You don't have to grant this mercy to me, this I understand. You are the Master not me. However, if you bring her, I will not feel lustful. Just saying her name to me this minute makes me sick to my stomach. I have no use for that horrible woman. I would like to make it clear that right now I do not agree with her price and even if I had agreed I would tell you she isn't worth it. I would rather endure your one-sided lust for all

149

time than have her touching me ever again. She ever comes near me in the future, I will be the one doing the biting this time. She will not enjoy my teeth in her perfect flesh any more than I did hers, that I promise you." I growled out in anger.

Master Jonas stood there with his mouth open in shock. "Are you serious, Mad Maxx? I thought you adored her. She was a gift from me to you. I wanted you to enjoy our lovemaking at least a little. I just don't understand this…" I interrupted him most rudely.

"I am going to say this one more time, Master. You bring her anywhere near me, I will do my best to rip her apart. She will have more to worry about than father time when I get my hands or teeth on her. Keep her the fuck away from me. Donor my ass. That bitch is a vampire like you. I know what the hell she is to you. I say nothing about your having lovers that are of the forbidden collars, but I will be damned if you will push them off on me. I will not tolerate that shit, Master. She does not have a collar on me last I checked. The day a fucking black collar will profit from my forced submission to you, or any other Dominant is the day I fucking go to the orchard. I have to tolerate being your donor but let me make this clear, I will kill any other of your kind that tries that shit on me." I braced for his backhand for standing my ground on his black collar lover Emma the called herself a vampire too.

Ja. I told you, I am a lot of things Meine Liebe, but a fool is not one of them. I figured out the two were into the same vampire cult and likely long-term lovers, after all how else could she have known he was a generous one in bed? She had fucked up and said so just before she bit me. I realized she likely was blackmailing my Master into getting her own taste of my Priceless blood, the stupid bitch. How Master Jonas ended that vixen's hold on him was not my problem to fix, nor my price to fucking pay.

I nodded in agreement. I was glad he put his foot down on Emma. Even at nine I could see that woman was there to hurt Master Maxx. She did almost nothing for the terror she was extracting from him. Any woman would have worked. Getting one that didn't want to suck his blood would have been a hell of a lot smarter, unless there was a motive in the first place. I was glad to see my Master had recognized that immediately just as my child mind had. Buh bye Emma.

"Master Jonas nodded with an expression of shame. "I wish you would reconsider Emma, my love. She has me in a tight spot. If I don't allow her to receive her price, she could open her mouth. Even as an Elder I could be sent from this Haus if she does. I do beg your forgiveness for not telling you the truth. I see you're not a fool. I just assumed your lust for the Frau would be strong enough to overlook such a small thing."

I shook my head with wickedness in my gaze at him. "I will speak to Emma for you Master. I assure you she will never open her mouth to threaten you ever again when I finish with her. I don't know why you didn't make sure to shut that trap of hers with your own hands, but Mad Maxx has talent at doing just that if it is a burden for your back. This is one service I am more than happy to provide you without expectation of any return. The fucking deed is the pleasure in itself."

My Master's eyes went wide. "Oh, meine Gott. Are you saying you want to kill Emma? Why Christian? All she did was show your great kindness and you're ready to set her to the orchard?"

I laughed out loud full of insanity "That was kindness? Ah silly Mad Maxx. What the hell was I thinking? Of course, you would see it that way, wouldn't you? What I saw was a woman that come to bit me and steal my blood for only giving me a kiss and hugs. Must have been a hell of a good deal for her. Not even to be asked for a hand job. Oh, wait, she may get an orgasm when I bring her the oral pleasure she never had to grant back. Fuck that bitch. She black mailed you so she could enjoy watching my shame and drinking my blood. All this so she could stay young and is not even silver. It matters not if she is young or attractive. Pure vanity for one already so damned blessed as she is. Disgusting. Truth is she could resemble an old husband and her future is secured. You had to bind me because you feared she would soil me. You knew she has the means to recover her spot in the Haus on the pleasure floor. Why would she want to? She was sleeping with you, one of the most powerful in the fucking Haus. This bitch wants for nothing and still she is never satisfied. This Emma has not a good heart or soul. She is a manipulator that would see you or I put down if she could gain from it. I am happy to put that shit to bed forever. Ask Felix, oh wait, you cannot. I took care of his ass the same fucking way I will this vampire bitch."

Master Jonas shook his head. "Nein, Mad Maxx, leave Emma alone. I will attend to her. You focus on other more important dings. There is no need for you to taint your hands with her blood. You're right. This is my doing and I will not allow her to worm her way into our bed by manipulating her position. She only thinks she has the power to bring me down. She is mistaken. I suppose I fell for her charms, not too many vampires around you know. Now that I have you for my lover, I no longer need her to keep my bed lively. I believe she forgot her bad behavior could someday come back on her. In fact, her cruel threatening me caused me to notice you walking by one day. Got me to thinking of replacing the wrong kind of lover with the right one."

I pulled up my trousers grimacing at the discomfort of his cage device. "Whatever Master. I say to you now if I ever see the bitch again, she will find out I am not in love with her anymore. However, I swear to you I can grant her that eternal youth she craves because the dead don't age." I turned and stormed off to the kitchenette to find something to eat, leaving my stunned Master to think over what I said to him. Hey, I hadn't had a damned thing in twenty-four hours, I was starving.

I got a sandwich, then sat down on the living room floor doing my best to study my schoolwork. I was still fuming about the despotic Emma when suddenly Maximillian tore loose and jumped from the boy.

"That is it. I am not sticking around for a thudding, Mad Maxx. This is your domain, not mine." He brushed himself off acting as if he were trying to wipe himself clean of my essence.

I shot a look down the hallway to be sure he and I were alone. "Stop being a crybaby, Maximillian. This Barnim maybe has a reputation that is mostly rumor and overblown."

Maximillian scoffed. "Uhm, better look in the mirror their whipping boy. That outfit doesn't lie. This Barnim plans to fuck the flesh up like Xavier did. I will not deal with it. You're on your own this time."

I groaned. "Oh, I am? If I take this alone, I could report you to Der Hund. Wonder how he will take your bailing on me."

Maximillian sighed. "Let me off the hook or chains or whatever these bastard pulls, and I will make it up to you."

I laughed. "Oh? Well then, I would like to know what you plan to do to make this up to me?"

The schwuler shard appeared to think a moment then smiled. "I take Master Claus and you can rest."

I started to argue but then thought about that for a second. "You swear it, Maximillian? I take Master Barnim's torture alone and you take Master Claus's crossdressing on your own? Then for one each of these disgusting Masters we get a breather. If you give me your word of honor, I take this deal."

Maximillian nodded. "Ja, I swear it on my honor brother. We can handle Master Jonas together. Master Drexel neither of us have to handle."

I startled at that. "Huh? Why? Is Der Hund getting one of the others to run the wheel for Master Drexel?"

Maximillian chuckled. "Damn for being the smart one, this time your dumb as a post. Master Drexel wants a human statue fool. We both step out and the boy goes catatonic. This will please that weirdo and neither of us need deal with the nightmare of his intercourse, ja?"

I let out my breath. "Ah. I never thought of that. Ja. Okay. I take this deal happily. Only this sadistic Master Barnim and sharing the load of Master Jonas. Hell, this is easy."

Maximillian frowned at that. "Not so easy. There is a serious problem Mad Maxx. The schwulers are fighting like a pack of cats. If we are to punish Cora for her betrayal, and get to the others that have it coming, we need these Masters to work together. We are causing much jealousy among them. This drives them further apart. We need to come up with a way to gang them up. Otherwise, Cora will run this Haus unopposed as Xavier did. That is why she and Peter used us, you know. Everyone knows the five never agree on anything. That leaves an open channel for the Head to get all he or she desires without a single voice against them. Cora thinks she has gotten this place of pure power. The best way to pay her, Peter, all of them back, is to stop her from getting away with this. The five Masters working as a team will neuter her from getting anything done in this Haus. She is a FemDom, day are schwuler Masters. They will side with each other and block her into a corner if we can bring them together."

I must give Maximillian credit. There was much validity to what he was saying. If our goal, besides breaking our collar, was revenge on those that brought us into this nightmare life. Then it was clear bringing our five Masters together rather than seeing them continue to drift apart was the way to start. The truth was if we didn't, Cora could even become a serious threat to our getting through the vote. She had to be neutralized and quickly as possible before she had any time to secure her new throne.

Maximillian and I would be through our first cycle with the Masters before she even took legal possession of the Haus head seat. Master Jonas was already well within our power through seduction. It would be up to me to bring in Master Barnim, and Maximillian agreed to bring across Master Claus.

I looked at the floor. "What about Master Drexel and Master Bladrick? I think I can maybe come up with something in our seduction for the statue lover but Master Bladrick that is impossible. He is impotent. Without the sex to bind him, then we can never be sure."

Maximillian cleared his throat. "Master Bladrick can be seduced by sexual desire too. In fact, he is the one among them that will not be able to live without us when I am through with him."

I nodded with a sudden understanding of his vision for Master Bladrick "You have my ultimate respect, brother. I can see what you plan to do, and I think you're a genius. Your sacrifice in bringing that most ancient Master to his knees before us deserves a medal as far as I am concerned. For what that is worth you may be the best shard of all of us."

Maximillian looked at the floor coyly. "Damn. What you said almost makes the nightmare of Master Bladrick worth it, almost. It is one thing to say I can do it, but another to go there."

I chuckled at that. "Don't I know it. Look I have to figure out how to tolerate becoming the statue, so I assume a mouth full of piss is a fair trade, ja?"

Maximillian shook his head. "We shall see, brother. For now, I say I will stay close tonight just in case you need a break. We work together in all ways. I am not Mad Max. I won't abandon you when the going gets brutal. You remember that when my turn comes."

I nodded with a smile at my most agreeable partner shard. "I hear you, brother. I will never leave you to suffer alone. Der Hund would shatter me even if I tried." We began to giggle at that when suddenly Master Jonas came into the room.

"Der Hund? I heard this name before. You said it in the dungeons, Mad Maxx. Who are you speaking to? I see no one here but I hear your voice for the last several moments." The Vampire looked at me with curiosity.

I shrugged. "Just reading aloud Master. That is all. I didn't mean to disturb your nap." I dropped my eyes to the schoolbook.

Master Jonas scoffed. "The psychosis working on you again, I think. I wonder if this sharing you with these others will set that off again. Well, we will find out. Barnim's time will begin soon. Time to go my love."

I looked up with a startle. "Huh? I thought we were not to leave till midnight, Master?"

My Master appeared shocked. "You okay Mad Maxx? It is midnight, don't you see the time on the clock? Did you lose track of it studying?"

I jerked my sight to the clock that indicated many hours had passed in what appeared to be only moments. I felt a chill run down my spine that I had lost hours somehow. I decided to let this slide and not report the strange symptom to my Master. I went to stand and noticed a wet spot on my stomach and front of my pants. I had been drooling heavily for much time without noticing apparently.

Master Jonas had lain down to sleep while I studied (he had a long night remember) and had missed my catatonic stupor. I didn't even realize I had slipped away from reality for almost five hours.

I rushed from the room to grab my overnight bag and take the muscle relaxers. I grabbed a towel doing my best to wipe off my bare stomach. I was frantic in my trying to hide the symptoms of my brain disease. I feared if Master Jonas noticed this, he may cause more difficulty with Master Barnim by refusing to hand my collar to him for his turn in the cycle. He was already nervous about sending me on my duties to each of them thanks to my last psychotic episode.

It was not that I was in a hurry to deal with this sexual sadist or the other perverts because believe me I was not. I was painfully aware I had no choice but to serve all these monsters at some point one way or another. No doubt the schizophrenia was a hurtle to my continued good health and all my future goals if I let it take control of me.

I needed to seduce all the Masters to make sure that before I ended up falling into madness during my next disease cycle, they didn't end up seeding the grass with me. I assumed it would be harder for the Masters to call the Guard on a lover.

Master Jonas guided me out of our apartment then turned to look at me. "Shit. I forgot to give you the muscle relaxers to take before Drexel tomorrow night. I'll be right back. Stay here my love." He rushed back inside.

I walked over to look over the banister to the floor below. I briefly thought of jumping to a most gruesome death when way below I saw Peter step out of his apartment in his robe. He was looking down too likely wishing he had me tied up in his fucking bed. Without me there to rape he apparently wasn't sleeping well,

I don't know what got into me, but I cleared my nasal passages and throat with vigor then spit the hocker off the railing aiming for Peter. I watched as this foulness made contact by landing right on the top of my cruel father's head. He looked up immediately to see me backing the fuck away in a shock that I actually hit the bastard.

Peter was pissed. He took off running for the stairs to come kick my ass for my trick. I went back to the apartment door looking all around for a place to escape. Master Jonas came out of the apartment handing me the pills. I saw Peter rushing up the last flight of stairs loudly cursing.

I reached out and grabbed Master Jonas and pulled him into a kiss of wanton passion pouring it on with all I had. My Master was wide eyed and quite stunned at my sudden aggressive interest in him. He began to return my adoration with much eagerness running his hands over my near naked chest and stomach. I moaned with feigned ecstasy as I watched angry Peter's stomping toward us.

"Jonas, you hand that fucking boy over for my punishment right now," Peter tapped harshly on Master

Jonas's back as he dropped to my neck panting out in heated desire.

My Master tore his mouth away from me, but kept me held tight in his embrace, suddenly losing his lust but quickly gaining irritation. "Peter? What the fuck is wrong with you? Get out of here. This collar is not yours anymore."

Peter snorted, "I am fucking aware of that, Jonas. You already stole him from me. Now this bastard spat on me from the banister. I will not allow this to go without correction."

Master Jonas shot a look of wickedness at me, and I dropped my sight to the floor. "First of all, Peter, I stole nothing from you. Your collar, uhm, Maximillian, was it? He was killed by the Guard I seem to recall. This submissive here is Mad Maxx the Priceless collar of the Elders. I know our collar didn't spit on you because he has been here entertaining me with his mouth for the last many minutes. The only spit leaving this boy was the stuff I was sharing with him."

Peter growled out in a pure fury. "Bullshit. I saw him spit on me with my own eyes. See this. He did that. Your precious Priceless has a thudding coming for it too. I demand he is punished right the fuck now." He reached into his hair then produced the slick, shiny spit wad on his fingers for Master Jonas to see.

Master Jonas snorted at Peter with disgust then without a word spun me into his embrace. I let out a loud gasp when he then pinned me to his closed apartment door leaning down forcing his lips to my own. He immediately returned to his heavy petting ignoring the fuming Peter.

Peter stood there unsure what to do for a moment, then yelled out. "Fine. I will remember this, Jonas. I will catch that fucking little bastard Mad Maxx out somewhere, sooner or later. I will punish him within an inch of his life the second I get a chance." Peter began to storm off back down the stairs.

Master Jonas pulled away from our kissing then winked at me. "You touch a single hair on this collar, Peter, then five very angry old sonsofbitches will have your ass for their supper. Best you never come up this direction again. You forget you place in this Haus and who you threaten. Do it again, and it will be the last fucking time you have a memory slip." Peter snorted loudly then tore off down the stairs soundly defeated in his bid to pay me back for my little "slip of my tongue."

I smiled at Master Jonas as he glared at me with some humor in his gaze. "You're a bad boy, Mad Maxx. Spitting on your father, really? I would think that a bit beneath you and at your age."

I shrugged. "Wasn't me Master. Must have been some other boy that bastard misused and raped, ja?"

Master Jonas leaned down kissing and fondling me for several moments. This time I didn't mind his affection so much. He had kept me from being punished even though he knew I did the crime. If he wanted to kiss and touch over that, beat the hell out of the tawsing I surely had coming from Peter. I happily returned his adoration without hesitation.

My Master finally pulled himself off me groaning out in frustration. "Shit, I can't believe I have to give you up from my bed to this fucker Barnim. Come on love. Let's go before the old buzzard starts bitchin that I am unfairly holding you after his clock begins. I continue this with you in two more days when you come home at last." I sighed wishing this night had already passed and the next two as well,

It was not that I liked Master Jonas more than the others as I had not even been with three of them yet, and I pretty much hated all of them period. But I had been with him long enough to know I was safe with him. He was not eager to see me killed, injured, or in a terrible amount of pain. I also didn't fear Master Claus nor Master Bladrick. I had been with Master Claus before, and Master Bladrick didn't have a bizarre fetish.

The other two scared me a great deal. I followed behind Master Jonas in pure fear keeping my eye on my brother Maximillian. He kept up by riding the shadows and whispering words of encouragement. I braced myself for whatever nightmare awaited me at the last apartment on the floor of the Elders. The head of the Haus took the top floor of the Haus all for themself, then the penthouses on the floor just below the top dog belonged to the other five Elders. We were nearly at Master Barnim's door, and it come open and the man came out into the hallway.

He glared at Master Jonas, appearing most vexed. "I thought maybe you decided to hijack the collar and run away with him. You're late Jonas. I waited almost fifteen minutes for my turn. You said midnight not daybreak."

Master Jonas scoffed. "Don't be a drama queen, Barnim. I had a problem with that fucking old Master of our collar. He started some shit back at my place. That caused a hold up. I apologize for it."

Master Barnim's eyes went wide. "Oh? Peter came up here you say. What the fuck was his problem? I thought you said he threw this treasure away?"

Ma Master nodded. "Oh, he did Barnim. That is the problem though. Sometimes these lower Dominants do shit impulsively then realize their mistakes. I had to run back to my house for something and come out to find him harassing our collar. I don't know what his problem is, but I don't care. He can't go fooling with things that are not his anymore. I sent the rat bastard running though, so no harm done."

Master Barnim cast a look at me with curiosity. "Tell me Mad Maxx, what this Peter want?"

I looked at Master Jonas who smiled then nodded allowing me to answer. "He saw me in this glorious outfit you selected. I guess he was angered thinking he still had the right to tell me what to wear. I suppose this because he was cursing me and demanding to know who had the audacity to dress me like, oh I better not repeat what he said Master Barnim. It was bullshit coming from a nothing and I don't appreciate it at all. Plus, it is a lie." I cast my eyes at the floor causing Master Jonas to giggle as he realized my head game with Master Barnim.

Master Barnim glared at me for a moment then stomped his foot angrily (like the pissy Frau can, you believe that shit?). "I demand you tell me what that sonofabitch said about the outfit I choose for you Mad Maxx. Speak it now I command it."

I sighed then winced. "He wanted to know the name of the idiot that dressed me like a schwuler pole dancer. He said that fool should be flogged soundly for it. I told him

163

my Master had impeccable taste and that he was jealous he never thought to display me in such a pleasurable look when he held my collar." I pretended to be ashamed of repeating such a terrible and truthful statement.

Master Barnim nearly blew a gasket over that. "That motherfucker. Jonas, I want that arrogant prick in chains. I demand he be thudded immediately for insulting me and my collar, Mad Maxx." He reached out and snatched the black leash from Master Jonas's hand while he demanded Peter's ass in the flog room below.

Master Jonas smiled at me with a look of thrill, and unsaid understanding of my game, in his dark eyes. "I will see to that right away with much pleasure, my brother. You need not stress about a thing. I am happy to handle this punishment for you. Take Mad Maxx inside to lose yourself in his charms. I will give you a full report when I have finished punishing that snotty Dominant that dares to question your most infallible taste."

Master Barnim snorted then began to haul me inside his apartment but stopped at his door looking back at Master Jonas. "Thank you for your aid in this matter brother. I apologize for the nasty things I said in your home this afternoon. I was tired and grumpy but there is no excuse. I will owe you one for standing up for me on this thing."

Master Jonas smiled while staring right at me. "I would ask you to be easy on Mad Maxx. He will be here to serve you all your remaining days with honor, adoration, and grace. Remember if you break it over false anger at your brothers, there can never be a replacement. If you can get the heart of Mad Maxx, you're more blessed than any of the rest of us. Good luck brother may the best man win it."

His toothy grin spoke of his honest love and concern for me without his saying another word.

I closed my eyes as the sexual sadist dragged me inside his home. I hoped that Master Jonas's well-chosen words of competition for something none of them could have, would work their magic to keep the cruel old Elders all treating me with at least some dignity.

Master Barnim and I traveled down his hallway to the room on the right. The door was painted black causing me to breathe a sigh of relief. I had assumed there was some kind of code in the Haus among the Dominants that all torture and blood rooms had red doors. That night I would find out one should never assume anything. My Master opened the door and immediately I nearly went running down the hallway screaming like a kid that seen the Boogie Man.

Inside that room the stone walls were dank and wet from being hosed down. A small drain was in the middle of the concrete floor. I was nearly hypnotized by the sight of red tinged water swirling down that hole in the floor. From the ceiling hung his chains with manacles bitten with bits of rust from many years of use in a wet environment. Bondage and torture furniture such as the horse were scattered about the large room. All of it appeared well worn from many an unhappy collar's visit to them. I stood there trembling in full on terror with flashbacks of my horrible visits to Xavier's torture chamber.

Master Barnim smiled with glee at my obvious fear. "Ah, you are an artist of rare form. I had heard your tolerance for torture was above average and I can see the numerous blade marks on your exposed skin. Correct me if I am wrong here. A straight razor, ja?"

I could do nothing but nod sure that I was about to lose my shit any moment before this man even touched me with any of his horrible tools.

My Master nodded, smiling even bigger at my response. "The one that did that to you was quite the fool. If you're going to cut up a prize, it should be done with a bit of artistic flair. There is no pattern to any of it that I can see, but then again, I only see part of you yet. Soon my beauty, I will see all of it. Tonight, I am in the mood for the hooks. We see what kind of humor I am in, but I am thinking electro play or even the sharps? These things I know should excite you. I was told even Xavier himself never punctured your flesh with more than a paltry pinwheel or the rake. Those are nothing. I would have thought the man had more style than that bullshit. Well, my Mad Maxx, you need not fret with your Master Barnim. I know how to open the true ability of the Priceless of legend. Shall we begin?"

I saw the large hooks hanging just behind the chains and I was already horridly aware of what he meant by sharps. Likely needles in sensitive places. *You know that one don't you Meine Liebe?* I decided the Guard could have their fertilizer. A bullet was quick. The pain wouldn't be followed by a rape. I was leaving. Fuck this.

However, Master Barnim had not sent over that horrid outfit to make a fashion statement. He was already aware I may be a bit nervous about our first night together as Master and submissive. I turned to flee but Barnim, who was still quite strong in his early sixties grabbed the chest harness and held tight to my leash. He laughed as I began to come at him ready to attack in a blind terror,

I was grabbed by both arms and lifted off the floor just as Master Barnim yelled out. "Olaf, Vilber bring Mad Maxx with me." I turned my head to see the two brutes that had been in my own employ were the ones gripping me without expression of even familiarity on their faces.

I almost went out of my mind in full on panic at this latest betrayal. I cursed and spit on the black collars while I struggled wildly. Nothing I tried slowed down their progression of dragging me into that room.

Master Barnim turned around and watched me battling with all my might to pull free of Olaf and Vilber. He laughed most wickedly then picked up a spider mouth gag and threw it to Olaf.

"Put that on the Priceless's head Olaf. That will keep him from spitting and pleading but not prevent his screaming. If you stick around boys, I will let you have some fun with his open mouth later after I am done with my own interests." Master Barnim winked at the brutes.

I immediately shot a look of warning at them both. I saw Vilber drop his head casting his eyes down in what appeared to be shame at his part in this horrible situation. Olaf, however, was smiling brightly with a glint in his eyes.

I glared at him with much hate when he forced on the gag whispering into my ear. "I told you one day I would make your suck my cock, didn't I? Looks like tonight I get lucky, and you learn your place once and for all."

Master Barnim pulled my attention from the evil Olaf when I heard the clank of the hooks as the sexual sadist demanded the black collars bring me forward to ready me for "suspension."

Chapter 35: Free Falling

I did my best to brace myself for the nightmare unfolding before my eyes. The big brutes Vilber and Olaf dragged me to Master Barnim's chains. The spider mouth gag kept me from pleading my case and reminding my Master that scarification of my flesh was forbidden by my collar contract with him.

I could see from his expression of thrill, even if I could have spoken, there was no care for a nothing in his eyes. He would not be granting me any mercy. It was more than a little obvious, this man was hell bent to use me in any fucking way he wanted. He was without interest in showing honesty nor honor in his vows to the sworn agreement with his brothers.

Master Drexel had been correct in his trying to warn the others about this monster Elder. Sadly, no one had believed him in what he swore he knew about this pervert. I closed my eyes and pulled deep inside as Vilber and Olaf positioned me under the hooks.

Master Barnim stood behind me pulling the horrible tools of torture tight while looking over the exposed flesh of my back. "He is thinner and smaller than I would have liked. Not much space to work with here. No matter, I can make do with what I have. Hold him tightly boys, this will be unpleasant. If he gets loose, I will string you up instead of him." I felt the thugs tighten their grips on my upper arms.

The sexual sadist dug the first foul hook into the flesh just below my left shoulder blade in my back. I gasped out in pain but refused to scream. He took his time feeding my tender skin onto his sharp hook. I could hear him chuckling, appearing to enjoy my trembling, and sweating that gave away my inner agony. He secured the cruel metal in my skin with a clasp over the top so that it could not slip out no matter how much I struggled. Without a break in his brutality, he then dug another hook into my right side in the same place.

Again, I gasped but held my wail though by now I was feeling faint. The piercing hurt more than you can imagine. I thought this was going to be the worst of it. I was wrong as usual. That bastard walked over to another table then came back with eight more of the horrible hooks on chains.

He had Olaf and Vilber take turns holding me still while one aided him in clipping the ends to a suspension bar above my head. It took almost twenty minutes or so for Master Barnim to thread each one of these horrors into the flesh on my back and upper arms. He pulled the slack from his chains on me forcing me to stand up straight or suffer terribly for it.

By this time, my blood rolled down my waist in small rivers. Terrible aching was sending up signals to my brain that this trauma was likely only the beginning of worse. Master Barnim's clock had only just begun. He had decided to start his cycle off with the most extreme of abuses. This was not looking good for Mad Maxx.

I kept my screams held in check by deep breathing and sheer willpower through the entire piercing process. I closed my eyes to aid in my focus. It took all that I had to ignore the burning, sharp cries of torment coming from my many nerve endings.

The black collars no longer had to restrain me. I could not escape Master Barnim's torment any longer. I was held in place by the chains that were now literally under my skin. I didn't dare to move to even attempt to remove my mouth gag for fear that he would do even worse than he already had.

I stood their shaking from the stress while I silently swore, I would kill all three of these men the second I got half a chance. I no longer cared if it got me shot by the Guard. Even Xavier had not been this cruel to me, but I had helped that man find his grave for doing less.

Master Barnim got the last of his cruel claws into my skin then came to stand in front of me. "You are indeed a treasure most rare, Mad Maxx. Not even a whimper while I penetrate you. I see I have met a collar worthy of my attention at last. Usually by now my victims are screaming like weaklings, but not you. I doubted the rumors that I heard of your Priceless powers but no more. Well, let's see how much further I can go before you too break under my harsh torture, ja? This will be fun. I have not been this excited since I first began my career destroying the beautiful creations of Gott." He grabbed my face demanding I open my eyes to look at him.

I glared at him full of hate and desire for revenge. This expression of insolence from my soul caused him to laugh with much humor.

"Ah. Nein fear from this one. I am impressed. You would like to rip me apart, wouldn't you? Well too bad it will be the other way around, Mad Maxx. When the sun rises, Drexel will find his turn ruined. I intend to damage you so badly that even holding still for that foul creature will be impossible. You can beg me to stop or show you mercy, but I promise you I won't stop." He reached out and removed the spider gag to allow me to offer up my pleas.

To his surprise I didn't plead with him at all. I spit in his face then called him a sting of foul obscenities, and dishonorably included his mother in my insults. I am not proud of that since I never met the woman. Perhaps she had been a saint, but to be honest, I doubt it. No good person could have been the parent of this bastard, I think. Still, that cursing of his mother was uncalled for and not proper under any circumstances.

Master Barnim didn't appreciate my lack of compliance with his command that I beg. He angrily went to his lever and began to roll the chains up. The hooks in my back and upper arms pulled me up off the floor until I was suspended at least a foot or more off the ground.

I groaned out in pure agony. My weight and gravity worked to pull me back to the Earth while the hooks and chains refused to grant such a mercy. The tension of my flesh pulling upward while my bones headed for the ground was hellish beyond description. My vision was filled with fractured images of the room, and the sound of a loud train deafened my ears. I was swooning from the pain, unable to reconnect to my fast-sinking consciousness.

I could barely respond when I saw Olaf come to undo my pants. Nothing was making sense anymore. My mind was whirling, unable to find a pivot to gain any understanding. The only thing that was making it through to my senses was the horrific agony in my back and arms. Those black collars had me stripped within moments without even an attempted kick from me for his hateful efforts.

The sound of a thudder colliding with skin and the sting of it rising to my brain brought me back from this odd place of disconnection. I let out a wail when the second swat crossed my backside. I suddenly come back from the abyss to find Master Barnim thrashing me soundly with his tawse. I was still hanging from the hook suspension and this monster was thudding me to add insult to my injuries.

I suppose only the pinata can empathize with that situation I found myself in that night. That horrid sadist used every damned thudder known to man on my flesh while I swung helpless to stop him. There was no doubt he was willing to destroy me to elicit the begging he was sure I owed him for his brutal efforts.

At first, I was able to keep my noises to groans or a few gasps with trembling. That came to an end when he pulled out his pinwheel and rake. I never could handle those two instruments of pain well, you see Meine Liebe, for every submissive there is one thing of torture that they never can overcome.

For me, a thudding from the well-trained hand will make me wail and piss me off. Piercing can put me near unconsciousness with my gasping and inability to breathe from the pain. Burning or branding will make me curse you and plan your execution. Electricity will make my flesh dance while I jell out in agony and call you names.

However, the cutters, those make me beg for death every time. This type of agony is the one I never could conquer. To this day, I cringe at even the sight of them instruments of torment most foul.

I watched my Master smiling with wickedness in his gaze when he retrieved the pinwheel from his torturing tools. I began to tremble all over unable to tear my terrified sight off this instrument of extraordinary pain. I suppose some like it, but I am not one of them. Master Barnim must have spoken to Xavier at some point to know this was my nightmare come to life. I say that because he nodded, appearing to already know of my inner fear without my saying a word of it.

"Ah, this little thing is something you are not happy to see. Tell me, am I right Mad Maxx? You seem unwilling to grant me the pleasure of begging for my mercy. I wonder if you are sorry now for such foul insolence to your Master. You finally realize I am not a man to be denied, ja?" He gently rolled that hellish wheel down the front of my right thigh looking closely at that wound Master Jonas put in me with his lancet for his dark pleasure.

I shook my head. "I beg you to leave that tool on the table, Master. I take all your other tortures but this one I ask for mercy to avoid the bite of it." I kept my wet eyes to the ground doing my best to brace myself for its stick in my flesh.

Master Barnim chuckled at my weak statement. "You ask my mercy and beg me to leave this pleasure for another day. You can do better than that, Mad Maxx. I have been working you for some time now and not a single worthy scream has come out of your mouth. I see that this instrument has your respect and terror. I would wish to see the power it can wield over you." He rolled it again a bit harder but still not puncturing my skin.

174

I took a deep breath then flashed a look at him. "I beg your mercy and offer my adoration of you in return for it, Master." I was in no hurry to couple with this disgusting Master but even that penetration was preferable to this one, and likely would bleed less.

Master Barnim laughed hard at that, then turned to speak to Olaf and Vilber. "You hear that? This foolish collar offers me the right of intercourse for my mercy. Can you believe the arrogance? I have this fool in hook suspension, he is bleeding like the knifed pig, and welted to black. Yet, he still thinks he can decide anything. He forgets that I can take whatever I wish without his permission. I am not only his Master, but I don't believe he could deny me in his current helpless condition to boot. I want to say pure insolence is what I am hearing spew from his mouth. Do either of you have any suggestions as to what I can do to bring this lofty opinion this Priceless seems to have of himself down a peg?"

Vilber cast his eyes to the ground quickly then said, "Forgive me for saying this Barnim, but I know this collar well. He is neither demonstrating hubris nor misunderstanding his level in respect to you. Mad Maxx is unwell, he carries much insanity. That is merely the pain speaking, not the boy." He said in a feeble attempt to aid in cooling the rising temper of my Master.

Master Barnim scoffed at this. "Oh? Madness has captured his tongue you say. What about you, Olaf? Do you know this forbidden silver as well as your partner claims he does?" He shot a look toward Olaf.

Olaf grinned with much evil in his smile. "Ja, I know him better than even Vilber does. The boy is not crazy. It is an act only. I seem to recall Xavier could get this disrespect to stop by cutting him to ribbons. That tended to soften him up to a compliant lamb." I glared at him with much hatred over his incessant need to see me fucked over at every turn no matter how kind or generous I had been to him.

I suppose to be fair I should tell you that no matter what Olaf or Vilber had said, Master Barnim intended to use those cruel tools on me anyway. Both the black collars could have begged for my mercy on their hands and knees themselves. That would have done no good either. That didn't excuse Olaf's taking advantage of this situation for his own personal insults to me. Had he been a real man then he would have taken this discord between us privately. I had already decided his takin advantage of my weak position was not something I would allow to go unpunished, if I lived that is.

This Master Barnim was blood thirsty by nature. That torture room's poorly sanitized condition, not including his unsterilized hooks and tools, indicated this brutal Dominant was not accustomed to his victims surviving his scenes." It goes without saying he had no reason to worry about slow acting infections, shock from blood loss, nor contagious diseases for the collars he tortured. He never intended for any of them to make return visits. It had become painfully clear to me that if anyone ended up in his clutches, then they had found their final stop in the journey of life.

Master Barnim ran his pinwheel for the third time down my thigh. This time he used much force penetrating the flesh with vigor. I let out a long loud scream with much panic. That brought out the true viciousness in the horrid Elder. He quickly grabbed my other leg. Using his full weight, he pulled downward with force forcing the skin in my back and upper arms to unnatural and unbearable tautness, held tight by the chains.

Then before I could even respond to the agonizing tearing at my flesh on those metal hooks, he ground the pinwheel into my left thigh. I let out a wail, loud and long that seemed to split my soul. Master Barnim laughed with glee then ran that wheel with even more aggression down my outer left thigh. He pulled even harder on me, adding more of his weight straining my chains and skin to hold the increased tension he caused.

Something went wrong within me. I heard a snap, or maybe a clicking. The world went red as the blood rolling off my flesh into the floor. I heard Christian screaming into my ears with the sounds of the demons of hell. I saw the shard of lust and anger come from through the bloody waters. His eyes shown with the brimstone of Satan himself. I stifled my own cries of pain unable to understand what the hell was going on.

Christian took a leap and threw me with force from the boy. I smacked into the wall feeling at once I may shatter into a million pieces. In my stunned state I fell to my knees unable to speak, breathe or move. I watched in pure horror while this murderous shard let out a scream that would frighten away the Banshee herself.

Master Barnim was laughing and using the boy to swing himself like a human rope. I saw Christian lift his pinned arms above his head and grab the chains attached to his back. He used them for stability then with all his strength he kicked our Master off him with his right leg.

Master Barnim had not expected this. He had assumed the boy was in too much pain to their such a bold move. He and his pinwheel went spiraling to the wet concrete floor with a thud. The Master was temporarily stunned, appearing to think he had slipped and fallen perhaps.

Christian let out another inhuman shriek then began to struggle on the chains that held him with much wildness. It appeared from my vantage the boy was having a seizure of immeasurable strength. His teeth gnashed and his torso contorted into unimaginable angles.

Blood from the ripping flesh on his back began to splatter everywhere as did sweat. It almost seemed as if he were a wolf that came from a dip in the pool and was shaking off its fur there was so much fluid flying through the air from that crazed boy.

"You let me the fuck off these hooks or so help me I will rip them the fuck out. You wanted to hear begging? Then open your fucking ears, Master. I beg you to kill me right this Gott damned minute. If you don't, and I free myself, then I would not want to be you," the anger shard yelled out as he reached behind him, undoing the clasps of the metal meat hooks.

Master Barnim shot a look of fear at Olaf and Vilber from his place on the floor, he was still on his ass below the struggling Christian. "Do something. He is going to free himself. Stop him."

Vilber shook his head, appearing to be in much terror. "I beg you mercy Barnim, but I cannot. Mad Maxx is insane I told you. He is going to end his own life and the other Elders will come looking for a black collar to slay for their anger. I cannot be a party to this dishonor any longer. I will eagerly await you punishment. Olaf you fool. This torture has gone too fucking far. You come with me or suffer for your stupidity. Can you not see this man intends to kill Mad Maxx. What the fuck do you think Jonas, Claus or even Drexel is going to do to your sorry ass when they come to claim the Priceless corpse? Fuck this. They will not be blaming Vilber, that is for damned sure." The black collar turned and ran from the room with much speed leaving his brother collar to his fate.

Christian let out another scream of frustration then I almost fainted when I see him rip the hooks from his left upper arm. Master Barnim yelled for Olaf to stop Mad Maxx once again. This time Olaf, who had been standing there with his eyes wide open in terror, turned and ran away, following his brother in flight from the scene of what he assumed would be my suicide.

Master Barnim sat there a moment unable to wrap his mind around the retreat of his helpers. Then he got up, nearly being kicked back down by Christian. He had been busy working on releasing his right arm from the hooks, but the shard saw him rising from the floor. He stopped his bloody work long enough to try to strike out with both his legs.

"You sonofabitch. I will be free shortly, then I am going to kill you. Do you hear me schwuler scum? I am going to gut you in your own fucking house. I do this for all the poor helpless children you have murder. I do it for the Gott damned health of humanity. You abomination, rat bastard, motherfucker, pervert," Christian wailed out as he began ripping the hooks from his right upper arm spinning with the fury of hell around in his chains.

Master Barnim ran to his lever and rapidly dropped the boy to his feet. Christian immediately took a run at the sexual sadist. His back was still hooked tightly to the chains. He was snapped to a halt abruptly the second he hit the end of them. He let out a shriek of frustration and agony but continued to pull against his restraints. The shard had lost his fucking mind. It was then I noticed he was foaming at the mouth with an expression of pure madness in his eyes.

I watched in stunned horror as he continued this dangerous berserker behavior appearing to not care for the damage he was causing the flesh. He was nearly ripping the hooks from his back by swiping his mangled arms with fury at the terrified Master Barnim. That Elder was beyond a shadow of a doubt afraid of the demon he had released.

Master Barnim apparently didn't have any previous experience with schizophrenics in a psychotic episode, that had a long history of torturous abuse, ja?

Master Maxx chuckled at that as did I, but my laughter was anxious. I recalled my own berserker moment against Debbie and Russell with some fear over my loss of control, which was not so different from his story of this sexual sadist.

Master Barnim kept his distance unsure what to do with the railing Christian. I watched my brother shard growling, howling, and wailing non-stop appearing unaware of his injuries, or his surroundings. I could see that he was functioning at the lowest of base instincts by this time. He would have torn anything within snatching distance to pieces, whether it be Master Barnim or a puppy. That shard was a pure animal without fear, feeling, nor care.

Then to my horror I saw Master Barnim walk calmly back to his tools of torture table. He dug through the implements of his fetish sweating and keeping his eyes on the struggling boy. I gasped out loud when that bastard grabbed out a hatchet with a long handle. He smiled while checking the sharpness of the blade. It was obvious my Master decided he needed to put down the ailing Priceless collar in his hooks.

I shot a look of extreme terror at my brother Christian. "Beware brother, Barnim has the hatchet. Brother, he comes to end the boy. Please scream for help, struggle to avoid the blade. Someone, help us." I fell to my knees watching helplessly as Master Barnim began his approach on the insane Christian.

My Master stopped just beyond Christian's reach holding that axe with a smile on his face. "Well, I admit I thought I would get to enjoy you longer than only three hours, but shit that black collar was right. You're indeed quite insane. Clever of old Jonas to hide that fact from all of us. Had I known I would have gone slower so I could at least enjoy fucking you a bit before having to send you to the lawn. I do regret that, but maybe I can take you down and get my interests filled before you go cold. Either way, it was a pleasure no matter how short." He lifted that weapon ready to swing it and end our life.

Christian at last understood my warning. He saw the gleam of that blade and began to back away. His guttural screams silenced immediately, and his expression became one of fear. Master Barnim slowly followed the retreating boy chuckling low in his throat with glee. Christian finally could back away from his attacker no further. The chains

181

and hooks prevented his escaping this violent death at the hands of Master Barnim's axe.

I let out a cry of pure despair when Christian cowered and tried to cover his head with his gory arms. There was nothing else could do. Even our strong anger shard was no match for weapons like the axe, straight razors, or guns. I heard him whimper with much sorrow at the loss of our long struggle for survival in this brutal world.

Then out of nowhere came our brother shard Maximillian. With stealth and speed, he pushed Christian out taking his place in the terrified boy. Christian shot a look of confusion at me kneeling their just as the door of the torture room come flying open.

Master Bladrick came through the open entry followed closely by Vilber. I shook my head in disbelief. Vilber had rousted the Elder and reported the horror that Master Barnim was inflicting. Master Bladrick had come running to see if this disturbing report was truthful. He stood there his foggy eyes open wide in complete startle at the sight before him.

Master Bladrick let out a loud bellow of anguish when he saw his collar Mad Maxx was beyond bloody, sweating, drooling and covered in welts, cuts, bruises with hooks still embedded in his back. Master Barnim stood there over him ready to bring the long-handled axe down to cut the tormented boy in two.

"What the holy Christ, Barnum. You drop that fucking axe now, you sonofabitch. How dare you? What have you done to this beautiful collar of ours? Meine Gott, this is a horror movie. You beast. Drop that weapon or I will call the fucking Guard and have your ass planted in the orchard

182

where you surely belong," yelled out Master Bladrick with a commanding voice that seemed to shake the room, it was so baritone.

Master Barnim flinched upon hearing Master Bladrick's order. He had been so busy trying to slaughter us he had not even noticed that his brother had caught him red handed (*okay pun intended there, clever huh? Nein? you have no sense of humor Meine Liebe*). He turned around with an expression of intense irritation on his face.

"Mind your business Bladrick, you old fart. This collar is full on schizophrenic. I am putting it down for everyone's good. Jonas pulled a trick on us all. This boy is only useful for fertilizer. I barely thud him and he lost his mind and went insane. Close the door on your way out or stay for the show. It matters not to me. I am not worried that the others will not understand this was for everyone's safety that I do this. This thing would cut your throat in your sleep no doubt." He came forward to lay Maximillian low with his deadly swing.

Master Bladrick turned to Vilber. "Retrieved that fucking axe from my brother. I grant you immunity from punishment for this command. Take it away from him now."

The brute Vilber didn't need to be given that command twice. He rushed Master Barnim and without much struggle wrestled that weapon away from the Elder. He was gentle as possible but firm in repossessing that deadly blade. Maximillian didn't uncover his head, nor did he move a muscle during this altercation. He was not dumb enough to incite any further anger from anyone.

Master Barnim glared at Vilber. "I will deal with you later, you sonofabitch. Bladrick, you have no right to barge into my fucking apartment and interfere with my collar time. Who the fuck do you think you are?" He turned his anger at Master Bladrick.

The Elder shook his head. "I was informed you were killing our collar. I am beyond offended to come here in the wee hours of the morning to find not only was the report true, but my dumbass defended you from your brother Drexel's accusations. He apparently knew more about your foul nature than I ever suspected. This boy is in horrid shape. Are those hooks in his flesh? I think so. You broke the contract and tried to murder our property. Barnim, your behavior in this matter will not go ignored nor unpunished. You are the one that has no right. You release the boy nor or I swear I will have Vilber put your ass in the chains, and I will show you why the name Bladrick once caused this Haus to tremble when I walked her hallways."

Master Barnim scoffed, "You wouldn't dare, old man."

Master Bladrick crossed his arms and nodded to Vilber. "Want to try me, brother? I dare you. I will make a believer out of you, that is a vow." Vilber took the axe, put it on the thudder table and picked up a fresh set of chains turning ready to comply with Master Bladrick's commands.

Master Barnim saw that and relented his position. "Okay, everyone calm down, ja? I release the damned boy. You will be sorry when he comes tearing across the floor to chew out your throat. I will stand here laughing as you lay bleeding to death from your foolishness. This kid is fucking insane, I tell you. Vilber come here and restrain this nut before he gets a few licks on me trying to get at Bladrick, ja?"

Vilber put down the chains then went to Maximillian holding the subdued, quiet, quivering boy by his bleeding arms demanding he be still. The boy nodded and kept his eyes to the floor offering no resistance. I rushed forward to enter with my brother to aid him in enduring the pain of the hook removal from the flesh.

We held each other's hand and took deep breaths while the vile Master Barnim removed each metal terror from our back. The pain almost made us faint from the overwhelming signals coming from every nerve. When the final one was out, we fell to our knees holding the boy up with our ravaged arms near swooning from the trauma of it all.

Master Bladrick approached looking down in pity at us on our hands and knees trembling and whimpering. "Oh ja, truly insane. A terrible threat. I am myself terrified of this tiny boy at my feet Barnim. Thank Gott you warned me. I would be most embarrassed to have my throat cut then bled out by a flea of this frightening speed and violence." He glared at Master Barnim with an expression of disgust.

Master Barnim stomped his foot in anger. "You came too late to see this monster in action, Bladrick. He ripped the fucking hooks out of his own arms while suspended. I swear I never seen anything like the shit I just saw from this crazy fucker. You have to believe me." He kicked me hard in the stomach.

I rolled to my side gasping and moaning on the floor at Master Bladrick's feet. "You sonofabitch. You have injured this submissive enough, Barnim. Keep your fucking hands, feet, mouth, all of you, the fuck away from him. Vilber, help Mad Maxx get redressed. He is coming with me," screamed Bladrick sounding beyond furious.

Master Barnim put out his arm to stall Vilber that had started reaching down to retrieve my spasming flesh from the floor. "You hold on a fucking minute, Vilber. Bladrick this boy is mine till midnight tonight. This is my rotation day. I took the damn thing off my hooks, and I won't fucking chop him up, this I swear, but I have not even gotten my couple yet. You cannot just come in here, order me around then walk out my door with my property, you old fucker."

Master Bladrick crossed his arms with a most evil smile on his old, cracked face. "Vilber, I told you dress to this collar. Do not disobey me again. As for you Barnim, I take Mad Maxx with me or we can go wake up Claus and how about Jonas, the boy's husband. Wonder how they will enjoy seeing this horror you made of their collar? You like this apartment and secrecy to rape, then kill pretty little boys at your leisure, do you? Want to keep this place safe? Then I suggest you shut the fuck up, hand me this boys leash, and back the fuck up. I will take him home, clean him up, and treat his grievous wounds. That buys you a few days for you to come up with some story to explain the puncture marks you swore to never leave on our shared property. Take this deal or we go stomping down the halls of the Elder's floor right this minute to awaken our neighbors ja?"

Master Barnim looked at me with a bit of fear in his eyes, finally realizing the serious infraction he had committed. "Oh, uhm, okay. I suppose I can couple with him my next rotation. Vilber, dress this collar. Are you full of molasses? You are slower than my grandmother, I swear it." He backed off while Viber lifted me off the floor gently pulling me back to my feet.

The two Masters said nothing to each other while they watched the brute help me get the bondage pants back on. When I buttoned them moaning out in extraordinary aching, Master Bladrick stared at Vilber.

"Well? Get his shirt, Vilber. I am ready to go. What the hell are you waiting on?" Master Bladrick looked around the room.

Vilber looked at the floor. "This is all this silver was wearing, I believe Bladrick."

Master Bladrick looked me over in shock. "Really, Barnim? You dressed this collar like this? Then rather than fuck him you decided to beat the shit out of him while he was being tortured? You are not only a fool, but you're also a joke. I don't know if I should laugh or cry. I lived all my eighty plus years and never have I seen a more cliched nor petty soul. I am truly disgusted, and with the life I have lived, that was a near an impossible task to accomplish. Come Mad Maxx, follow your Master if you can fucking walk." Master Bladrick grabbed my black leash and jerked me, demanding I be silent with a hand gesture.

I quietly did as commanded, grateful to not be cut into two, bad enough our mind is, ja? I felt faint but capable of mobility. I would have been happy to crawl, slink, or even slide out of there face first to avoid being anywhere near Master Barnim another second.

Vilber stayed behind with the irritated sexual sadist. I decided that he was a black collar brute I would not kill since he did save my life by telling Master Bladrick of my deadly situation. Olaf however, he was the dead man the second I got any chance at him.

Master Bladrick and I left the apartment door and the Elder stopped at the banister appearing out of breath. I dropped to a kneel, slow and painfully behind him, as is protocol realizing this was intense anxiety that old man was demonstrating. He had appeared sure and in control with Master Barnim, but I could see the truth at last. That was an act. This horror had upset Master Bladrick to a near heart attack. He stood there gripping the banister railing breathing deep, holding his chest with one hand and my leash in the other. He leaned forward, closing his eyes trying to still his nerves.

I said nothing. I was in too much pain to even speak, to be honest. I could barely breathe myself; the agony was riding me with such harshness. I didn't know if I would survive. Master Barnim's hooks and instruments of terror were foul, unclean, and full of rust. I had open wounds everywhere. Worse, my only hope for treatment was a man well past eighty, that was having a panic attack only five steps from the door of the man that near killed me only moments before.

Then the door flew open, and Master Barnim came into the hallway. He flashed a look of fury at me kneeling there. Without hesitation he came lumbering at Master Bladrick. He stood there with his back to me "whisper yelling" at the Elder.

"I changed my mind Bladrick. I demand you bring Mad Maxx back. I want to fuck him. You can watch if you like, but I will have my rights. Once that prissy Drexel and monster Jonas see his wounds they likely will throw a silly fit over this nothing I do tonight. I can see them keeping me out of the rotation for a bit. I demand you bring him back inside to service his Master right this minute before those bastards' can end my fun with him." Master Barnim got right into Master Bladrick's face, then snatched my leash from the still panicking Elder man.

Then Meine Liebe, I saw something that to this day I still have trouble believing. I was watching my Master Bladrick's trembling hands when I saw him give me a little-known hand gesture. This slight movement of his fingers indicated he wanted me to push or shove someone out of his way. I sat there only a second before Maximillian, the perfect submissive, took the wheel and obeyed his Master command without hesitation.

I stood up and took off running right for Master Barnim bracing for the collision with him. In a single smooth movement Master Bladrick snatched back my leash from the sexual sadist's hands. I plowed into the brutal Elder with such force he rocked forward leaning over the banister for a moment. Then to my shock, Master Bladrick kicked Master Barnim's feet out from under him sending him spiraling over the edge down the six flights of stairs to his gruesome death below.

Master Barnim's screams of terror echoed off the walls for several moments until with a loud crash his voice was silenced forever more. I stood their staring in shock over that railing unable to comprehend that man far below lying dead in a pool of his own blood was an Elder, that another Elder had commanded me to help him kill.

I shot a look of bewilderment at Master Bladrick. He smiled then put his fingers to his lips hushing me for all time. I nodded then dropped back to a kneel and bowed my head. I was more than happy to be at this man's feet. I felt deeply indebted to this man that granted me vengeance against one that had killed so many others just like me. He reached out and patted my head like he would a pet dog.

"You are indeed a treasure my boy. If only I were still a young man, the romance we could have had. Such a spirit you have. Tis a curse to meet you too late in my hour to truly enjoy your gifts. Oh, but youth is so fleeting, ja? I can only gaze upon your beauty and remember what once was but will never be again; like for Barnim down there. Well, I never liked the brute anyway. Good riddance to that trash, I say." He chuckled at that then stifled his smile when he saw Vilber come running from the dead Elder's apartment.

"I heard screaming, Bladrick. He was so angry he hit me over the head with his mallet, then went to chase you down. I thought, oh hell, I thought, wait, where is Barnim?" He shot his eyes in both directions down the Elder's hallway, blood running down the side of his head from his own blow from the sexual sadist.

Master Bladrick frowned then pointed over the banister. "He did come at us. We ducked and the dumb bastard went flying over the railing Vilber. Barnim was a damned fool. To come running at us like a madman. Wake up the others. This must be dealt with. I will take Mad Maxx with me. When Claus and my brothers have assessed the problem, tell them to come see me for the story in my apartment. I am too fucking old for all this excitement. Mad Maxx needs some care, or he will be dead as Barnim in a few days. Can I trust you to do all this for me, Vilber?"

Vilber nodded, appearing stunned to stupid. "Ja, I go get the others. I will relay your message, Bladrick."

Master Bladrick nodded. "That is good of you, Vilber. Come by to see me in a few days. I will take you to sup with me at the Great Hall. You earned a special reward for saving the Elder's Priceless Mad Maxx from one that was insane with blood lust. This a worthy price for your honest service to our precious collar?"

Vilber's eyes went wide again as he stuttered out. "Ja, I am most honored by your favor Bladrick. Though I am unworthy of it."

My Master chuckled with much bitterness at that. "Gott damned right you are. You are a sorry worm, Vilber. Do not think I am so old; I am not aware your information about the condition of my beloved silver came from your being present to injure him in the first place. It also is not lost on me that had you been a decent man you would have come to find me the second those nasty hooks went into my property, not waiting until the boy went mad from the pain of Barnim's torture. I will take you to supper for finally waking up to do the right thing. Just remember, I will never forgive nor forget your slow actions this night that has led to serious danger of infection or death from shock for my submissive. I know that demonstrating your true loyalty lies with your own pockets and not with that of me or any of my brothers. If he dies, you will be joining my brother Barnim in eternal rest. You are dismissed."

I winced at the truest words of my wise Master Bladrick. Vilber had not gone to seek out aid when he was aware Barnim's actions breached his contract with the others. I too could not forgive the black collar for his cruelty, and his breaking of his oath of loyalty to me for all time.

I despaired a bit in my aching heart that I would have to seed the lawn with this big brute right next to his brother Olaf. I really did like Vilber, despite his flaws. No one is perfect, Meine Liebe, but in this case, I could not let my affection for the man blind me to the fact this adoration was not reciprocated. Vilber went for help because he feared his name would be drug into the mess when Barnim killed me, and the Elders went hunting for heads to chop off.

I followed behind the slow walking Elder feeling more decrepit than he appeared. Many of my injuries were still bleeding and the ones that had congealed burned with the flames of hellfire. I felt even more miserable when I found myself wondering if Vilber would have joined in with Olaf to defile me if Barnim had given him half a chance.

"You better be a fuck more concerned with who they will get to replace that dead bastard, Mad Maxx," I heard the voice of Mad Max running alongside us startle me from my dark thoughts.

Maximillian struggled a bit trying to get as far away, inside the flesh, avoiding the sadistic shard as possible. "Get the fuck out of here, you motherfucker. Do you not see we have enough to deal with as it is? Who the fuck let Christian off his leash by the way? He nearly got us chopped in two," whined out our submissive shard.

Mad Max growled, "I am not a motherfucker, but you are a schwuler fatherfucker. If we are done with the pleasant greetings, then I would like to point out that what I say is important despite this pitfall. As for Christian, Der Hund sent him, dumbass. That shit was a close call. Der Hund thought we were a goner, so why not send in the only one of us that cares not for what he does in his effort for revenge, ja?"

Maximillian sighed. "Ah, ja. There was wisdom in that idea I have to agree there. Okay, tell Der Hund I will speak to Master Bladrick. I have something I was hoping to avoid that will seduce this old husband. My flesh is not in good condition, but I will have Mad Maxx aid by taking the pain while I get into this Elder's mind and heart. He seems to have much sway. We capture him, then make sure the one voted up is not another fucking sexual sadist, ja?"

Mad Max rolled his eyes. "Holy shit, you are going to do this thing, Maximillian? Well, you are not only the schwuler you are fucking disgusting. I guess though after sucking our father's cock all this time you're just twisted enough to do about anything."

I had to step in on this one. Mad Max and Maximillian tend to argue quite a bit which is expected given their reverse natures. That said, what Maximillian was planning to endure for the good of us all was pure hell for him. He was demonstrating his selflessness and true dedication to Der Hund's mission by sacrificing himself like this. I couldn't just sit there and allow our sadistic brother to take this beautiful heartfelt thing Maximillian was doing for us all and shit all over it.

"That is enough, Mad Max. You say another word about Maximillian or what he offers to do to fix our serious problem, I will jump out of this boy and shatter you into a wall. Der Hund can bust me into star dust for it, but I will be Gott damned if the likes of you will bad mouth the talents and skills of this most perfect shard among us all. He has saved us enough times to be deserving of your respect and quiet tongue." I snorted out feeling my chest heat up with anger at this non-empathetic psychopathic bastard I called brother.

Mad Max's eyes went wide "Seriously? You are gonna take that queen's side? Ficken mich. You have spent too much time with him. I think you have become infected with his female wiles. Damn, Mad Maxx. I told Maximillian he could have the next female we get but you know what? I think you need one more. You're turning schwuler too."

I reached the boy's mangled arm out wincing to swipe at that bastard. "Fuck off, Mad Max. I have been at the wheel when this schwuler sex happens now. Maximillian is not schwuler. He is well trained. There is a fucking difference between desire and duty, you useless cocksucker. He doesn't enjoy that shit any more than you or me, or Der Hund, any of us. Go bother Christian or Max or your cousin the Devil. We are busy here and Maximillian has a foul duty to perform tonight. I will not allow you to disturb him. In fact, if ever you insult him again, you come through me first. When I finish with you, there will only be need for one X in our name when I bury you."

Mad Max glared at me but stopped his gait letting us pass on. "Ja? You think you can beat me, Mad Maxx? Ha, you will take the beatings I hand out stupid, fatherfucker. I hope the both of you are happy fucking each other. I will make sure to cry at your wedding, arschloch.

Maximillian sat their next to me in stunned silence for a moment then looked at me and said, "If you ask me to marry you, I will say ja, Mad Maxx, but just for the record, I cannot wear white."

I raised my eyebrow at that weird thing he mumbled to me. "Annette doesn't count. We are still a virgin; I swear to it on a bible."

He shook his head, "Then you'd be lying most foul. It is not because I am no virgin that I cannot wear that dreadful color brother. White makes my ass look huge. It would ruin our wedding photos."

I turned to look at him then we broke out in insane laughter at this most inappropriate time my brother chooses to tell such a stupid joke. After all, we were already feeling fevered from a likely infection setting in, and weak from blood loss. If that were not enough, we had also helped send one of the securely seduced Elders to his death. This was a time of great upheaval. Nothing was assured, not even the sunrise.

Master Bladrick looked back at us as the boy giggled at bit from our silly humor within. He seemed a bit startled by this but didn't ask any questions. He finally reached his apartment on the other side of the hallway across the huge open area of the Haus stairwells. He opened his door and led us inside without a word.

His place was simple and comfortable for an old bachelor husband. He had a television, many dusty shelves filled with magazines and books, with an old well-worn couch, recliner, and loveseat. None of his furniture matched up. There was an old shaggy tan throw rug under his aged coffee table. I could tell this man of wealth had once been a fellow of less. He didn't care about him the air of old money nor the hubris of one of them. I hazarded a quick look at his hands and noticed they were well worn from years of hard labor in his youth.

Master Bladrick took me straight to his bedroom and master bathroom without stopping for a rest. His room was like the rest of his place. A twin bed of a simple wooden frame, a dresser with a broken mirror, and more stuffed bookshelves, decorated his private space. I noted his pictures on the wall were of fields, farmhouses, and an occasional painting of some nude young boy.

I winced at those paintings, recalling the fact that this seemingly kindly old husband was not our grandfather, nor a favored uncle. He was nothing more than a perverted Kindersolestor like all the rest of the scum in the Haus. At least he had been before old age and cancer had stolen his prostate. Thanks to that, he no longer could gain an erection.

His lust had remained intact despite the removal of the structure the allowed for engorging of his manhood to complete any sexual acts with it. Since his seventieth birthday, more than fifteen years ago, he had been forced to do nothing more than watch his brother Master Drexel molest the statues or gaze wantonly upon the fresh male kind without a way to do anything about his lustful interests. This fact had made his worthiness among his lovers null and his importance with his brothers less.

You see, men are weird about things like impotence and sexual disfunction, Meine Liebe. They are so quick to assume if they cannot get a hard on, all sexuality is over for them. That is not only stupid, but also not even physically truthful.

We had been studying medical journals for a few years. When seeking information about causing temporary impotence so we could kiss on the girls in the washroom, we accidently found out a man need not have an erection to have an orgasm.

Ja. This mercy is possible even after the catastrophic removal of the prostate or impotence caused by high blood pressure or diabetes. That is if their lover is patient and willing to endure the unexpected difficulties that may come from the misfunctioning male organ, they can have a thing called a retrograde orgasm. That is an orgasm that the male feels but there is no release of sperm because all the fluid runs back into his abdomen.

If this is true, then why had Master Bladrick gone so long without a single lover in a Haus where he could demand any collar satisfy his lust no matter what. Well, that is simple. Almost no one knows this shit. Often not even the doctors will tell the patient that he can still gain climax through oral stimulation. A simple blow job without ever expecting him to engorge to be exact. Ha, now the next question, why does no one tell anyone? Ah, that, Meine Liebe is the secret.

In a retrograde orgasm the sperm or seminal fluid, if there is still a prostate if not there is neither of these things, runs back into the man's abdomen. That does not mean there is nothing to indicate there has been orgasm. Most often the male will accidently release his bladder or even throw a bloody tissue in the place of his seed at the moment of apex.

Worse than that, he will not know he is about to reach that point as he once did when he was viral. That means he cannot warn his lover that he is about to piss or bled in their mouth. There are very few women or men on this Earth willing to get a mouth full of such foulness after employing many minutes of oral sex on a flaccid penis to provide for an orgasm in an old husband.

The doctors and medical staff usually never mention that this retrograde climax is possible to keep marriage from breaking up when the wife or husband, hey I have a husband ja, refuses to adjust to this disgusting situation that brings pleasure to him with a heavy price paid by the lover.

Anyone who would do such a kindness is either in serious love, got one weird ass fetish, or are like your Master, desperate to get the fuck out of their nightmare metal. Maximillian had agreed with me that to give Master Bladrick this foul release would not only empower him among his brothers but would likely bind him to us in his gratitude for all time.

The trouble was, saying he could endure such a hellish thing and actually engaging in the deed is two different things. We both understood there was the possibility that once done, Maximillian could find the act too nasty for him to tolerate, but then we would have a Master demanding such an act from time to time. You know, it is like opening a can of worms.

Anyway, as we entered the ancient schwuler's bathroom I could feel Maximillian bracing himself for this difficult task best as any of us could.

I looked at him with worry. "Are you sure about this, brother? We are pretty injured. If you wish to wait for another day, I will not hold it against you. No one could."

He shook his head. "If you wish to sleep, go ahead, brother. You endured Barnim's hell for me, I will endure this one for you. Best to capture this Elder fast before the others come knocking, asking shit about the death of that bastard. If we wait, then maybe he turns us over to save himself when questions get harsh? Besides do you really think Master Drexel will give a shit we are injured? Nein. He will collect our collar shortly, then our chance to be alone with this Elder has passed for good. This is the best chance we have. It is now or never."

I knew there was wisdom in his words. I nodded then smiled. "I respect your good judgement in this. I will wait here while you do what must be done. If you need me, I will be right here guarding your back, brother."

Maximillian smiled, appearing relieved. "You're a real friend to me, Mad Maxx. I must say I appreciate that Der Hund choose you rather than that bastard Mad Max to be my partner."

I chuckled. "Uhm, you already have me seduced, brother. Maybe you should be focusing on that old man coming at the boy with his bandages and ointments? We can kiss and cuddle later when we are alone."

Maximillian snickered. "When the fuck are we ever along, brother." We both laughed at that truth as Master Bladrick told us to kneel with our back to him while he sat on his commode putting on his glasses to look over our damaged back.

He took a deep breath. "This is very bad, my boy. I think you will need a good shot of heavy-duty antibiotics with several rounds of pills. This may save your bacon. I will need to call in the Haus doctor on this damage. It is beyond a simple bandage and Tylenol."

I nodded my head. "As you wish Master. I thank you for your mercy, and for saving my life."

Master Bladrick sighed as I kept my kneel but turned to face him. "That business with Barnim, we must never speak of it Mad Maxx. He is not the first bastard that found his death thanks to his daring to fool with me. I have never been caught ending those Dominants in this Haus that dared to push their weight around on me. I intend to die with a nice clean reputation despite the many trees that grow thanks to my craftiness. Can I trust you to never reveal the things that happened this morning? Will you swear it on your word and blood to keep my confidence?"

I smiled with much wickedness in my gaze. "I swear it on my word and swear it in blood with another secret that can stay between us, ja?"

Master Bladrick's eyes went wide at my cryptic words. "What is this you say? Another secret? I don't understand."

I pushed myself between his legs still smiling with evil. The Elder was shocked to paralysis by my forward behavior. I began to undo his trousers and he reached out and grabbed my wrists with much fear in his eyes.

"Nein, what the hell are you doing, Mad Maxx. I cannot do a coupling with you. I am rendered useless. I would ask you to stop embarrassing me and yourself with such brazen and very cruel behavior." I shook his hands loose and pushed his arms away.

"I am a Priceless Master. I possess a special prowess that can bring even the disordered to ecstasy. I grant you this very secret and special joy for all you have done. I will be capable of giving you back your thrill by turning back the clock for this moment, but you must never question my ability again, and remember only Mad Maxx can do this this. I will make you my lover no different than Master Jonas, Master Claus, or Master Drexel. Lay back and relax. Close your eyes and let me take you to your youth. I will now give you pleasure that you thought was lost." I continued my disrobing this foul old husband took a deep breath, then began my revolting task reminding myself the freedom was worth any price I had to pay.

Within only a few moments of my professional oral skills the Elder was panting and sweating despite the stillness of his manhood. I did my best to think of other things while my Master's muscles began to grow taunt with increasing interest in my tongues activities at stimulating what he was sure was long dead. I did notice that preforming oral sex on a man without an erection ability was very much like attending to the female's clitoris with only slightly larger space to work with.

I closed my eyes and pretended Master Bladrick was the luscious Annette moaning on the washroom counter, quivering to my touch. Then without warning I was torn from my fantasies when a sudden burst of blood-tinged urine rushed into my attending mouth. My first instinct was to pull away puking from this most hideous "explosion" of my Master's broken lust mechanisms.

However, I willed myself to keep attending his interests until his retrograde climax had completed. Master Bladrick had lost the ability to penetrate but he had gained the comfort of an unusually long orgasm in return for his heavy lost. I was already aware what would happen based on my research on the matter, so I was prepared for that disgusting situation.

Master Bladrick grabbed my head holding me hostage to his groin. He started wailing out in pure pleasure and much surprise when what he thought was a long-lost orgasm ripped through his dusty loins. Almost eight seconds passed while I endured him filling my mouth with his nauseating fluids. I nearly vomited but held my breath so the smell of it didn't send me over the edge.

When at last he was spent he released me. I immediately rushed to the sink and spit that shit out. I turned on the faucet stabilizing my rolling stomach, taking several mouthfuls of water trying to wash the taste of his urine out of my mouth. I did my best not to seem grossed out, but this was the first time, so I doubt I did a very good job at it.

Master Bladrick was still sitting there on the commode moaning out and oddly chuckling under his breath. I thought this a strange behavior, but I was too busy trying to find a way to get my tongue to stop suffering. I saw his toothpaste and with much relief used some of that on my finger to clear the worst of it from my taste buds.

I was vigorously rubbing this minty flavored paste into my teeth, tongue, and inner cheeks when I let out a yelp. Master Bladrick had stood up then approached me from behind. I was so busy freaking the fuck out I missed his approach. He had wrapped his arms around my waist and embraced me in a tight hug. I suppose he forgot for a moment I was ripped up like a gutted fish.

Master Bladrick leaned down into my ear and whispered. "I swear I am in love with you. I had an orgasm. You are the Priceless of legend. I have my manhood back when I never thought such a thing possible. For the rest of my day, no matter the request, you ask your Master Bladrick, and it shall be yours Mad Maxx. To think Barnim almost destroyed you, my treasure. Pure horror."

I gasped and shuddered from the agony of his pressing into my angered flesh. "I thank you Master. I can do this for you upon your request, but I do ask one small favor in return for granting you such a mercy."

He moaned out and kissed the back of my head. "Anything for you. I would kill everyone in this Haus if you asked me to."

I chuckled at that. "Well, maybe I ask for this Haus to be a little roomier the next time I take you back to your youth but for now, I would ask that before Master Barnim's replacement is voted in you consult me with full disclosure of this Dominant's temperament."

Thankfully Master Bladrick pulled off me. "Ah, I swear I love you even more. We think alike, my love. I love this plan of yours. It is time for the brothers to work together before that bitch Cora comes into her power and disrupts this Haus. Your beautiful and clever. Consider this request not only granted but since I am the one that chooses the candidate you will aid me to choose one that will work with our plans, ja?"

I turned around staring at him with my mouth hanging open, also to air the damned thing out. "What? I say nothing about Mistress Cora or the other Masters. I have no plan I was merely worried about getting another Master Barnim."

He interrupted me. "Sure, you were. I am an old man, Mad Maxx. I didn't get here to the top being a foolish one, now did I. It is not too hard to see what you are up to if I only stop to think about it. If I were a Priceless young boy, that wanted to be free of this shit show Haus, then I would be thinking of a way to capture the Voting Council. I would need to break my collar. There would be nothing I wouldn't do to get out from under disgusting old men sticking me with their nasty fetishes and aged dicks. Well, my darling, let me help you do that. My last big game in my long life of debauchery and waste, ja? I have spent my life subjugating your kind to their knees. Just this once I will aid one in finding his feet instead. I will be one of the foul beasts demanding your favors but at least you will be off me when either that silver busts or the worms come for their dinner. Either way, I am excited to do this with such a worthy partner in my final days. What a fine swan song?"

I shook my head. "Master Bladrick, I think you say much, and I appreciate all of it, but you will live many years yet. There is no need to get yourself into such danger over the likes of me. I say this with respect."

Master Bladrick smiled with much bitterness while stroking my cheek. "Ah, your too beautiful for words my love. I do not have many years. I am dying. The doctors told me I have a slow growing cancer in my colon. I have less than nineteen months to live. My brothers do not know this, and I ask your silence on this secret too. You have just given me comfort and joy when all I could see is pain, terror, and disease. I draw strength from your struggle and unexpected thrill from your touching. For that my love, I bow at your feet and give you my undying loyalty for what little time I have left." He knelt before me, taking my hands, and kissing my knuckles while I stood above him gasping in pure shock at his words.

He was about to say something else when there was a loud, excited pounding on his door.

Master Jonas's voice rang out in a pure panic. "Kick the fucking door down, Wilber. Mad Maxx may have killed Bladrick too, you fool."

Chapter 36: Frozen

I looked with terror at Master Bladrick. "They think I killed Barnim. The Guard will be called. Help me, Master." I fell to my knees then forward into the prostrate position filling with fear over Master Jonas's words to Vilber at the door.

Master Bladrick glanced at me with surprise then yelled out. "Don't kick in my door, you bastards. I am not dead. Give me a fucking minute and I will let you in like human beings rather than the brutes you are." He pulled out of my ankle embrace and took off to let the two of them inside his apartment.

I go back to my knees shivering. My wounds were filling with fever and fear was in my soul. I had no shirt and was covered in my own blood by Barnim's cruel attentions. I wrapped my arms around my chest hugging myself close, trying to find warmth where none could be had.

The trembling grew worse by the second. My stomach flip flopped bringing tears to my eyes. A sickness was overtaking me there in Master Bladrick's bathroom floor unlike anything I had felt before. This was a mix of pain, fatigue, fear, and hopelessness. Within a flood of emotions began to rise, threating to drown me then wash my corpse away to the sea of nothing.

I realized with much horror this was a psychotic episode trying to onset. I wildly sought something to hold on to, hoping against all hope to find a way to ground myself before I was overtaken. Not sure what the hell I thought could be found to prevent the inner undertow that was holding me hostage. That didn't prevent me from seeking the answer anyway.

Then I thought of the cold father helping me sometimes in the early days of Peter's reign. I would lose my shit after he forced his lust, and he would put my head under the faucet to end my freaking out. I jumped up and rushed to the tub. without even removing my bondage pants or boots I turned on the flow of the shower then got inside closing the curtain behind me.

I stood their shivering in my clothing while the frigid liquid run-down my head soothing my flayed flesh. Blood, sweat, and tears swirled down the drain along with my rising madness. This was my last hope of maintaining my grip on reality.

The agony of every wound mixing with the shocking sensations of that temperature shift pulled my quickly shattering thoughts to focus. It appeared to be working to stave off yet another trip to that nightmare world behind the brutal one in which these foul men held me captive. I had to keep my head on as straight as possible. It was my only chance of survival in the pathetic situation in which I was trapped.

As I battled off my madness, I could hear shouting and excited voices in the next room. I knew that Master Bladrick was confronting Master Jonas. There was no doubt he was giving him the explanation of why the sexual sadist Barnim's corpse was turning cold on the first floor of the Haus. This was not my place to answer such questions. Master Bladrick had send that man over the edge not Mad

Maxx. If he desired to blame me for the murder, then there was nothing I could do about it.

No one would ever take my word over the Elders, and I knew this for the truth. I had to trust my Master wouldn't pin this death on my soul. Master Bladrick had found his manhood returned by our submissive shards talented mouth.

Surely, my Master wouldn't wish to see the boy hauled away for execution for that reason alone. I silently thanked my brother Maximillian for making his timely sacrifice. I realized it may be the only thing preventing our own untimely demise.

Maximillian shuddered next to me, appearing to be like me holding his breath. "I am happy to do it whenever need be, brother Mad Maxx. I ask only that you can bail out this fast-sinking ship in return. Do you hear that strange electrical noise in the distance? I heard this in the cells below during my eight months as Hemmel's and the black collars' punching bag. I fear this is that illness of confusion the flesh suffered all this time trying to overtake us again."

I nodded. "Ja, I hear it too. This is that shattering that disfigured Der Hund, I think. This water seems to be sending it back to wherever it comes from, but I wonder brother, will we have to keep the boy in this cold rain for all his life? What do we do if when I shut off the shower the sickness just comes right back?" The flesh trembled and its teeth chattered from the freezing temperature.

Maximillian groaned out. "Then keep the boy in the drink I say. Better to be chilly and wet all our life then to be chained to the wall in a cell down below."

Then I saw a shadow come into the room followed by a second. I couldn't make out the features through the foggy shower curtain but based on the heights I assumed it was my grumbling, Masters. I didn't move from my soggy spot fearing that enough time had not passed to wash away the madness to completion yet.

"Mad Maxx, come out of there. What the hell? Are you in the bath with your clothing on? Boy, what is wrong with you," I heard Master Jonas jell out in surprise.

I winced at his words that seemed too loud in my ears. "Forgive me, Master, I cannot take the pain of my injuries. I needed relief from the burn of them. I beg you for a few more moments of this mercy of cooling my agony," I called back while wrapping my arms around myself again, trying to brace against the chill.

Master Jonas came forward and ripped the curtain back. He glared at me shivering, soaked to the bone staring back at him in full terror. I saw him look me up and down with shock filling his expression at what his eyes told him of my physical state. He reached out and killed the faucet.

"Bladrick, my Mad Maxx is ripped to pieces. This is far worse than even what you told me Barnim has done. This tub is filled with blood. His wounds are serious. Call the Haus doctor. I am taking my man out of here. Tell that rat bastard to bring his medications and stitching to my apartment. Get me a Gott damned towel. Beloved come with me so I can dry you off. We are going home this minute." My Master reached his claw towards me.

I whimpered a bit but took his offered hand fearful of refusal of my blood bonded Vampire Husband. He pulled me roughly from the tub then snatched the threadbare towel that Master Bladrick offered to him. I cried out in pure agony the second Master Jonas touched me with that oversized rag. He ignored my sounds of agony while continuing his attempts to try and sop up my wetness.

Master Bladrick stood there watching this scene of unreality. "I will call the Haus doctor, Jonas but you will not be taking Mad Maxx anywhere. He says here with me. I saved him from that creature Barnim's blood lust, so I claim his time. I also take tomorrow for my own day in the cycle with our shared collar. Drexel can wait to take his turn when my time is done. I noticed no one bothered to include me in the schedule. I let this slide before, but no more. I can attend to this collar's grievous injuries just as well as you or any of my brothers can," he growled out to Master Jonas sounding irritable.

Master Jonas stopped his towel assault on me to turn and glare at Master Bladrick in disbelief. "Are you serious, Bladrick? This boy is cut to ribbons and all you think about is your turn in the cycle with him. This is insanity. I am takin him with me to be attended to by his man and that is final."

Master Bladrick shook his head fuming with much anger. "You forget that I am second in command, Jonas. You don't order me around, not in my own house or anywhere else. You also seem to think you're the sole owner of this boy's silver. Well, you are not. You have already spent most of the week with him. You cannot use this situation to disrupt the possession of his other Masters. This I won't allow." He crossed his arms blocking his bathroom door ready to fight to keep Master Jonas from leaving with me.

The Vampire threw down the dripping towel and I knelt immediately awaiting the outcome of this latest battle among the Elders "You are old Bladrick. Mad Maxx requires medical treatment and rest. This stress is not good for him. I will not stand aside and let you allow infection to set into these deep wounds he has."

The eldest schwuler chuckled bitterly. "I am indeed old, Jonas. So are you, so are Drexel and Claus. I don't intend to treat him myself. I will call in the Haus doctor and put this boy to bed immediately just as you would do. I intend to care for my collar as if he were my own son. I was the Dungeon Master of this Haus for forty years, Jonas. I have attended injuries far worse than these over the many years. I can handle this just as good if not better than you ever could. Drexel is not going to be thwarted his turn another few weeks or whenever you bother to deem Mad Maxx well enough for a return to his rounds. I know the tricks to get this boy back on his feet without endangering his continued existence. You have no such skills; I am sure of that."

Master Jonas shook his head "What the hell do you know of any abilities I have or don't have, Bladrick? You are offending me in all the ways you can find tonight. I will have to believe you when you say that Barnim came running and slipped off the banister, but this shit you spew about knowing the way to heal quick, that I must call you out on as exaggeration. You don't know this collar like I do. He is Priceless. He has special problems that need tender love and care." Master Bladrick interrupted him with a loud long laugh.

"Oh, is that so? I tell you right now, I know of what special problems you are speaking. You think I am unaware of that boy's mental illness? Christ, old friend, I would hope you knew me better than that. I was not born yesterday; of that no one can dispute. I know Gott damned well he is schizophrenic or else he would not be the forbidden silver in the first fucking place. I say to you that I am with you Jonas in your bid to help Mad Maxx be the first and only Priceless collar to find his way out that front door without his metal. I am not your enemy, nor am I capable of forcing my disgusting lustful interests on him while he is in this bad state, unlike you, Claus, or Drexel. He is safe in all ways in my home for the next two days. I say to you I can offer him peace, quiet and attend his agony unlike any of the rest of you can. I have the experience, the time, and I know how to keep a fucking secret too. Now that you know I know, what exactly is it that makes you so hell bent to overlook my true interest in seeing this boy well? I did fucking save his life from that trash leaking his life blood on the floor downstairs, didn't I? what the fuck more do I need to do to prove my loyalty to this silver collar, and your ultimate goals Jonas?" Master Bladrick smiled with wickedness.

Master Jonas shot a look at me with my eyes gazing at the floor. I had stood there silently shivering and slightly cowered. The whole discussion I had been watching the crimson tinged water dripping on Master Bladrick's fuzzy bathmat almost in a trance. Whatever the two Elder's decided no longer mattered to me. I was feeling faint and to be real honest needed to lay down before I fell the fuck down.

The Vampire growled out. "Alright Bladrick, enough of this argument. Call the Haus doctor, then come help me put Mad Maxx to your bed. He looks very weak. You are right, there is no reason we should not work together. You are my brother, and I am grateful that you saved our Priceless treasure this night. I only ask that you grant me the right to aid you in attending my man during this short convalescence." He turned his attention back to Master Bladrick.

The Elder nodded. "Fair enough, brother Jonas. I can always use an extra pair of hands and clearer eyes. I am going now to call the doctor. Have him stripped of these wet clothes. I meet you in the bedroom in a few moments." Master Bladrick took off to his telephone.

Master Jonas reached out and stroked my trembling cheek. "Are you strong enough to get your boots and pants off or do you need aid?"

I tried to speak but nothing came out. When this happened twice, I gave up and dropped to undo the soaking of my boots. My Master watched my clumsy slow work at removing my sopping outfit. He then attacked me once again with that towel, making me squirm and groan in pain from it. I had never been so grateful in my life when he decided I was as dry as possible at last. He took my leash and pulled me out of there demanding I get into the single wood framed bed in Master Bladrick's stuffy room.

I didn't give him any quarrel about this command. I was not feeling good at all. I quickly rolled face first unable to bare the pain of laying on my ravaged back. I could do nothing but moan and whimper in pure agony, helpless to fight with even a fly any longer.

Thankfully, the Haus doctor arrived within a short time. He had been downstairs granting his expertise in determining the death of Barnim. He shot me full of merciful pain killers and then cleaned out my open wounds. With rapid skill he closed the worst of them with stitching. Another round of antibiotics was ordered along with a warning that I need much rest and antiseptics daily until the danger of infection had passed. I fainted halfway through this process of sewing me back together for what seemed to be the hundredth time.

I awoke several hours later to find Master Jonas asleep in a wooden chair that had been brought in from the kitchen. Master Bladrick saw my eyes open. He put his finger to his lips to hush me then come over to me looking over my angry black and blue back.

He whispered to me, "Are you hungry Mad Maxx? I will call the black collars for something to eat. You need to regain your strength and have a full stomach for your medication to work properly. The doctor wants you to rest but I think you should attempt to get out of this bed. I command you to try to take at least a short walk around the apartment. I have found lying around too much slows the healing. The key to regaining your health is to get back on your feet as rapidly as possible. I will be with you to help you move if you need it." He backed away from the bed to allow me the space to follow his order.

I groaned in pain as I used my arms to push myself up off my face. The worst of the burning and stinging had settled into utter soreness with horrid stiffness in my shoulders. I slowly managed to maneuver to a sitting position. I kept my eyes to the floor grateful that I had not been taken by the reaper in the night. My grievous injuries reported to my nerve ending that my gratitude may not have been well placed. I hurt like hell.

I put my legs over the side of his bed feeling I may swoon. Part of that was caused by the doctor's painkillers, but some of that was from the trauma. Master Bladrick handed me a light bathrobe to cover my nakedness and slide over a pair of slippers for my bare feet. My head was pounding with each heartbeat. I cursed the dead Barnim for his cruelty. Had he not already found his grave I would have sure as hell sought him out and hung his ass by his own hooks until he expired. This was indeed horror.

I stood up and followed the silent Master Bladrick from his room. Master Jonas didn't stir from his slumber in the chair. I shot a look of worry at the Vampire, but my Master shook his head using a hand gesture demanding I follow him without speaking.

Once we were in his living area, he turned to me. "Jonas sat up all morning and most of this day attending your injuries Mad Maxx. He needs his rest. Now you kneel there next to my couch, and I call in for that food. I could use a little something myself. It is good to see you up and getting around on your own power. I know that for many days you will be sore with pain, but this will pass. You're a tough one. Those scars you wear tell me this is not your first time encountering this kind of torture. You'll be fine I think, as long as we can keep infection from onsetting, ja?"

I nodded. "Thank you for your mercy, Master. I heard you keep Master Jonas from taking me back to his apartment. I won't forget your kindness." I winced while slowly dropping to a kneel as he commanded.

Master Bladrick chuckled. "Ah well, I know you will pay me back in a short time for that. I have no worries after experiencing the extent of your skills. I am aware Jonas, and the others are slaves to their lusts. He thinks holding you away from Drexel and Claus's interests would be a kindness, but I know Jonas. You already seduced that man to near stupidity. He thinks he can take you back under his black wings and you're better off. However, we both know he wouldn't keep his beasts at bay and making prissy Drexel wait longer to taste you is not smart. If you're to suffer the foul touching of one of your Master's without the rest, you surely deserve it needs to be that bitchy statue lover. Then when you have captured Drexel, you and I can pull these wild cats together as the trusting brothers they should have been from the start. Do you think you can be ready for my old partner's tomfoolery by midnight tomorrow night?"

I kept my eyes to the floor listening to his wise words with dread in my heart. "Ja, I will do what must be done to please Master Drexel despite my condition. Breaking my metal is all that matters to me. If I had both my arms cut off and my legs too, I would insist to continue what needed to be done to find my freedom from this hell hole."

Master Bladrick grinned. "Ah, true Priceless to the soul. You can see nothing but that door to escape the life of subjugation. I would be lying if I said seeing this struggle of yours with my old eyes isn't a pleasure all its very own. That said, I must warn you. Drexel is not a gentle lover, Mad Maxx. I will do my best to curb the fools brutality as much as possible but there is no sure way to know if he will listen to my advice."

I looked up at my Master in a startle. "Wait, I thought that you and Master Drexel were a pair, Master. Won't you be there when he takes his rights? Can you not make sure he minds his manners with me?"

Master Bladrick frowned. "Well, ja I was his partner when I had no choices, my beauty. You have returned to me my own manhood. I no longer am a prisoner to that idiot's weirdness of love with the fake life. I am so grateful for you setting me free that I not only aid you in breaking your collar, but I also granted you a moment of mercy. I took this day for myself in the cycle to prevent him getting his nasty hands on you for another day. It was a calculated risk since doing this thing keeps me from being there to keep him honest with you. I have faith that you can handle Drexel's couple, despite his odd proclivities. He is no Barnim, nor Xavier. He doesn't do the violence of even Jonas. I believe you'll be a bit horrified by his touching but not physically injured by it. He is a weird one, my love, but not a threat to your life or flesh."

I sighed. "Then so be it, Master. I will do what I must to seduce this, Master Drexel. I know you have done much for me in the last twenty-four hours, but I would beg to ask the mercy of pain killers to aid in my seduction work with him."

Master Bladrick shook his head. "I would readily grant that mercy, Mad Maxx, if I could. I cannot be sure of what scene Drexel will act on. You need to be clear-headed to manage him. Pain killers could be dangerous to your success with him. I do apologize for having to deny this to you but in time you will thank me for it."

I groaned. "As you wish, Master. May I ask you, is being a Dominant worth all this pain? It seems the closer I get to being the Master in this Haus the worse things are getting. Is this the way it is for all those the break their silver or is this horror because I am leveled Priceless?"

I knew I should not have dared to ask this question. I had to know if everyone was picking on me, or if this nightmare was typical for the Dominant trainee. The paranoia that the whole Haus was in a conspiracy to trap me in my metal had been driving me to near madness.

During the exchange between Master Jonas and Master Bladrick the night before regarding their joining forces something bothersome had occurred to me. While they made their deals, I had tried to think of a single Dominant I knew, or heard of, that had worn a collar in this place. I couldn't come up with a single name. This made me suspicious that no one had ever passed the test nor the vote.

I had begun to worry that like anything in the Haus the story that a submissive could rise to the lofty place of the Dominant was an illusion. Mad Maxx was no longer a foolish boy that believed all he had been told. I took the chance that Master Bladrick would be honest with me and tell me the truth when so far no one else had been. Okay, to be fair, Annette had not lied to me, but all the others were dishonorable.

My Master dropped his gaze to his shoes and shifted uncomfortably. "Uhm, well ja and nein, Mad Maxx. You see, no one has broken a collar in the last sixty-five years. Most never survived the testing. Those that did never received the unanimous vote."

I let out a yelp of terror. "None in sixty-five years? This means I have no chance either. The training is all a lie, isn't it." I began to tremble in full on despair upon hearing the honest answer I had known all along but never wanted to admit.

Master Bladrick rubbed his forehead. "I ask you to calm yourself, my love. I tell you now that you will break that collar and be the first to rise in sixty-five years. I will be truthful and tell you I am the number one reason no silver has risen in the Haus all six decades. I made sure that those that made it to the vote were stopped. I have always known this Haus cannot survive if we allow people their freedom after abusing them since childhood. Think of what would happen if enough angry ex-silvers ran throughout these hallways seeking revenge against those that raped, beat, and misused them for years. It would destroy this place in only a short time. I told you last night that I have spent my life destroying your kind, but as my last act I will raise you to your feet. Well, that you have no choice but to believe. With me standing on your side, then your chances of breaking the collar are real for the first time since I took the job of Dungeon Master on my seventeenth birthday. You must move all the others that block your path or that can end your bid. That is something I cannot do for you. You must believe me when I tell you, others that have ran for the bolt cutters managed to capture all the other votes, but day never were able to sway the cruel Bladrick. That my love was those silver collars' undoing, all of them. Unlike you, none of them could give me a single reason to believe they earned the right to stand before me as my equal. Mad Maxx, I see you rise with the wounds of hell on your back.

Your mind is near busted from brain disease. Everyone in this Haus has signed up to fuck you, kick your ass, take advantage, or even try to kill you, and yet you got out of my bed to prepare for yet another rape. All this so you can walk out the front door like a man rather than scrape on your knees for all your life. That, my love, I respect so much you have won my heart and stayed my hand to prevent your rise. That is all I will ever confess to or say about this subject so never ask me again."

I dropped my head onto my raised knee fighting back the urge to cry with all I had. "I thank you for being honest with me, Master. I choose to trust you, but I beg your mercy in this. If you desire to betray what you tell me this moment in the future let me know. I would rather hear a painful truth than a glorious lie. I suppose that you say I already knew but refused to accept. I needed to believe there was a way out of my nightmare or I never could have survived this long. Even though it was obvious I was the real liar. If some silver had gained such an ascension, then no doubt I would have heard that name from every mouth in this place. That lucky ex-silver would be viewed as the hero to all us that have short, brutal lives on our knees at the will of their Dominants. I of course never heard a single rumor, gossip, nor story of such a man or frau in all my time in the Haus. I have been the fool, and I must face I may still be one if you're merely telling me what I want to hear."

Master Bladrick came across the room and laid his hand on my bowed head. "Nein, my love. I don't stroke your ears with the flames of dishonesty. I will stand aside and let you fly or fall on your own merits. I add further that if I still had any real power in this Haus, I would use it to aid your bid for freedom. As it is, I can only hinder you or not, nothing more and nothing less. The rest is up to you. Last night I saw a boy willing to go to the extreme without hesitation in an effort to repossess his soul from these hounds of hell around him. I have faith that these old foggy eyes of mine will pour with the tears of happiness over your freedom soon enough. Nothing on Earth would bring me lasting peace more than watching my Mad Maxx handed the sacred bolt cutters. If anyone can do this, it will be you." He leaned down, then kissed the top of my head.

I sniffed back my unmanly tears before they could fall and nodded. "Thank you for believing that Master. I am just so tired already. I still have so far to go."

My Master sighed, "Ja, sadly this is truth, my love. Drexel will be here tomorrow for his turn with you. Try to focus on staying calm, resting, and regaining your strength. When you finish your first rounds, we will meet to discuss the choice of a replacement for Barnim. You will need to seduce the fresh Elder bastard right away without giving the others a chance to block your attempts. If we can get all the Elders to join forces, then you have a chance at blocking Cora when she tries to halt your rise. It is the only way, my love. For this I apologize but I doubt even in your own errored beliefs did you ever assume the Haus would allow you to get away easily."

I looked up at my Master feeling a bit faint again. "Nein, I knew it would be difficult. Not even Mad Maxx is that big a fool to believe otherwise. That said, I wonder, you already have someone in mind to replace Barnim?"

Master Bladrick sat down on his couch next to me with a loud groan appearing to suffer from his old bones. "Ja, I do my love. There are only two in this Haus that qualify for this position. The Dominant Leo and the eldest current Dungeon Master Hemmel. Leo has strong ties to Cora and the head council member Gretta. Dungeon Master Hemmel has allegiance to your ex-Master Peter. Neither candidate is a good one for your bid, but both can be bought to side with the brother Elders, even Leo."

I moaned out in much pain upon hearing this latest horrible news. "Meine Gott, Master. Are you sure there is not another choice? I swear I would choose any other foul Dominant in this Haus over those two."

Ma Master nodded. "You and I agree on that point but my love there is no others that qualify. Leo was dungeon Master in his youth just long enough to meet the requirements. He just celebrated his fifty-fifth year. Dungeon Master Hemmel has turned fifty-seven and has served many more years than required for the position. Leo is known for his backstabbing and perversion with the young boys of this Haus. Master Hemmel is a hard bitten, brutal, and cruel man with no qualms about crushing his enemies or rewarding his friends. It will be a tough call for you to choose. I seem to recall I granted you that honor. Think about this for a week and decide wisely. If we pick the wrong man, he could destroy our well laid plans with little effort."

I did my best not to vomit at the idea the I would have to provide for the lusts of one of these nightmares on legs. "Master, I will need to speak to both of them prior to making my choice. I think if I have a moment or two alone with each it may help me decide which is the better of the worst."

My Master nodded. "Ah, ja, that is good thinking. Okay, I will arrange to give you an opportunity to have a meeting with Hemmel and Leo when my next day of holding your leash comes next week. That way none of the brothers will be wise to our arrangement, Mad Maxx. I can only hope your instincts for survival are strong enough to weed out the one that can help rather than halt us."

I put my head back onto my knee. "I fear both will be a hindrance. I can only choose the easier to control, but I know these men already. I can assure you anything they promise us would be a lie. We will have to work around them and watch our backs always."

Master Bladrick chuckled. "Well, that may be the truth, my love, but at least they won't be putting hooks into you like the monster Barnim, ja?"

I scoffed with much bitterness. "Hooks hurt less than a knife in it would, Master. I will recover from this, but maybe I won't be so lucky with the hateful Master Hemmel or the rat Master Leo. I would ask you to take good care of your health and stave off the reaper as long as possible if I could be so bold."

Master Bladrick appeared startled by that statement. "Oh? I would like to ask why you say that. I already told you I have prevented every silver from the bolt cutters all my life. If I were to die, then you'd be assured I can hinder you or anyone. Does this mean you trust me completely? Could I be so lucky as having earned such a gift from you so quickly?"

I shook my head and raised up to stare into his wizened face. "Nein, I never lie Master. It is not trust the causes me to desire your continued existence above ground. Though I will say I have to believe you and I do. The reason I say this for truth is that I realized just now if your gone then both Master Hemmel and Master Leo will rise, not just one of them. That I cannot deal width. So, I again beg of you, stay with me long as you can. I am willing to give you plenty of reasons to put off your date with the grave."

Master Bladrick stared at me with a strange expression that seemed to be awe. Then without warning he leaned forward and grabbed the back of my head. I was pulled to him slowly with gentle strength, then engaged with him in a deep kiss. To my surprise the Elder was skilled at this display of affection and unlike Master Drexel, had all his teeth. *I know that seems like an odd thing to notice but unless you have kissed someone without them, don't judge me. It is something that just grosses me out, even more than being forced to endure being explored by the mouth of a husband well in his eighties.*

Master Jonas came into the living room to find me and Master Bladrick deep in a mouth embrace. I don't know how long he stood there watching before he cleared his throat loudly. He was trying to announce his presence without being too rude, since he was a visitor to Master Bladrick's home and on his collar clock to boot. Master Bladrick let go of my head. I quickly retreated back to my kneel at his feet while he wiped his mouth off grinning like a mischievous boy.

"Oh, I apologize Jonas. I didn't know you had awakened," said Master Bladrick, while he leaned back onto his couch to get comfortable.

Master Jonas shot a wicked smile at us both. "Apparently you didn't, that is pretty obvious. Should I go back into the room and give you more time to fondle my man, Bladrick, or are you satisfied for now?"

Master Bladrick feigned indignation at that. "Your man he may be any other time but not today. This beautiful boy is my lover until the clock strikes midnight tomorrow night, Jonas. I am far from satiated with him. You can stick around and watch if that brings you some pleasure, but I warn you I have waited a long time to not have to share my treasure. This day and tomorrow, only I will be allowed to lay a finger on him. I have been holding back for many years. I did this to allow all you a chance to win the hearts of the silvers available. I am now out of my retirement. I am a stud most rare and Mad Maxx is the object of my unbridled desires. He will be worthless from my lustful affections. He will never find any of you worthy of his attentions when I am finally satisfied." He began to chuckle at his weak attempt to sound as if he were intending to fuck me till his dick broke off, because his dick was already broke long before I ever came along.

The Vampire chuckled at Master Bladrick's bullshit. "Well shit. You are here to ruin my beautiful marriage to this boy. I should have known it is always the quiet one, ja?" he teased back as he sat down on the love seat looking at my mangled back with some concern in his expression.

Master Bladrick stopped giggling. "Mad Maxx, go back to my bed and lay down for rest. I will call in that food.

225

Jonas or I will be in shortly to attend your medication and wounds. I wish you to sleep, be calm, and let your worries go for this short time of peace. That, my love, is a directive."

I did as he told me without quarrel. That night and the next day, Master Jonas took turns with Master Bladrick in attending my injuries. Master Bladrick had me get out of his bed for short walks every few hours during the daytime. I was kept calm with tranquilizers and pain killing drugs. All loud noises, and stress of any kind was kept far from my convalescing flesh. This more than anything else sent the oncoming psychotic break back to the dark recesses of my mind.

Master Bladrick had been truthful when he told Master Jonas he knew how to heal the wounded quickly. It was not my skin that was threatening my life, it was my psyche. Thankfully, that Elder knew this and did all that was humanly possible to give me time to regain my foothold on reality. I could have used many more days of this pampering (*I say that but remember my bar for mercy was low back then Meine Liebe*), but that was something that was beyond even this powerful Elder's control.

Other than some mild pawing from Master Jonas, until Master Bladrick caught him and demanded he stop molesting his collar, and a few deep kisses from Master Bladrick, I was free from serious sex acts.

While I was grateful for the break, I did worry that this was not going to help me manage the pain of a couple with Master Drexel. I already knew nothing was going to put that old schwuler off, not even a mangled back. This fear of another painful intercourse situation was compounded when four hours before midnight even my muscle relaxant medication had been denied me. I was confused by this sudden refusal of any kind of mercy by Master Jonas and Master Bladrick but there was nothing I could do about it.

Just before midnight Master Jonas came to the bedroom and kissed me good night and goodbye. He appeared nervous. That was not helping me feel any better about this scary situation I was heading into blindly. I wanted to ask him why everyone seemed to dislike Master Drexel so much and all of them cringed when his strange fetish was brought up. I found my words frozen in my throat as the Vampire released me from his embrace then left the room briskly.

Master Bladrick came in after his retreat. He took up my leash telling me to grab my things. We were headed out. I stood up feeling a bit of fear, noticing I had nothing but a bathrobe and slippers to wear.

"Master, forgive me, but did Master Drexel send anything to wear for his pleasure?" I shuddered when I realized the answer to the dumb question was the lack of being offered any outfits earlier that day.

Master Bladrick frowned. "Drexel will put whatever the hell he wants you to wear on you when you get there, my love. That idiot is moody. You never know what he will desire at any given moment. The artist is like that you know. Drexel fancies himself such a creature. Just do whatever he tells you and it will be over before you know it. The key to seducing my brother is to keep your mouth shut unless he tells you otherwise. He doesn't like to be called out, questioned, or criticized. Do as I say, and he will be putty in your hands."

I looked at the floor as I stood up off the bed to follow my Master. "You mean I will be putty in his Master. Isn't that what the statue is made of?"

Ma Master nodded. "You already understand, that is good. I will worry about you less now that I know you will play your role without quarrel. We must go but do know I enjoyed our time together more than I ever thought I could. I look forward to seeing you tomorrow at midnight."

I began to walk behind my slow-moving Master feeling very confused by that statement. "What? I am to be with Master Claus after Master Drexel, ja? Did the schedule get scrambled up?"

He chuckled with glee. "Nein, you are to be with Claus after Drexel. I am far too old and sick to live alone anymore, my love. Thanks to you I decided to change my roommate. I am moving in with my brother Claus when the sun rises. I had been living with Drexel but now that you have freed me of his control, I can join one that is closer to my temperament. He and I are closer in our ages, and his fetish is one that I can appreciate. Drexel was fussy, difficult, stingy, and prone to pissy fits. Claus is easy going, lazy, and enjoys peace. I was thrilled when he told me having me with him was a dream come true for him. Now I will have the aid I need to remain semi-independent, and Claus will no longer feel the demons of loneliness in his final days. We have our Priceless collar to thank for our sudden good fortune. Once again, I say I see you at midnight tomorrow, try not to despair for this harsh leash. When Drexel bothers you think of the loving arms of your two biggest admires awaiting you when this dreadfulness is done."

I rolled my eyes behind him where he could not see me. "Ah. This is great news Master. Thank you for the mercy of it." I didn't mean a fucking word of that shit.

Master Maxx spun me around to look at him for a moment "I have to say this, really? This old fart thinks that the idea of two old men waiting to paw me is something wonderful to look forward to after the lustful attack of a third one. I am the one they say has insanity, but I have to ask this, who is the judge of the crazy? I would like to meet that guy and kick him right in the fucking hoddensack." I nodded that I agreed, we both should kick that guy in the nuts for calling us nuts.

He kissed me on the forehead then turned me back around in his lap. He snuggled me close and took a deep breath.

"I have seen many vile things in this world Meine Liebe. There is not much anymore that surprises me. Drexel, Xavier, Barnim, and Jonas, add in my father Peter. Well, they define the word perverted and sick. However, the day I met your mother Debbie in the Haus four years ago, I swear I started to believe in the devil for truth. If someone had told me that one day, I would be sitting in that horror's home holding her daughter in my lap calling her my own blood bonded frau, well I would have stabbed them in their eyes for being so rude. Yet here I sit and so do you. I often think that you and I are merely comic relief for the Gotts in their boredom. I actually started believing that the night I became Drexel's collared lover, nothing on Earth could have prepared me for the fool."

I looked back at him in surprise. "You met my mother when I was six. How Master?"

He chuckled then ruffled my hair. "Damn it, Meine Liebe. I will get to that when the time in my story for meeting your mother comes. Stop being in such a hurry, ja? I tell you that I did meet her and have known of her foul nature longer than I known you, Meine Frau. I have the sad distinction of probably knowing all the worst people in this world. I have even been intimate with a few of those that should be shot as monsters. Thankfully, disgusting Debbie is not one of them. So, you want to hear this story in total, or do we stop now, and you can hit the floor for sleep?"

I shook my head. "I wish to hear the story in order thank you, Master."

He chuckled. "Good enough, then we go back to maybe one of the damned weirdest nights of my young life, Master Drexel the statue lover.

Master Bladrick and I walked down the long hallway back toward the dead Barnim's apartment. To my surprise he stopped at the penthouse just next to the monster's dwelling. I realized Master Drexel was the sexual sadist's neighbor. That had to be how he knew of Barnim's brutal nature when none of the others seemed to be aware. I stood behind my Elder Master doing my best to steady my nerves.

I shot a quick look at Maximillian as we stood there waiting for Master Drexel to answer his door. "We jump from the boy together the second that this weirdo goes for the couple. I take your hand now so that we can get the fuck out of here the second the petting gets serious, ja?"

Maximillian nodded. "I would be lying if I didn't say this is the one Master I was looking forward to. Neither of us must endure that nasty schwuler sex. The flesh can go into a trance while you and I grab a beer and chase the women."

I chuckled at that fantasy scene. "Women? I thought you were about to marry me, brother? We haven't even cut the wedding cake and already you're cuckolding me. Damn, I thought you loved me Maximillian. You did nothing but play with my heart."

Maximillian shrugged. "What did you expect of me Mad Maxx? You marry me as the child bride before I knew anything of the ways of the world. I have grown up and found I desire to know the world. Try not to despair my love. I will go and sow my wild oats but one day I will be ready again to settle down with you."

I frowned at that trying not to break into laughter at our stupid playing. Hey, I was stressed the fuck out with thoughts of the creepy statue fucker, nothing wrong with a little humor, ja? "I will wait for you Maximillian, but I warn you now, I am a jealous husband. When you return, I will hunt down and kill all your previous lovers."

Maximillian's eyes went wide at that. "Oh? Then I make a list of names of all my conquests right this fucking second for you. Where the fuck did, I put that pen." We both started to giggle at our banter causing Master Bladrick to glance back at us with a raised eyebrow.

Master Drexel opened the door. I trembled a bit at the sight of that skinny, toothless, old man with that weird hawkish face. He looked me up and down then glanced at Master Bladrick with his beady eyes.

"He looks pretty good to me, Bladrick. I can hid all those ugly bruises with a bit of illusion easy enough, I think. I think you have done an amazing job bringing him back from death. Though it shouldn't have happened in the first fucking place. I told all of you Barnim was bad news. Now you won't be so quick to discount what Drexel has to say I bet. Near cost us this work of art though, didn't it?" Master Drexel sputtered out in his high-pitched voice.

Master Bladrick nodded. "Ja, you were right to put up the warning flags. I already apologized to you plenty for discounting your sage advice brother. I would like to give you a fair warning in return for your service to all of us though. Be careful with Mad Maxx when enjoying your rights with him. He looks good but when you get the robe off, well Barnim was nearly successful in sending this collar to the orchard. I ask you kindly to be gentle and fair."

Master Drexel scoffed. "I am always gentle and fair. I have no one complaining of my interests in them that I am aware. Not now, not ever."

Master Bladrick snorted. "Drexel, your lovers cannot complain now, can they? Be easy on him, I mean it brother. This is a living breathing creature. Go easy on him. If you break this one, it is forever."

Master Drexel snatched my leash from Master Bladrick's hands and pulled me roughly toward him. "I do believe your time with our shared collar is up Bladrick. I was not at your apartment telling you what you could or couldn't do with your own property. I will thank you for showing me the same respect. Good night." He pulled me in behind him and slammed his door on Master Bladrick.

His living area was filled with odd looking furniture. His couch was a weird orange cube thing and his sitting chairs orb shaped of deep blues. Even his lamps were strange with sharp angles and ugly color matches such as lime green with yellow. The flooring was of the modern art deco to match up with his entire scheme.

On the walls were paintings of various art methods from cubism to realism. The subjects were all of parts of the human anatomy most the male legs, faces and genitalia. I grimaced at the overwhelming mixes of color clashes and harsh scenes in every corner of his apartment. It was disturbing, I cannot express the strongly enough, Meine Liebe.

As I followed this weirdo down his long hallway, I found myself actually missing the simpleness of Bladrick's home or even the creepy Vampire's home. This place made me feel confused, nervous, and disconnected. There was a strange smell in the air that was similar to that of an old attic or dusty closet that held many chemicals with no ventilation.

He took me through a bright blue door. The room was huge and wide open. All around were mannequins. Some of them looked plastic and others seemed to be made of cloth or soft materials. They were like his paintings, mostly male. I shivered when the schwuler arrived at the center of the room. All those human dolls were staring at us with their creepy lifeless eyes.

Master Drexel told me to stay still until he comes back. He dropped my leash and headed for the back of that room to a doorway. I watched him open it and go inside leaving me alone with the spooky lovers of my Master. I cast my eyes at them staring mindlessly at me. I felt a chill run down my spine when I noticed a platform of black just to the right of me.

I could see that it had an adjustable tabletop, and bondage ropes for ankles attached to two round bars sticking up from the floor. I could see that Master Drexel would use this odd mechanism to bind his lifeless sex partners to keep them propped and still for his coupling. Yikes!

I was shaking in my house shoes over this upsetting situation when Master Drexel came back out of that door carrying a large olive-green bag. I watched him set it on his adjustable sex table then begin digging through it. I didn't dare say a word. I took Master Bladrick's advice and waited for Master Drexel to tell me what he desired rather than incite the anger of one not accustomed to empathy for the living.

He pulled out a large container about the size of a small paint can that was dark grey. Then he took out a small clutch looking purse. He picked both these items up and came back toward me. I was really trembling by this time, never taking my eyes off that canister.

Master Drexel walked behind me. I heard him drop the grey bucket thing on the floor. He stood there a minute in silence. I did my best to remain calm, but I wasn't sure what the fuck he was up to. I stole a look behind me best as I could. I saw into the canister. It was exactly what it looked like, paint. I wondered what he needed that shit for.

Then he cleared his throat startling me with the sudden noise in that quiet creepy place. "Mad Maxx, you can remove that robe and the shoes now please."

I winced at that command but knew better than to deny a Master their desires. I unbelted the soft cotton bathrobe Master Bladrick loaned me. I shot a look at Maximillian letting him know we would be jumping from the wheel shortly. If this schwuler wanted us naked a couple was sure to be coming soon.

I heard Master Drexel gasp when my scared and stitched back was in his full view. He came around the front of me looking me up and down with what appeared to be disgust. His eyes settled on my chastity device. His brow furrowed and he clicked his tongue appearing angered at that sight.

"Jonas is a bastard. Bad enough I have to look at that shit Barnim did to this work of art without having this metal eye sore too. I swear this pisses me off to near fit status. How the fuck is an artist supposed to work when the canvas is damaged, and his brushes locked up in a cage? Humm?" He looked at me holding his weird little green clutch purse crossing his arms at me.

I shrugged. "I will do my best to please you despite these hindrances, Master. I am sure an artist of your legend shall have no problem finding pleasurable use of this material despite it being of substandard quality."

Master Drexel's eyes went wide. "Ah, you have heard of my skill then. I knew it the second I saw you, Mad Maxx. I said to myself, Drexel, this collar has a deeper understanding of art than the usual brute in this Haus. So, you worship art the way I do then?"

I looked at the floor. "I dare not ever compare myself to one of your lofty heights, Master. I am but a novice with skill only as to the tools for artistic expression, not the

235

talents of the one that can wield them to create masterpieces."

Master Drexel smiled at my statement "You are beyond beautiful, Mad Maxx. I have tasted your lips and thought of nothing since. I saw your ability to mimic perfection in Jonas's bed after that disastrous blood bonding many months ago. I won't lie and say I have not looked forward to this night with fevered fantasies ever since. Well, then I say we get started. You are correct. I can work around this horror of Barnim and ignore the chastity device of Jonas. Illusion is my middle name. Now, you hold still. I wish to paint you, Mad Maxx. You will be silent and still for my desires that is a directive." He walked back behind me to his paint bucket.

I nearly passed out when I realized his saying he wanted to paint me was literal. He didn't intend to create a fake image on a canvas. I was the fucking canvas. I braced myself for the application of his grey paint on my flesh.

I heard him unzip the purse to remove his brushes to begin his art on my flesh. I shuddered when the pervert grabbed my around my waist to steady me. Then instead of the softness of the artists brush I felt a sharp stick in my backside.

I turned around with a start to see Master Drexel holding up a syringe staring at me with a smile. Within mere seconds I felt weak all over. I tried to open my mouth to scream but my jaw would not respond nor would my arms or legs. Nothing was responding. Then my knees gave way. I began to fall to the floor helpless to stop my decent. Master Drexel caught the swooning boy. He laid me on the floor with gentleness and stood over me staring into my vacant eyes.

"Don't worry, Mad Maxx. Your muscles are paralyzed but I give you no anesthetic. You will remain conscious but incapable of movement. I didn't give you enough to require a ventilator so some crude movements should be possible if you focus hard enough. However, I command you to be still and let me do all the work. In about four hours or so I will give you back your will, but for now, I will have what I want without worrying that you'll argue, fight me, or piss me off. Now, I believe I was going to paint you. Hold still this may be a little cold." He chuckled as he went to retrieve his paint can leaving me there unable to move even to blink in the middle of the floor.

I took Maximillian's hand and nodded that it was time to flee the flesh. We took a run but bounced off the barrier of the wheel. Maximillian whimpered in terror while I railed trying like hell to find a way out of this nightmare situation.

No matter what we tried we could not get out. That paralytic drug had trapped us both inside the boy. In great horror we saw Master Drexel kneel over us and begin to paint our skin the color of his statues.

He was right. That paint was cold. We not only could see, hear, and taste like normal; we could also feel.

Chapter 37: A Shot of Ingenuity

I laid their stuck, staring at the ceiling paralyzed from even swallowing thanks to Master Drexel's shot of some paralytic drug. He reached out then turned our head to the side, so we didn't drown in our own drool. This was a nightmare that we never expected.

I could see and feel his paint brush covering our skin with his "statue" paint. Maximillian and I continued to beat on the walls of the flesh trying like hell to abandon him. Neither of us wanted to be in there when Master Drexel did whatever foulness he planned to enact on the boy.

I looked at my panicking brother. "Okay, Maximillian, we are trapped. There is no way out of this shit. You try to move the wheel and I will see if there is some way for us to turn ourselves off when Master Drexel comes at us. Do not call Der Hund whatever you do. Best he never knows of this dishonorable situation we are in. If Master Drexel intends to end our life, then brother let me say it has been a pleasure to serve at your side."

Maximillian's eyes were wide in terror, but he nodded. "Same goes for me, brother. I will keep pushing the wheel to move. No matter what comes I am here by your side, and I have your back. I swear this on my soul."

We both took a deep breath then began our agreed tasks. I saw Maximillian using all his strength to move the flesh even a little bit. I closed my eyes doing my best to focus on going to sleep within the boy. Nothing we did worked. It didn't take long for us to realize, like it or not, we would have to feel, see, hear, and remember this sexual assault. There was no escape this time.

Master Drexel finished painting the front of us, then rolled the boy to his face. The cold paint chilled our skin and burned our wounds. Each stroke on our ravaged back felt like a million bee stings. Despite our nerves loud reports of pain, we could not even cry out that his actions were hurting us.

Maximillian and I were under too much stress from that agony to focus any longer on anything else. We finally gave up our struggle to find a way out. We grabbed ahold of each other, melding into one single shard, then braced for the coming terror. We strengthened each other by uniting. It was our last-ditch effort to prevent Master Drexel shattering us for all time.

Master Maxx turned me to investigate my face. "This Master's abuse of us was the worst we had ever encountered in all our days, including the ones of Gerard's brutal bondage. You Meine Liebe understand why I say this, I know. Nothing is worse than being trapped within yourself, unable to even speak or brace the flesh for cruelty. Even in the worst ropes and gags you can flinch or cry. This helps to allow your letting your attacker know when they go too far if nothing else. More than that, you can believe that there is a chance of escape if you struggle hard enough. It is not even important if that is not true. You thinking it helps keeps down that hopelessness. Master Drexel had takin away even the illusion of any control. You remember this horror from when you convalesce from that head trauma Russell did to you, ja? Your voice box was smashed, and the doctor gave those horrid parents of yours muscle relaxers. Ah, I see that look in your eyes. You know exactly what I am talking about, don't you? The horror of being this kind of helpless, there are not strong enough words to relay the trauma of it when being beaten, tortured, or raped, now is there?"

I winced, then nodded. He was right. I had suffered many cruel, brutal, and painful events but nothing compared to the true terror of being physically paralyzed while being assaulted. Especially when you are conscious enough to feel the whole thing but unable to cry out.

He nodded with a look of pity. "Well, Master Barnim had taken me to the deepest of all tortures I had suffered to that point. Master Drexel, he was about to take me to the worst of the raping I had ever endured. I had only just been able to prevent a psychotic break from my last severe trauma. I was sure this latest horror would be one that sent me right into the throat of the Mother of Madness for all time." He turned me back around in his lap and took a deep breath in preparation to relive his nightmare at the hands of Master Drexel.

"I have no idea how much time passed while Master Drexel painted me like one of his statues. I drooled on the floor on my stomach damning my existence with all my soul. He covered every inch of my flesh from the bottom of my feet to the top of my head. He kept that crap out of my hair but the rest of me was colored granite.

He took eye drops, and every fifteen minutes or so he would pick up my head and put them in my eyes, so they didn't dry out. Ja, he had sedated me so deeply I couldn't blink nor close them or my mouth with my own power. I could breathe, but it was shallow, and I wondered if he had only added a tiny bit more if I would not have had to be ventilated to keep me from smothering.

When he was finally satisfied, I was painted enough he picked up all his paints and brushed returning them to his satchel. Master Drexel returned quickly. He checked to see I was dry enough to not smudge, then rolled me to my back once more. He stood above me admiring his handiwork at creating the Mad Maxx "living statue."

He laughed. "You are breathtaking, Mad Maxx. A true masterpiece. I need to find a way to preserve this moment for all time. I don't like the photographs, but I don't have the time to capture you on canvas before the medication wears off. You hold still, hahaha, while I go get my camera. A couple of shots will aid me in my drawing you latter when I have more time, ja?" He rushed off leaving me there helpless yet again.

Master Drexel returned with his camera. He moved my head, and tried to position me in a way he could that would make him happy. No matter what he tried I didn't seem to be the vision he wanted me to be. He never took a single photo thanks to his irritation at my lack of compliance with his desires. I could do nothing but take his constant pushes, pulls, rolling, and verbal assaults. I wasn't even able to apologize for being unable to meet his wishes.

Sweat had broken out on his forehead from all his attempts to move my dead weight around on his floor. He sat down next to me. He appeared at last beaten in his bid to obtain his desired pose. I stared at him while he wiped his forehead sighing in obvious disgust.

"I give up. This has never worked. I cannot find a way to get any fucking human being to be as perfect as my statues or mannequins. I had such hope for you since you're the Priceless collar but even you are worthless as pure art. You see capturing life is the hardest thing on Earth, Mad Maxx. I see a movement in the living that speaks to my heart but before I can save that on canvas, it disappears for all time. I cannot get anyone to hold that pose for more than a second. Then I am stuck painting that image from the horrid photographs. There is no depth in a photograph like there is in reality. A copy only of perfection, like an errored mirror image. I grow weary of it all." He sighed then reached out and ran his hands through my hair.

At that moment suddenly I was able to make a light guttural sound in my throat that was quick and barely audible. Master Drexel pulled his hand back as if I bit him rather than whimpered out loud. He sat there appearing stunned for a second then reached back out grabbing a handful of my hair to pull it up and stair into my glazed eyes.

"I told you to be still. You will not make another sound, or I will beat you for it. I know you can hear me, Mad Maxx. I will not tolerate this insolence." He dropped my head to the floor with a hard thud.

That hurt a great deal. The floor was merely painted concrete. I began to wildly think on that statement Master Bladrick made during the dinner in the Great Hall, and again when dropping me off with Master Drexel. "If you break it then this one cannot be glued back together." I began to become afraid this Master would not realize that dropping my head or beating on me could kill me, unlike the statues he seemed to care for so much.

Deep terror filled me when I saw the irritated Master Drexel stand up and leave my field of vision. I wondered if he had gone to retrieve a thudder or other tool of torture. He returned in only a few moments. I could not see what he had retrieved but I heard metal hitting the floor as if he had dropped something next to me.

He leaned down into my face smiling with wickedness. "Well, I may not be able to find the pleasure of savoring my Mad Maxx statue by photo, but I am able to enjoy this snapshot while it lasts, ja?" He grabbed the sides of my jaw forcing my mouth open then he spit into it.

I could do nothing while Master Drexel quickly dropped his lips to mine, then began kissing with vigor. I wanted to throw up from the sensation of his tongue exploring the inside my head. He did this for several minutes before pulling up and spitting into my mouth again. Yuck, just fucking yuck.

I laid their damning all existence while I watched Master Drexel open his little green clutch that held his syringes and other sharps. He pulled out two small needle shaped objects with a smile on his face.

He showed them to my frozen eyes. "The contract says we are not to pierce your flesh, but Barnim already ignored this agreement beyond calculation. I personally like my lovers to have some decorations that are skin deep. I am going to put these needles through your nipples, Mad Maxx, but you need not be upset. I will remove them when I am finished with you tonight. The wounds will heal without permanent problems. I warn you; this is between you and me. If you tell anyone about it, then I will make sure you are punished so severely you will think Barnim a saint. Now, you can disagree with me over this. All you got to do is shake your head nein and I will have to relent to your refusal. I don't like to do anything against another's will. I give you two minutes to tell me to stop." He giggled knowing Gott damned well I couldn't move enough to even beg him to end any fucking thing he wanted to do to me.

He sat there watching me for any sign of movement. I did my best to try but I was still unable to even make a sound. When his time allotted for my refusal passed without hesitation that rat bastard took his thrill of piecing my nipples with his needles. I had endured much worst pain only a few nights before, but this was not pleasant let me tell you. I could feel the whole process of his digging into my sensitive parts. Within I yelled like a little bitch, but the boy laid their silent, staring, and unable to respond to my inner turmoil.

Master Drexel admired his cruel piercing a bit then picked something up. I finally saw this thing, just as he pulled my head up to buckle it in place. It was a fucking spider mouth gag. I realized he was preparing to force himself on me. Since I could not respond on my own, he was making sure to keep my mouth from closing during his oral rape.

Just when I thought it couldn't get any worse than this shit, he reached onto the floor and grabbed the metal thing that made all that noise when he dropped it. I saw with great disgust he had a spreader bar to aid him in completion of his coupling with me.

I was helpless to stop him as he strapped that bar in between my ankles. He then pulled me up by my arms harnessing my wrists to the bar. I was now held in a sitting position by use of this restraining device. My gagged head rolled limp and useless staring down into my lap unable to lift by my own power.

I groaned within at this horrid solution to his sexual assault on me while paralyzed. I had suffered so many unwanted sexual assaults by this time I was not that upset anymore when one of these hideous creatures violated me.

This one, however, bothered me a great deal. I could not brace myself, tell this Master if he was being too rough nor even control my breathing to aid me in getting through the nightmare of it. I managed another soft whimper when he grabbed my hair lifting my head forcing his cock into my useless mouth. The rape had begun, and there wasn't shit I could do about it.

Master Drexel took his time with his brutal oral penetration. He thrust himself into my head harshly forcing himself as far as he could go into my throat. Then he would often hold me there, cutting off my ability to breathe for several moments saying many perverted things under his breath. I was terrified he intended to smother me with his manhood since I could not even signal him that I could hold my breath no longer.

He pulled me off him several times to spit in my mouth. This revolting behavior of his made no sense at all to me. Thanks to the fact that I could not swallow, there was tons of my own spittle pouring everywhere from this horrid sex act. I found the whole act not only humiliating, but painful (my throat was sore for a week), and beyond disgusting.

Just when I was sure I couldn't take another second of this nightmare, he pulled out and let go of my head. Without any gentleness he kicked me in the side, sending the boy to the floor. Master Drexel lit on the flesh grabbing me by my upper arm forcing me to my face bottom up. He turned my head, so I didn't smother him, then took his mount without any mercy.

I endured his brutal, harsh thrusting doing the best I could to think of other things. The pain of it kept me from ignoring it completely like I had hoped to do. The bastard was so rough I was sure he was bound to puncture something and send me to my grave. Had I been able to speak I would have begged him to be a bit easier with his lust, but as it was all I could do was pray he was quick.

I have told you I don't believe in any fucking Gotts. That night I was not disappointed. My prayers were not answered. Master Drexel decided he wanted to enjoy all the positions of sex he could within his restriction of the spreader bar and my paralysis. I was forced to endure his drawn-out sexual assault where each time he was reaching his apex, he would stop, reposition me, then begin his intercourse with me all over again. I was near madness by the time he began to cry out that he was "cuming."

I closed my eyes in relief that this horror was nearly over. Then realized with great excitement I closed them by my own power. I was thrilled, despite Master Drexel still being in the throes of his brutal sex with me, that at last I was awakening.

Master Drexel moaned out then finally reached his orgasm with much racket. I ignored him by focusing on moving anything I could. To my dismay I found that only my eyelids and jaw appeared to be working under my control.

I flexed my face muscles around the mouth gag and blinked to distract me from his foul statements of lust. Then to make my humiliation complete he withdrew his couple and violated me further with his fingers in the most perverted ways. *I swear to you Meine Liebe, if he had not been my Master, I would have killed him the second I was able. He was nothing but a fucking schwuler pig.*

I thought to myself that seduction of this foul beast was going to be a real challenge. I had no intention of ever going through this torture with him in the future. There was no fucking reason for him to trap me like this in the first place. I can go into a catatonic like trace anytime I want. Doing that would grant me the mercy of not being aware of any of his outrageous interests with me. This bullshit of shooting me up with paralytic drugs was not only dangerous for ending my ability to breath, but it was also psychologically damaging as hell.

I laid there unable to prevent his nasty violations of the boy. I distracted myself by thinking of ways to convince this idiot that he needed to leave his needles in his purse. I thought of the nipple piercing and wondered if maybe this was not something I could use to bring him to the table for an agreement, or at least a demonstration, with me before he came at me again like this. I knew I would lose my shit if this ever happened to me again.

Finally, he tired of his sickening games with the flesh. He removed his spreader bar and spider gag, then laid down next to me pulling me into deep kissing. This time I was able to respond back clumsily. That surprised him apparently. He pulled away then looked into my eyes.

"You can move?" He waited for me to say something or respond.

I blinked but could do nothing more.

He furrowed his brow at that. "It has only been two hours, Mad Maxx. You shouldn't be able to move anything yet. That metabolism of yours is too fast. I need more than three hours at a time to enjoy my rights with my collar. I would give you more of my drugs, but I fear it may stop your breathing. This is not good news for either of us. I don't like my lovers to move or react. I also like to take my time without feeling rushed. If I cannot drug you to stillness, then I see no use for you in my bed. This is most disturbing. I will need to think on this problem." He got up and took up his restraining tool leaving me there still helpless to await his next nightmarish attack.

While I awaited Master Drexel's return, I found I could move my jaw fully but with much effort. My shoulders would quiver with total focus and my right toes trembled. I could also make soft noises in my throat but no words. I managed to roll my head every other attempt. I was coming back from total paralysis pretty fast but not quickly enough as far as I was concerned.

I was working hard to return the boy's control to the wheel when I heard Master Drexel returning. I stopped my attempts to do anything. I thought it better I play completely paralyzed just in case he decided to shoot me up with more of his numbing cocktail. He made it clear he was most unhappy about my hurried recovery. I was in no hurry to end up completely helpless again or worse overdosed in his selfish efforts to continue his molestations without my right to choose.

I sent the boy into a trance by holding real still staring without blinking as if still drugged to the gills. My Master came close to me looking me over. He snorted then kicked me onto my side. I was not able to respond much at all yet so not responding to that openly was not hard to do. Inside though, I have to admit, I was doing some cussing. That foot of his fucking hurt.

"Well, this is good news. I thought for sure that you had awakened. I guess it was just the random movement that some have from time to time. I see that the drug is holding despite my fears. You are under my spell deep as when I first stuck you with my needles. Speaking of needles, I need to remove my bars, ja?" He reached down and slid his needles from my nipples chuckling at his taking cruel liberties like this with me.

Then I heard someone else entering the room. I willed myself to stay in this "fake trancing" despite a sudden terror that Master Drexel had invited others over. I could not fight off anyone with only the slight use of my jaw, blinking, and small twitches.

I saw Olaf and Vilber suddenly standing over me with smiles on their faces. I immediately heated up with much anger within. I was getting tired of these two showing up every time I was suffering tortures most foul. I began to wonder if every Elder had their numbers on their "call if you need help fucking over Mad Maxx" rolodex.

Olaf snorted. "Well Drexel, he looks stiff to me. I mean Vilber and I don't mind aiding you in moving him, but I don't think you're going to need much restraining muscle this time. The boy is out cold still."

Master Drexel joined them staring down into me frozen eyes. "Ja, I think I panicked over nothing but a random reflex behavior. Since you two are here pick him up and haul him to the spare bathroom. Wash off this paint. I want to start over with a new color. It looks like I have enough time for one more masterpiece before the drugs wear off and ruin the fun. Hurry this up, then bring him back to me. I'm going to choose another paint and maybe a different set of the needles. I bet I can pierce him through that chastity device without much trouble. You can stick around after you bathe him to assist by holding him up for my pleasure, ja?"

Olaf chuckled with evil, "Sure thing Drexel. Whatever you need, Vilber and I are your men. Hey brother you grab his legs, I got his shoulders." The brutes fanned out and lifted me from the floor.

The two black collars carried me to Master Drexel's spare bathroom. I was alone and heavily drugged to stillness in their care without any supervision from my fucking idiot Master. I knew this would not likely have a good outcome for me. I continued to keep my eyes fixed and maintained my silence hoping against hope the brutes would just do their jobs honestly without taking any advantage of my helpless state.

At first, I thought that day had decided to just mind my Master's orders without any funny business. The black collars sat me on the floor leaning me up against the wall. Vilber started the water in the shower and Olaf dug in the vanity for towels. I sighed a breath of relief over their appearing to be task oriented only. Then Olaf threw the towels on the floor, turned, and closed the door locking it behind him. I felt my mouth going dry. That sinister move right there was bothersome.

Olaf tapped Vilber on the shoulder then said, "Okay fuck this. Mad Maxx cannot scream, fight nor run. I say we have some fun with him, then smother this sonofabitch once and for all. Just think Vilber, we can finally be free of him. What do you say brother? You in or out?"

Vilber turned and looked at me sitting there staring at him. "Olaf, I am sick of him too, but killing him? That is a bit much, don't you think? Hell, he will be dead soon enough. Two nights ago, we saw him tortured near to death and tonight he is shot up with Drexel's poisons. This fucking kid can't last long with all these old fuckers messing him up like this every few nights. Why not just wait until they end him? No need to risk ourselves over this nothing silver collar."

I heard that shit loud and clear. Vilber had never liked me, just as I suspected. He was not against seeing me dead. He just didn't want to get his hands bloody doing it. It took all I had not to groan out at my sadness that not even he had ever liked me. That was a nasty blow, but I had already started to suspect it when I saw him aiding Barnim in his torture.

Olaf scoffed at that. "Ficken Dich Vilber. I want to be the one that sends this bastard to hell. This situation is perfect. Think on it a moment. He will know it was us that killed him. You are aware Drexel's medication allows them to feel, see, and hear brother. In fact, we kind of have to end this idiot now that he has heard anything I said. If we let him come out of this, he will surely tell that fucking freak Vampire or Claus. Do you want to taste the chains or worse, just speaking our minds? I don't."

Vilber suddenly looked afraid. "Oh hell. Your right Olaf. I forgot he is paralyzed only. Gott damn it. We are in a lot of trouble. This little motherfucker is sure to tell. I suppose you are right. We must take him out to still his tongue for all time. Drexel will think he overdosed him like he has done so many times with all the others. Better hurry up and get to finishing him off though before that weirdo comes to see what is taken so long."

Olaf smiled widely with much joy in his expression. "Ja, now you're talking sense, Vilber. About fucking time. Okay, but look before I smother him, I want to fuck him for a minute. Then when we pounded on his chest to make it look like we tried to resuscitate him I poked out his eyes. I tell you I hate them since the first time I saw him."

Vilber let out his breath looking at the door nervously. "Fine, get to it but hurry up damn it. We really don't have time for all this bullshit, Olaf. I wish you'd just let me cut off his air instead of all this perverted stuff."

Olaf came to me. "Get over here and hold his head a minute. I want a taste of a Priceless Vilber. Whatever the hell this boy has, it drove Peter near mad. It made Barnim jump from the banister. Jonas, Claus and Bladrick have become fools over him. Xavier died trying to break him. You really going to pass up an opportunity to find out what the hell was so special about sex with this strange scarred up kid? Open his mouth and I will start there, then we can flip him over and solve this mystery, ja?" Vilber came over and grabbed me by the hair on top of my head while Olaf undid his pants.

Vilber forced my mouth open wincing at the scene of rape unfolding. "You can fuck him, then tell me later about your discoveries. We don't have enough time to grant me a turn so you will have to make it count for us both. I say hurry up, then I strangle him. No more fucking Mad Maxx to deal with anymore."

Olaf laughed. "You're a true friend, Vilber. I owe you one for allowing me this pleasure." He forced his manhood into my mouth harshly letting out a moan of thrill.

Vilber held my jaw tight while Olaf thrust with brutality holding my head by my hair. I closed my eyes then focused all my will on my mouth. With all I had, I bit down with all the strength I could pull from my soul. I broke loose of Vilber's hold on me and firmly gripped Olaf's cock with my eager teeth.

The brute Olaf let out a wail of agony. I refused to let go my hold of his dick even as he reflexively punched me in my face several times. Vilber panicked and tried to pull me backward off his partner's prick. This only served to let my embedded teeth pull the surface skin off his part. Olaf screamed even louder in pure pain of the most heinous kind.

Vilber finally came to his senses. He wrapped his arm around my neck then pinched my nose, cutting off my air. I was forced to open my mouth for a breath within a few minutes or perish from smothering in his grips. I had to unclamp my teeth from Olaf's near severed cock thanks to this trick.

Olaf fell backward, holding his bloody groin crying out wildly. Vilber let me go. He threw my still paralyzed flesh to the floor running to aid his partner. I heard Master Drexel began beating on the door sounding upset while demanding that the door be unlocked at once.

Vilber shot a terrified look at me. For a moment I thought he may come try to finish me off rather than mind my Master's increasingly angered commands. I glared back at him daring him to come end me the way he wanted to. I made damned sure my gaze conveyed if he didn't, I was fucking going to end him and that Gott damned Olaf the second I got half a chance.

Instead, he whispered to Olaf, "Put your cock into your pants, idiot. Don't say a fucking word. Let me do all the talking, fool. You should have just let me kill the demon. I told you there is something wrong with this boy. The Devil owns his soul. You cannot fuck with Satan's spawn without getting your ass burned." Olaf groaned but did as Vilber demanded.

He did his best to get to his knees. I watched him trembling and breathing hard in front of me. I saw his hands were covered in blood as was the front of his pants. He looked up at me. I smiled then winked at him with wickedness in my eyes. Then to his horror I stuck out my tongue and licked my lips, clearing up his crimson fluid on them.

Olaf's look of terror was enough to make up for his sexual assault. I was sure I could live a thousand nights with the memory of his frightening eyes. He finally understood that I was indeed the Demon that Vilber had tried to warn him I was all along. Olaf knew that for him, the reaper would be wearing my own face. He and Vilber were dead men. The brutes clocks were now ticking down to their sunset.

Vilber opened the door to the railing Master Drexel. That pervert came rushing inside to find Olaf on his knees, me on my side, and his hot water running into an empty tub. He looked at Vilber that stood there with his eyes to the floor, sweating bullets.

"What the hell is going on in here? I heard shouting and crying. Why is their blood on my collars face. Olaf? You hit my property?" His gaze settled on Olaf's red hands.

Vilber spoke up with extreme steadiness. "Nein Drexel, the collar went into a seizure. Olaf was trying to keep him from swallowing his tongue but got bitten in the process. The Grand Mal was powerful. I fear he may be a bit confused and disoriented when he comes out of his state of paralysis because of it. I have seen such a thing before from others that you brought down like this."

Master Drexel nodded. "Ja, seizures do happen, so what? Mad Maxx seems okay now. Wait, maybe another can happen quickly. This gets on my nerves. I like peaceful places. If you two are done with the stupidity and yelling, then get him into the shower and clean off that paint like I told you to. I will stay here and keep an eye on him in case he goes into the spasms again. Get to it. I don't like all this noise or movement. There are too many living people in this apartment for my peace. I want you two out of here as soon as my collar is cleaned up. Hurry this up, damn you."

Vilber pulled the injured Olaf to his feet. "Get up, brother. You heard Drexel. Help me get this silver cleaned up."

I sat up suddenly then slowly turned my head to look at the stunned Drexel. That I could move surprised me as much as it did him. "I can bathe myself, Master. Thank you for the mercy." I choked out with some mild coughing from the cruelty shown to my throat by those men. The rat bastards Drexel and Olaf were on my shit list for truth.

Vilber stared at me while Olaf closed his eyes taking deep breaths, appearing to be in a great deal of pain. "The seizure must have awakened Mad Maxx."

I turned my attention to him with a big evil smile breaking across my face. "What the hell are you doing here? When did you arrive? How did I get into this bathroom? I cannot remember anything."

The black collars shot looks of confusion to each other. I reached out my still half numb arm and pulled myself up to stand. Then with a mild limp I got into the shower and closed the curtain ignoring all of them. I wanted that crap paint off me and Drexel out of me that second.

The truth was I had already tired of dealing with them. I was gonna kill all three in due time, so there was no reason to spend any more than necessary in their company. I see no value in talking to dead men.

I had already swore I would bury the black collar brutes outside the Haus doors, and Master Drexel? I was going to make damned sure he would soon be in a place where the living could bother him no longer. This schwuler could not be seduced thanks to his unnatural affections that threatened my life, plus he was beyond disgusting. I believed he may even enjoy being fucking dead but first I needed to kill another. You see, I couldn't have both

Hemmel and Leo rising. I didn't need five Masters. I thought even four was four too many.

You see, it seemed to me that the shit in the Haus kept rising to the top. Well luckily, Meine Liebe, I had lots of experience with the enema by this time. It seemed that an expert with such a cleansing device was just what this place needed, ja? I nodded my head that I agreed it was time for my Master Mad Maxx to clean the Haus.

I finished my shower while the three men stood their scratching their heads. None of them knew what to do about the boy's early and unexpected recovery. I let that hot water run down the flesh ignoring the biting, burning, and sharp pains being reported from almost every inch of me. That damned paralytic drug Master Drexel put into me tingled within my tissues, making an already agonizing situation worse. I was ready to blow my gaskets, there was no doubt. I had enough of this bullshit for truth. Heads were about to roll.

When I stepped out of that tub Vilber handed me a towel, staring at me with a dumbfounded expression on his face. I snatched that damned thing from his hands, then glared at Olaf. That brute was doing his best to not demonstrate the horrible pain his cock plagued him with.

I began to dry off, never taking my eyes off him. "You know what, Master. I think I need a bit of a stroll to walk off the medication you gave me. Could I beg your mercy to borrow your men here for an escort. I only need a short one, maybe only down this hallway and back? I need to collect a piece of art that I believe you will find pleasurable from Master Jonas's apartment." Olaf and Vilber shot frightened looks at each odder.

Master Drexel smiled at me perking up from his brooding "You say you have some artwork for me to view? Now this sounds interesting indeed."

I smiled most brutally while still staring at Olaf. "Ah, ja. I can assure you Master; this may be a masterpiece of your dreams. I would of course be honored to have an artist of your lofty character to look and let me know if this is not the most sublime of anything you ever set your sights on."

My Master nearly squealed in delight. "I must see this thing of which you speak, Mad Maxx. Ja, take Olaf and Vilber out of here and get this beautiful item. You brutes, go with my collar and see that he obtains my work of art safely."

I nodded. "I will need my robe Master, unless you desire, I wander the Haus naked. May I please go get it?"

Master Drexel smiled while looking sheepish. "Oh, meine Gott. Of course, get the robe, Mad Maxx. Olaf and Vilber will await you at the front door. Will it take long to get this piece of art?"

I pushed my way past the stunned black collars. "About thirty minutes, Master. I will hurry, so I can assure you. Perhaps you can collect that next color of paint for my flesh while you wait?"

Master Drexel nodded. "I can stay busy. You hurry up. Get going."

I rushed to the statue room. I grabbed my robe and then snatched that fucking green clutch purse of my Master. I dropped it into the pocket of the robe while sliding on my slippers. I would not tolerate being shot up again by this beast. He would notice it had gone missing, but I was not worried. The artwork I was bringing back would make him forget all about his nasty syringe tricks. I rushed to the door with my deadly escorts. They didn't know it, but I was about to make them keep their vows to serve me or find themselves growing a fucking tree in the Gott damned yard.

I allowed the two big black collars to go out first. I followed closely behind. No one spoke a word as we headed for Master Jonas's apartment. When I was certain we were out of earshot of Master Drexel's door I halted my steps.

"Both of you can stop right this fucking minute, you bastards," I said with force to the brutes.

They stopped and turned around looking at me with anger in their eyes. Olaf had been limping and Vilber had been sullen until this point. I could see they still wanted me dead more than anything on Earth. Luckily, I had a way for them to pay me back for the service they stole while getting that blood lusting off their chests at the same time.

"What are you waiting for? Go ahead and tell the Elders about what happened back there in the bathroom. Do you think they will believe you, Mad Maxx? No one cares about what comes out of that pretty mouth of yours, only what goes into it," Olaf growled out while grabbing his crotch moaning under his breath.

I chuckled full of demons. "Oh? Well, I guess now you know how great I am at sucking cock, ja? How'd you like that blow job service motherfucker? Tell you what, I get on my knees right here and we can finish what we started? Or have you had enough of your taste of the Priceless? Oh wait, this time the Priceless tasted you, didn't he?"

"Ficken Dich, Mad Maxx," Olaf bellowed.

"Here I am, you rat bastard. You can try to fuck me if there is anything left of your prick to do it with." I threw out my arms baiting him to come at me again and see if he didn't get the same results of it.

Vilber winced at that. "Look both of you cut the bullshit. Mad Maxx, are you going to tell Jonas on Olaf and me? Is that why we are headed to his apartment? Olaf is a fool, but I am not. I know all you have to do is claim this thing happened and this idiot's cock carries the proof of it. What will it take to keep your mouth shut and let this incident slide into memory?"

I laughed at that. "You bet I will keep what you both did in my memory, fucker. As for what will keep my mouth shut, well that is easy. I want you to kill Dungeon Master Hemmel. This very night. I don't care how you do it, just make that bastard is worm food. Otherwise, we go wake up Jonas. What is the penalty for the rape of a silver by the black collars, I seem to forget."

Olaf scoffed. "It is death for the silver and the black, fool. You tell Jonas then the Haus kills your dumbass right next to us."

I shook my head. "Ah, but you are wrong there. Vilber, my dear, do you want to educate your dense brother on why if I tell my Master Jonas about this raping shit, you both grow grass, but Mad Maxx will be watering it only?"

Vilber looked at the floor with fatigue. "Olaf, you're the fool. Mad Maxx is a Priceless. The Haus never kills them outright unless they kill someone. If that boy tells his Husband, we are dead. The Guard will use us as fertilizer."

260

I smiled. "You better listen to Vilber, Olaf. For a change he seems to have a brain. Now, the clock is ticking. I want Dungeon Master Hemmel to find his peace before the sunrise. I would run to make sure that happens if I were you. I have to return to Master Drexel for now. When I collect his morning tray, I better be hearing that the worthless Hemmel died in his fucking sleep, or I know two black collars that will find their eternal rest."

Olaf growled. "Pick another task to pay back the blow job, Mad Maxx. How is killing a man equal fucking service."

I turned around to return to Master Drexel apartment "You are dumb as you look, Olaf. If I tell, two men die. I demand the life of this perverted Dominant to save two worthless ones. It is more than a fair trade. Don't do it and I say it has been a pleasure. One way or another the fields demand blood. It matters not if it be you or Hemmel. I will get him later on my own anyway."

Vilber called out to the retreating boy. "Wait a minute, Mad Maxx. We kill this Hemmel, and we are even again? This situation is paid for and dropped?"

I turned around for a moment. "Ja, you kill him, I keep my mouth shut like it should have been left tonight around you Olaf. However, you forgot that I told you when you made your oath to be loyal to me in Peter apartment if you ever betrayed me, I would kill you. Consider yourself on borrowed time Vilber. Olaf you too. When I break my collar, I'm going to kill you where you stand and bury you outside the Haus doors with my own hands. See you in the morning or maybe not, up to you. good night brutes." I turned back around and rushed back to my Master's apartment leaving the upset black collars to contemplate their fates.

You see I had decided to raise Leo to replace the dead Barnim. The reason was quite simple. When Cora, Gretta, Peter, and Leo had started their game to gain Cora the Head seat of the Haus, all were supposed to profit if it succeeded. I noticed that Cora once raised put Peter and Gretta on the seats of the voting counsel. Leo had been neglected of any elevation in status for some reason. I could only guess that the other three had not trusted him enough to take him along for their ride.

This surely had old Leo feeling damned neglected, angered and no longer in line to go anywhere in the Haus. I had been aware of his lustful advances toward me since the early days of Peter's reign. Back then the idea of that nasty schwuler fucking me made my blood run cold in my veins. I had even once taken punishment to avoid having to suck the motherfucker's cock. I had chosen to give Peter head rather than submit to his desires to have me for his intercourse.

Well, I no longer had quarrel with enduring any nasty sexual assault if it would assure my eventual freedom from my collar. Leo had both the potential for my easy seduction and the anger to break off ties with those who left him behind. If I could demonstrate that I had elevated him to the position just under this Cora, well his loyalty would be assured. If nothing else, he would fear the wrath of Master Jonas if he dared to fuck me over.

Master Hemmel on the other hand had tried to uncollar me, called the Guard on me, and beat the holy piss out of me for eight months. I was helpless in a straight jacket, leashed to the wall, and still he used a heavy hand. This sadistic bastard did all this because Peter paid him. He was the pansexual and not a schwuler so seduction was possible but could prove difficult. Though reasons alone made him a worst choice than Leo, but the biggest excuse to send this sonofabitch to the orchard was simpler. He knew I had been diagnosed with schizophrenia. That information could put me on his leash rather than the other way around.

I had decided I not only would not raise him to the status of Elder, but I needed his mouth shut for good. That attack by Olaf and Vilber gave me the leverage to end Dungeon Master Hemmel's threat to my continued dash for the front door. With those two doing the dirty work on this murder, I could focus my attention on Master Drexel. Then I could move on to capture Leo's loyalty the second my rounds finished with Claus the next day.

I smiled with great joy that in a short while Master Hemmel would be no more. I was a bit disappointed his eyes would not see that I reached out to send that fucker to hell where he belongs, but hey you can't get anything you want.

I knew Olaf and Vilber would make sure the deed was done. They had no choice. Both knew me well enough to realize if they failed, I would stop at nothing to see them dead themselves. They didn't fear I could kill them when I broke my metal. The black collars, like everyone else that was over twenty in the Haus, knew what I had refused to believe. No silver ever sees the bolt cutters unless they are well born.

Olaf and Vilber didn't think I'd live long enough to even see the collar selection, Vilber made that clear in Master

Drexel's bathroom. Too bad for them, I was going to be an exception to the expected. I made a vow to them I would kill them the second I was free of my subjugation. Of course, you know Meine Liebe, I am a man of my word.

I took out that green clutch full of sharps and paralytic drugs and hid it under a fake plant in the fancy hallway. I then returned to Master Drexel's door and knocked lightly. The old creepy schwuler came to let me in before I could knock a second time. I saw him searching the flesh seeking out this work of art I had promised him. I merely chuckled and walked inside right past his curious eyes. I took a seat on that hideous orange cube couch of his. I think it was a couch, this guy was super weird.

Master Drexel stood there with his arms crossed, becoming angered rapidly. "Well? Where the hell is this Masterpiece you promised me, Mad Maxx? I also would like to know if you took my sharps pouch. I cannot find it anywhere. You know stealing from your Master is a serious crime. I could have you taken to the chains for it."

I nodded while smiling at him. "Ja, you could. I wonder though if after I am punished if you would still be allowed in the rotation? I do believe you committed a crime of your own, Master. Your agreement with my Masters said no flesh penetration. My chest tells me that you broke this contract. I seem to recall the penalty is also quite stiff. In fact, stiffer than your syringes made me. I took your medication in equal payment for the service you stole. I will keep them and neither of us need to suffer any further punishment. I say that with respect."

Master Drexel appeared incensed by my words. "How dare you? I am your Master. You don't have the right to demand anything from me. I own you."

I clicked my tongue. "Oh, now there you are wrong Master. You don't own me. I am your submissive but not your slave. You were at the collaring ceremony, I do recall. You're honor bond to provide equal services in return for the services I provide for your pleasure. You punctured my flesh. I took your sharps because you gave them to me. I have the fucking wounds to prove it. Perhaps we awaken Master Claus. He is the acting Head of the Haus. I think we should ask him for a ruling on this. I think I have the right to things you stick into me. You seem to believe you can do such brutality without paying me for my pain. What do you think? Master Claus will surely be capable of settling your breaking of the Elder agreement of the Priceless silver."

Master Drexel's eyes lit up with fires of fury. "You little bastard. Are you threatening me? If you are then I would be afraid if I were you. I can have you trapped in the collar with only a flick of my wrist. Then I can spend my life waiting for another chance to fuck you up. Do you know who you are pissing off Mad Maxx, or does your name say it all?"

I shrugged. "Master, I do not intend to insult you, threaten you, nor end your right to my services to you. I simply say you punctured me, and I took back what was owed. Nothing more and nothing less."

Master Drexel scoffed. "Okay, then keep them. I care not a bit. I can get more of them without any effort. Then next time, I maybe give you enough to stop that breathing of yours. Still willing to piss me off?"

I dropped my eyes to the floor at that. "I see I have anger you, Master, but that is not my intention either. Now I do owe you a service to replace your pleasure of peace and quiet. Oh, I know what. If you come with me to the room of statues, I can show you that work of art I promised you. Is this a fair trade ja?"

Master Drexel fumed a few moments, but his curiosity got the best of him. "Fine, but I warn you though. If this art is not everything you swore to me, I will be tempted to throw you over the banister to join that pig Barnim. Get up and stop stalling. I want to see this art you claim is so fucking fantastic it will bring me to tears of joy."

I stood up with a smile. "As you wish, Master." I followed the nasty Elder down his hallway listening to him grumbling under his breath while calling me many foul names.

That wasn't very nice either. This man had only an hour before been most intimate with me in almost all ways possible between us and already he was ready to call it quits. Well, you just can't please some people. I must say the way he was speaking about me I began to think he didn't even like me a little bit. I had decided to let him live if he was able to appreciate my artistic skills, but the way he was grumbling I was starting to believe maybe I would kill him even if he did.

Anyway, we entered the statue room and as before he stopped in the center. He turned then crossed his arms like he always does this.

"Where is this artwork, Mad Maxx? You are really starting to piss me the fuck off." He was already pissed off.

I glared at him full of fury of my own. "If you wanted a fucking human statue, Master, all you had to do is ask me. I am the Priceless. I have powers you cannot even imagine in your most fevered dreams. You say to me that no matter what you do there is no way to capture perfection from real life. I say to you Mad Maxx can. I will demonstrate this skill for you. You saw it in Master Jonas's apartment. I will become your statue on command. I will not move, speak, nor give you quarrel. However, when I become this for you my limbs are not only posable, but they also stay that way no matter the awkwardness of it. In a moment I will demonstrate this art for you but first, I warn you, if you pierce my flesh anywhere again, I will not have to tell anyone about you. This trance I go into can become dangerous if I am awakened too suddenly. You hurt me like that, I will likely kill you with my bare hands before I can stop myself. You vow to me this minute to never do such cruelty and I will make all your darkest dreams come to truth."

Master Drexel's eyes went wide "What is this you say? No one can do what you say. I have had many try to act but they always give way or wear out of the pose." I interrupted him rudely.

"I asked you to vow no piercing nor breaching the contract, Master. Do that and I will show you I can do the impossible. I didn't ask you to just take my fucking word like you expect me to," I growled out at him.

He flinched at my sudden aggression. "Ja, okay, I vow I will never break my agreement regarding the brother's Priceless collar again. There, now show me. I don't believe a word of it."

I smiled, calming immediately. "One more thing before I become the living statue of your desires. I must be awakened by a sudden drop in temperature. A cold shower will do the trick. You need not call any aid. If you take my leash and pull me hard, I will follow you mindlessly. Take me to the tub, turn it to full cold, then force me in it. I will come to in short order. Just back up, sometimes I spasm wildly. Are you ready?"

Master Drexel scoffed. "I have been fucking ready for some time now."

I nodded then closed my eyes. Maximillian and I split apart rapidly. We secured the wheel so it would stand on its own without orders from its shards. Then we took each other's hand and bailed out of the boy. We hit the ground free of the flesh at last. I turned around to see Mad Maxx staring into the nothing. He was standing perfectly still, unable to do anything without another there to move him from the outside. His head was empty without any guidance.

Maximillian and I watched the bastard trying to speak to the catatonic boy. We giggled a great deal when the Elder finally approached him and backhanded the flesh. It didn't move an inch nor react. Master Drexel gasped at that, then grabbed his wrist pulling it out straight. The boy's arm didn't return. He stood there holding it out, never appearing to tire of the position.

Master Drexel tried to get Mad Maxx to flinch, cry out, or stagger on his own. After about thirty minutes he finally realized we were indeed the human statue of his wildest fantasies. He let out squeals of joy. We kept our hawk eyes on him as he positioned the boy in various poses. He was in obvious thrill upon finding he held them exactly, never complaining nor moving out of them. No matter how impossible or uncomfortable appearing Master Drexel found his living work of art more than willing to comply.

When the Master rushed off to grab his easel and canvas. Apparently, he was eager to paint rather than violate us again, thank Gott. Maximillian looked at me with a yawn.

"I was kind of hoping we would have to kill this bastard. I am going to get a fucking shower brother. You mind watching this idiot for a bit?" He stretched and yawned again.

I nodded then felt my own yawn coming on. "Ja, I watch for now, but I get that shower next. Hey, did we pack a toothbrush?"

Maximillian chuckled while dropping to the floor appearing suddenly sleepy. "I think we forgot it. No matter. We use our finger like with Bladrick. I am such a tired brother. I think I will nap a second before that shower. You watch first, then I spell you soon, ja?" He closed his eyes, appearing to fall asleep before I could even answer him.

I sat down next to him, feeling a terrible fatigue filling me as well, I did my best to keep my eyes open, but something was wrong. I couldn't stay awake. I slid to the floor next to Maximillian drifting away to wait a minute. Shards cannot sleep outside the flesh. No one would be there to take the wheel when Master Drexel ran that cold water. The boy wouldn't be able to awaken if I couldn't stay awake. I did my very best to hold off the coming slumber, but I was just so beaten.

Chapter 38: Out with the Old and in with the Old

I have no memory of what happened for the next twenty-one hours of being within Master Drexel's clutches. Over the years I have done my best to recover the time, but nein. When we fell asleep, the catatonic boy didn't record a damned thing of what happened to it. At least not in our mind. The flesh, however, it told a tale of the cruelest abuses.

Maximillian and I had been worn to exhaustion by the combined brutality of Master Drexel and Master Barnim. We didn't mean to fall into slumber, but there was no stopping it. A tired shard cannot be allowed to run the wheel. That has always been the rule for this very reason. Neither of us realized we were so tapped out. This led to a near disaster for our mission thanks to this idiot statue fucker.

Worst of all, that bastard Master Drexel didn't keep his oath of no piecing our flesh while I was unconscious. He had told Olaf and Vilber he intended to puncture me through the chastity device. He did carry out that threat. Not sure what he used since I took all his sharps but my manhood and hoddensack carried the foul wounds and much pain. He had no issue ignoring the contract of no piercing the skin he had with his brother Elders either. Master Drexel was not a man of honor by a long shot.

There was incredible agony, cuts, bruises, and punctures all over the flesh. Based on the amount of damage discovered by the shards when they re-entered, it was apparent this sonofabitch spent a great deal of time violating the boy with implements of torture most foul. And nothing was off limits. It is beyond disgusting that Master Drexel took complete advantage of a very sick person.

You see Meine Liebe; it turns out this catatonic behavior is a one of the severest symptoms of this disease called schizophrenia. Back then, I didn't know of such things, but looking back on it I can say this Master Drexel had been a truly rotten bastard of the worst kind.

I am grateful that I have no memory of whatever nasty shit he did to me during that missing time though. I am not sure I could live with it if I did know. I cannot stress enough how perverted this cocksucker truly was. A true predator. I think even the mannequins and statues would need therapy after being forced to endure his lustful touching.

When Master Drexel didn't show up at midnight to trade off my leash to Master Claus and Master Bladrick, they came banging on his door. They found the odd schwuler panicking when he had been unable to awaken the flesh in his freezing shower. That selfish bastard had allowed the catatonic stupor to continue too long. Enough time had been allowed to pass to cause Maximillian and I to fall deep into the throws of peaceful sleep. There was no waking us until we had recovered fully.

Had Master Drexel tried to revive us within only four hours, then we could have easily recovered. We had mistakenly assumed he would be a decent human being and revive us for a meal or sleep. If you think of it that would have been almost a full seven hours of our being his living statue. He had not even been concerned when over twelve hours, and then twenty, passed without the boy even blinking.

I was told by Master Claus when I awoke that he attempted backhands and near drowning in the chilly shower. Nothing was stirring me. The three schwulers called Master Jonas, praying that he had some kind of cure for this frightening lack of response.

Master Jonas arrived and found he too couldn't rouse me. The Vampire called in his private doctor while the two eldest Elders blocked Master Drexel in his room threatening him into silence over his accidental discovery of my diagnosis. They informed me the statue pervert was willing to keep his mouth shut but unwilling to lose his new plaything to the Guard over the Haus rule of no mentally ill collars allowed.

The doctor arrived and gave me many shots of valium. For most of the night the four Master's sat around the bed watching the "frozen" Mad Maxx lay in the bed not even blinking.

Der Hund had lost communication with Maximillian and me. He had become worried when neither of us responded to his calling us. This caused him to come out of hiding to check on our welfare. Likely he assumed we had gotten the boy killed. He found us too deep in our slumber to awaken no matter what he tried. Caught in a terrible bind he had no choice but to call in our brother shards Mad Max and Christian.

Der Hund told me he gave Mad Max and Christian strict orders of "no funny business." That was a useless command. The sadist and the anger/lust shard were hell on wheels singularly. Together, well Meine Liebe, that was a full-on disaster waiting to happen. The reaper heard those two jumping into the boy and likely got a hard on. There was no doubt that blood was going to be flowing through the hallways of the Haus. The vicious shards took to the flesh and the boy awakened just before the sunrise. This guaranteed it was the sunset for a few that had it coming.

Christian and I struggled with each other to take the wheel thanks to the crowded space. I was most unhappy that the two schwuler shards decided to take a vacation day when the work of seduction was still far from complete. I told Der Hund that Christian, and I were not the boys to be calling on when it comes to nasty sex with the man, but he would hear none of it.

I looked at my brother sitting there feeling the same disgust as me. "Well, like it or not we have to do the job those pussy Max boys could not."

Christian nodded. "Do you see what they let Master Barnim and Master Drexel do to the boy? I think maybe we should have been called in sooner, brother. This shit right here has got to stop or there won't be anything left to reach the collar selection. This flesh is a mess. Ouch, what the holy hell has this Drexel done to us, brother?"

I had to agree with him that Maximillian and Mad Maxx had allowed things to get out of hand. Stitches, punctures, and foul sexual practices were not acceptable. This was bullshit that even the shitty father of ours never pulled. These idiot Masters were not only disgusting, but they were also not careful with their playthings. Thank Gott, Christian and I were finally there to stop this abuse before it was too late.

I shook my head. "He goes too far, that is what he has done to us. I say we kill this beast immediately. I don't care what Der Hund says. We cannot wait till he gets a second chance to end our life. Besides, are we to go catatonic once a week? I think not. Fuck this schwuler pig."

Christian smiled with murder in his eyes. "I am with you, brother. I even have a plan to end his reign of terror in this Haus. For now, though we must decide if we kill Master Claus and Master Bladrick as well,"

I liked the sound of that, but I knew that too many dead men from the top may bring down the roof on our heads. "Ah, I like the way you're thinking brother, but why waste them when days are already ripe for the buzzards? I say we kill Master Drexel, Master Jonas, Leo, Olaf, Vilber, and hell, let's take out our father Peter too. If we have time, we throw Cora from the banister and stab Gretta in her eyes as well,"

Christian giggled wildly at that. "Carefully speaking dirty to, brother. I am just a young man. I cannot control myself yet. It is too crowded in the boys head for me to gain erection without embarrassment in front of you."

I glared at him with irritation. "You keep that cock to yourself freak. I swear to Gott if you pull any of that nasty schwuler shit with me I will beat you to death and piss on your bones. I am only interested in Annette, fool."

The killer shard smiled with evil. "Ja, Annette. We can go find her. This time I get to fuck her, and you can wait your turn."

I felt a stir of interest in that idea. "Now you're speaking my language. We kill Drexel, then go find Annette. The rest of these idiots can wait their turn to meet our anger till we have curbed our own lust."

Christian nodded with much joy. "Ja, I think this is the greatest plan I ever heard. They are hailing us, brother. Play the role that nothing is amiss and leave the murdering to me." He winked at me with much mischief in his expression.

I opened my eyes to see Master Jonas glaring down at me with a look of concern. He was startled when he saw I was starting to respond on my own at last.

"Oh, Claus. Bladrick. Drexel. Mad Maxx is awake. Love. Can you hear me? If so, nod your head," yelled out Master Jonas in apparent excitement.

I nodded then reached up to grab my forehead. "Ja, I can hear you Master. Not so loud I beg of you. My head is splitting." I groaned out from the agony washing over the flesh from Olaf's blows, Master Barnim's torture, and Master Drexel's god only knows what cruelty.

The other three Masters come running into the room with a look of relief and thrill in their eyes. They assumed their prize was back from the void and ready to resume their game of abuse. Well, those fuckers were wrong this time. I was back alright. Hungry for their blood. I was gonna make them all sorry that they didn't leave me in that statue state forever.

I looked about and realized I was in Master Jonas's bed. It seemed the men had carried me home, then laid me out for their care. I looked down and saw I was naked, as usual the scum, with much left-over paint, bruising and many cuts everywhere. They didn't even bother to clean me up from the foul raping of Master Drexel. This was beyond ridiculous.

I glared at Master Jonas. "I would like to have a shower, Master. It seems I am in a disgusting state of uncleanliness. If you could be so kind to allow this mercy, I would be most grateful."

The four Masters looked at each other appearing confused by my request, then Master Claus answered, "If you think you're strong enough? Mad Maxx you just suffered a serious psychotic attack. You have been out for four days. The doctor thought you were lost to us, Should you not maybe rest a bit longer?"

I sat up with a groan. "I was asleep four days, you say. I think then I have rested enough. I would beg your pardon, Masters, but I am hungry, I feel disgusting, and could use the mercy of some clothing. I think getting out of this bed and into a shower is better medicine than resting another week."

Master Bladrick smiled with glee. "That is my boy. Let him out of this bed Jonas. Claus, call down for a meal. Let Mad Maxx get up. He says he is feeling better. I think we let him do whatever he feels strong enough to do. There is no reason to baby him."

Master Jonas looked at me with some concern. "Bladrick, I think he needs more time for convalescing. We let him continue his rotation with Drexel and look what happened. This boy needs more time off the clock. He is not well,"

Master Drexel scoffed. "There you go again, Jonas. This was not my fault. None of you told me he suffers the madness. I had no idea this was a symptom of it. Had I known things might be different."

Master Claus interrupted him. "You would not have done anything differently had you known. Drexel. You adored this symptom a great deal by the look of the boy. So, I for one desire you to shut the fuck up. Your whining over this past many days has gotten on my last nerve."

Master Drexel crossed his arms. "Ficken Dich, Claus. I would have called all of you right away. I am already beyond angered that all of you knew this shit but kept Drexel out of the mix. That was bullshit and all of you know it. I own this boy as equal as any of you. I think knowing he is an idiot was important information to share."

Master Bladrick growled out in pure irritation. "He is not an idiot, Drexel. He is mentally ill. There is a fucking difference, fool."

Master Drexel snorted. "Is there? Psssst, the boy thinks he is a statue. That is stupid. Call it whatever you want. Dumb is what it is."

Master Claus glared at Master Drexel. "Oh? Mad Maxx goes out of his way to mind his Master's dark desires. He got injured in his attempt to please you, Drexel. That is why he is sick right now. You're the one that loves to fuck the statues and you there to call him the idiot."

Master Jonas put up his hands and yelled out, "Enough, Gott Verdammt. I wasn't pointing any fingers at anyone. Mad Maxx has schizophrenia. He is going to have difficulty from time to time. That is the price we pay for holding the forbidden silver. I told all of you this already. Now, are we going to fight like children or are we going to work together to keep our collar alive and well? I thought we all agreed, as brothers do, this as a team. Are we going to show dishonor and break our vows so quickly?"

The three Elders suddenly hung their heads in shame over Master Jonas's stern statement. They all looked at each other and mumbled quiet apologies for their heated words. I sat there watching the drama feeling more and more irritation building. I cleared my throat loudly causing them to look at me once more.

"I apologize for continuing to repeat myself, but I would like to have that shower, and dress please, Masters? I think I have earned it." I said with force in my tone.

Master Jonas nodded. "Ja, okay you may get out of this bed for your hygiene and dressing, but I must insist to be at your side. You may fall or otherwise injure yourself, Mad Maxx."

I glowered at that bullshit right there. He is a fucking pervert. "As you wish, Master. I thank you for your mercy." I said without meaning a word of it.

He moved out of my way. It took all I had to pull the flesh out of that bed and get to Master Jonas's bathroom. That fucking Master Drexel really fucked the boy up. Cocksucker that he was, the Vampire was hot on my heels.

I was able to get that most refreshing shower, though I admit the work of cleansing was slower than a snail's pace. I let that water roll down our flayed, bruised flesh like a mother's milk to a starving kid. I was really starting to love the bathtub. If only I could live in one maybe for my entire life, it would have improved slightly.

When I finished, Master Jonas handed me a towel. He never took his eyes off me, not even when I brushed my teeth and attended my other hygiene rituals. The Vampire Elder stood leaning up against the wall, silent as death watching me like the predator he is. Downright nerve wracking if you ask me.

When at last I felt like a shiny new penny, that had been run over by a train, I may add, I limped down the hallway to the room with a grey door. I turned around to see Master Jonas following me. This guy was not going to give me a fucking bit of privacy, that sonofabitch. I reached into my closet and quickly picked one of his Vampire outfits to cover my nakedness.

He sat on my small bed while I dressed, then did my best to cover the bruises and cuts all over my face with the makeup he had given me. When I finished this long process, I almost looked like a human again, albeit an undead one. He smiled at me when I grabbed my hat then limped over and knelt at his feet to demonstrate I was through with my tasks.

"Ah, your beauty always takes my breath away my love. I was beyond horrified to see what that dreadful Drexel and criminal Barnim did to my treasure. Yet, a little soap, water and makeup fixes a world of sins, ja?" He grabbed my chin to hold up my bowed head closely looking over my artistry with his powders and eye pencils.

I did my best to swallow down my intense irritation at his statement that a little illusion made all this horror done to me alright. "Thank you for the mercy, Master. If you could be so kind, I would be very hungry. May I please have something to eat?" My stomach felt as if it had shrunk, then kicked many times, the hunger was so bad.

Master Jonas nodded with a large smile. "I am most happy to grant that request, my love. You have refused food for all four days. I would love nothing more than to see you eat until you bust. I know that Claus wanted to call in the meal, but I think I have a better idea. Let's go to the Grand Hall for our dinner. It is time the Haus sees that the Elders are now the most blessed men in this place. Of course, that is if you feel up to such excitement?" His eyes searched my face for his answer.

I smiled back realizing everyone – except the Elders, Olaf, Vilber and Peter – thought me long dead. "As you wish Master. I feel strong enough to attend the Great Hall, but I will need to eat soon. I am worried that this light headedness could cause issues if not dealt with quickly." I was aware that going without food for all those days was not a smart move.

Despite my less than perfect health, I was happy to be offered the chance to leave the Elders' floor at last. I had always hated trips to the Great Hall with Peter. The only good thing I could be assured when we went there was hearing all the gossip. I needed hearing of the death or fine health of a certain Dungeon Master. I dared not ask about such things outright at of risk being tied to his death if the black collars did their job.

If no discussion of the untimely demise of Hemmel was mentioned over the plates of supper, then I had dark work of ending the existence of the two big brutes immediately. *Hey, I am a man of my word, right Meine Leibe? Huh? I cannot hear you. Ah, not speaking I see. Damn, I was hoping to get to swat you. You are getting better at knowing your place I see. Too bad for Mad Max.*

Master Jonas grinned showing all his pointed teeth. "You will sit right next to you Husband and eat right off my plate, my love. Let this Haus be shocked, stand on their heads, and made to wish they were so fucking lucky as the Elders."

I nodded smiling back with much evil in my expression. "Your pleasure is my own, Master. I will grab a coat and follow your commands. Thank you for this mercy." I got up and selected the long black coat with a hidden pocket just inside the crimson liner. Master Jonas gasped when I turned around with a look of adoration on his face.

"You take my breath away, my love. I swear I have never seen anything more magnificent in all my long days. To think you are all mine, well mostly all mine." He frowned, appearing to be thinking about that but took up my leash, then lead me down the hallway to the living area.

He took no time to greet his brothers with his latest idea. All the Elders became excited at that. They would finally getting to show off their "plaything." The need to incite the jealousy of others is rampant among the Dominants of all levels. I have never understood this need but then again, I think they are all the ones that are crazy.

They all wanted me to believe I have this schizophrenia shit, but between you and me, I must tell you I am not insane. I was just navigating a weird world. The second I got a break from them I was perfectly fine. You see I am not sick at all. These people are the schizophrenics, and the Haus is their insane asylum. Somehow, I got stuck in there, maybe by accident I am not sure. Whatever the mix up, it was indeed most disturbing to grow up around so many madmen. Thank Gott it never did rub off too much. You know that nutball shit can be contagious if you're not careful. Mad Max was not contaminated but I think Maximillian maybe wasn't so lucky. I swear that shard is not only schwuler, but he is also bent in all the wrong places too.

Anyway, as I was saying, the Elders all went cuckoo over this idea of showing off their Priceless collar in the Great Hall. Master Jonas told them to hurry to their apartments and dress for this "historic stepping out of the Elders.' I quietly dropped to a kneel awaiting my Masters orders, unsure of who was the current holder of the leash.

Master Drexel, Master Claus, and Master Bladrick all rushed from Master Jonas's apartment to change into their finest outfits. Master Jonas chuckled as he watched the excited old men rush off like Frau who were just told their dream husband had called seeking a date with them.

He stole a look at me kneeling there. "Normally, Christian Axel, I would have you aid me in dressing but today only I give you a break. You sit on that couch and relax. I worry this may be too much excitement too soon, but I trust you will notify you Husband if such fatigue overcomes you at any time during this trip. In fact, I make that a directive. I'll be back in a short time." He walked over and forced a deep kiss on me. Yuck, Vampire spit, fucking disgusting.

I watched him hurry to his room for his grooming. I didn't hesitate. I rushed from his apartment in stealth heading for the fake flowers just down the hallway from his front door. I pulled up the fake flora and found the green clutch of Master Drexel right where Mad Maxx and Maximillian left it.

I smiled full of demons when I opened it. I rapidly removed one of the loaded syringes. I dropped the paralytic drug into my hidden pocket, rezipped the purse and returned it to its hiding spot. Then without a second hesitation returned to Master Jonas's apartment, quiet as a snake in the tall grass. No one had seen me nor had Master Jonas realized I took a quick little stroll down the hall. I took my seat on his couch to await my dinner escorts.

I shot a look at my brother Christian that was smiling back at me. "Ready to attend the debutant ball, brother? Looks like we are the guest of honor. Do you think these boots are comfortable to do dancing in?" I chuckled at my bullshit teasing him.

Christian laughed wildly. "Ah, I think we have a full dance card, brother. No worries, blisters are more tolerable when they are gained for a good reason. I have just the medicine to cure our ails. This is going to be a night one of them will regret but none of them will soon forget. Hahaha!"

I snorted. "You are a dirty rotten bastard, Christian. I think I am starting to like you a little or maybe I am just hungry. Either way this dinner will be a thrill for a fucking change. I tire of nothing but despair. About time we had some fun too."

He nodded. "Agreed. However, you need not try to pet my ego with kind words, Mad Max. Go find Annette and let her do the stroking, fool. You just get the boy through the meal, and I handle the rest." He winked at me then pulled back to allow me to run the show, until it was time for his expertise to be required.

I heard Master Jonas call out for me just as I was about to give Christian a taste of my verbal assault. I sighed but got up to see what the creepy ass Vampire Husband wanted this time. I moved swiftly and found him sitting on his bed wrestling with his cuff buttons. He smiled his spooky grin at me when I came through the door then rushed to kneel at his feet.

"Ah. My love. I ask you to button these cuffs. I never could get this blouse to comply without much struggle though it is my favorite." He held out his arms to allow my attendance of his desired service.

He watched me with much adoration in his expression as I patiently worked the tight buttons through the eyelets. He then stood up and went to his dresser. He came back with the large bloodstone broach he wore the day of our collaring.

Master Jonas had me attach this to his high collar. I was tempted to run the needle of it through his Adam's apple. It took all I had to hold off Christians overeager attempts to grab the wheel to make this impulse a truth. Damned boy kills everyone without thinking, you know.

Master Jonas grabbed my head before I could return to my kneel the second his broach was in place. He pulled me into a lustful kiss with pawing of the boy. I swear to you, Meine Liebe, I wanted to kick this creep in his hoddensack. I was in no mood for this heavy petting at any time with any fucking man.

I suppose he could tell my tensing up indicated I was not going to pretend to enjoy his molestation. He pulled back rather quickly with a look of surprise on his face.

"Christian Axel? What is going on with you? I kiss you and you are supposed to kiss back, not go stiff without a shred of affection for you Husband and Master." He glared into my eyes.

I scoffed. "Mad Max not Christian Axel. You bark up the wrong tree, Master. This cat is no pussy."

Master Jonas's eyes went wide in shock. "Huh? this is a mask I fondle and not Christian Axel?"

I smiled with much wickedness. "I am neither a mask nor am I Christian Axel, Master. I am a nightmare come to life. You bring Annette in here, then I will show you a demonstration of my affection, the most sublime. Otherwise, I suggest you get your fucking hand off my cock and tongue out of my mouth. I am no schwuler."

Master Jonas immediately backed off me, thank Gott, looking me over with suspiciousness. "Mad Max is your name you say. This is the mask from the torture room with Egon I believe."

I smiled over that beautiful memory of beating that black collar to begging. "Ah, ja. That would be correct Master. Pleasure to meet you, well not so much as to meet you so intimately."

My Master frowned at that. "I accept that. Thanks to your illness you have many minds. However, what I don't understand is what the hell you are doing here, Mad Max. This is not the time for this attitude when alone with your Husband. Bring me my Christian Axel or even that one

286

called Maximillian. You don't belong here in my bedroom."

I grinned with evil. "I agree with that most fully. I don't wish to be in your bedroom or anywhere near your bed, Master. I have no choice. Der Hund says that Master Drexel fucked up that crybaby Maximillian. He called me here or the boy would still be stuck in the void."

Master Jonas furrowed his brow. "Drexel injured my Maximillian. What about Christian Axel? Did he hurt him too?"

I laughed till I coughed on that one. "All of you disfigured Christian Axel, Master. You're all a pack of fools. Der Hund never rides the flesh thanks to the brutality in this world. I for one don't mind cruelty, just as long as I am the one holding the thudder."

Master Jonas sat back a bit. "Ah, shit I think I am starting to understand all this. Der Hund, he you call Christian Axel, right? He sent you to fix something, didn't he?"

To that I nodded. I raised my eyebrow. "I tell you already, Master. Maximillian was injured. He sleeps to recuperate. I was Der Hund's only option, so here I am."

My Master nodded. "Ja, I heard you say that, but I seem to recall in the dungeon below you said there are six of you. Maximillian and Der Hund, then you, make only three. There were three other choices. Why is this one called Mad Max? You are clearly the one that dishes out the pain rather than taking it."

I frowned at that. "There were six of us. Now there are five, Master. The masochist Mad Maxx sleeps too. Der

Hund destroyed Max. Good enough for that pansy. I never liked him anyway. Christian is the only other one, and if you meet him, you have met the boy for the last fucking time. You saved him in the yard. Not a smart move if you ask me. I would have let the Guard shoot him."

I saw Christian flash me a look of anger at my saying that, but I didn't care. He was stupid to run around like the dumbass over finding out Peter was our father. It would have served him right to be killed. You don't commit suicide over something like that. You enact murder over it. That is what I would have done anyway.)

Master Jonas sighed. "What if I wanted to speak to Der Hund. Can I get an audience with him? I can order or direct it can I not? I am your Husband and Master."

I scowled at that bullshit right there. "Ja, you can direct it if you wish Master. I would be careful pushing your weight around with such a dangerous meeting though. Der Hund doesn't like you very much. Your bullshit blood bonding, and cruelty of taking his choice by bondage, that didn't win you, his heart. I would like to give you the kind advice of leaving that core of ours alone. I believe you have done enough damage. I say that with respect." I noticed even Christian was getting agitated that Master Jonas would dare to order Der Hund to speak to him.

M Master nodded. "Okay, then I ask you when will Maximillian return to me?"

I shrugged. "How the hell am I supposed to know that, Master. I am not the designer of this weird shit. I am only a slave to it."

He smiled. "Then I wish that meeting with Der Hund. In fact, you call him right now. That Mad Max is a directive."

I shot a look of hate at the creepy bastard. "Your funeral, Master. I do this as you demand. See you on the other side." I closed my eyes and Christian and I flew from the boy just as a very angry Der Hund arrived to ride the flesh.

The boys eyes opened, blazing with the fires of hell. "Here I am Jonas. Have you lost your fucking mind calling me here. What the holy hell are you doing fucking with my Max boys. They serve you and your foul brothers with all they have and still this is not enough for your flea riddled carcass?"

Master Jonas chucked at Der Hund's insolence. "Ah, there is my smart-ass Christian Axel. I call you to ask when Maximillian will return to my bed and why you sent your assassin Mad Max. I suspect this killer Christian is with him or not far behind."

Der Hund crossed his arms then spat on Master Jonas floor. "They come to kill Drexel, Jonas. That beast must go. None of you others will end him to protect and defend your collar. Therefore, I send my boys to do it. I cannot have that monster drugging the flesh every week for puncturing, and perverted sex acts. I also cannot allow a catatonic fit every few fucking days to appease that beast. We cannot survive long that way. You stay out of my way, Jonas, or next time, I send them looking to slay a Vampire."

I thought for sure that Master Jonas would have a fit over Der Hund's brazen statement of murdering the statue fucking Elder. That was not the case.

Master Jonas grinned with evil. "Fair enough. You be careful that your Mad Max and Christian don't get caught. I will not stand in the way. You are correct. Drexel must die or you will not live long. I can see the evidence of that written all over you. However, I asked when I could expect my lover Maximillian to return. Answer me and I turn my blind eyes without any further quarrel."

Der Hund seemed a bit stunned that Master Jonas was giving his blessing. "When Drexel is worm food, I will awaken Maximillian. He must have his rest from this revolting shit those fetishers did to him. Another day or two at the most I think."

Ma Master growled out in fury over that. "I do not wish to wait another day or two for my special services. This Mad Max is not any good to warm my bed. I command you to return when I call you and you will attend my interests anytime, I ask for you. Even when my Maximillian is back from his slumber. My feeding from your blood must be from the source. You are the boy's core Der Hund. I require your attendance at least twice a month or whenever I need a transfusion. I need this done before Claus comes for his leash rights tomorrow."

Our core grew beyond furious at this command. "You cannot tell me how to run my own head, Jonas. I refuse to obey this command. You keep your hands off the boy or deal with the cold Mad Max for the next few days. Maximillian was designed to please the Masters. He will be returned shortly. I am not interested in your foul touching twice a month nor ever. I demand punishment rather than comply with your orders."

Master Jonas grinned again, appearing to be expecting that response. "Fine, the punishment shall be you trapped in that metal for life, Christian Axel. You can avoid my blade and my bed, but your masks will serve my lust for all their lives. I will keep them alive and well for many, many years to come. I only need to chain the boy to a wall in a cell below. He will be kept alive, and I will drain him slowly. His being mad, sane, happy, sad, matters not to me."

Der Hund's face fell into the expression of extreme fear. "You wouldn't do that. I thought you said you love me. If I am trapped in my metal, you will never find the female Priceless, Jonas. She will never be leashed so you can be cured of death."

Master Jonas nodded. "I do understand, Christian Axel, but I told you many times now. I don't like things that I cannot have, held under my nose. I can be a most generous Husband or a most brutal one. You choose that, not me. I am helpless in this matter. I must have the core to meet my blood lust. If I am stuck with the masks, then the feeding is no good. I may as well drink water from the tap. You come to me for my special requirements, then I can buy enough years to live till you find our Frau. You are worthless to me to obtain the dream of a female Priceless if I die of old age disease while waiting. I ask you Christian Axel, you still desire punishment rather than obey my directive?"

Der Hund fell into a kneel at his feet. "I believe I have no choice with you, as usual Jonas. You play a dangerous game with a shattered mind. I mourn not for you or me when this bomb blows into a million pieces instead of only five."

291

Master Jonas chucked with much vigor. "Don't be so dramatic, Christian Axel. You survived that attack of the strait razor, Xavier, Barnim and now the disgusting Drexel. I will even bring the frau of your choice to our bed to ease this burden of yours. I heard the name Annette. Is this a frau of some interest of yours? If so, I say name her and I bring her in place of Emma."

Der Hund gasped "You would do that for me? Ja, this Annette is the Frau of my choice, but I must beg your mercy and allow me to approach her with such an offer first?"

Ma Master nodded. "I grant that mercy the second you start calling me Master, Christian Axel. You are not above the masks. You wear my collar like all the others. You show me the respect of my Dominance over you, or I call the fucking Guard to have you taken to the cell right this minute. Save this insolence of yours for our tristes where I encourage your anger. Right this minute though, I have you on your knees. That is your place. Better never forget it either."

I almost died when I saw our Core and leader nod then say. "As you wish, Master. I respectfully request you allow me to visit with this Annette to seek her interest in joining our bed. Thank you for the mercy of it in advance." He lowered his head to demonstrate his submission to the Vampires will.

The creepy Elder's smile nearly broke his face in two on his victory over Der Hund. "I grant your most polite request, Christian Axel. I even grant you time to seek the girl out shortly. I will hold off Claus until midnight but come dark you will show up at my call ready to submit to my interests with or without this Annette. Fail me, and I will know it. Don't push me on this. I am very serious. I offer no second chances."

Der Hund nodded. "I understand this, Master. I will not fail to mind your command. Thank you for your mercy."

Master Jonas pulled Der Hund up from his knees and forced him into a deep passionate kiss. When he finished violating our core with wanton molestation for several moments, he allowed the boy to return to his knees.

"You are released Christian Axel. I desire to speak with Mad Max now." Master Jonas watched as the boys eyes closed. Christian and Mad Max rushed inside to fill the void left by our rapidly retreating core, Der Hund.

I opened my lids to glare at this cruel man that dared to abuse our Core like that. "I am here Master. You requested to speak with me."

Master Jonas smiled with thrill "That was quick. Ja, Mad Max, you intend to end Drexel this night? I demand to know how."

I nearly choked when he said that. "Master, I am not sure this is something you would desire to have knowledge of in advance."

Ma Master scoffed. "You are wrong about that. In fact, I think Claus and Bladrick should also be included in this murder of Drexel. None of us like this foul man. He, like Barnim, was raised by that dreadful Xavier. They hate him, Mad Max. His death would be a mercy to all of us. So, I demand again to know how you plan to end this man."

I smiled with glee. "I will stick him with his own paralytics, then watch him fall down from a distance that will leave more than bruises Master."

Master Jonas laughed with evil in his sound. "Ah, you stole his medication? Clever boy. Okay, I will speak to my brothers and make sure they stay out of your way. Make sure no one sees your tomfoolery though. If you are caught, even Claus cannot save you."

I nodded. "I only ask that you stay out of my way when I send him to hell Master."

My Master looked at his lap. "Wait, if you kill Drexel with Barnim already dead, that leaves only Leo as a brother that can rise. There is also Helga and Heidi, the dungeon twins as well, but they hate Bladrick with a passion. We will never get those two harpies to play ball with the blocking of Cora that Bladrick suggests." He seemed deep in thought, and I took this chance to ask.

"I beg your pardon Master, but what about Hemmel? I thought he was with Leo to rise. Won't he be the one to move up with Leo, or was Master Bladrick in error when he told me there are two men for the openings?" I winced, hoping I didn't overstep my bounds a bit there.

Master Jonas groaned. "Well, ja, Hemmel was to rise but the fool went and had a fucking heart attack in his sleep four days ago. Found dead and stiff in his bed. Poor little silver frau of only nine years old was chained to his bed soiled to all hell. Didn't matter though, since Hemmel already killed the sad thing with strangulation. I was told the excitement blew his valves. Too bad he didn't die sooner. At least now everyone knows why there were so few female silvers ever salvaged from the slave dungeons over the last ten years since that cocksucker took headmaster. He was raping them to uselessness before they ever reached auction. Can you believe that monster? What a pervert, forcing himself on children like that."

I glared at him with much hate. "Ja, what a pervert. Nine years old is disgusting but thirteen or twelve, well that is an old man isn't it, Master?"

Master Jonas looked up at me with a start. "Oh hell. I forget your age, my love. You seem so much older than your years, you know. Besides, I didn't take your virginity. Peter your father did."

I nodded., "Ja he did by raping me. His forcing himself on me made it okay for everyone else to do the same I suppose. I just turned fourteen, actually forty-one too. Thanks for clearing that misunderstanding up for me Master."

Well, at least it turned out that killing Hemmel was a better move than I ever had hoped. Who can say how many poor children he killed.

Master Jonas stood up ignoring my most true statement. "Well, we waste time sitting here, Mad Max. Let's get you some dinner, shall we. Then you can get rid of Drexel, find Der Hund's choice of distraction frau, and then I make him my supper, ja?" He smiled while tapping the top of the boys hat.

I looked at Christian. "We need to add the twins Helga and Heidi to our hit list and fast. Can you work on a way to end the two of them so close to the death of Drexel, Barnim and Hemmel?"

Christian nodded. "I already know just what to do. The girls are straight, ugly as a Billy goat and super jealous of each other. Looks like the boy will be stepping out as the gigolo instead of the Schwuler on this one."

I had to chuckle at that idea of our seducing the woman for a change. Sadly, this would not be a fun task even if it was trying to capture the affections of the right gender of our preference. If you ever saw those two, you maybe would beg to differ. Neither of them looked like the female, nor any male of worth either. Even I wasn't hard up enough to desire the H-twins' affections.

Ja, these ladies were, the American way to call them, real hound dogs. Ja, like that mother of yours. Meine Liebe, you ever wondered if maybe you're adopted? I think you must have been. Anyway, back to the story. Stop distracting me. I will never get done telling this tale if you keep doing it. Do it again and I will thud you with my can.

For the record I never said a thing nor moved a muscle. Mad Max is such a nut. Just saying.

The schwuler Elders were banging on the door before my Master and I could even relax a second on the couch. I was told to answer the door. Master Claus came inside wearing a red gown with many jewels and blue opera gloves. He was able to pull off this strange clash in color most beautifully if you could ignore his white mustache and portly gut. He took his seat next to Master Jonas to the sounds of my HusDom giving him many kind compliments.

Behind Master Claus came Master Bladrick dressed in a smart looking tan camel hair suit jacket with alligator shoes. He was maybe the only one of us dressed even close to normal in fashion, even if it was a bit out of the modern fashion for the seventies.

I was about to close the door when Master Drexel came pushing his way in. That idiot was dressed in a pure white outfit with what appeared to be glitter in every crease and edge of it. It hurt to look at the toothless old weasel, the color was so bright. I felt my stomach flip flop when he grabbed my leash, pulling me harshly toward him.

"I want to hold Mad Maxx's leash, Jonas. He looks stunning tonight, and his white face matches my outfit," he whined out, refusing to let my chain go.

I dropped to a kneel, praying that Master Jonas or any of the others would save me from following behind this bastard. I was going to kill him after dinner. I needed to get something to eat first. If I didn't, then I would be joining him on the stretcher shortly after, when these neglectful Masters forgot to feed me for another several hours.

Master Claus roared out, "Let Mad Maxx go, Drexel. I will be holding his leash to dinner. I am not only still awaiting my turn on the cock, but I am head of this Haus until morning comes and Cora takes the throne. This night I will be honored as is my right with this Priceless collar on my heels." He looked around at his brothers to see if any of them wanted to despite his claim to my leash for this historic walk to the Great hall.

None of them dared to argue with Master Claus. He stood up then approached me demanding I stand. He took my leash into his gloved hand then turned to the others.

"Come on brothers. Let's go show this Haus who the real Power is around here." He waited till I opened the door for him then took off pulling me along behind him.

As Master Claus took up the front, the other three Elders surrounded me like a pack of wolves. Master Jonas was on my left, Master Bladrick on my right. Master Drexel took up the rear. Drexel was probably staring at my ass, that nasty sonofabitch.

I felt very small in the center of these old men. However, I had been gaining height rapidly. I was no longer the tiny kid I had been, but still I had many years left till I was large enough to tower over most in the Haus. In fact, I am likely the tallest of them all these days. That night I was only just barely big enough to be seen traveling with this pack of rule makers of the highest level.

The silver collars fell to their knees, and the blacks retreated in every direction as the brothers come barging down the staircase. Dominants took to the walls staring in awe at the boy dressed like Master Jonas, wearing a bat collar, was walking on a black leash behind Master Claus.

I heard the whispering breaking out all around us. The whole Haus thought the Priceless collar was growing a tree in the orchard. Yet, here he was, brazenly being led around by the Elders themselves. Confusion, thrill, and fantastical rumors were already rushing around the nosey inhabitants within the Haus walls. No one had ever seen nor heard of such a thing as what they were witnessing that night coming down the stairs headed for the hallway and Great Hall.

I could see this interest and wagging tongues were swelling the old schwulers' chests with pride. They were the only ones of their kind to own a collar in all the Haus's history. This special honor was enhanced by the identity of the one held. Not only was I the Priceless, but I was the oldest living one and most infamous ever known in their memory. Yeah, only fourteen, yikes!

I was infamous back then for many reasons (now for even more but that will be discussed later). First my scars, especially those ones on my face, made me the most recognizable person in the place. Second, I was the only Priceless collar ever leashed, and then tossed. Stepping out as the only collar ever held by the Elders, further elevated me when you realized no other silver could claim five, now four, Masters at the same time.

I was also the youngest full submissive ever allowed in their written history and the only Priceless that had been enrolled in the Dominant training program. Many recalled I had survived Xavier's brutality and more remembered he died while taking his special services in public with me.

In the two years since my cruel collaring with Peter I had moved up the rungs of the Haus rapidly. I arose from a nothing, insolent slave called Christian that no one would purchase from the dungeons, to become Mad Maxx the Brutal, Priceless Collar of the Elders. There was not a single collar (silver or black) nor Dominant in that Haus that didn't recognize I was a legend in the making by this time.

I am sure that Peter and Agnette were kicking themselves for allowing me to live. They had their chance when I was helpless that eight months in the dungeons having that shit fit. The calculated risk of keeping those Elder schwulers busy to raise their girl Cora was going to bite them both in the ass. I guess they just assumed I couldn't hold my own with these shady scumbags that called themselves the power of the Haus. Well, they were wrong. I am Priceless, and thanks to that, there is nothing I cannot do.

When we walked into the Great Hall packed up like that, all the chattering and eating stopped in that room. All eyes were on us. I could see Peter sitting at a table with Gretta, Cora, and Agnette. They thought themselves so brilliant. They were about to be schooled.

Master Claus demanded to be sat far away from the table of the Voting Council scum. We took our seats with Master Jonas insisting to sit me between him and the crossdressing Elder. I didn't give a fuck where I sat. I just needed something to eat. I also wanted a rifle to blow the heads off everyone sitting in that Hall. Okay, a bloody thought I know but I really hated this trash you, know? Plus, not eating makes me crabby I suppose.

I was allowed to place my order and believe me I could barely pay attention to anything else waiting for my food. As the Elders giggled and whispered among themselves enjoying the watchful eyes of everyone in the Hall, I noticed a table where Leo sat alone. He appeared upset and lonely. I kept my sight on him noticing him casting disgusted looks at Peter table. I could see even from my vantage he had been betrayed most callously by those he thought were his friends. I saw my opportunity. I am not the seductive one, but I do know how to bring on the desire for revenge in another person, that you can be assured.

I leaned over to Master Jonas to whisper in his ear. "Master, if you would allow it, I think I should go fetch

Leo to join his brothers. It is a true shame to see one of his status, sitting without a friend, ja?"

Master Jonas smiled with a sharp toothed grin. "Ja, my love. Go get our newest brother. Tell him to come home at last." I nodded then took off to bring in my next conquest, the rat bastard Leo.

I saw Peter and Agnette stop everything and stare at me as I walked past their table ignoring them. Cora and Gretta were still chattering until they noticed the sudden irritation of the other two. Then they also turned the focus on the limping Priceless collar strolling by.

"Where do you think you are going, Maximillian," scoffed out Peter.

I ignored his statement since I am not that boy. This caused him much irritation. Agnette then did her best to stop my progression.

"Maximillian, you better said something to you. Get your worthless ass over here and kneel or be taken below for such insolence," my useless mother called out trying to sound stern.

I didn't even flinch but kept up my journey to the table of Leo. The old schwuler had noticed my approach and kept looking around trying to figure out where the hell I was headed. He had not determined I had any business with him, nor would he have ever thought that. All my time of knowing him I had made it clear his attentions were not appreciated nor permitted. Boy was this going to be his lucky night.

I reached the seemingly confused Leo. "Hello, Master Leo. I have been sent by my Honorable Master Claus,

Master Bladrick, Master Drexel, and Master Jonas to extend a welcome. They request the pleasure of your presence at their table where you belong."

Master Leo looked around appearing stunned then furrowed his brow. "Huh? Maximillian, I don't understand what you are saying. Is this a cruel joke? I am not bothering you nor anyone else. Please show some mercy and leave me to my own private meal."

I shook my head. "Master Leo, I must apologize and beg your forgiveness for it. For starters I am Mad Maxx not Maximillian. I also am here to inform you that you are to be raised to Elder the second you accept the offer. This honor comes with an apartment on the Elder's floor, four loyal brothers, and your turn with the Priceless collar as your personal pleasure submissive. Swear the oath of brotherhood to the Elders and take my leash. If you do this, I will follow you and submit to you as my Master. Ignore this generous offer and I walk back unescorted to elevate another in your stead."

Master Leo's jaw dropped to the table. "Wha..what? I am being called to be an Elder? You submit to me? I can have you for my own, and move to the Elder's floor? I must have fallen asleep. Am I dreaming this."

I chuckled with some humor over this idiot's response. You see only the Elders know what qualifies for a raise to that status, so Leo wouldn't know he was a candidate. "You are not dreaming, Master Leo or do I merely call you Leo? I say again take my leash and I bow to my newest Master and brother to the Elders of this Haus. Or I walk back to rejoin my Masters and serve their pleasures alone."

Master Leo's face broke into a huge smile. "I say come here and kneel before me Maximillian, uhm Mad Maxx. I swear to the oath of loyalty to my brother Elders and desire to submit and take your leash." He turned in his chair as I approached and knelt at his feet.

The tables next to Master Leo's had stopped anything to watch this display. They now began to clap in thrill as Master Leo took up my black chain and stood throwing down his napkin onto his plate.

He slightly bowed at his cheering witnesses, then pulled on my leash lightly. "Come with me, Mad Maxx. I go to join my brothers for dinner." I stood up and limped in quiet reverence behind the newest Elder and my replacement Master.

I was feeling pretty miserable that even after all that time trying to escape Master Leo's lust, I was subjugated to it anyway. Then he did something that changed my mind about him for all time. He walked by Peter's table slowly making sure to give them time to hail him.

He stopped when Peter called out to him. "Leo. Bring that boy to me. He has a thudding coming for spitting on me a week ago. Then he walks by this table in insolence. I demand punishment."

Master Leo stopped then looked back at me standing there with my head bowed, waiting for him to turn me over for a thrashing. "Are you speaking of my submissive Mad Maxx? Ah, I see you think you have the right to tell me, the Elder Leo, what to do with my own property. Well, forget it, Peter. Mad Maxx belongs to me this time. You tossed this beautiful boy away the second you no longer had any use for him I seem to recall. I doubt he spit on you because you are not worth such an honor. I know he ignored you because you see this submissive is Priceless. He is only interested in quality. Maybe one day he will step down off his lofty cloud, but I doubt it. He is too picky I know, but he is the best you know. He will only bother to speak to those of the finest status. That leaves you, Gretta, and Agnette out. Cora, we shall see about you, but I bet he won't bother with you either. Funny thing about these high caliber submissives, they are so damned likely to hold grudges for all their lives. I do believe he owes every single one of you a severe ass kicking. I know I will aid him in doing it. Since, now I understand how he feels being so badly used as we were. You all enjoy your meal. Hope you choke on it, oh hell I mean, I hope you enjoy it." I looked up at Master Leo with a startle to hear him say what he did.

It was of great interest that he used many of the same words to Peter that Peter said to him the day I refused to give Master Leo a blow job over a year before. I had completely misjudged Master Leo as nothing but a predatory, perverted, schwuler. Well, to be honest, he is still all those things too. Turned out the man did have a backbone after all. He wasn't even afraid of Cora even though by morning she would be Head of the Haus at last.

I suddenly realized he had been playing a role assigned him by Peter and his co-conspirators. He had likely even been directed to demand that blow job, then say those things in the torture room all in a plan to get me to side up with Peter. I had been the fool to fall for the entire thing.

Peter scoffed, while Agnette and Gretta gasped. Then Cora spoke, "Take that thing out of here Leo and remove your slimy self while you are at it. I am getting indigestion just looking at the two of you."

Master Leo smiled with evil at that. "Well Cora, I am surprised you feel so arrogant to speak to your brother Elder in such a nasty tone. You will be sorry for such an insult soon enough. I am happy to remove myself and my beautiful submissive from your sight. Your horse face may frighten him so badly he will need medication to aid his sleep from the nightmares. Come Mad Maxx, this conversation grows stale, and the view leaves one wanting as well," He tugged on my leash and took off leading me away from the stunned Dominants that had betrayed the ones that now had the power to crush their plans.

I had to stifle a giggle that Master Leo recalled I had called Cora a horse face the day I blew a gasket in the Great Hall during the days of Xavier. I was incredibly grateful that Mad Maxx and Maximillian had judged the two candidates correctly. Master Leo without a doubt turned out to be the right man for the elevation and Master Hemmel the correct one for the grave. Too bad we didn't get him fast enough to save the poor nine-year-old female silver. Oh well, she was his last victim. Had Olaf and Vilber not fucked up in Master Drexel's bathroom, more would have followed her to the orchard than already had.

Speaking of serial killers, I was more than ready to help the third one in a single week find his way to hell. Master Barnim and Master Hemmel were finally where they could hurt no one anymore, but I thought day could use some company. I sat down in my chair between Master Claus and Master Jonas, quietly watching the Elders in a friendly welcoming of Master Leo to their ranks.

My food had arrived while I was fetching Master Leo. I kept my eyes on my Masters but shoveled the food into my starving mouth. I ate anything the black collars brought and even aided Master Jonas in cleaning his plate. The Elders laughed about the incredible appetite of a growing boy and spoke of their own days as youths.

I felt sweat breaking out on my brow now that my aching stomach quieted. The pain that had been muted by overwhelming hunger came to my consciousness. I was hurt all over, and in the most personal of places I felt the ravages of brutality most cruel.

The desire for revenge rushed from my black heart to every vein in my violated flesh. I glared with extreme hatred dripping from every pore at Master Drexel. I vowed to myself that statue fucker was going to sleep in a casket tonight, Gott damnit. He had to go.

When at last the Elders had their fill of food, wine and conversation, Master Claus informed all of them it was time to leave. Master Drexel, as expected, whined that he wanted to hold my leash. I shot a look of caution and nodded at Master Jonas when Master Claus vetoed that notion.

Master Jonas spoke up. "Brother, let Drexel hold the damned leash. will you? If it makes him happy, I see no harm in it. Bladrick, don't you agree? It is time for peace among us. There will be many dinners here in the Great Hall with our collar. We take turns with the leading him like we do with our nights, ja?"

Master Leo looked around at the others. "Mad Maxx wasn't just tempting me then? He really is shared among the Elders?"

Master Drexel snorted. "Ja, we all share this collar, fool. You will have to wait your turn like the rest of us. I will say Claus, Leo is new. I think he should not get put ahead of me in the rotation. I will throw a fit if he is. I mean it."

Master Claus sighed. "Christ, Drexel. You are like a kid. Leo is new and never got his taste of his new apartment nor his collar rights. You are so selfish. We want to welcome our newest brother with open and sharing arms, not insults."

Master Bladrick scoffed. "I am with Claus and Jonas on this. You can hold the leash, but you don't get to kick Leo from the cycle. He gets the boy after me and Claus. You already had your turn Drexel. Live with it."

Master Leo looked at the table. "Nein, it is okay, Bladrick. I do thank you for thinking of me, but I waited to have Mad Maxx's priceless special services for my own a long time already. I don't mind waiting any longer. It is a pleasure I never thought I would receive. I am not a greedy man. Whenever my turn to have him for my own comes, it is a dream come true, for that I am most patient I assure you."

Master Claus smiled, as did Master Jonas and Master Bladrick. "Ah, you are a most wonderful brother, to be so willing to work with us on this complicated matter Leo. You need not worry. You will have your rights the day after tomorrow at midnight. Drexel you will be the next on that schedule. You may take Mad Maxx's collar Drexel, if that will shut you the fuck up but on the other business, I will hear not another word of it," said Master Claus sternly.

All the Elders stood, and Master Drexel rushed over snatching up my leash. I sighed but followed behind that rat bastard. He again took up the hind end of the pack. I listened to the Elders telling Master Leo he could take the deceased Barnim's apartment right away. I watched the silvers fall to their knees and the blacks run for the hills.

I shot a look of hate at Olaf and Vilber standing silently guarding the door as we began our climbing the many stairs to the Elders' floor. The big brutes looked at the floor avoiding making eye contact with me. I wanted to kill them both, but I realized there were too many more important ahead of them in need of weeding out of the Haus.

Once we had made it to the fifth-floor stair grouping I reached into my inner pocket and popped off the needle guard of Master Drexel's pre-loaded syringe. The other Elders were all busy with their conversations and the statue fucker was deeply involved in listening to them.

In a single quick movement, I rushed forward and jammed the needle into Master Drexel's bright white backside pushing right through the material of his clothing. He let out a yelp then turned around full of fury to verbally attack me for doing whatever I had done to him.

However, the paralytic drug is a fast-moving sonofabitch. His words were frozen in his throat. I dropped the offending weapon back into my pocket as I watched the Elder quiver for a moment. He swayed, then dropped my leash as his ability to move began to leave him. I smiled wildly as he crumbled then rolled down the stairs unable to stand, grab anything or even call out for help. Buh bye, Drexel.

Screams most sublime rang out in the stairwell as Drexel rolled past the traveling silvers and blacks. His neck snapped around the fourth set of steps. I watched his statue like form roll head over heels all the way to the bottom without a single attempt made by anyone to stop his decent. I have to say Meine Liebe, seeing that bloody scene, now that was art.

The other Elders had realized by the first screams coming from the collars traveling the stairs with us that their odd brother had found his eternal rest. They stood next to me unable to tear their eyes away from the sight of Master Drexel slipping away to his nasty end. When at last he came to a rest without any sign of life, they looked at each other in silent shock.

Master Jonas shot me a look then said to Master Claus. "Well Leo, you can choose between Barnim's and Drexel's apartment. It seems our brother had a heart attack or slipped. Mad Maxx, did you see what the hell happened?"

I shook my head feigning sadness. "He turned around, grabbed his chest, and tried to say something. Then he dropped my leash and fell down the stairs. I am not a doctor, but I would say that he saw the reaper calling and was in a hurry to get to the land where no one speaks anymore. At last, he found that peace and quiet he complained could not be found in this world."

Master Bladrick chuckled at that. "You are one evil little bastard Mad Maxx. You better give me that syringe before the Haus doctor gets here." He held out his hand while I turned over my empty evidence to him.

Master Claus grinned. "Good work, my love. Okay brothers. Let's go to my apartment for a drink to celebrate, errr, mourn the loss of our brother Drexel. May he rest in pieces."

Master Leo looked at all of them a bit nervously. "You meant him to be killed? I don't understand. Why?"

Master Jonas scoffed. "You never knew him, or you wouldn't that Leo. I expect you to keep this secret or we make sure you join the statue lover, ja? Come with us to Claus's place and we will explain this shit to you. Mad Maxx, you are released to attend that matter we discussed. Return when you have secured that silver collar or be ready to suffer for it."

I nodded. "Your wish is my pleasure, Master." I rushed down the stairs pushing past all the gathering nosey collars trying to get a look at the dead Elder Drexel.

I was on my way to see Annette. It was time for me to repay that favor I owed her.

Chapter 39: The Green Fields and Baby Lambs in Annette's Eyes

I pushed my way through the fast packing up crowd. It seemed everyone in that damned place wanted to get a look at Master Drexel's corpse laying there at the bottom of the stairs. Well not Mad Max. I had seen all I wanted to see of that rat bastard, trust me. I didn't even caste a glance at the white clad schwuler that I had sent to find his grave.

He always wanted to be the center of attention. I always aim to please my Masters. I am the Priceless after all. I made sure he finally got his wish. Sonofabitch that he was. No one appeared able to take their eyes off the statue fucker that late afternoon.

I got through the rushing crowds and ran fast as my limping would permit headed right for Annette's apartment. I hoped she was still alive. The sorry truth of the House is that the female silvers are often killed or sold out to the invisible people faster than males. I was aware her Master had done the illegal collaring with her at age fourteen but that didn't assure she wasn't already discarded by a fickle Dominant looking for fresh flesh.

You see Meine Liebe; I had already admitted many nasty truths to myself. One of them was that a full submissive's collar didn't save no one. I was a damned good example. I had already been tossed after only one year.

At some point that Master of Annette's would tire of her affections no matter how perfect her service to him, nor beautiful the girl may be. Then, without a remaining virginity she would be sold off to the circuit. After that, off to the camps with her.

All the silvers, boy or girl, would eventually end up this way. Very few made it to the age of twenty in the House. A silver needed to possess a very special talent or become blood bonded to their Dominant. That was their only chance. Even that didn't promise anything. The very few that survived to adulthood could be assured by age thirty to be sold out if unlucky or if their Dominant was an honest one, they perhaps could get tarnished to black.

To be tarnished is a bad thing, but to be painted black is the pleasure submissives dream come to truth or to break their metal. It is their only chance to live to old age.

Now when I was only the boy of eight, I was taken to the dungeons like all the others. After we all had been assessed for a few weeks the Dungeon Master had us all lined up. This was the "color selection collaring." The Dungeon Master walked past each kind calling out either "this is silver" or "this one is black."

There were two black collar brutes following each carrying a bucket. One bucket held the silver collars and the other carried the blacks. Each of us stood, some trembling, others praying. Among the scared children was the collective "please dear God" don't let me be cursed to wear silver.'

Even in the dungeons we all had heard the truth of the pleasure submissive. They got used up and rarely lived to see their adulthood. The black collar got a guaranteed job, good treatment, retirement and could marry without fear of the forced sexual congress of the Dominants. To be selected black promised you'd live a long, peaceful life with choices and the rumor was you even had the right to leave the House.

Ta be selected silver assured a life of toil, subjugation, rape, beatings, and for all your agonies, in the end you end up a whore sucking cock in the work camps of Russia. Not a happy ending for most. If you were careful, pleased the Master/Mistress well, and did your job, then maybe you have children with them, get painted black or even break the metal.

Still not good odds, and life would be harsh without much choice. The silvers were hostages to the House and could never even go outside the walls of it without a Dominant escorting them.

When the Dungeon Master tossed a silver at a kid there would be many tears and often wailing from them. When they tossed a black at the feet of a boy or girl, they would display gratitude. I wasn't worried Meine Liebe. I was cut all to shit, ugly, and worse, insolent as hell. I assumed I would be selected black or even sent away.

Then my turn came. The Master stopped in front of me ignoring the cries and weeping all around him of those selected silver.

He looked down his nose at me then yelled out, "this one is silver."

I swear to God, I stood their several seconds even after the black collar assistant threw that shiny metal collar at my feet unbelieving what he said. There was no way I had been chosen to serve as the pleasure submissive. Yet, there was the evidence at my feet.

When the Master finished his rounds, he and the brutes came down the rows locking the selected colored collars around the kids' necks. When they got to me, I broke from the line and ran away. I'd decided I wasn't wearing any fucking collar, silver, black, maroon, or multi-colored. Oh, hell no.

Well, I was a tiny boy back then. I had no way to get out of the rock walls of the dungeon's classrooms and cells. It took them no time to catch me and haul my ass to a cell. In there I was held down and that damned silver collar locked around my throat. I spent several weeks in isolation refusing to accept even the collar much less the duties of the pleasure sub.

Of those children that stood in the lines with me so long ago, I can only name a handful of them chosen silver that still live today. The very few survivors are no longer wearing shiny collars though. They were all the lucky ones and escaped to black. If they hadn't, I would be counting them among those that grow trees in the orchards.

Only Prince Ryker had been well born in my year of being sold in. He had not even survived collar selection to break his metal. The House was just no place to be labeled "exploitable," no matter your gender or pedigree. Not when the ultra-wealthy have no care for anything, not even another's good welfare or life.

I was not a child anymore, not mind nor soul. I knew that Annette's illegal collaring almost guaranteed she would be tarnished and circuited unusually young. The poor girl was simply no match for the manipulations of her adult Master. She would have accepted his bullshit secret full submission collar whether she wished to or not. Had

314

she refused he would have auctioned her off, and then maybe she would have been bought by the likes of Xavier, Hemmel, Barnim or even Drexel.

In a place that abused children for more than two hundred years, serial child killers with enough money to avoid detection had created a haven. Those four men had likely put many a tiny child to their earthy beds. I almost squirm to think of the amount of innocent blood spilled in their torture rooms. If all the corpses rose from the orchards, I imagine the place would be packed wall to wall with them.

I stood there at Annette's door unsure what to do or what to say. I didn't see her among those running to view the dead statue fucker. That was not a good sign, and I knew this. I guess I was afraid to find out. I had loved the girl since the day she gave me her adoration without asking for a service return.

She had been the only one in my life that kept her word to me. No one had ever been told of that morning in her Master's closet. The girl called "nobody" was my dream and had given me the reason to fight on. If I found out she had been tarnished or put to the yard, I didn't believe I could handle it.

I knew I couldn't stand at that door all day. I braced myself for whatever news I would be handed as I knocked. I had to pound three times before finally I heard her Master yell out, sounding irritated, that he was coming.

Within a few moments the man answered. His eyes went wide upon seeing me there. I assumed it was not every day you see a silver collar dressed like the Vampire outside your apartment. I looked at the floor quickly cursing under my breath for forgetting my strange attire. This man would likely freak out wondering what the hell kind of nut was hanging out in the halls.

I glared at this short haired man of a heavy build in his early thirties. He was clean shaven with dark brown eyes and a weak chin.

To my surprise he gasped then said, "Mad Maxx, my God. To what do I owe this magnificent pleasure?" A huge smile covered his face with an expression of thrill. Huh? What a weirdo.

I shifted feeling my nerves fray with my next statement. "Master Stefan, I was sent by my Master Jonas to inquire about your silver trainee Annette." I cleared my throat trying to keep my eyes on my boots in case he gave me news I couldn't face without tears.

Master Stefan grunted. "Oh, I was hoping you come to see me Mad Maxx. Instead, you want to speak to my worthless trainee. What the hell does Jonas want with Annette? He looking to add a little fat to his diet?" He laughed with a great deal of humor at his cruel insult to the girl.

I held Christian tightly, he and I wanted to throttle that rat bastard for daring to call the luscious Annette fat. "Uhm, Nein. I do apologize, Master Stefan, but he saw her in the hallway and thought he may find some sport with her. He sent me as an offer for exchange," I lied.

That man nearly fainted. "Huh? He would be willing to trade off the Priceless Mad Maxx for my piggy trainee. That is like offering platinum for coal. Has Jonas lost his mind?"

Again, I had to pin Christian to the wall as I replied, "I again apologize to you, Master Stefan, but one cannot assess the desires of another. My Master finds value in your trainee. His desire is my command. If this offer is good for you then say ja or nein?"

Master Stefan laughed loud and long. "Well hell, ja. I take this amazing offer of trade. Fuck, I would be insane to say nein. When does he want this exchange to take place?"

I stole a glance at that nasty fucker staring at me with lust in his eyes, "My Master wants your trainee this very night. I will come to you tomorrow morning to finish his side of the arrangement. I will need time for the proper preparation to meet your needs."

The burly Master nodded. "Deal. I'm calling Annette right now. You can take her this minute. I will be awaiting your return by, let's say ten in the morning?"

I nodded. "Master Jonas wishes to keep the trainee for two days. I'll return tomorrow morning and the day after that in equal service. I'll be here at ten. If you can call Annette, I would appreciate your mercy. I need to be getting back or you will be taking your rights with me forced to gaze at far worse bruising than you already witness."

He chuckled. "Ja, I heard you endured Barnim. Well, you look better than I would have expected, given his reputation. You got lucky he fell to his death. I lost a lot of money betting you wouldn't last two weeks as the Elders' property. That is okay though. I will take out the loss on you when I get you in my bed."

317

I had to stifle a shudder as I replied, "As you wish Master. I beg your pardon, but may I have Annette?"

Master Stefan sucked in his breath. "Ah shit, ja. Annette, get your fat ass over here now."

I waited there holding my breath, praying that she would be in good health. I stole a look up and saw the girl not only was alive, but she was also more beautiful than I had recalled. It nearly took me to the floor to see maturity had made this female gorgeous. I fell in love with her all over again.

She saw me and dropped to a kneel, appearing to tremble a bit. She likely thought I'd come to tell on her regarding our single triste the year before.

"I am here Master. You called?" She stole another look at me standing at the door.

Master Stefan never took his eyes off me as he said, "Go with Mad Maxx and serve Master Jonas's orders. Be aware this means I am handing your leash to the Elder. You will mind him no matter what he commands. You somehow caught the powerful man's eye. You are one lucky bitch. You return to me in two days. Now get the hell out." He kicked at her, missing her by the way, luckily for him.

She nodded then stood and come toward me with tears in her eyes, "As you say Master. Thank you for your mercy."

Master Stefan looked at me again. "See you at ten, Mad Maxx. I intend to use my time to the fullest. Be ready for a real lover of incredible eagerness. I am not an old, used up man like you are used to. I promise you; I will discover all the secrets of that forbidden silver of yours. I cannot wait to see if your couple can really be as dangerous as everyone says it is. I am excited to explore the possibilities."

I nodded then smiled at him full of demons as I replied, "Oh, I am looking forward to it, Master. I will be here right on time. In my embrace many say everyone find all their darkest desires met to completion. One could even say my lovers tend to find themselves in another world. I assure you by tomorrow night you will understand why I'm leveled Priceless."

Annette stood there with a look of shock on her face as she listened to our strange exchange. I signaled for her to follow. She didn't argue but took her place traveling swiftly behind me. We hauled our tails away from the prying ears and eyes of her Master. When we got to an empty hallway I stopped. I looked around to see if I could spy a closet or somewhere private to tell Annette what the hell was going on. I couldn't have her walking blind into the nightmare of my Master Jonas's blood room or her witness my disgrace unprepared.

She stood there trying to figure out what I was up to. "Mad Max, you got a leash to your Master Jonas for me? Why would you be so kind?"

I was near stunned by her statement. "What? Aren't you upset that I'm possibly taking you to be violated by my Vampire Master?"

Annettes pretty eyes lit up. "Nein, I hope he kills me Mad Max. Then I won't be sent away to the camps. I have heard he often drains the collars of all their blood, and they die a mercifully quiet death."

I almost choked. "What? Are you saying you want to be killed by the Vampire?"

She shook her head, tearing up again as she replied. "I don't want to be killed at all, but it is a better thing than the life I have coming. She looked around to make sure we were alone. I am fully soiled Mad Max. My Master, he wouldn't take nein for an answer. When collar selection comes, he is auctioning me. I have nothing to trade for a new collar. That means I am finished. I would rather be dead than tarnished to the camps. Your Master can grant me the mercy of a painless death."

I watched the beautiful girl weep for a moment. Then before I could stop myself, I pulled her into an embrace feeling my heart break for her. I assumed that she was already a goner and off to the camps. I had not guessed wrong. She was soiled beyond repair and heading to a fate worse than death.

She cried for a moment into my chest then pushed me off her and growled angrily, "Are you stupid, Mad Max. What if someone saw you hugging me? We'd both get sent to the dungeons, fool. Besides, I don't want you touching me ever again. Your couple was more brutal than even my Master's. In fact, I never want anyone touching me again. I hate this sex stuff. You were right. You tried to tell us that day in the bathroom. I wish, oh Gott, Mad Max, what am I going to do?" She fell to her knees in a full-on crying jag.

I saw a closet door just up from where we were. "Come on Annette. Not here. This way. I need to speak to you right away, where no one can hear. Please, get up. The others will stop viewing the dead Drexel soon and be returning to this hallway. We don't have much time."

She looked up with a startle. "What? The Elder Drexel is dead? How?"

I smiled. "He crossed me. Come on Annette, please?" I put my hand out offering to help her back to her feet.

Annette furrowed her brow but took my hand and followed me to the safety of the storage closet. Once inside I turned on the light. I cracked the door to watch for traffic return. I took off my hat and took a deep breath then turned to the pretty submissive to lay it all on the line with her.

She stared at me, with a curious expression on her face as I said, "Look Annette. Master Jonas cannot couple with me for his blood lust unless I am lustful too. He has allowed for a third person in our bed and this person must be a female."

Annette shook her head. "Female? Why? Are you saying, Master Jonas needs a boy and a girl to feed his blood lust?"

I looked at the floor. "Uhm, nein. He isn't interested in the female. I am. I cannot find lust for my husband or any male for that matter."

She gasped then let out a cry, "You mean you are straight?"

I sighed and said, "Ja, I lied to all of you. I am straight, Annette. I find sex with the man a burden and revolting. But I endure what I must to break my metal. But this Master, he needs me lustful for his blood drinking fetish. That is why he requires a female present."

She looked at the floor, her eyes filling with fresh rain as she said, "Oh my God. You poor boy. This is horrid. You are taking me to Master Jonas's bed because, oh nein. Mad

321

Max, I already told you I just can't bear to couple with you again. I just can't. Don't ask me to do this. If you ever cared for me, please understand. It is not you. I am just so disgusting." She began to wail uncontrollably as she said that.

I winced over her words, but replied softly, "It is okay Annette, calm down. I don't need you to couple with me. I only wish I could. You are not disgusting. I would do anything to have you for my own. Sadly, my penetrating anyone is forbidden. I need you there to help distract me and set off my interest only. You will not have to endure my lusts, nor grant me any type of release. Basically, you get me excited, then Master Jonas will, uhm." I looked at the floor unable to say another word.

Annette glared at me and said in an angry sounding tone. "Rape you like he always does. Like my Master does me. Like all of us silvers endure everyday of our worthless lives, Mad Max. Just say it. Say it, we are nothing to them. Your Master rapes you. You don't even like sex with a man, but he cares not. He makes you lay there and take it anyway. He is a monster. They all are. I hate them. All of them. Look at your beautiful face. The Master beats you even though you always do what they want. They kill the silvers and never lose any sleep. Why? What did I ever do to deserve this? My mother died, that is what I did. I was fucking born. You too, Mad Max. All of us are cursed. I wish I was dead. God help me, but I do." She began to weep uncontrollably again.

I pulled her to me holding her tight while she let her pain go. I said nothing as she beat on my chest, railed, begged for death, and cursed. I knew how she felt. This horror of others touching against our wills was beyond vile. Annette needed a moment to let out the crushing agony of her foul existence.

I calmly stroked her back when her cries lowered to sobs and shudders and said, "Annette, I cannot say anything to take back what these criminals did to you. I wish I could make you whole again. Words are of no help to a broken heart, this I know. If you think you cannot do this thing, I ask of you. I will understand. I am not a Master. I am Mad Max and I love you. I always have. I'll give you a choice. If you wish to return to your Master, then go. If you want to die, then I will help you find your peace without judgement. If you come with me to ease my burdens, I offer you the same in return."

She looked up at me with a start. "How can you offer me an ease to my burdens, Mad Max? I heard you back there talking to my Master. Your Master has traded you off like a whore to take my spot. I don't have to fuck Master Jonas nor the Priceless. But I assure you my Master will rape the hell out of you. He will beat you too."

I smiled while looking into her gorgeous eyes. "Ah, my beloved, you don't know me very well. Look, once upon a time, you and I trusted each other completely. Did I betray you or you me? Nein. I must ask you to have faith in me that I am always a man of my word. I tell you I can give you a gift most rare. Only if you choose to grant me the favor of easing my own nightmare. For this small price, I promise to return the service by granting you a life free of your Master's lustful touching and cruel words. I cannot change the past, but I can give you a happy future."

Her eyes went wide. "A happy future? But Mad Max, that is not possible!"

I interrupted her, "Ja, Annette, it is. Because I can get you painted black, my love."

She gasped and replied in a near squeak. "You can do that? I dared not to hope for such a dream. Mad Max don't be so cruel. You are a silver like me. Even your Master Jonas cannot set me free as powerful as he is. Only my Master has the ability, and he'd never agree. Especially since he would have to admit to his illegally collaring with me. Trust me Mad Max, that's something he won't ever do."

I chuckled softly then pushed her blond hair out of her face as I replied, "I asked you to trust me, Annette. I am Priceless. I can do amazing things, even paint silver to black with the hand of a dishonorable Master. Will you grant me the mercy of your lips during my darkest hours for this precious service return? Ja or nein?"

She closed her eyes and sighed. "Ja, Gott help me. I accept your offer. I will not ask you another thing. I'm not agreeing to do it for the black collar though. I honestly don't believe you can do what you promised me, Mad Max. I will have to end my life soon and I am coming to terms with it. I will find the bravery to do it before the auction, I know that."

I shook my head with confusion. "Then why the hell would you bother? This thing I ask you is not going to be pretty, and I am ashamed to have you there to witness my humiliation. If not for a service return, then why are going to do it?"

She smiled bitterly. "I do this for you because I love you too, Mad Max. I suppose I always have and always will. I wasn't sure of it until just now. After that horrible thing we did last year, I couldn't stop thinking of you. The way you make me feel beautiful and desired. I dreamed of you so many nights. I would listen to hear for any news of you in the hallways. I mourned deeply when everyone said you were dead. I thought of ending my own life not realizing it was over losing you. Then tonight I heard you were alive, and I couldn't stop smiling. No matter what mean thing my Master said I was floating on air. Here I am with you and my heart beats like a wild creature within my chest. You hold me in your arms, and it feels right. I can see the skies I miss so much in your blue eyes, my love. I know that if I died right this minute, I would be at peace if the last voice I heard was yours in my ears. I would do anything to ease your burdens. Your pain is my own. I can say if this that I feel for you is not love then there is no such a thing."

I pulled her into a deep passionate kiss that was honest. I kept Christian from ruining it by holding that lustful bitch to the wall. She melted in my arms. Annette was the most beautiful soul I had ever known and for that second, I could lie to myself, believing that she was all mine forever. Then reality came calling us both back from our cloud of fantasy.

I heard a shout from a loud female black collar to another that the dead Elder was being removed. She was ordering everyone back to work. Annette and I pulled out of our loving embrace and watched for a chance to escape that closet without being seen. The moment the coast was clear we hauled ass, headed straight for the back stairwell to Master Jonas's apartment.

We walked in silence, our heads bowed. Everyone we crossed knelt or bowed causing Annette to giggle a few times. She was not accustomed to this strange ritual of the silvers toward their Priceless. It had become so common to my sight I no longer even noticed it.

All I could do was think of saving my precious Annette from the circuit. I had a plan, but it was a tricky one. I was unsure if Master Jonas should be let in on it, or if this would be best left to my own counsel.

By the time I reached my Master's apartment door, I knew what to do. The plan was to be kept out of the Vampire's radar. Something about his and the other Elder's quick approval of Drexel's murder wasn't sitting well within me. They seemed more ready than me to see that statue fucker gone. I wondered if they hated him so much why they didn't just kill the bastard. I needed to slow down a minute and look around me. I worried I had traded one conspiracy for others to take power for yet another one.

That examination of the evidence would have to wait. Master Jonas had demanded Der Hund show up for this horrid schwuler fetish sex. I already had to keep my nerves in a bind without adding more twists to my mixed-up brutal world.

I knocked on the door and Master Jonas opened it quickly.

Annette bowed her head, appearing scared as the Vampire smiled at the two of us standing in his entry. "Ah, she is a vision Christian Axel. I see you have good taste in the selection of females. I take it this is Annette?" He grinned even more widely, showing all his pointy teeth.

I nodded, never looking up from the floor. "Ja, Master this is Annette. I beg you allow us entry. She has agreed to do this for me, but her Master requires she be gone for two days."

He looked startled for a moment then said, "Two days? Christian Axel we only need her here an hour. What the hell am I supposed to do with her the rest of the time?"

Annette spoke up, "I can stay with a sister collar if my presence causes issue. My Master is remodeling. I fear he has taken a bit of advantage." She lied for me, demonstrating she was indeed a loyal heart.

Master Jonas snorted. "Damn right he has. What was his price for this twice a month arrangement, Christian Axel?"

I smiled. "Looking after his silver for the next two days Master."

My Master groaned. "Of course. He is auctioning the girl, isn't he? Well shit. Guess we must take what we can. Come inside you two. I have to say selling off such a beautiful silver is a foolish thing. Oh well, we'll wait to see who buys her collar. Then we can work out a new arrangement with the winner next month, ja?"

Annette and I walked in while I shot her a look of caution. "Ja, Master. We can do that. Annette you will be sure to report the new Dominant to my Master, right?"

She looked at me then smiled. "For Master Jonas and Mad Max of course. I am honored just to be granted such a gift as to please a man of his level."

Master Jonas's ego was stroked immediately. "I like this girl, Christian Axel. Okay, she may stay for two days in your old room, if she is quiet, I will keep her safe. You, my love, will be busy with Claus then Leo. So that means I will be stuck dealing with her till you get home. You will owe me for this favor."

I growled a bit at that. "Oh? I would think I already more than pay that debt tonight, Master. What more can I give you than blood. I say that with respect."

He chuckled. "There is my Der Hund. To think I didn't even have to call you. Good boy, I was prepared to thud you if you'd forgotten my directive. I'm thrilled you've decided it wasn't wise to give me trouble."

Annette looked confused but I smiled with wickedness at his strange statement. It was with much thrill I realized that Master Jonas couldn't tell one of us shards from another if we played our roles carefully.

"I will need to use your washroom a moment Master. I need to prepare if you would grant me the mercy of it?" I cast my eyes to the floor to make sure he didn't read in my eyes I was not Der Hund.

He nodded. "Ja, go get ready for our pleasure business. I will entertain Annette till you're ready. Oh, and Christian Axel, go ahead and remove your clothing. There is no reason to redress after your preparation ritual, ja? When you are ready, head for the room and wait patiently on the bondage bed. We will be their directly."

I winced then shot a look at a frightened Annette. "It will be okay, Annette. Do not be afraid. Neither my Master nor I will harm you. All you need to do is be the beautiful girl you truly are. That is the way to lift my burden."

She nodded. "I can do that Mad Max. I'll see you soon." She looked down, doing her best to remain stoic, but I could tell this was a disturbing scene for her and she hadn't seen anything yet.

I rushed to the bathroom to call the core. Christian and I are not the ones for this type of work. I was terrified that Der Hund would expect us to try to do the impossible. Master Jonas would know we were not him. The results would be a lifetime in our metal. This was some serious shit, and I won't lie, I was ready to bail and say fuck it. Let the boy go catatonic for good.

I flipped on the light and nearly had a heart attack. Maximillian and Mad Maxx stood there with Der Hund awaiting our presence. Once I recovered my breathing I completely relaxed. The boys were finally awake. This disaster was sure to be averted with two schwulers around to fix this problem.

Der Hund appeared to be deep in thought. "Okay, Jonas expects me to be there tonight but that will never happen again. I tend to be nasty in my temper like Christian, but this will require the schwuler sex with fake lustful interest. That is Maximillian's realm. However, he also cuts and drinks our blood. The taking of pain is Mad Maxx's domain. Ah but I tend to be of the quick wit too, like you Mad Max. In fact, he thought you were me thanks to your sarcasm. I have the perfect plan. You two, get in there with your brothers now." He pushed the shards inside with Christian and I.

The four of us were together for the first time in almost a year. It was fucking crowded as hell. All of us struggled to try to find comfort when suddenly our edges began to bleed into our brothers. Within only moments we were one shard with four minds.

Der Hund grinned. "Ah here he is. Master Mad Maxx the Brutal. This is the answer to our prayers. I now realized it will take all four of you to attend to the Elders, this insane Vampire and to seduce the H twins, Leo, and others too. The anger, lust and murdering of Christian will fulfill the Vampire's commands and smite our enemies. The seductive submissive of Maximillian will bring Leo, Stefan, the H twins and whoever stands in our way to their knees. The tolerance for pain and cool-headed planning of our targets will be attended to by Mad Maxx. The lack of empathy, ability to punish, and cruel strategy to thwart Cora, Gretta, Agnette, Peter and all the Voting Council will be Mad Max's thrill. Ja. Each of you hold a piece of me within him. Jonas will never be able to tell the difference with all the facets of me covered but not the real thing present for him to abuse. Twice a month you all meet for the blood fetish then when the fierce couple begins tonight Mad Max, and Christian, you will immediately break from the boy. I forbid the flesh to be coupled with my most dangerous shards within it. Mad Maxx you and Maximillian will shoulder such things, but you will break out when the killing begins. I will not have my most sensitive shards brutalized either."

We smiled back at our core full of the demons of our disease, "Your will is our own."

I attended my duties of preparation for this nightmarish scene then quickly went down the hallway to the red door blood room. Master Jonas and Annette had not yet arrived. I took my place on the bondage bed doing my best to brace for the coming disgusting acts of the Vampire.

I heard Master Jonas and Annette come through the door. My Master was in his robe and Annette was fully dressed in her pink sundress with white stockings. I smiled at her trying to help her to feel more comfortable. I could see the look of sheer terror in her eyes.

Though she had been involved in threesomes with her Master and sister collar before, this one was not exactly what she was experienced with. I knew she would be a bit more than disturbed by it. Really, there is no way to prepare anyone for this thing Master Jonas does. I wisely decided to just let her learn as it went along.

Master Jonas approached me and began to bond me to his bed. He gazed deep into my eyes thinking he maybe could see if I was Der Hund or not. I glared at him with hate lent the boy by Christian.

When he finished his last rope on my ankle, he frowned at me then said, "I think maybe I go get Emma to let her drink from you too."

I growled out full of fury. "Ficken Dich. Leave that whore at home."

He smiled. "There you are Der Hund. Ja, you're angry. Now for the lust, ja? Come to me beauty. Kiss and stroke this boy but remember, no touching him below the waist. Just do as I told you and all will be fine."

Annette came forward and sat on the bed next to me with her a sad look in her eyes. "Ja, I will do as you commanded Master." She leaned down then began kissing me with much passion.

I kissed her back feeling the heat of lust prickling my skin, then raising in my loins with vigor. My memory of the couple with this gorgeous girl ran through my mind stuck on repeat like the torn film in a projector. I wanted to take her so badly I began to pull against the ropes ignoring the bite of them. Annette gasped a bit but didn't pause from attending her duties.

As with Emma, I only flinched when Master Jonas cut into my arm with his lancet. I ignored his foul sucking at the wound. I was completely enraptured with the beauty instead of that beast. Annette could see this disgusting display and for a moment hesitated then started to pull away. I whimpered full of terror that she would remove the only thing that could bring me any mercy during this horror scene.

She saw my desperation. Annette swallowed hard, closed her eyes, then pushed her lips back to my own. I was swept away once more by the gentle touch of her soft skin and ecstasy of her playful tongue. Then I felt Master Jonas removing the ropes. The time had come for his most brutal blood coupling.

My right arm was free as he worked to release my right leg. I used the arm to stroke the back of Annettes hair. She immediately responded with a much wilder mouthing of my own. He released my other leg then came around the bed to get my last rope. He could see that our kissing was deeply involved.

He growled out sounding irritated. "Annette. I said to remove your clothing. Also, you move out of my way so I can release, then rebind Christian Axel in a better position. Take that dress off while I attend this knotwork." Annette backed away appearing fully terrified.

She was trembling but nodded then reached up to undo the buttons of her dress. I investigated her expression and saw the hundreds of nights of humiliation and despair. I know I couldn't allow myself to be another one of her worst nightmares.

With as much bravery as I could muster, I yelled out, "Nein, Master. I want Annette to stay dressed. It is the fantasy not the reality with her. I've never seen her naked before. Allow me to focus on imagining her beauty without seeing it. Maybe, next time I'll get a chance to see if my fantasy is reality, ja?" I lied since I had indeed seen her flesh, but not recently, so not a total fib, ja?

Annette shot a confused look at my Master as he asked, "Christian Axel? Are you sure about this? The girl is not ashamed to be naked for your pleasure. Why would you turn down the thrill of it?"

I nodded. "I don't want to grow bored with her too fast is all. Master, I beg mercy. I will lust for her for a longer time if I get to enjoy her slowly, I think."

Annette shot me a bitter smile of gratitude and I smiled back at her while Master Jonas finished unbinding me. He then had me put my arms behind my back as with Emma despite Annette being fully dressed. I kept my eyes on the mattress, realizing this was the moment of my biggest fears.

The woman I loved would soon be witness to my being sodomized by my Master. I did my best to console myself that if she truly cared for me her feelings would not change no matter what she saw. The shards within broke apart. Christian and Mad Max jumped from the flesh leaving Maximillian and me to deal with the coming rape.

Annette returned to bed, then pulled my face to hers kissing me with all the heat of a lover. I closed my eyes and joined her in this wanton act that would go unrequited for all our lives. Master Jonas, as before with Emma, watched this for a moment. Then when he saw that I was eager to mount the gorgeous girl he crawled up on the bed and removed his robe. I felt him running his hands over my flesh before he dropped down and began kissing me on my back and shoulders.

When he moved to my neck, he whispered to Annette to allow him to take my lips. She moved her attention to my ears while Master Jonas pulled me into his lustful tongue embracing. Once again, I could not tell one touch from the others. I had become overheated with passion and desirous of release.

Master Jonas then began pushing my head down indicating the time had come for his oral stimulation. I didn't bother to hesitate this time. This would happen and all that would do is slow down the inevitable. Annette had given plenty of blow jobs I am sure, and I had even given her oral stimulation once myself.

To my utter surprise she waited till I began giving Master Jonas head then she crawled behind me and reached around my waist. I moaned out in both shock and thrill when she grabbed my cock and began to stroke it with the talent only a pleasure submissive can provide. I expected Master Jonas to roar out for her to stop but to my great relief he allowed this to continue. She kissed my back while sending me straight to lustful heaven with her most skilled hand.

I admit I had a bit of trouble focusing on Master Jonas's interests with my own raging through my teenaged hormonally challenged brain. I was getting close to finding my orgasm when to my irritation Master Jonas pulled me off him and told Annette to back off her most appreciated behavior.

He pulled me around to position me for his mount with my own climax thwarted immediately. I groaned out and sought out Annette with much panic washing over me. I was agitated both by the loss of my apex so close to the moment and by this most unwelcome intercourse on the heels of it. I was terribly ravaged by Drexel's cruelty only four days before. I had not even gotten close to healing. This penetration was assured to be unpleasant, not that Jonas gave a damn, mind you.

Annette sat there looking at me with much pity while Master Jonas pulled me into position. She dropped her eyes to stare at the bed with tears running down her cheeks. I assumed she was demonstrating her empathy over my shame.

Her trickling tears turned to rivers, and she flinched to a cower when I let out an agonized wail. Master Jonas had entered me, most brutally. I knew this blood couple was gonna be rough, but this was worse than expected. I have no idea what Drexel did, but I assumed it was something that would make my job as the pincushion horribly painful for many days to come even with lubrication.

Master Jonas took a rest when I continued to yell out in agony after he'd being thrusting for several moments. "Relax Christian Axel, stop this nonsense. What's wrong with you? A little moaning is sexy, but you sound like a wounded cow. You're starting to hurt my feelings."

I whimpered back. "I apologize Master, but I think I am not ready for this. Please mercy, I am injured. It hurts."

He scoffed and said flatly, "Oh shut the hell up and do your job Christian Axel. The pain will pass and if it doesn't, too bad for you. Annette, get over here and silence this idiot. What good are you? I can't enjoy myself while he acts like a fool."

Annette came forward and grabbed both sides of my head, planting her lips on my panting mouth. Master Jonas resumed his sexual assault with harshness totally ignoring my obvious cries of agony. I could not help but begin weeping loudly. I didn't wish to have my Annette see that, but the tears came despite my best efforts.

Upon realizing I was growing despondent, she realized she had to do more than just kiss me to draw my attention from that terror. Annette pulled away from my lips and put her mouth next to my ear.

Then she whispered, "Come with me Mad Max. Do you see me? I am in the fields green and lush. I want to pick the flowers for our table. Tonight, I am making your favorite meal for dinner. You haven't forgotten my mother is coming to visit us, have you? Do you smell the cooking on the stove. Oh, the sun is so bright on our faces. Here my love, take my hand and run with me till we drop in the soft grass. Can't you feel it under our bare feet? In the air are the many ducks flying. Ah, how sweet! They are calling for their mates. The wind is cooling our sweaty faces. I love how you look so handsome when you smile like that. Listen, can you hear it? The church bells from town. It must be noon. Hurry my love, give me a kiss and we can return to our little cottage. I will sew and you can read to me. You have so many important books, ja? I'll call our dog to join us." She kissed my ear, and I felt her trembling lips were wet with tears.

I gasped, then grit my teeth as my Master's thrust grew rougher. I did my best to focus on my Annette. She calmly spoke of the vision of the life we would never have together. Her voice wavering with the sound of her own sorrow at feeling helpless to end this nightmare. Master Jonas continued to ignore my wailing, oblivious to my torment.

Instead, he increased his brutal assault banging on my ravaged backside with all his strength sending me straight to hell.

I focused all my attention on Annette. I listened hard while she described her twirling in her new dress. She was holding a baby lamb, asking me to pet it with her. In the lids of my tightly closed eyes, I began to see the colors of her beautiful world. My nose drank in the smell of supper she'd cooked for me waiting on the table of our pretend home.

Ah, Meine Liebe, for a moment I was there with her. No more pain, no more darkness. Just my beautiful Annette, a loyal dog, baby lambs and green land without walls far as the human could see. I staired into the blue-sky with her watching the fluffy white clouds. I smiled for a moment, but suddenly the sky went black, and it began to rain blood.

I screamed out as unimaginable pain gripped my flesh. Master Jonas had grabbed my shoulders and slammed himself into me with all his might in his bucking orgasm.

Annette wrapped her arms around my neck and held on tightly making hushing sounds into my ear. She was begging me to be silent before I ended up thudded for my insolence.

Master Jonas moaned out in thrill then leaned down across my back wrapping his arms around my chest. "I like this, Annette. At first, it was bothersome, but I must admit, your screaming turned out to be a real treat. I don't know what she did but bring her back next time. I approve of her techniques very much." He breathed out sounding dreamy.

I shook in pain praying for my heart to stop with Annette holding my head and Master Jonas gripping my chest. I briefly considered suicide again. This was a most unexpected horrific experience thanks to that God damned Drexel.

I had not even been offered the mercy of muscle relaxers nor pain killers. I then suddenly recalled with much terror; Master Claus would be looking to rape me in only another two hours. I was fucked, literally.

These horrible realizations caused fresh tears to erupt. I had some trouble catching my breath. Master Jonas had not bothered to uncouple for starters and the pain was unbelievable. I couldn't stop trembling. My anxiety was too high. It threatened to rip me apart at the seams.

Annette nodded. "I will come here twice a month if you wish it so Master. That is if Mad Maxx will be happy with that?" She didn't unhide her face from my own and I could hear her sniffling from her own crying.

Master Jonas pulled up then got off me, thank fucking God. He chuckled while undoing my wrists. "Christian

Axel does what I tell him to do. His opinion matters not, Annette. I say you come back then you do. Isn't that right my love?" He swatted my backside with a laugh.

I nodded then choked out. "As you wish Master." I this it is best to quell my tears and ignore the violation pains that burned like fire with the sharpness of a blade.

Master Jonas then gasped loudly. "What is this? Blood? Christian Axel? Why are you bleeding? Oh my God, there is tearing and injury here." He'd finally realized I had been screaming like that because something was very wrong. Okay more than what was usually wrong during his cruel assaults.

Suddenly Master Jonas let out a bellow that sent Annette to her face in prostrate and me to my back in terror. "Drexel, you fucking snake in the grass bastard." He grabbed his cock and fell forward shouting as if in great pain.

I shot a look of terror at the prostrated Annette who stole a confused, horrified look at me. Master Jonas got off the bed then ran from the room cursing Drexel and holding himself as if his manhood was about to fall off.

I could hear him knocking things off onto the floor in his bathroom down the hallway. I couldn't move from my position due to the sheer agony in my hind side. I was left wondering what had Drexel done to me and now Master Jonas. Annette lifted to her knees the moment she decided we were alone.

She crawled over and wrapped herself around my panting chest hugging tightly, "Oh my God, that was horrid Mad Maxx. I am so sorry, my beloved. I never knew it could be so awful," she wailed while clinging to my ravaged flesh.

I shook my head and panted out. "It is okay Annette. Please let me go. I am in a lot of pain. The things I suffer in my Masters' beds are bad, but normally not this bad. Something has gone wrong this time. I think Drexel did something. Please, my love, if Master Jonas catches you, he will hurt you. I will be alright I promise."

She looked up with worry in her expression, "What could Drexel have done to cause injury, I thought you said he died? Why would he even attack you in the first place? Seems to me the worst thing he could have done, he and all the others already do. What I just saw was a true nightmare. I will never be able to get this from my head. The Master was hurting you and wouldn't stop no matter how much you begged him to."

Master Jonas came barreling back down the hall cursing loudly.

I whimpered to Annette. "Please, get off Annette. He is coming. Don't let him catch us like this. He's capable of far worse than the things you already have witnessed."

Annette pulled away and took to the floor in a silent kneel. Master Jonas stormed into the room carrying a tube of something in his claws.

He glared at me for a moment then growled out at Annette. "Get up and go to the room with the grey door. I need to attend my collar and your presence is no longer welcomed. Go now." Annette moved with speed to do as he demanded.

I was wide-eyed and frightened, and in much agony, as he approached me his eyes red with anger. "Fuckin Drexel glued a nasty chemical to you, my love. He fixed it so that the next time anyone caused friction it would breach his trap. Obviously, he set this trap thinking it would get Claus, but he got me instead. Luckily, he has done this before. I have the antidote here. Now I need you to be still while I neutralize this shit. I brought something for the outer spots that've been hit the hardest, but I also have some of it in a prepped enema. When I curb your pain superficially, you will go to the bathroom and take care of the internal mess. I'll notify Claus of Drexel's betrayal. You'll need a few days off from rotation so you can heal. He and Leo will have to wait, I am sorry to say. Nothing can be done. The girl can stay here for her two days, but you will be in a chastity device until she leaves. Do you have any issues with that? If so, then you can take them up with my torture tools," he said just before he demanded I roll over for his treatment.

I did as he ordered and found the pain cut in half almost immediately. Then I went to his bathroom and followed the remainder of his instructions. After all that foulness was completed, he bent me over his sink so he could treat the entire affected area with petroleum jelly. The Vampire said several times that I was to keep coating myself with it. He told me doing it this way would encourage quick healing. I was beyond exhausted and more than horrified over this humiliating situation.

To this day I have no idea what that bastard did or how he did it. Master Jonas didn't explain any of it to me. The only good thing that came from it was I got a full three days off from the lusting of the schwulers. That bought me the time I needed to take care of my Annette and start my work toward seduction of the ugly Mistresses Helga and Heidi.

You may find it interesting, I sure didn't at the time, but my lack of being capable of sodomy caused Master Jonas to be a lot less interested in my activities. With my chastity device secured and my other coveted ability shut down for "healing." Only oral attacks could be forced. He is okay with a blow job but tends to dislike the idea that would be all that was possible for now in his intercourse with me. Thanks to that, he pretty much kept his hands off me for the next few days. Of course, I was still forced to sleep in his bed, held hostage in his cuddle though all the nights of my convalescence.

That first night after the attack from the late Drexel, I was worn out, in a lot of pain, and to be honest downright embarrassed that my poor Annette had been there to see such a nightmare. I was questioning my wisdom at having asked her to do such a task for me in the first place.

I was held hostage in the snoozing Master Jonas's clutches thinking what a fool I was when I saw Mad Max and Christian motioning me and Mad Maxx to join them. Obviously, the boys were in the mood for a group discussion. I told Mad Maxx he could stay with the flesh, and I would go see what the boys were wanting to bitch about this time.

I jumped from the boy and joined them in the restroom for this discussion. Mad Max glared at me with a lot of irritation in his eyes while Christian stood there his arms crossed shaking his head in disgust.

342

Mad Max clicked his tongue then said, "What the fuck went wrong, brother? I heard you cried like a little bitch over that schwuler sex. I thought you were a whore of the highest caliber. What was that shit about?"

I didn't appreciate that insult but calmly replied, "Well smart ass, that is apparently what happens when you are left in charge of attending to the hygiene of the boy. Did you even bother to scrub at all before the Vampire's blood coupling? If I'd been allowed to examine our flesh, I would have found and removed that shit from Drexel left behind. That is why this job of handling the lovers is mine and not yours. You are sloppy. Now the flesh has a chemical burn. Not good and stop calling me a whore. I am a proper pleasure submissive, but you are nothing but a common cocksucker."

Mad Max shook his head. "Ficken Dich, Maximillian. I'm telling you I cleaned the flesh completely after Drexel finished raping us. That stuff must have been internal or something. Whatever it was it didn't kill the boy, so drop it. The reason I called you here is I wanted to make sure the two of you knew that come ten tomorrow, Christian and I will be riding the flesh. You and Mad Maxx can relax until we are done with Master Stefan. Oh, and you are a whore. Call it whatever you like."

I rolled my eyes. "Okay, whatever motherfucker. Call me a whore if it makes you happy. I do my job just like you do fool. I am more than glad to jump out of the boy while you two villains do what you do best. Just make sure you save our poor Annette."

Christian chuckled at that. "What the hell do you care if we save Annette, schwuler boy? Oh wait, I know. You want to share dress patterns and do each other's hair, ja?"

Mad Max laughed hard at that, then high fived Christian as he said, "Damn, you are truly evil. We need to party together real soon."

Christian laughed back. "Oh, I intend to at ten in the morning. I believe we both have a date, ja? Then we show these schwuler boys the way real men fuck another man."

I scoffed and replied, "You know they say those that fear the schwuler do it because they are afraid, they are schwuler themselves. I know no matter what happens I prefer the woman in my bed. I am not ashamed of being called the schwuler for being good at my job. I know it isn't the truth. I also don't need to prove it to the like of you or anyone. You simply cannot prove the truth when others refuse to believe it. No doubt I am the only real man in this bathroom. I don't question my sexuality like you two seem to."

That pissed off Mad Max and Christian. They both began cursing while denying either had a single schwuler bone in their skin. I just stood there with my arms crossed refusing to hear a word of their protest. I pointed out it wasn't me, Maxmillian, that seemed obsessed with schwuler sex like they seemed to be. I thought nothing of it. Well, to be honest, I hate the job, but I don't like cleaning the toilet either or doing the laundry. I still must do it.

"I am not into schwuler sex, Maximillian. You take that back now," yelled out Mad Max.

I shrugged as I replied, "Oh? I only point out the truth of it. I never sit around thinking about sex with my husband. I also never bring the subject up in conversations. I would rather forget that shit. Seems that every time I see either of you that is all I hear come out of your mouths. Why? You don't call me the foot massager, the tailor, the conversationalist, or the Master dresser? I do all those things just as often. But you bring up the special services as if that is the only service, I provide for the Masters' pleasure day and night. Well, you know better. So, I say again, you are the ones hung up on sexual tasks. That means you both are secretly titillated by these nasty men touching me. Now if you two are quite satisfied, I need to get back to bed. I am fucking tired."

I turned to leave when Mad Max snorted out, "You mean you're tired from fucking, you whore. Don't forget to suck the Vampire's cock in the morning before coffee." He and Christian giggled with evil.

I flipped him the bird, then jumped into the boy for sleep. I watched the two of them take to the shadows.

Just as I drifted off to my slumber, I head Mad Max call out of the darkness, "Not even in your wildest dreams schwuler boy. Sweet dreams about ass coupling, you pervert."

Well for his information that night I dreamed of Annette's pretty eyes, the flowers in her fields of imagination, and making love to her under the bright blue skies. I awoke with a raging hard on for the girl thinking only of sneaking from that room to slip into her bed. I just knew I could change her mind about her insisting she never wanted to have sex with me again.

I am a gentle and generous lover, unlike that brute Mad Max. What an idiot. His unbridled and unthinking lust ruined it for the rest of us. If he oversaw the lovemaking around here, shit, we'd have to be a schwuler because no females would ever want us touching them.

I was just about to do exactly what I was thinking when Master Jonas stirred next to me.

He woke, then looked at me with concern. "How are you feeling, Christian Axel? Any better than last night?" He stared at me while stretching.

I winced and replied, "I'm still very sore. Thank you for asking, Master." I felt better but I wasn't fucking telling him that.

He nodded. "I am raw too. Fucking Drexel, I hope the Devil sticks a red-hot poker up his ass for all time."

I snorted and said, "Well, this morning I know exactly how that would feel Master. I would beg you to allow me to go downstairs to the kitchen for my breakfast. I think walking will aid me in healing a bit."

His eyes went wide in surprise. "Christian Axel, you haven't slept even three hours. Are you not tired? All night you tossed and turned. I couldn't sleep myself with all your trips to the bathroom love. What about the girl? Aren't you afraid to leave her here alone with me?"

I chuckled at that as I said, "Master if you could do anything foul to Annette with your cock cooked like that then I would bow in respect and so would she. I believe she will be fine resting. She is about to end up at auction. That kind of stress would get to anyone. I beg you allow me to quietly go down for our breakfast tray and a stroll around the House. I am in the cock cage, and anything else is busted or burned the fuck up. I cannot get into much mischief now, can I? I also would like to go see if Egon is around and see what he knows about the latest gossip. I think being seen would be helpful to further the idea that Mad Maxx is alive and well, ja?"

Master Jonas yawned loudly. "Okay Christian Axel. Go ahead and take your meal and stroll. No funny business. It is now nine thirty. Be back here by eleven. I need more rest. If I awaken to find my Husband is not home your ass will hurt worse than it already does at the end of my tawse."

I nodded then got out of the bed throwing on my clothing from the night before. "As you wish Master. I will be back by eleven."

I left my sleepy Master and rushed to the room with a grey door. I knocked softly and Annette bid me entry. I stood at the door keeping my gaze to the floor. She sat up in the bed, her hair a mess from a rough rest, with much sleep in her eyes.

"Annette I am going down to the kitchen then to see Egon. I will be back at eleven. I will bring you something to eat when I come back. I ask you to stay in this room with the door locked. Make no noise and Master Jonas will not awaken. I hate to leave you alone, but it cannot be helped. I also would like to thank you for last night." I took a deep breath trembling to keep down my despair of the memory of that foulness.

She nodded then looked at the floor. "Mad Max I have no words. I know those days in the bathroom with us girls we thought you schwuler. That was funny for us, and we made a lot of sport of you over it. I have now seen that horror in the flesh, and I feel the ass for my part in anything I said that may have hurt your feelings. There is no excuse for such meanness, so I won't offer any. Just know that to my dying day you have my deepest respect. None of us realized you are one of the only ones of your gender in this House that can utterly understand the pain of the female silver. For what it is worth, you said you worried about my seeing your humiliation. I only saw the one I love suffering and I was their helpless to help him. You have nothing to be ashamed of, but I cannot say the same for everyone from Ben to Geraldine and sadly me. You're the only one of us with a decent heart. I never once heard you say anything ugly about anyone first. After what I saw, and now know what you go through every day of your life here in this House, well my love now, I realize you really are the Priceless."

I smiled at her. "Thank you for saying such kind words that I surely don't deserve. Annette, promise me you will do what I told you. Await my return and don't unlock this door or do anything rash. Do me the honor of spending this time we are parted dreaming of the dog and cottage in the flower fields. When I return, I'll bring you a fantasy come to truth. I ask you once more to trust me. I have done so much evil in my short time. I beg you to allow me this one chance to do something that proves my life worthy of having been lived. Swear to me I will find the girl I love safe and sound in this bed at eleven and one-minute past."

She nodded. "I know you are up to something because you are due at my Master's apartment at ten, but Master Jonas didn't approve this trade. I told you I ask no questions and I say nothing. I keep my word. Mad Maxx, I swear to you I will do whatever you say. I'm merely grateful to have another day to bask in your eyes. I won't miss that for the world. Thank you for caring so much for me. I wonder how I got so lucky?" She looked up with tears in her eyes.

I bowed my head and replied, "I only gave you equal service for the one you granted me, Annette. See you soon my love. Lock this door and pet our dog a million times for me." I took off down the hall ready to earn my right to call myself a decent human being.

I slipped over to the fake flowers and removed Drexel's green clutch. I took out another of his pre-loaded paralytic syringes. I re-hid the purse then rushed to the back staircase after dropping the needle into my hidden jacket pocket.

With much speed I traveled to the kitchen and ordered breakfast for Master Jonas and my Annette. I picked up the tray then headed down the many hallways. I arrived at the door of Master Stefan and knocked.

He opened the door smiling with glee. "Ah, you are right on time Mad Maxx. I can see you're a submissive of good manners."

The boy staggered a second while Mad Maxx and I jumped out and Christian and Mad Max crammed inside.

The flesh shook his head to clear the transference fog then smiled with much evil. "I have a lot of good qualities Master. May I come inside?"

Master Stefan stood there appearing a bit confused by the minor tremor, but then motioned me to enter. I walked past his curious eyes.

"What is with the tray? I thought you were staying for two days. I didn't order any food." He pointed at my breakfast tray.

I grinned with pure mischief. "Well, I was sent to offer a new business deal between you and my Master. He wanted an answer and breakfast before I am released to attend your every desire."

Master Stefan scoffed. "Huh? Wait a fucking minute. I sent my worthless trainee, and I don't see the bitch here yet. I held up my end. What the hell is with this stalling?"

I knelt and cast my eyes at his floor faking that I was upset over his distress. "Oh, I do apologize for my clumsy delivery of this message Master. I would beg you to listen to what I have to say. It will please you a great deal I think."

Master Stefan stood over me staring down with an expression of irritation. "I am fucking listening, Mad Maxx. Out with it before I beat your ass and send Jonas my own message."

I nodded. "My Master killed a black collar by accident a few years ago. He owes the head Black collar Mistress a tarnished collar of the same worth. He noticed your trainee is of the same age, build and quality as the one he owes. He is growing fatigued at the constant demands he replace what he broke. He is in a terrible bind and sent me to ask you what it would take to tarnish this trainee to black. I am to return with the certificate right away if you agree to this deal. He said if you did this for him, he would owe you any favor you wished for it."

Master Stefan gasped. "Well, I guess he would indeed. To tarnish that trainee, I would have to swear a collar she doesn't have now, wouldn't I? That would hurt my reputation if it were ever discovered. The price for such a risk would be most high."

I sighed as I responded. "That is what my Master said. He authorized me to accept any offer within his power for such a relief of his situation with the assurance no one will ever hear of any dishonor of the honorable Master Stefan."

Master Stefan took a seat on his couch blowing out his breath. "Any offer within his power, huh? Now that changes things a bit. What if I said I wanted to sit with him at his table in the Great Hall every meal?"

I nodded. "That could be arranged easily, Master. This is a fair trade."

The greedy man snorted. "Wait a second, you agree too fast. I also want to be seen strolling with him in the garden."

I nodded again. "Ja, I say once more this can be arranged, Master. Master Jonas is rather fond of you. I think that is also a fair trade."

Master Stefan sat forward then grinned with much lust in his eyes. "I also want a leash to his submissive, the Priceless, once a week for my own pleasures, no questions asked, and no boundaries given."

I looked up glaring in irritation as I spit out, "I say this also can be arranged Master. Anything else? I will warn you he will require the certificate in advance. He wishes to pay off the head Mistress quickly. If you do this for him, I'll take it to him, then I will return with his agreement in writing. Once the deal is sealed you can begin your leash privileges with me, no further quarrel or hindrance."

He laughed. "Deal, I will go get the certificate and fill it out this second. You stay here, I'll be right back."

I smiled. "I wouldn't dare to go anywhere without that paper, Master. I am happy to await your pleasure."

The brute ran off to a back room practically singing in happiness over his good luck. I reached into my pocket and flipped off the top of the needle. I laid down the tray of food waiting patiently for my new lover to return to me.

Master Stefan came back within fifteen minutes or so with the certificate that announced to the House his trainee, I mean submissive, Nobody's silver was tarnished to black for all time. He signed it in front of me. All the while he disgustingly bragged of what he intended to do to me sexually.

I smiled coyly in silence while he completed the form. When he handed it to me, I looked it over to make sure it was legitimate and fully filled out.

Finding it complete, I laid it on the breakfast tray then looked up at him with a wide smile on my face. "Before I go perhaps you would like a demonstration of the pleasures you soon will enjoy during all your tristes with my forbidden silver?" I stood up while I said that with the storm clouds of murder filling my mind.

Master Stefan grinned with thrill, "Hell ja, I would!"

I grabbed him roughly pulling him into a lustful kiss. He pawed at me wildly as I slowly backed him toward his couch, never breaking our embrace. The man panted and clawed like a beast making it difficult for me to move him backward. Then he realized where I was trying to get him to go.

He broke from our mouthing with a large smile of glee. "Ah, you intend to please me with that pretty mouth of yours. Silly Stefan is a slow thinker before he has his coffee, ja? I'll go sit down for you. All you had to do is say so Mad Maxx." He rushed to his couch and sat down spreading his legs while dropping his pants to his knees.

I walked toward him reaching into my pocket. "Well Master, I have to say, you weren't bragging. You are definitely more eager than my old dusty Masters." I dropped to my knees then took up his manhood in one hand and swiftly jammed Drexel's needle into his cock with the other.

Chapter 40: Love's Sacrifice

"I pushed the plunger of that syringe in with the quickness of a flea's jump. Master Stefan let out a loud yell and leaned forward, backhanding me with much force. I fell to the floor nearly unconscious. He rose from the seat ready to beat the stuffing out of me, but that medication of Master Drexel's is fast acting shit.

His attempt stalled with speed. The foul Master Stefan shot a look at me when he noticed that his limbs were not responding. Like that old statue fucker Drexel, he trembled a minute, then fell back to his sitting position. All he could do was stare unblinkingly at me. Stefan was unable to move even his eyelids.

I lifted myself off the floor. I saw that the syringe had been thrown across the room when I hit the ground. I collected it then put the guard on the needle and dropped it back into my pocket. I chuckled as I returned to the paralyzed Master Stefan. He was stuck sitting there with his pants around his knees.

I sat down by him and gazed into his glazed eyes as I said out loud so Master Stefan could hear. "Well Christian, what do you think? I bet you a million dollars this bastard won't live to see the dusk."

Christian laughed hard as he responded, "Ah, I bet you a million dollar he doesn't live another hour."

I shook my head then replied, "Ficken mich, Christian. I believe I've just lost a fortune to you! I happen to be capable of seeing into the future. It is another superpower of the Priceless perhaps. It's become clear you have won this bet. Obviously, I'm going to owe you a million dollars. Thank you, Master Stefan, you just lost me a minor fortune. Oh well, I guess it only fair that I take out that loss on you before my brother Christian comes for what is owed him, ja?" I said this loudly so I could be sure he heard me betting on the survival of the helpless, just as he had done to me.

I got up and walked around looking at his pictures on the wall. I noticed one of him with an elder woman of great resemblance. I smiled as took that photo from the hook.

I held it before his frozen eyes then sat down next to him again. "Ah, this is your mother, right? She is so very lovely Master Stefan. Bet she would be then proud of her son if she knew he was nothing but a child molester of the little girls and boys, ja? That is a mother for you. Their unconditional love is eternal, isn't it? My own mother, she loves me like yours surely loves you. In fact, she treats me just like you treat your submissive Annette. You know, it warms my heart that a mother's love for her son is the same as Master Stefan has for his loyal submissives. While it's true I am going to let Christian kill you in a few moments, I'm a torn now that I've seen you have a sweet mother that will mourn. It honestly breaks my heart. After all, a mother should never have to cry over the loss of a child. So, tell you what. I am going to grant her mercy. I'm going to put her picture in your hand for you. That way when they find your corpse it will be reported to your mother that she was the person you were thinking of as you died. Oh wait, shit. You are too large for a little boy such as me to place in a more dignified position. I suppose my tiny size didn't matter to you a moment ago. Hell, you viewed me as big enough to fuck, ja? Just like Annette or her sister collar who was only fourteen years old. You know, I wonder where Annette's sister has been hiding out? I haven't seen her in the halls in a long time. Oh, that's right. My memory is so poor, I almost forgot. I suddenly recalled you sold her off to the invisible people. Ah that poor girl was surely raped to death. then buried in an unmarked grave somewhere in the barren lands outside of Moscow. Silly me, I should shut up my discussion of facts you are not interested in hearing. Since I'm aware the horrific fate of the little girls you defiled doesn't bother you, I will get back to my actions of returned kindness to you Master. Here you take this picture of your mother. Ah, and let's put your other hand on your cock. My goodness. It looks like you are masturbating, doesn't it? Well, it's natural that you die holding the one person that loved you and the only thing that that you ever cared about. Gee, I hope no one misunderstands and thinks you were jacking off to a picture of your mother. Do you worry this position you are in may appear scandalous?" I pretended to be deep thought over that possibility while I wrapped his right hand around his flaccid cock.

I saw water start to stream down his frozen cheeks.

With a smile of evil I said, "There, there Master Stefan. It is far too late for tears. You never cared about those helpless children while you raped them. Mad Max always provides service to all his masters in equality. So, you can be assured, I feel nothing for the pain you suffer, you cocksucker. I love watching you suffer with the knowledge that you are finally getting empathy for the innocent ones you have defiled. You are not worthy of regret nor sorrow

356

from anyone but maybe that foolish mother of yours. But before you die, I want you to know, the Priceless ends your life in the name of Annette, her sister Judith and all the many children before them you destroyed. I noticed their pretty faces neither grace your walls nor trouble your memory. When you get to Hell, tell the Devil Mad Max sends his respects, ja?"

I went to the tray of breakfast and removed the plate I got for my Master Jonas; he never eats breakfast. I put the plate of food on the table. I took a chunk of the sausage off the meal. I went to the stilled Master Stefan that was weeping heavily. I pulled away from the wheel and let Christian loose.

Christian forced opened Master Stefans mouth and shoved that piece of meat down the Dominant's throat. He couldn't swallow the air blocking chunk thanks to Master Drexel's medication. Christian stood over him watching the life drain out of the Stefan's eyes with a gleeful smile on his face. Within five minutes, without a struggle or even a whimper, Annette's Master died.

Christian gasped and said, "Well shit! There wasn't anything to that. I was hoping to see more fight out of him. I thought a man choking to death would be violent."

I growled in irritation. "Ficken mich Christian. I let you have all the fun killing that bastard and still you're bitching. Although you do have a point. We'd better make it look like he did fight with the reaper, ja? I suppose he should appear more disheveled."

Christian took a step back to examine the scene as he replied, "No one is going to find him for days. By then, Annette will safely be out of the House. They will be disgusted when they see he was masturbating to his mother's photo. No one will suspect us. I say we leave this piece of shit to rot as he is. Besides, if they do an autopsy, that medication of Drexel's will be found in him anyway. The House will never allow such a deep investigation over a Dominant of such low status. Instead, the leaders will cover their asses by claiming Stefan was a pervert that got what he had coming. I say we leave it be and let the Laws of the House cover up the crime for us, ja?"

I nodded as I responded, "Makes sense to me but for the record I think you are insane."

Christian snorted then replied, "Fuck, haven't you realized we all are. We have schizophrenia, dumbass."

I said angrily, "Do you believe that brother? Really? Surely you know that is a lie. Everyone tells us lies, especially that crooked House doctor. I tell you; we do not have schizophrenia."

He shook his head. "My God, we are further gone then I thought. I wonder if we need more medication? I think standing here in front of a man we just killed arguing with ourselves looks damned bat shit crazy to me. Seriously, you can't get any more insane than that."

I pushed Christian away from the wheel. "Shut the fuck up, idiot. There is no arguing. I say we are perfectly sane, and we are. You back the fuck down and let me manage the work. You need a rest. The only crazy thing we have done recently is not fuck that sexy Annette till the boy's dick falls off. I will get to the dungeon and seek out the H twins then we go home to get into that beauty's panties."

Christian had been sullen about my pushing him out of the way, but he brightened at that idea, "For truth? Don't you be stroking my cock with a tease, brother. You said I get to have her the next time she lets us have sex with her. If you give me the wheel to fuck Annette, then I'll forgive you for pissing me off."

I picked up the rest of the breakfast tray and stuck the black collar certificate into my hidden pocket as I replied, "Like I give a shit if you forgive me, Christian. I will beat the holy hell out of you just for the sport of it. You can have Annette when I am done fucking her. I got her the certificate of freedom so she will want to reward me, the Mad Max. Not you, the idiot Christian. All you did was shove meat down a man throat. Hey, wait a minute! You are a schwuler." I laughed over my clever insult as I went to the door to see if the coast was clear.

Christian was beyond livid at my words but not that I cared. That fool hadn't earned Annette's gratitude. I was the one that had to endure that nasty kissing and touch that brute's cock. I was going to enjoy her adoration first and if there was anything left of her he could have my leftovers.

I was about to sneak out the door when suddenly Maximillian and Mad Maxx threw me and Christian to the wall with force.

I recovered before Christian and yelled out, "What the fuck are you doing, schwuler boys?" I was furious they had hijacked the boy.

Maximillian smiled at me as he replied, "Time to seduce the H twins, monster boys. Your job is done for now but keep your fangs handy. Never know when a little killing might come in useful. Oh, you'd better not touch Annette, you freaks. She already said nein. You'll mind the lady, or I personally will shatter your ass."

I was gonna slap that prissy shard around, but the boy took off out the door headed for the dungeons. Christian and I were forced to race behind him trying to catch up.

The boy rushed down the crowded hallway. Silvers dropped to their knees all around me slowing down my wild run. I was cursing several of them under my breath when I saw one of my targets heading for the stairwell that led to the bowels of the House. I jumped, then nearly tripped two small silvers that fell to the ground near terrified to see me barreling down on them.

The squatty, elderly, ugly woman I was running to catch turned around to see me hauling ass at her full speed. Her eyes went wide when I approached, then fell to my knees at her feet dropping my head with reverence. She stood there looking all around appearing to be seeking the Elder or Voting Council member that caused such a dramatic display of honor from the Priceless collar.

When she was satisfied, she could spy no such member of the House, she looked down at me. "Mad Maxx I presume? Are you kneeling to me? Surely not."

I nodded. "I am sorry, Ma'am. You seem to know me, but I don't know you. I apologize. I was trying to get a better look at you, and well, I was stunned by the vision. Forgive my stupidity and clumsiness. I am only a young man. I know not how to woo a female of worth."

The elderly female's eyes nearly bugged out of her head, which made her even uglier as if this were possible. "Who sent you to have sport with me Mad Maxx? Jonas? Claus?

Bladrick, ah yeah that rat bastard. He is behind this. Well, you go back to your Master Bladrick and tell him I am not amused. How dare he try to make fun of Heidi like that."

I looked up with a dreamy look and a stupid smile. "Mistress Heidi? That is your name? How beautiful. I don't understand why you would think any Master would send me to make sport of you, Mistress. You must have a mirror somewhere. What man wouldn't chase you down and kneel at your feet."

Mistress Heidi grunted. "Boy, you are truly a Priceless collar indeed. I bet old Bladrick wishes he was still the young man. A tongue of silver within his reach and his useless cock which could never enjoy the stroke of it. Ha, good enough for him. You get the hell out of here, Mad Maxx. I have no time for games. I have little silvers to subjugate and the sweet sounds of them crying for their mothers to enjoy."

I frowned and feigned a pout. "As you wish Mistress. Could I beg your mercy for kneeling at your feet again soon? I understand you are very busy, and I don't assume myself even worthy of such a joy but if you would grant me this kindness, I would be forever grateful."

She scoffed. "Persistent cuss, aren't you? Well tell you what, Mad Maxx, you want to kneel at my feet come back tomorrow morning and I will be here. I will take you down to the dungeons and put you in my chains. When I finish beating you, then we see if you still want to kneel at my feet."

I smiled brightly. "Thank you, Mistress. I will be here. You are a true Goddess to allow me to bask in your glory."

Mistress Heidi's mouth dropped to the floor. "Did you not hear me Mad Maxx? I said I am going to thud you till you wish for death."

I nodded. "Ja, I heard your words. The sound of the dove calling always catches my attention. I am not even worthy enough for your thudder, yet you are willing to grace me with your skillful hand. I will wear your stripes with honor. Mistress."

She stood there appearing flattered, finally, hell's bells. "Master Bladrick didn't send you then?"

I shook my head, still staring at her with adoration. "Nein Mistress. I told you I saw you from afar. I was smitten immediately. I dared not to even expect the thrill of your communication much less your heavy hand. You have made my day."

She laughed hard at that. "Boy, I am old enough to be your grandmother. I don't believe a handsome boy such as you would bother with my old bones. I am a lot of things, but a stunner is not one of them. I do in fact have a mirror, Mad Maxx, and that bitch don't tell lies, like the Priceless collar does."

I grabbed her hand causing her to startle then lightly kissed her knuckles still in my kneel. "Older women are my fetish, my beauty, and thudding my thrill. You are my angel fallen from Heaven, Mistress. I understand you may not believe me but that matters not. I can live all my days with the vision of your gorgeous face within my memory. Thank you for the mercy of it. I must go before my Master grows irritated at my insolence. I will be here tomorrow with my heart hoping that you bring me the love you promised me." I got up and ran the other direction as if in a hurry to get back to my Master's apartment, leaving the confused Mistress to absorb my words of seduction.

When I was certain that I was too far from her sight I slowed my gait then looked at Mad Maxx. "Damn, she is uglier than I recalled. For a moment there I thought maybe I was trying to seduce one of the Elder schwulers. I couldn't be sure of the gender."

Mad Maxx nodded looking stunned. "Dear Gott, you don't think we are going to have to sleep with her, do you?"

I cringed. "Fichin nein. I am not touching that, yikes."

Mad Max ran up alongside me. "Ha, I knew it. You agreed to fuck old ugly Claus and nasty Bladrick but think to refuse Mistress Heidi. At least she is a woman, you fool."

I snorted at the sadistic bastard. "Christ, Mad Max. None of us is sure she is a girl. You go back there and look for yourself, then come back and assure me. Either way though, I assure you I am not fucking Claus or Bladrick."

Mad Maxx frowned. "Maximillian is right on that one. They fuck the boy fool, not the other way around. Trust me, there is a huge difference."

Mad Max looked back at Christian that had just caught up as he yelled to him. "You hear that brother? There is a difference between fucking the man or being fucked by one."

Christian nodded. "Could have fooled me. Hey, did any of you notice that you idiots are talking to yourself aloud? I think maybe that doesn't look good for the boy."

Suddenly filled with the feeling of horror, I stopped and looked around me. The silvers in the hall were trembling in fear. I had not realized I was indeed speaking to my brothers with the boy's voice. I stormed off down the hallway cursing all three of them while Christian and Mad Max chuckled over my stupidity. No wonder everyone thinks we are fucking nuts.

I looked at one of the clocks on the House wall. I saw that I still had another thirty minutes before I had to be back to Master Jonas's service. I rushed to the stairwell to check on Egon's welfare and loyalty. I got down there to the torture rooms in record time. I had barely started checking the rooms when, to my shock and horror, Peter came out of the branding room with Agnette.

I turned to rush back the way I came. Egon would have to fucking wait. I didn't want to risk a confrontation with Peter while holding a spent syringe, a black collar certificate, and a breakfast tray. Well, I was in no hurry to see my parents under any circumstances, to be completely honest. I was almost on the stairs when my worst fear was realized.

"Halt Maximillian. You stop right there you little bastard," I heard Peter yell from behind me.

I winced but kept moving faster trying to rush up the steps. Peter took off running after me. I yelped then tried to push my way past the crowd going up and down the old stone walkway. He easily caught up and halted my bid to escape by grabbing the back of my jacket.

He held me tightly as he shouted with glee, "I got you, you little fucker."

I said nothing while he dragged me to the hallway of the rooms where Agnette stood smiling with humor. I kept my eyes to the floor when Peter reached her. He snatched up my black leash pulling it forward with harshness. I almost dropped my breakfast tray but wisely remained silent.

"Well, look what I have here Agnette. I seem to have found your insolent son creeping around the torture rooms. I wonder, did he finally get a bit of remorse for denying me that thudding he has coming?" Peter chuckled while my mother grinned appearing thrilled at my situation, bitch.

My mother stared at my bowed head as she replied, "Nein, Peter. I don't think he is seeking to grant you what is owed. I believe he is here to insult us both some more. I would give him more than a thud for such grievous behaviors."

Peter chuckled full of evil. "Ja? Well, my dear what would you suggest instead of my tawse then?"

Agnette scoffed. "I hear he hates the pinwheel and other cutters. I say take him to the sharps and cut the boy up till he learns to mind his betters."

I shot a look of both fear and hate at my mother. "I beg your mercy, Master. I must be back at my Master's apartment right away. He will not be pleased with your scaring my flesh either."

Peter laughed loudly, as did Agnette. "Ah, there we go. Finally, a little respect at last from this useless submissive. Do you hear this bullshit, Agnette? Is that a rat on his collar? I think that rodent is a most appropriate representation of this thing." He reached out and flipped my bat collar with a disgusted expression on his face.

She roared in laughter at that as she said, "Ja, a rat with leathery wings. Nothing but vermin."

I kept my eyes on the floor wondering if I should have saved that syringe of Drexel's for a more worthy target.

Peter got his laughter under control then said, "I think you are right, Agnette. I'll take this bastard to the cutting room for a little reminder of who is the one that broke him in."

He dragged me by leash heading for the torture room labeled "Blood Sports."

I fought his lead wildly while yelling out in a terrified tone, "Nein, nein. You cannot do this. I will tell my Masters. They've sworn to a rule against tearing my flesh. I swear if you dare to cut me Master Peter, the Elders will rip you a new asshole!"

Peter turned around and shot a smug glance at Agnette as he replied, "I didn't grant arrangement nor agreement with your Masters. I can do this as my choice of punishment, Maximillian."

I shook my head. "Nein. You do it and you will find out that my Masters won't care that you didn't. I promise if you proceed, they will punish you more fiercely than whatever you intend to do to me, Master."

He glared at me as he said angrily. "Fine, I will not use the sharps then. Besides, I've decided on a better torture for your punishment. Agnette, my love. please follow us." He dragged me to the last door of the torture chamber hallway.

This door had no label on it. It was the room the Dominants used for private meetings or for forbidden sexual tristes. I was hauled inside behind Peter. Agnette took up the rear to push me forward when I tried to back up. Once inside she closed the door behind us.

Peter turned around as he smiled and said, "Drop to your knees and suck my cock, Maximillian. Do it the way I taught you and maybe if you do a perfect job, I won't beat you with my tawse after I'm satisfied."

I shook my head. "Nein. I'll take your tawsing. I'll never grant you my sexual artistry ever again Master."

He chuckled. "Oh ja? Well, I've heard tale your about to break that ratty collar. When you do then, I think you've forgotten we have a contract that will make me your Master once more. I guess that fact slipped your mind thanks to the burden of your psychosis, ja? Eventually I will force you back to your knees and you will do as I command. Agnette, be a dear and retrieve one of the thudders from the back wall please."

Agnette took off in a near run, appearing eager to get the torture tool for Peter. I stood there in silence. I mentally told Christian he had better come up with a plan to kill these two soon. I was fucking sick and tired of my mother and father's cruel treatment.

Suddenly the door flew open. To my shock, in walked Master Leo. He cast his eyes around the room and for a moment appeared as if he was going to leave. The shady Elder stopped dead in his tracks when he spotted me being held hostage by leash by Peter.

He sounded confused as he asked, "Peter? Why do you have the Priceless in here with you?"

Peter scoffed as he replied, "I am giving a correction lesson to this insolent collar. This situation is none of your affair Leo. So, get the fuck out, you are wasting my time."

Master Leo put his hands on his hips and smiled evilly as he said, "It's not my affair, you say? Oh, I beg to differ my old friend. You see, I am an Elder now, and that means you are in possession of my property without asking for my permission. I will be getting the fuck out as you rudely demanded, but not without first taking back what belongs to me."

I shot the Elder a pitiful look of fear and whimpered out, "Master Leo. I did nothing wrong. I was merely minding Master Jonas's commands to seek out Egon for my training session. I swear I was not insolent to this honorable Dominant."

Master Leo nodded then replied, "Ah, I believe you Mad Maxx. Peter, I know my submissive has only the best manners. Seems I recall not too long ago you bragged the Priceless of such high-quality, common faults were beneath him. He wouldn't dare to behave poorly toward you or any of his betters. So, again I say to you, hand that boy to me, his Master. Refuse my demands this time, and Peter, believe me when I say I wouldn't want to be you."

Peter pulled my leash harshly and he snarled out, "I tell you Leo the submissive is telling lies. Only a few days ago he spit on me, then ignored my commands to attend me while supping in the Great Hall. You know damned well, I am well within my right to punish this little bastard with or without your consent." Agnette moved closer as he said that and handed a tawse to Peter.

Master Leo sighed, then with much irritation in his voice said, "Peter, I've already told you I don't believe he did spit on you. As for ignoring you in the Great Hall, he isn't wearing your fucking collar anymore. You tossed it, remember? That means you don't have the right to demand he attend you in the Great Hall unless his Masters command him to. Now that we have settled all that bullshit, give him to me. Or do I need to use that tawse you're holding to knock some sense back into your empty head?" He finished his statement turning red with much anger. Wow, the guy was easily pissed off, never knew that before.

Peter looked at Agnette for a moment then frowned and said in an irritated tone, "Fine, take the bastard. He's not worth fighting for, anyway. Besides, as I told him already, he may not belong to me today but when he breaks that metal, I will get him. I hope you are listening to me Maximillian. Go ahead and enjoy this tiny victory while you can. Just make sure you practice getting to your knees because I am going to make sure you stay there for the rest of your life." He threw the leash at me with such force I nearly dropped the breakfast tray, again.

Master Leo glared at Peter with a smile of victory on his face as he said, "Come to me Mad Maxx. Peter you are a fucking fool. You are taking out your anger on this boy, but it's not his fault you threw his amazing collar away. Truth is, if he does break his collar, I would run for your life if I was you. If I was him, I would feed the buzzards with your carcass right after I threw down the sacred bolt cutters. Hell, I am thrilled that I will get a front row seat to watch it happen. I tried to tell you the boy is a real Priceless. You fucked up thinking him fake and that mistake will come back on you in the worst way, you'll see. Leo on the other hand, will wisely treat Mad Maxx with respect and kindness. In the end, you will die, and I will get to enjoy the love and loyalty you tried to take with force from this beautiful boy." He motioned me to come to him as he insulted Peter.

I dutifully minded his hand command. Master Leo grabbed my leash with speed. He didn't even attempt to use humility as he looked over me with a gleeful expression on his face.

I kept my sight to the ground feeling sick to my stomach over all this open talk of Peter's betrayal and criminal misuse of my trust in him. Peter and Agnette stood there glaring with hate at a very happy Master Leo. I just wanted to get the hell out of there, but Master Leo wasn't granting the mercy of leaving.

All of us stood there locked in an uncomfortable silence for several moments until I finally I dropped to a kneel then politely said, "Master I beg your mercy. I must return to Master Jonas's apartment with his breakfast. Can I receive your release to attend your brother Elder?"

Master Leo looked down at me, appearing to enjoy my subjugation to him a great deal as he said flatly, "Nein. Not yet my love. First, I command you to grant me special services."

I was startled in pure shock. I heard Agnette gasp and Peter grumbling at that, then stammered in response, "Master I must again beg your mercy. I am convalescing from Master Drexel's cruelty. I will be happy to attend all your pleasures when your clock begins at the end of the week. I believe Master Jonas's called and explained this issue to you?" I was wondering if Master Leo had lost his mind.

He nodded and replied, "Ja, he did explain the issue to me my love. I assure you I am sensitive to your difficulties. That is why I am requesting you grant me the pleasure of your mouth till I find my climax. I promise you its only superficial penetration I seek, and I dare say won't compromise your injured areas, ja? I do believe I had the right to demand such a pleasure anywhere and anytime. I have taken the oath of the Elders, and we own your collar equally. So, I command you to mind my orders right this minute. Do it the way you did it to Peter so long ago, when I was forced to watch. Peter informed me I would never know such delight. Get to it Mad Maxx or would you rather I turn you over to Peter so you can endure his undeserved punishment?"

I laid the tray in the floor and responded, "As you wish Master."

Before I could reach for his fly Master Leo, pushed my hands away. I waited patiently for Master Leo to undo his pants damning my existence at this most humiliating situation I had found myself in.

Peter and Agnette stood their ground in silence. Both seemed to be frozen in shock until Master Leo released himself and I began attending to his service request. Peter snatched Agnette by the wrist and took off rushing for the door. No doubt he was in a big hurry to leave the scene of this most unexpected blow job show.

Master Leo held up his hand demanding both Dominants halt their attempts to retreat.

Peter stopped his rapid flight and growled out angrily, "Leo, dammit. I'm not going to stand here and watch this shit!"

Master Leo panted out, "You and Agnette will not leave till I release you or I'll happily see you receive five lashes for denying an Elder's orders. You made me watch and now you are getting an equal service return, motherfucker." With that he emitted a loud moaned of thrill making damned sure Peter thought my skills were sending him to incredible rapture.

Peter and Agnette wisely ended their plans to leave. I have no idea if either of them watched or looked away or what. I was busy doing my job. It didn't help that Master Leo grabbed my hair on both sides of my head blocking my view of my parents.

It's unclear if he was not satisfied that I could do my work without his aid or if this move was part of his interest in thoroughly pissing Peter off. To add insult to injury, Master Leo moaned and panted nonstop. All the while, he yelled out torrid descriptions of his enjoyment of my perfect skill in attending to his lust.

I normally would have felt terribly humiliated over this disgraceful display. However, I got through the indignity of it by reminding myself that nothing pissed Peter off more than his having to endure another taking what he thought was his.

Peter honestly believes he was the one that had endured the difficulty of breaking my will to the silver. Ha, I am sure that was a burden for the pervert, whatever. Being made to listen while another yelled out my name in ecstasy, surely was grinding his nerves something terrible.

I turned off my emotions and focused all my energy on granting my Master Leo the pleasure service he requested. This did the trick because, after only suffering this shame a few moments he began to reach his orgasm, much to my relief.

My heart raced fueled by stress as the Elder held me hostage to his groin. I closed my eyes tightly trying to ignore the foulness while he emptied his lust into my head yelling out loudly of his pure bliss. To my disgust, Master Leo didn't release me from his hold right away. He spent several moments shouting out praises that I would rather not repeat, thank you.

After demanding I swallow his foul seed, he relented his grip on my hair allowing me to break from his manhood. I returned to my kneel and kept my eyes to the floor while he readjusted himself. He was breathing raggedly and still making comments about my "amazingly artistic" talents at providing the oral services.

I did my best not to vomit as I practically whispered, "I beg of you Master. If you are satisfied, I need to return to Master Jonas before I am disrespectfully tardy. I thank you in advance for the mercy of your releasing me from your employ for this task."

Master Leo let out a final sound of thrill then said, "By all means, Mad Maxx. I release you and look forward to exploring the rest of your sublime services this weekend. Be assured you have more than satisfied your Master. Tell Jonas I will be by later today for that book he promised to lend me. Go on now. Better hurry along."

I grabbed my tray and hauled ass without being told twice. I had enough of that crap. I was pushing my way through the crowd headed with speed to leave the torture rooms when I heard the voice of Egon hailing me.

I almost didn't stop beyond irritated at the most unexpected calling in of Master Leo's rights. I halted and turned around just as Peter slammed into me. Without any attempt to catch myself I collapsed onto the floor. The tray fell with a loud crash spilling food everywhere.

Without thought I yelled out, "God dammit!"

Peter stood above me glaring hatefully as he said, "Get up Maximillian! I wouldn't want you to give your Masters any excuses to prevent you from breaking your collar. See me after you do. Then we can explore just how angry I truly am."

I glared back and growled out without fear. "My name is Mad Maxx, Master. Maximillian is dead because you threw him away."

He snorted but didn't respond to my statement. I watched him rush off to the stairs, my mother on his heels. To my relief neither of them stopped nor looked back. I groaned at the loss of Annette's breakfast, while I stood. I did my best to pick up the empty tray and discarded food. I sighed as I watched the mass of collars and Dominants stomping Annettes's breakfast into a mess. Not one of them paid any mind to the food scattered at their feet on the concrete floor.

Egon rushed over with a grin on his face as he exclaimed, "Oh my God. It is you Mad Maxx. I thought you were dead. I'm so happy to see you are still alive after all." He sounded thrilled to see me.

I nodded. "I wonder about that sometimes, Egon. I am glad to see you too. I was hoping you'd be agreeable to resume my lessons, but this time I require no seduction training. Instead, I'm in need of thudding skills. You still open for an arrangement?"

Egon nodded with a bigger grin. "Hell ja, I am. Egon is your man. Just name the day and time and I am all yours."

I smiled bitterly, "Let me get back to you on that. Things have become a bit more complicated since last we saw each other. I serve four Masters these days. My schedule is booked. Oh shit, one of those greedy bastards is coming this way now. I better haul ass before he has mine. See you soon Egon." I'd seen Master Leo, closing, and locking the back-room door about to head my way.

I was in no mood for giving a second demonstration of my oral abilities. I turned and tore up the stairs giving up my attempts to make sure my Annette had something to eat. I decided that since I had managed to get her painted black and granted her revenge. That would have to be enough to show her how much I truly cared.

I made it back to Master Jonas's apartment with five minutes to spare. I went inside to find the place quiet. I could hear the Vampire snoring all the way in the living room. I sighed a breath of relief then went to the grey door. I knocked softly. Annette opened the door looking much better groomed.

He pretty eyes were wet from tears. She had been weeping. Based on how puffy and red they were, quite a bit I expected.

I reached out and stroked her cheek, softly as I asked, "You okay Annette? Is there anything I can do to comfort you in your sorrow?" I watched as her eyes filled with rain again.

She shook her head then replied. "I was just thinking how much I would miss you when I get sent to the circuit or I get brave enough to commit suicide. I wish so much I had not taken you for granted back in the days of our washroom antics. I am a dumbass for not seeing the wonderful boy that was right in front of my nose all along. I was so in love with my Master back then. He was only using Judith and me. Why couldn't I see that?"

I chuckled as I said, "Oh, Annette don't beat yourself up over such silliness. All the adults take advantage of the young here. You are only human. Master Stefan did to you what Peter did to me. We are not fools my love. We are victims. May I come inside a moment? I am in a chastity device, and I promise I will respect your space. I swear it."

She giggled despite her tears then replied, "Mad Maxx, you make me laugh. How can a girl say nein to such a romantic request to enter her room?"

She backed up and I walked inside closing the door behind me. I reached into my pocket then took out the certificate but kept my eyes on the floor.

I took a deep breath while she stood there staring in confusion at the paper and then I said slowly, "Annette, I am a man of my word. I did what I promised for your service last night. That said, before I give you a release from that metal nightmare you wear, I beg you would do me a few favors that surely, I have not earned from you." I held my breath waiting for her to ask me to continue.

She shook her head, appearing quite perplexed. "I don't understand. What did you do? As for favors you've requested, I will happily do anything for you, my love."

I looked at the black collar announcement as I replied. "I hold in my hands the announcement that you are no longer silver, but black. It has been filled out and signed by your Master Stefan. Annette, as of this moment, you're free of suffering the fate of enforced sexual services." I handed the certificate to her.

She reached out and took the document, staring at it with her mouth hanging open in stunned silence. I watched her read it, then re-read it again as if she was having difficulty believing her eyes.

Suddenly her cheeks became soaked with salty happiness. Her mouth broke into the most beautiful smile I had ever seen in my life. Annette looked up from the paper with a squeal, then jumped on me pulling me into a passion-filled kiss.

I closed my eyes enjoying the spectacular feelings of her lips on my own. Annette pulled and panted into my mouth. With a muffled moan she grabbed around my neck pulling herself up onto me. I realized, in thrill, she was offering to engage in sex with me.

It was then, I was awoken from my lustful stupor as my growing erection was cramped by its metal cage. The girl was willing, but the Mad Maxx was unable. God damned Jonas!

I gently pulled her off me sighing with much regret as I stammered out. "Annette please. I will be injured if you don't stop this. I want you so bad I am about to break my cock off in its cage. Don't you remember? I told you I am chaste."

She got a look of horror on her face as she glanced down at my crotch. "Oh, my love. I apologize, I forgot." She backed away while I turned to the door tugging at my pants groaning in sheer agony over my pitiful encasement.

Annette stood quietly with patience while I calmed down my interest. Once I was able to breathe without fear of breaking off my manhood, I turned back around able at last to enjoy her beauty with my eyes only.

She smiled sheepishly as she said, "I do apologize for that Mad Maxx. I was just so thrilled. You gave me a dream I never thought I could hope for. I will be free to live my life without being forced to have sex or other horrid services to some cruel Dominant. I can have a house of my own, with a dog, and baby sheep. Oh, you saved me. I will never be sent away to the circuit of camps. But wait? How did you get my Master to agree to this impossible blessing?" Her eyes suddenly went from rapture to thick clouds of grief when she noticed I was staring at my boots silently.

Annette wailed out, "Mad Maxx, you traded yourself for my freedom, didn't you? Nein, I cannot bare it." She flew at me grabbing me in a tight hug as she wept like a baby.

I stroked her back trying to hush her terror as I whispered in her ear, "Nein Annette. I did no such a thing. Please stop crying. This is the time to celebrate not one for tears of sorrow. Your free, my love. Just think. Tonight, you will watch the brilliance of the sun setting with your own eyes, not your memory."

She pulled from our embrace and glared at me with her wet eyes as she said, "Ja, I will but my beloved Mad Maxx will be roped to a bed being used like a mare. After the monsters finish that, they will cut and beat him for no other reason than for twisted pleasures. How can I even consider the joy of peace knowing I leave the boy I love to suffer like he surely does."

I chuckled holding back my own tears overhearing her speak my terrible truth as I said, "My love you never allowed me to voice the favors I hope you will grant me. I beg you to hear what I ask. If you do honestly love me, you will do me the mercy of seeing my wishes fulfilled. If you were to be so generous, it would bring me the peace I've happily obtained for you."

Annette nodded and replied, "I am listening."

I sighed then said, "First I ask you to leave this room and apartment after we are done speaking. I beg that you don't go back to Master Stefan's house. Instead go directly to the black collar head mistress and turn the certificate over to her. I want you to start your new life without taking anything from your past with you. Second, I beg you to refuse any offer from my Master Jonas might make. I don't wish to ever see you entangled in his perversions any further. In fact, I ask you to take a job that requires you to live outside the House walls. You can go to the garden, stables, or do the shopping. Anything but one that puts you where the Vampire can get to you easily. I've managed to grant your freedom with much difficulty. That's why I never want to see you anywhere inside this hell hole again. Last, if it pleases you, leave the House altogether. If you do, I then ask you get the baby lambs and a dog. Go out in the world and find a good husband. I beg of you to live happily all your days, my love. Do your best to forget this horror you've suffered. And you must erase Mad Maxx from your memory. I want you to vow to all these things in blood. If not, I'm sorry I cannot grant you this gift of freedom. It would be a useless gift if you cannot do all the things, I've asked of you." I looked away feeling my heart breaking in my chest over the demands I had made of her.

She whimpered in reply, "I cannot leave you here or just forget you. Listen to me. If you saved me then there must be a way to help you escape also. Then we can leave the House together and we will get the cottage, the baby lambs, and the dog."

I interrupted her barely holding it together as I said in a stern tone. "Annette, please stop torturing me. I am the Priceless. That means I cannot be tarnished or painted black. I promise I will break my metal in time, but even when I do, I will be a Dominant not a submissive. You are now forever a black collar and forbidden to me in this life. If we were ever caught in each other's arms, I would be punished severely but it would be death for my beautiful Annette. Please swear in blood to all I've asked, then I want you to run away from me and never look back. I need you to say you understand that we are saying goodbye forever."

Annette shook her head wildly as she breathed out in the stressful tone, "I can't do this. I just cannot leave you."

I chuckled bitterly and replied calmly, "Surely by now you have realized that everything has a price. That is the first lesson you learned while enduring all the horrors you've encountered in this place. Tell me my love, what made you think the most precious thing on earth, wouldn't be so expensive you'd have to give up all you own to possess it? Freedom is worth it, you'll see. I do want you to know I will think of you and the green fields for all my days with a smile on my face and joy in my heart. You have given me the strength to fight on through the many dark days ahead. The outside world of colors and peace I had forgotten. Annette, you unselfishly gave that dream back to me. I now return the favor by setting you free. You go live. Be assured, you have earned your happiness and my eternal love. I ask you to love me back by granting me my favors without further hesitation. You must go before I forget myself and try to hold on to something that was never meant to be mine. As I have said, you deserve better than that, and now you can have it."

She sobbed but nodded her head while looking away. I smiled then stroked her cheek for a moment. She took my hand and held it to her face snuggling tightly whimpering with much shuddering. I walked over to my makeup case. With tears threatening to erupt I opened it and removed a broach. I poked her finger and then mine own. As we mingled our blood, she repeated her vows to do all I had asked her to do including forgetting me. She broke down hard when she got to that part though.

Remaining stoic while I listened to her denounce me, I knew she needed me to be strong for her. Once the terrible promises were made, she and I kissed. I held her in a tight embrace for what was to be the last time in our lives. I felt her heart beating with vigor into my own chest and marveled at the glory of her scent.

With much regret I pulled her out of our embrace then smiled as I said sadly, "I can see the sunrise of tomorrow in your eyes my beauty. Now do as you've sworn to me and never look back. I never want to see your beautiful face wandering the halls again."

She nodded then turned from me while clutching her certificate with a tremor. "No matter what you made me say, I will love you forever Christian Axel. I only swore to forget Mad Maxx, but Christian is who you are. And that boy, I will always remember." Before I could reply she fled the room, not even closing the door behind her.

I watched her flee until I couldn't make out her shape any longer. I closed the door and immediately fell to the floor in a weeping jag. I swear to God, nothing I ever suffered before that moment had hurt as bad as having to let Annette go.

After several moments of suffering there by the door on my knees, I crawled to the bed. Without breaking from my quiet grieving, I pulled the pillow and blankets off. Like a mother cradles her child, I held them in my arms. I covered my face and took deep breaths drinking deeply of her fast-dissipating scent. I thought for sure I was going to die right there that very moment from the heart break.

You see, Meine Liebe, I did love her. Well, I still do. I made her promise to leave the House because I knew Master Jonas would eventually find a way to get her to agree to help him seduce me for his nasty ritual. If I allowed her to return for my comfort, sooner or later, the vampire would hurt or even kill her. Jonas had made it clear he didn't like competition for my affection.

Annette had it and he knew he never would. I feared when he discovered my honest feelings for the girl, he'd end her. Of course, I made her promise to never answer his call if he found her demanding she return to our blood couplings. Even the powerful Master Jonas had no ability to force the black collared Annette to mind him, but I couldn't be sure Jonas wouldn't find a way around the House Law. I felt better knowing she was now beyond the reach of every Dominant regardless of their power for all her life.

I saved my lover, but I lost her by doing it. I could never be painted black thanks to my status as Priceless. If I didn't break my metal, I would be silver for all my life, however short or long that would be.

To this day, I don't know the true fate of my beloved Annette. She was a woman of her word, Meine Liebe. She told me she was leaving the House and never coming back. I can be sure she hasn't. I like to believe she left and is out there somewhere in Germany with a handsome man, lots of healthy children, and a comfortable home.

Wherever she went I just know a loyal dog lays at her feet and baby sheep flock her fields. Annette was the dream of freedom for Mad Maxx. You Meine Liebe are the dream of peace for Christian Axel.

Master Maxx (Maximillian at that moment) kissed the top of my head and sighed. I turned and looked at him, seeing that he had tears in his eyes. I assume it must hurt to lose your first love. I wouldn't know.

Christian Axel still lives to this day, and to this day we are connected by our children and their children. It is one of the only deep wounds he and I don't share, losing a loved one. I'm happy to not share this pain too, thank you very much.

I was surprised to look up and see Mad Max and Christian standing their watching me. I was also shocked to see even the hateful sadistic shard had tears in his eyes. He had loved her too, so I guess it was only to be expected. I was stunned to realize that bastard had any feelings that could incite the rain of a broken heart.

Mad Max wiped his eyes dry then said, "Well get the fuck up schwuler crybaby. Don't you have dicks to suck or some shit? If you've nothing better to do, then I suggest you make that fucking sharp in your pocket disappear. We get caught with it we will soon be growing strong roots for the tree basking in that sunrise you saw in Annette's eyes.

I nodded, "You are a heartless, bastard Mad Max. I know you are right, but can I not have a fucking second to mourn."

Mad Max giggled. "Grieve over what, fool? The girl was about to be killed. You saved her life. Now you want to cry because she's not here to tease us with what we never get to have. I think not. Get up. You should be happy for her and working to get us out that fucking door behind her. You told her freedom was expensive, but you seem to think we get that for cheap ourselves? You are not only a schwuler, but you are also an idiot."

I hate to admit it, but that motherfucker was right for a change "Ja, I hear you. No need to shout."

I crawled over to the vent for the air and pulled out the cover. I took out the sharp then dropped it inside watching it drop too far down to be seen or retrieved. I replaced the thing, then crawled back to the tear drenched bedding. I stood up and remade the bed. I was about to leave the room when I saw something sticking out of the waist of my pants. I pulled the item free, unable to figure out what it was or how it got there.

To my surprise I discovered it was a picture of the beautiful Annette. She was smiling brightly and holding a bouquet of blue flowers.

I turned it over and, on the back, she had written, "When the darkness comes, think of the sun on your face while I pick flowers for our table. I love you Christian Axel. Forever I am yours, Annette."

I felt my chest seizing up as a fresh wave of despair rushed over me as I read the words I longed to hear. Apparently, that sweet girl had snuck the photo into my pants as she was saying her final goodbye. I had been too busy holding my shit together and enjoying the sensation of holding a woman to notice her placing it there.

I kissed the tiny photo then carefully placed it into my hidden pocket.

I carried her world of colors with me everywhere I went until the day I broke my collar. She had left me, but in true pleasure submissive fashion she returned my service by granting me one of equal value. She gave me something to hold on to and focus on. Thanks to her I was able to reclaim my hope and unconditional love for another. Annette reminded me that life was meant to be lived, and not just about mindless survival.

After making sure I had hidden all the evidence of my plot that freed Annette, I went to the living room.

I had just grabbed one of my schoolbooks to study when Christian sat down next to me and said, "Well, one good thing, no one around anymore to claim that virginity I didn't get the pleasure to lose."

I groaned out loud as I replied, "Leave it to you to find the bright side to every toadstool. Get away from me. You smell like blood and rot." I kicked at him.

He laughed bitterly, then responded, "Well you know what they say, ja? You are what you eat, Maximillian."

I threw my book at him and yelled out angrily, "I mean it! Get the fuck away from me, you murderer. I am sick to death of both of you. Don't you and that psycho you hang out with have kittens to torture? Or perhaps you'd prefer to stroke each other off to the sounds of the suffering souls of this House." I kicked out at Christian with more vigor as I said that.

Suddenly, Master Jonas's angered voice startled me out of my attack on my brother shard, "Christian Axel, what the hell? Who are you talking to?"

I fell immediately to my knees shaking in terror. I kept my eyes to the floor as the irritated Vampire came into the room.

He stood there eyeing our surroundings for possible intruders as he said, "Well? I asked you a fucking question. I saw you throwing your books across the room and heard you screaming obscene things. I also witnessed you kicking violently but there doesn't appear to be anyone here."

I shook my head. "It was nothing, Master. I apologize for disturbing your slumber. I must submit to your punishment for this vulgar display."

Master Jonas took a seat on his fancy sofa then said with a sigh, "You were hearing voices. Ja, that is who you were talking to, isn't it? It's just like when I took you to the dungeons to see Peter. I am worried the madness is returning."

I shot him an anxious glance and replied, "Nein, I don't hear any voices. I was angry with Christian. He was teasing me. He and Mad Max are bullies. I should be punished for fighting too loudly, but please don't send me back to the dungeon."

My Master raised an eyebrow as he responded, "Wait, you are not Mad Max nor Christian. You don't sound like Der Hund either. I must assume I'm speaking with Maximillian."

I nodded. "Ja, Master. I am Maximillian. Please, I beg your mercy." I fell to the prostrate position; almost positive he was going to haul me downstair.

Master Jonas chuckled and replied, "Get up, Maximillian. I refuse to punish you. I'm not angry, I'm grateful to see you have returned to duty. Der Hund had reported you were injured by Drexel and no longer available to attend to my pleasures."

I raised back to my kneel stance and said, "It was fatiguing to attend to the interests of Master Drexel and Master Barnim. I swear I've recovered completely. If that fact pleases you, then I would remind my glorious Master there will be no need to bother calling doctors. I couldn't be of service to you if you decide to send this worthless submissive to a cell dressed in a straight jacket."

He laughed hard and replied, "Now that is bullshit. If I had any sense, that is exactly where you would be, because that is the only way to keep you and everyone else in the House safe. Be that as it may, I've decided to keep you here in my apartment where I can enjoy you anytime, I wish. Besides, you cannot break that collar if you remain leashed to the wall of a cell. You tell Mad Max and Christian, I order them to leave you alone. I command them to stand aside and allow you to do your job. In fact, you tell them that their Master says this thing I order is a directive."

I flashed a look of surprise at my evil brothers as I said, "Ah, I will need to ask Der Hund about enforcing your directive, Master. He is the only one that can control the behaviors of the shards."

The Vampire growled out in fury, "Der Hund answers to his Master Jonas, just the same as all of you must. He doesn't control your actions, I do. Are all of you listening to me? I am the boss, and you will obey me. I mean it Mad Max and Christian. I won't tolerate either of you teasing Maximillian. He perfectly provides the services I demand. The rest of you are fucking useless to me. I will not tolerate losing him to stress and fatigue ever again. I catch any of you upsetting Maximillian, I will take them down to the chains and make the shard responsible sorry for it. I mean it." I flinched as he continued yelling while glancing about the room as if seeking to catch sight of one of the shards.

Mad Max leaned into my ear and whispered in a suspicious sounding tone, "Oh my God. This motherfucker is insane, Maximillian. First, he thinks he's a Vampire and now he is talking to the God damned walls as if he can make them mind his crazy orders. You'd better watch out.

Touched people often kill people without the understanding they are wrong. Mad Maxx and you better keep that mad man calm and happy. Maybe we'll get lucky and in his delusional state he starts to believe himself able to turn into a bat. Then we can force him to jump from the banister like Barnim, ja?" He snorted, then crossed his arms.

My eyes went wide as I yelped in response. "Shut up, the Master will hear you, Mad Max, please stop trying to get me into trouble."

Master Jonas gasped and stooped down to stare into my eyes as he said, "Huh? You fear the Master will hear? Dammit, what did Mad Max just say to you Maximillian?"

I shook my head keeping my eyes to the floor, "Nothing worth repeating, Master. I think you should send him to the dungeons though. I will happily take him there for you. No doubt that will scare the foolish Mad Max. I beg you allow me to take him for a tour. He obviously needs reminding of what happens when he doesn't mind his Master."

The vampire shook his head in disbelief as he asked, "Are you saying if I send you to give Mad Max a tour of the dungeon, he will stop bothering you?"

I nodded but kept my eyes to the floor as I replied, "Ja, that is the only thing that scares that squirrely bastard. I beg your mercy. Let me take him down to the cells for about an hour or so. I'm certain that will shut him the fuck up, and I say that with respect."

Master Jonas smiled and caused me to flinch as he patted my head saying, "Okay, then I order you to take him to the dungeon, Maximillian. Listen here, Mad Max, the dungeon you are about to tour is where you will end up if you keep bothering Maximillian. You are going to learn your place. I promise you boys, making this Master angry isn't a smart thing to do. Now get going Maximillian. Oh, and bring back my supper when you return. I will call down to the kitchen and tell them to be expecting you in one hour."

As I took to my boots to mind his command, he slapped my backside. His lustful touch caused me to move with speed for the door. I didn't need to be told twice to mind him.

I raced down the hallway toward the back staircase, Mad Max run up alongside me and said, "What the fuck was that all about Maximillian. I am not afraid of the dungeons. Also, you know damned well the Master can't hear what I say to you. Why did you lie to him like that?"

I shot him an evil grin as I replied, "That Vampire thinks himself so clever, brother. He believes he has dominion even inside our head. I think not. I realized that I could tell him anything, even a fib, about how to handle us. You noticed he bought it. As you said, the man is fucking nuts. All I need to do is play by the rules of the madman. If the Vampire believes fairy tales and made-up shit as he goes along, so can I. So, I told him you fear the dungeons to get him to send me below. Once we are there we can work on the seduction of Helga. Geez Mad Max, I would've thought you'd figured out my clever plan. You are perhaps the meanest of us all but you sure not the brightest."

He growled out in response, "Wait a damned minute. I thought you got Heidi this morning. We've already seduced Master Stefan, then killed him. I believe then you gave Master Leo that blow job. After that you said goodbye to that fox Annette. We haven't had a moment of sleep thanks to the chemical burn, and I don't recall eating anything in a long time. Aren't you tired and hungry yet, schwuler boy? Oh, I know, all that cum guzzling filled your stomach earlier, right?"

I frowned as I yelled back, "I swear to God, can you get any more disgusting? Shut the fuck up and get off my back, Mad Max. I am just trying to do my fucking job. I don't know about you, but I don't want to be wearing a silver collar till I am one hundred. You either get with this program or get on your knees. Our rotation from Master to Master begins again in only two days. This is not a lot of time to seduce those nasty old twin birds down below. If we are to meet our deadline, sleep and food will have to wait. Oh, and just so you know there are only twenty-five calories in sperm. Like it or not, that gross diet food will have to do since we keep feeding all our substantial meals to corpses or the floor."

Mad Max rolled his eyes and replied, "Holy shit, you are going soft in the head. Twenty-five calories? Seriously? Where the hell did you learn that foul information? It's obvious you need medication, nutball. Mad Maxx, are you in there? Or did Maximillian eat you? Maybe he did and that's why he isn't hungry, ja?"

Mad Maxx came forward and took the wheel. "I am here, brother. What the hell are you squawking about? I told Maximillian to say that shit to Master Jonas. Trust me. I have a solid plan. Maximillian is crazy though, like the fox. So back the hell off, sicko."

Mad Max chuckled and replied, "Ah, well, the knowledge that Maximillian has the craziest bastard of us

391

all to do all the thinking for him makes me feel better. I am done with this shit. You sonofabitches call if you need me. Otherwise, I am going to look over brochures for funny farms. I want to make sure the one we end up in has all the pretty nurses and the television has color."

I rolled my eyes and said, "Got news for you brother, you need not do that shopping. We are already in a madhouse and our roommate is fully delusional. He thinks he is a Vampire and also our husband. I'm telling you, if this isn't the loony bin then I am more than a little frightened for humanity. Move on Mad Max. While I would love to chat with our psychiatrist Dr. Freud about the problems you have with your mother, Maximillian, and I have a date with a troll. We see you back at the castle Dracula later."

Mad Max stopped dead in his tracks turning pale as he stammered, "Holy shit, you are right, we are still in the insane asylum. I remember we got sent there for burning down Gerard's house. That explains everything. Oh fuck, that does explain everything, doesn't it?"

Me and Maximillian giggled over our screwing with Mad Max's head like that. We high fived each other since usually he is the winner of these little mind games we play. Not this time. That sadistic shard was left freaking out on the third-floor steps thinking we were still stuck in the institution back when we were a little boy. Well at least that would shut his ass up for a bit. We had work to do, and his constant pecking was slowing us down.

We arrived in the dungeon a bit out of breath from all the rushing downstairs, no elevator, go figure. I stepped back and let Maximillian retake the wheel. This seduction business was his domain. No one can wrap another around a finger like that shard can.

I went down the rock wall hallway that I had traveled for many years in my early childhood. I knew this place like the back of my hand. The draft played in my hair making me shiver. I still hated this place of my nightmares worse than any other spot in the House. Okay maybe I hated the interior apartment doors painted red or black slightly more.

I spotted the woman called Helga right where I recalled her to always be this time of day. No matter the year, this female could be clocked. She was that rigidly scheduled. I walked over to the desk where she sat reading her magazines. I could hear the distant laughter of children in a stone classroom down the corridor. She was on break while her twin sister Heidi took over the submissive protocol teaching duty.

She looked up to see me walking toward her and frowned. "Mad Max, well, I never thought to see you here again, not in a million years. I assumed you had your fill of the cells and moved on up."

I smiled then approached her desk looking down with a coy smile. "Mistress Helga, you're a refreshing sight for sore eyes."

She scoffed. "Now there is a line of bullshit if I ever heard any. What the hell do you want? Surely, you are not here for a stroll down memory lane. I have heard quite a bit about you over the last few years. Seems we had a Priceless under our noses. I never would have believed it of you, but there you are, I am impressed."

I shot her a look grinning with mischief. "Not yet you aren't, Mistress. However, let me take you to a more private place and I can show you the powers I possess that you regrettably overlooked."

Mistress Helga grabbed her chest as if in shock. "What is this you say. My God. You are a Priceless indeed. I say that because you are quite obviously insane!"

I nodded. "Mad as a hatter, Mistress. More than that, I am crazy for you." I flashed another coy smile then looked rapidly at the floor.

She snorted then stood up. "Okay is this some kind of game you're playing with me. I tell you right this minute I don't like being made fun of. You state your business here then be on your way or I'll beat the crazy out of you Mad Max."

I looked around wildly then back to her with evil in my gaze. "I play no games, Mistress. I think of you all the time. You are my wet dream come true. I always thought of you all those nights when I was locked away in my cell. I confess I've come into my puberty with your eyes in my fantasy mind. I've waited a long time to show you that I am the man of your dreams too."

I walked around the desk, and she began backing up with a look of fear in her expression. "Mad Max, you better get the hell out of here. I think you are psychotic. These things you're saying are not proper. You mind your Mistress, I mean it. You leave or I'll thud you."

I grabbed her and pushed her into the wall behind the desk, forcing my lips onto hers. She initially tried to escape my grip, but I tightly clutched her ample waist. Within only moments she was kissing me back with wantonness and vigor.

I have to say this was maybe as gross a seduction as any I pulled on my father or Claus, but hey sucks to be me. I do what I must do to get the mission complete. Even kiss Mistress Billy goat. At least she was a girl for a change, I think.

I moved to her neck then whispered in her ear. "Still think I'm insane Mistress or making sport of you? Be my lover and I'll show you the Priceless perfect service. I can take you away from this place to another world. All you must do is say ja."

She shuddered then moaned out in passion. "Ja, I say ja. I wish you to take me, Mad Max."

I pulled back smiling just as she grabbed me with strength by the sides of my head. I nearly fell forward to my knees as she pulled me into a kiss, she initiated this time. She was exploring my mouth with her tongue when the sound of someone coming down the hallway caught her ear.

The Mistress pushed me away and seemed to be terrified as she harshly whispered, "Hurry up and hide under my desk. That is my sister Heidi. Shit, I'll never live this down if she catches me." She pointed at the small space behind her chair.

I nodded then dropped to my knees and crammed into the opening. Mistress Helga sat in the chair, then pulled it up grabbing her magazine. She opened it and pretended to be busy leafing through it. I was trapped between her legs. All I could do is hope the Mistress Heidi didn't discover me. That would not be good for my plans to seduce them both.

I listened and heard Mistress Heidi come to the desk. They began to discuss the recently recruited slave collars and then I heard another voice join in. I listened hard and realized it was Mistress Gretta. That bitch was their inquiring about a few of the new slaves. She was trolling the boys looking to see if any were high born or of expensive metal.

I had to hear their talk of these poor little kids as if they were nothing but pieces of furniture without thoughts or feelings. It made me sick to my stomach. I wanted to rush out from under that desk and kill all three of them. Far as I was concerned, they were nothing but nasty slavers and a waste of air.

Then Mistress Helga shifted in her seat, and I saw she wasn't wearing panties under her knee length skirt. With a great deal of evil, and much disgust, I decided to make life a bit difficult for my new lover. I was going to add a little sensual torture to the torturer herself.

I quietly leaned forward and put my head between her thighs. I had to fight back the bile as I began to employ my priceless oral talents on her exposed female sex organs. The Mistress let out a loud gasp and her legs shook around my ears. She dared not reach down to pull me off her or she would risk being caught.

Mistress Heidi saw her sister seize up and let out that sound of sudden surprise. "Helga, are you okay, sister? What's wrong?"

Mistress Helga took a deep breath. "No nothing, nothing. It's ah, just my old knee injury kicking up, I ah, it is nothing." She gasped again and went tense as I increased my actions on her sensitive clitoris.

Mistress Gretta sighed. "Oh, it is the cold weather you know. It gets into my bones too. Hurts like hell. You know they say if you drink a hot toddy before bed it helps." She kept on prattling about home remedies nonstop.

Mistress Helga's thighs were quaking, and her breathing was shallow. I could tell she was nearing her climax very shortly. I attacked her joy button with more rigorous attention and reached out stroking both her ankles with the softness of a lover. She moaned out involuntarily causing Mistress Gretta to pause her never ending chatter.

Mistress Heidi appeared concerned. "Sister, you're bright red. Are you sure you're okay. Is the pain that bad?"

Mistress Helga could hold back no longer she spasmed in orgasm and yelled out, "Ja, ja. Oh, my God. Ja, holy hell I'm cuming." Her tenseness released as she fell forward in her seat slightly.

I backed off wiping my mouth and stifling the giggling that was about to break out of my throat.

Mistress Gretta and Mistress Heidi were quiet apparently confused by her screaming out like that. Mistress Helga sat their panting, appearing to be suddenly quite foggy eyed. She leaned away from her desk, appearing desperate to catch her breath.

Then Mistress Heidi cleared her throat. "Ah, sister, are you alright? Should I call the House doctor?"

Mistress Helga groaned, "Nein sister. I have never felt better. If you two don't mind, I would like to enjoy the rest of my break in solitude. Thank you, ladies, for your understanding."

Mistress Gretta whined, "Wait a minute. I wanted to ask more about that little brown eyed slave you said is expensive metal."

Mistress Helga bellowed out, "Get the fuck out of here, Gretta. Are you deaf? I said I am on break. Heidi, take this woman out of my sight."

Mistress Heidi gasped, "Ja, sure thing, sister. Gretta, come with me. My sister's knee is bothering her. Let her be so she can rest." I head the dungeon Mistress grabbed the bitching Gretta by her arm and haul her away off down the hallway.

Mistress Helga watched them until they were gone from her sight, then she pulled back her chair and stared at me. "What the hell did you do, Mad Maxx?"

I shrugged. "I apologize, Mistress. Not my best work I know. I could do better if I had more room to work with."

Her eyes went wide. "Wait, that was not your best?"

I nodded with a wicked smile. "Not even close, Mistress. I ask you again to be my lover. If you say ja, then I can be free to show you the truth of my talents at the Priceless services."

She nodded with her mouth hanging open. "How can I say nein to that? Ja, I think I may be in love with you already."

I crawled out from under her desk then kissed her cheek just before I began to rush off the way I had come. "See you soon, very soon, my love. I will be dreaming of you until then."

I was almost out of ear shot when I heard her let out a loud whooping noise.

I smiled at Mad Maxx when I heard that. "So, I have bagged the old hag Mistress Helga, brother. You ready to seduce the harsh Mistress Heidi in the morning?"

He nodded with an evil smile. "Does a fish have gills, brother? I was built for this shit."

We headed out of the dungeons headed back to Master Jonas's apartment thinking we needed to brush our teeth badly. It had already been such a busy day and it was barely past noon.

I was about to head up the stairwell when suddenly I was grabbed. A huge hand covered my mouth as this person dragged me kicking and struggling under the steps, into the darkest corner. Fear overcame my good senses as I realized no one had seen me being abducted. Try as I might, the stranger managed to stifle my attempts to cry for help.

To Be Continued in Book 5: Leo's Lamb

Alexandria May Ausman began demonstrating severe psychotic episodes while still in her teens. She was abandoned by her family after being diagnosed with Paranoid Schizophrenia at age sixteen. Forced to struggle with this devastating illness alone, she has suffered medication resistant symptoms, numerous hospitalizations, homelessness, exploitation, and an uncaring mental health system.

Despite the hardships, Alexandria managed to raise two healthy children to adulthood and has four beautiful grandchildren. She obtained a bachelor's degree in psychology and held a job as a child abuse investigator. In

2003, she began a career as a diagnostic psychologist while working towards a Master's in psychology.

Alexandria never forgot the experience of 'slipping through the cracks.' She worked tirelessly to help people suffering severe mental illness and/or all types of abuse have access to necessary services for over seventeen years.

In 2017, she was published and became a professional model of "goth fashion.' and won the World Gothic Models contest in 2018. She holds the title of World Goth Queen for   life.

Alexandria began writing several series of fictional novels after a catastrophic return of psychotic symptoms in 2019. She obtained the Killer Nashville Falchion Award as Best Southern Gothic writer in August 2023, and is a finalist for her book Delusion of the Collar and the Key.

Today, Alexandria is retired, and homebound due to crippling symptoms of Schizophrenia. She currently lives in Tallahassee, Florida, with her loving husband and a loyal support dog.